THE
MERMAID·
IN THE BASEMENT

OTHER NOVELS BY GILBERT MORRIS INCLUDE

The Creole Series

The Singing River Series

The House of Winslow Series

The Lone Star Legacy Series

Visit your online bookstore
for a complete listing of Gilbert's works.

THE MERMAID IN THE BASEMENT

A Lady Trent Mystery
Book One

GILBERT MORRIS

THOMAS NELSON
Since 1798

NASHVILLE DALLAS MEXICO CITY RIO DE JANEIRO BEIJING

Published in Nashville, Tennessee, by Thomas Nelson. Thomas Nelson is a registered trademark of Thomas Nelson, Inc.

Thomas Nelson, Inc. books may be purchased in bulk for educational, business, fund-raising, or sales promotional use. For information, please e-mail SpecialMarkets@ThomasNelson.com.

Scripture quotations are from the King James Version of the Bible.

"The Darkling Thrush" by Thomas Hardy.

Library of Congress Cataloging-in-Publication Data

Morris, Gilbert.
    The mermaid in the basement / Gilbert Morris.
        p. cm.—(A Lady Trent mystery ; bk. 1)
    ISBN: 978-0-8499-1891-9 (softcover)
        1. Actresses—Crimes against—Fiction. 2. Women private investigators—England—Fiction. 3. Aristocracy (Social class)—England—Fiction. I. Title.
PS3563.O8742M47 2007
813'.54—dc22

                                        2007041005

Printed in the United States of America

07 08 09 10 11 RRD 6 5 4 3 2 1

To the Curlin Family
The family is in trouble in America—but the Curlin Clan gives me hope. God sets the solitary in families, and it is a tremendous encouragement to me when I think about all of you—alive and well and serving God! So here's to you, Curlins:

Jay Curlin—a man after God's own heart!
Bonnie Curlin—a true handmaiden of the Lord!
and the wonderful, beautiful kids—

Gabriel, age 8
Charity, age 10
Kit, age 18
Adam, age 17
Jason, age 17
Gideon, age 14
Benjamin, age 1

⚜ ONE ⚜

As Clive Newton made his way along Drury Lane headed for the Old Vic Theatre, he felt the rush of excitement that always came when he attended any of Kate Fairfield's performances. As he crossed the intersection, the cobblestones were still gleaming from the light evening rain. He tossed a halfpenny to the crossing-sweeper, a small boy who swept away manure and mud. The boy bit the coin, then gave Clive a snaggletoothed grin. "Thankee, sir!"

A woman wearing a revealing dress, her face painted, appeared out of the shadows. She attached herself to Clive's arm and winked at him. "Come along wif me, husband. I'll show yer a good time." Shaking his head, Clive moved away, followed by the harlot's curse.

Hurrying along the street, he was struck by the fact that all classes of society mingled in London's streets. One expected harlots to be in the Seven Dials district or in the Haymarket, but it seemed odd that on this main thoroughfare, the rich and the poor, the good and the evil, formed a strange confluence. Some of the women, illuminated by the gaslights, were past their prime; most of them were rattle-cheeked and slack-bodied. There were some young women who came from the country to seek their fortune, but most of them sank to prostitution.

The theatre crowds—filled with respectable women of wealth, their

1

jewels flashing in the reflection of the gaslights—stood side by side with the poorest of London. Homeless children, or Street Arabs, no more than eight or ten years old, swarmed the street. Some pulled at the sleeves of men who whispered crude invitations.

Clive moved southward into the Strand. He passed large bills advertising dramas, musicals, concerts, and recitals with names of current favourites in giant letters: *Ellen Terry, Isabella Glyn.*

Reaching the Old Vic, Clive pressed his way into the crowded foyer. Massive crystal chandeliers threw their blazing candescence over the crowd, and from the hands and necks and headdresses of the women, jewels flashed. Diamonds sparkled in elaborate coiffures, at arms, throats, wrists, and hands. The foyer became a river of activity, pale shoulders gleaming amid the brilliant colours of silk, taffeta, voile, and velvet dresses, while the uniform black of men's dress made a violent contrast. Not all of the crowd that gathered in the Old Vic were wearing diamonds. Intermingled with the wealthy were men and women dressed in plain clothes. Indeed, attending the theatre was one of the few instances of true democracy in England!

Clive hesitated, taking in the scene, then impulsively turned and made his way to a doorway that led from the foyer. He walked down a narrow corridor that opened into a large area backstage. He stopped short, watching the actors, actresses, stagehands, prompters, and others necessary to putting on the production of *Hamlet* move about. They reminded Clive of a swarm of ants rushing about frantically in aimless activity. Moving toward the row of dressing rooms, he stopped before one of the doors and knocked. A voice called out, and he stepped inside. His features lit up at the sight of the woman who had risen from her chair and held a handkerchief in her right hand. "Clive, what are you doing here?"

Katherine Fairfield, a reigning star of the production, was no more than medium height, but her carriage was so erect that she seemed taller. She was wearing a dress that was not intended to be particularly revealing, being fitted to the fair Ophelia in the play, an innocent young girl, but Kate's spectacular figure could not be concealed even beneath such a dowdy exterior. She had dark red hair, enormous dark eyes, and diaphanous skin the envy of every woman in London. Just the sight of her had an effect that reached across the room, stirring him, but she repeated with a touch of irritation, "What are you doing here?"

"I wanted to see you, Kate."

"Well, you can't see me now. The performance starts in a few minutes."

Clive moved forward and put his arms out, but Kate frowned and shook her head. "There's no time for that now."

"But I haven't seen you in four days, Kate."

Kate Fairfield was adept at handling men. It was her stock in trade. She smiled and put her hand on Clive's cheek. "After the performance. Come back then."

༄

Disappointment swept across young Clive's face, but he knew her well enough to obey, so he left the room, closing the door behind him. Kate stared at the door and then laughed. "Young fool!" Then she turned back for one final look at her makeup. A muffled announcement came to her: "Curtain—five minutes!" She turned and stepped outside. Seeing a tall, dark-haired young man leaning against the scenery, she walked over to him and smiled winsomely. "You'd better be careful, Dylan."

Dylan Tremayne turned to face Kate. He was a strikingly handsome man of twenty-seven. Exactly six feet tall, his athletic form was unmistakable through the tights and close-fitting tunic of his costume for the part of Laertes. A lock of his glossy, coal black hair curled over his forehead. He had a wedge-shaped face, a wide mouth, and a definite cleft chin. His most striking feature, however, was the strange blue of his eyes. They were exactly the colour of the cornflowers that dotted the English countryside, and they made a startling contrast against his jet black hair and tanned complexion. Dylan had served for several years as a soldier in India. Despite his Welsh roots, he was so deeply tanned by the sun that he never paled.

"And what is it that I need to be careful about, Kate?" he asked. He turned and watched the woman carefully, with something guarded in his manner. "And, by the way, why are you tormenting young Newton like that?" His voice was smooth, and his choice of words gave evidence of his Welsh blood.

"He likes it, Dylan."

"In love with you, ay?"

"Of course he is. Every man is—except you." Kate studied Dylan carefully. He was the one man she had encountered who had resisted her charm. He had become, in effect, a challenge to her womanhood. It amused her to toy with men, but Dylan had resisted her advances—and this piqued the ego of the actress. Actually, Kate did more than "toy" with men. Her mother had been abused by a series of men, and she made it her burning ambition to see that this never happened to her daughter. She'd set out to instill in Kate from the beginning that a woman must *conquer* men. "Draw them by your beauty, then use them! Take what you can from men and laugh at them when you cast them off!" was the advice she gave Kate—who learnt her lesson well.

"You shouldn't torment the young fellow, Kate. I think it's green as grass, he is."

"It amuses me." She suddenly smiled, took his arm, and pressed her body against him. "You'd better not give a good performance tonight. Ash won't like it. He's jealous enough of you as it is."

"I'll be as bad as I can, me." Dylan grinned.

Kate reached up and pushed back the lock over his forehead. "Why don't we go to my place after the performance?" she whispered. "We could get to know each other better."

Dylan could not miss the sexual overtones of the invitation, nor the edacious look in her eyes. He shook his head, saying, "Not into that sort of thing anymore."

Kate Fairfield's eyes glinted with anger. "I don't believe you're as holy as all that."

"It's only a Christian I am—and not the best in the world, either."

"Everyone knows you're preaching, or something, down on the waterfront in some sort of mission work."

"It's what the Lord wants me to do, though I don't know why. There's plenty can preach better than I."

Kate Fairfield stared at him, and she wasn't smiling—indeed, Dylan saw a small stirring of sadness in her eyes. She did not like to hear talk about God or religion, and releasing her grip on Dylan's arm, she shook her head. "You're a fool, Dylan Tremayne!"

∿✤∾

The play fascinated Clive, but his eyes were fixed on Kate while she was onstage. He knew the drama well and followed it almost unconsciously. All the rest of the actors seemed drab and pale compared with the luminous quality that Kate possessed. Her hair caught the lights, and the clean bones of her face were ageless, a hint of the strong will that drove her visible in the corners of her lips and in her eyes.

Clive had seen *Hamlet* many times, returning night after night, always for the sole purpose of watching Kate. There was something in her that he had never found in any woman, and she created in him a desperate loneliness and a devastating sense of need so that he ached for her.

Finally the play ended with the stage littered with corpses, and the curtain calls began. Clive applauded until his palms hurt when Kate took her bows, but he couldn't help but notice that Dylan Tremayne received much more appreciative applause from the audience than did the star of the play, Ashley Hamilton. He did not miss the angry looks that Hamilton shot at Tremayne and muttered, "Dylan makes the star look bad. I wonder if he knows that."

The crowd began to file out, and Clive passed through the side door, then made his way backstage. He saw Kate surrounded by the usual crowd of admirers and shook his head impatiently.

"Hello, Clive. How are you tonight?"

Clive turned to see Dylan beside him. The two had become friends of sorts. Clive had chased after Kate for weeks now, haunting the dressing rooms and the theatre. Dylan had invited him to a late supper on one of those nights when Kate had gone off with someone for dinner, and the two men had continued to dine together when Kate fobbed young Newton off.

Dylan had a fondness for the young man and had gently tried to warn him about Kate, but to no avail. "I'm waiting for Kate," Clive said, hopefully.

"A bit of fatherly advice I have for you, " Dylan said. He had a smooth voice that could show power at times, but now his tone was merely confidential. "Put Kate out of your mind, yes? It's a nice young woman you need. Court her and marry her."

"I can't do that."

Dylan shook his head. "You are naive, Clive. Don't you know Kate Fairfield eats innocent young fellows like you?"

"I don't want to hear talk like that—" Clive was interrupted as Ashley Hamilton walked up to them. The actor was half drunk, and he glared at Dylan. "Well, you ate up the scenery again tonight, Tremayne. You'll do anything to upstage me, won't you?" Ashley was a fine actor—or would have been—but he had a drinking problem that cut the edge off his fine talent.

Dylan said mildly, "You're twice the actor I am, Ash. Sad it is to see you waste your talent. Why don't you stop drinking?"

Ashley glared at him with red-rimmed eyes. "You're nothing but a hypocrite! Why don't you go down to the docks and preach instead of cluttering up my stage?" He turned and walked away unsteadily.

Elise Cuvier had stopped long enough to watch the encounter between Hamilton and Tremayne. She was a small woman but well formed, with bright blonde hair and enormous brown eyes. The bony structure of her face made strong and pleasant contours. She served as Kate's understudy, and she had a dissatisfied look on her face. She said, "You were wonderful tonight, Dylan."

Dylan shrugged. "Thank you, Elise."

Elise turned to Clive and said, "Mr. Newton, I hope Dylan's giving you good advice about Kate."

Clive frowned at the actress, then wheeled and moved away.

"Trying to warn him, I was, about Kate."

"He seems like a nice young man. He needs to find another woman."

"So I told him."

"Kate enjoys destroying men." An unhappy expression crossed her face, and Dylan said gently, "You'll get your chance, Elise. It's a fine actress you are. Don't get discouraged."

Her eyes seemed to glow with a sudden inner fire, and her lips drew into a thin line. Her voice was no more than a whisper as she said, "Not unless Kate dies."

"Don't be saying that, Elise! She's bad, but the good God loves her."

"I could strangle her, Dylan! She's got everything, and I've got nothing!"

Dylan reached out and put his hand on Elise's shoulder. "It's a hard world, the theatre."

"It's dog-eat-dog! Actors and actresses will do anything to get a better part—lie, cheat, steal!"

"There's more to life than acting, yes?"

"Not for me," Elise said, and a vehemence scored her tone. She suddenly looked up at Dylan and gave a strange, harsh laugh. "If I believed in prayer like you, Dylan, I'd pray for Kate to die."

Tremayne stared at the young woman, and words of rebuke came to his lips. But he saw the adamant cast of her features. She was a beautiful young woman, but there was a hardness in her that he hated to see. He was a compassionate young man, and for a moment he stood there wondering if he might say anything that would mollify Elise's obvious hatred. Finally he said gently, "When you hate someone, Elise, it doesn't really hurt them. It's yourself will bear the hurt."

"I know that's what you believe, but I don't."

"Hatred makes people ugly."

Suddenly Elise laughed. "You're preaching at me, aren't you, Dylan?"

Dylan grinned, which gave him a boyish look and made him seem even younger than his years. His lips turned up at the corners, the right side more than the left, and he admitted ruefully, "Right, you! But you ought to be used to it by now."

"Don't you ever give up on anyone? I think you've tried to convert everybody in the cast. As far as I can tell, you haven't made any progress whatsoever. We're all headed for the fiery pit, Dylan. I don't think it's possible for anybody in our world to live a godly life."

"I'd hate to think that, because that's exactly what I want to do."

Elise stared at him, a mixture of wonder and disbelief on her features. "Have you always been like this, preaching and reading the Bible and talking about God?"

"No, indeed not. I grew up rough, Elise. Rougher than you can imagine. As a matter of fact, I was practically reared by a family of criminals."

"I don't believe that."

Dylan shrugged. "True enough it is. My father was a coal miner in Wales. He and my mother died of cholera when I was ten. I was turned over to an uncle whose chief fun in life seemed to be beating me. He made me go down to the coal mines when I was no more than a boy. I stayed there until I couldn't stand it, then I ran away and came to London."

Elise stared at him. "What did you do? Did you have friends here?"

"No friends, me. Mostly I starved. I wandered the streets and stole food and slept in alleys and under bridges. Then a family named Hanks took me in. I didn't know they were criminals at the time, but I soon enough learnt. They taught me how to survive. I stole with the rest of them. I was the smallest, so they'd put me through a small window in a house, and I'd go open the main door for the rest of the family to come in. We'd steal everything we could."

Elise stared at the young man. "How long did that last?"

"Until I ran away when I was seventeen. Went into the Army, I did. Then when I came out, I was almost starving again, and somehow I got a job working in the theatre. Tried out for a part." He laughed ruefully. "And here I am rich and famous." He gave Elise a warm smile, and the young woman understood why women flocked to him.

"I think you will be succesful. You've got whatever it is that makes people look at you. Some actors are like that. When they're onstage, the audience can't look at anybody else."

"Oh, I don't expect I'll be doing this forever."

Elise shook her head. "Well, *I* will be! It's my whole life, Dylan." She glanced over at Kate and said, "Look at her toying with that poor young fool! Doesn't he see that she's nothing but a carnivore?"

"I think the old saying that love is blind is true. In for a fall, that boy is!"

❧

Kate had let Clive into her dressing room. She changed clothes behind a screen, and when she came out wearing a gown of apricot-coloured silk with delicate lace a shade or two deeper, Clive went to her at once. "I have something for you."

"Really? A present for me? What is it, dear?"

Clive reached into his pocket and brought out a small box. He opened it, and saw Kate's eyes grow wide, and heard her catch her breath. "It's . . . beautiful!" Kate took the ring, an emerald-cut diamond, and slipped it on her finger. "Why, I hardly know what to say, Clive!"

"A little token of thanks would be appropriate." Clive held his arms toward her, and she willingly walked into them. Her lips were soft and yielding under his, as was her body. He drew her closer, but then suddenly the door opened, and Kate quickly drew back. Clive turned to glare at the man who stepped inside. He knew him, of course—Sir William Dowding, the producer of the play. He was tall, and at the age of sixty-five had gained a little weight. Still, he made a powerful impression. He had grey hair and light blue eyes, and now his lips were twisted in a cynical grin. "Have I interrupted something, Kate?"

"Oh, Sir William, come in. Look, Mr. Newton has given me a gift."

Dowding looked at the ring. His eyebrows lifted quizzically. "Well, that's a beautiful stone. You must be quite a wealthy man, Mr. Newton."

Clive felt anger rushing through him, for he felt that Dowding was laughing at him. He knew, of course, that Dowding often took Kate out after the performance. He was a powerful figure in the world of drama, and had made his wealth in steel mills. He also had a wife and three grown children. It infuriated Clive that an old man, which is how he thought of him, would dominate Kate.

"Let's go, Kate. I'm hungry," Clive said quickly.

"Oh, I'm sorry, Clive, but Sir William came earlier. He wants to discuss my next play. It's very exciting."

"But you promised—"

"Oh, I know, dear, but he's my employer. He has great plans for me, and I can't offend him."

Sir William Dowding laughed. "Perhaps another time, dear fellow. Come along, Kate."

Clive was an amiable young man, but under the surface of that amiability lay a temper that sometimes escaped. It did so now as he stepped forward and ripped Kate's hand away from where it rested on Dowding's arm. "Miss Fairfield is dining with me!"

Sir William Dowding was not a man who liked to be crossed. His eyes suddenly turned cold, and he said, "Who is this puppy, Katherine?"

"Puppy! You call me a puppy!" A red curtain seemed to fall before Clive's eyes, and he shouted something in anger. He doubled up his fists and started for Sir William, but Kate had come between them. She put her hands on his chest and said urgently, "Clive, I've told you how it is. This is business. You can come back after the performance tomorrow. We can go out then, but I have to talk to Mr. Dowding about my next play."

Kate took Dowding's arm, and Dowding gave Clive a triumphant smile as the two walked out. Clive, still blinded with rage, followed them out shouting, "You think because you have money you're something, but you're not a man!"

Kate turned, and her face was twisted with anger. "Clive, you're making a spectacle of yourself. Now behave!" She turned, and Clive watched the two leave.

Most of the cast had witnessed the scene; Ives Montgomery, who played Horatio in the production, was standing beside Dylan. He was a tall, slender young man with a deep tan and flashing white teeth. "Young Newton's getting an education. It won't kill him." His expression turned sour, and he shook his head sadly. "Kate used me up and tossed me aside like a peeling of an orange. Well"—he shrugged his shoulders— "I survived. Come along, Dylan. Let's get something to eat."

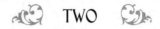 TWO

The late afternoon sunlight filtered down through the large chestnut trees, throwing a latticework of light and shadow on a small young boy and a large dog. David Trent, the future Viscount of Radnor, was tugging at the huge mastiff. The large creature stood looking at the seven-year-old, then with obvious affection licked the boy thoroughly on the face.

"Oh, stop that, Napoleon!" the boy cried. "You're not playing the game."

Charles David Trent had a wealth of fair hair with a distinct curl in it. His eyes were the dark blue one sees sometimes offshore, with just a touch of aquamarine. He was lean, with the hint of a tall frame concealed within his small body and revealed by the length of his fingers and his relatively long legs.

"Come on now. You've got to be a French dog." David pulled the mastiff around and, with much huffing and puffing, pushed him into position.

"Now I'm the Duke of Wellington, and you are the nasty old Frenchman Napoleon. We're going to have a battle, and I'm going to win."

"Woof!"

"That's right. Now you stay right there. I'm going over to that tree, and when I get there I'm going to turn, and I'm going to charge you on a horse. I'll be waving my sword, and I'm going to kill you."

11

"Woof!"

David ran toward the tree quickly, but he did not get far before Napoleon loped after him. With a cry, David turned and threw his arms around the dog's neck. The big mastiff fell on the ground, and the boy crawled all over him. His face flushed with excitement, David cried out, "I win! You're dead, Napoleon, you nasty old Frenchman!"

From the shadows of the barn, a young man approached. He was a lean young fellow of fifteen with a thin expressive face and watchful green eyes. He wore a pair of tight-fitting trousers, neat black boots, and a red-and-white checked shirt. Sandy hair escaped from under his loose cap. "Wot yer doin' now, Master Trent?"

David loosened his grip on Napoleon, rose, and sat down on the big dog's side, whereupon the dog grunted but did not move.

"I'm playing Army."

"Are you now? Yer a soldier, are you?"

"Yes, I'm the Duke of Wellington, and I just whipped Napoleon here at the Battle of Waterloo. My mum read me the story out of the history book this morning. I won, didn't I, Napoleon?"

"Woof!"

"Well, a'course yer won. An Englishman can wallop a Frog any day."

David was a rather literal young fellow. "I didn't say anything about frogs."

Danny Spears, the groom for Viscountess Serafina Trent, laughed. He said in his definite Cockney accent, "Don't yer know nuffin'? We calls Frenchmen *Frogs*."

"Why do we call them that?"

"'Cause they eat 'em."

"They eat frogs alive?"

"No, I suppose they cooks 'em, but it just shows 'ow backwards they be."

"Did you ever eat a frog, Danny?"

"Wot do yer fink I am? The closest I ever come to it was jellied eel. Now there's a proper dish for you!"

"I'd like to try a frog. Maybe we could catch one."

"Nah, you hafter go at night and stab the boogers."

The young future Viscount of Radnor's mind shifted rapidly. "I want to ride Patches."

"Well, yer can't."

"He's *my* pony."

"I knows that, but your mum says yer couldn't ride 'im today."

David glared at Danny and stuck his lip out in a gesture of defiance. "When I get big, and when I'm the Viscount of Radnor, I'm going to do everything I want to do."

Danny Spears laughed, a cheerful light in his eyes. "Blimey, boy! Not even 'er Majesty can do that."

"Yes, she can. Queen Victoria can do anything she wants."

"Well, you just keep on thinkin' that, Master Trent."

David leapt up off the dog, and Napoleon got to his feet. "Let's go down to the stream and see if we caught anything on the line."

"Righto." Danny reached out and took the boy's hand, and the two started across the emerald yard. April had brought a brilliant green to the grass, and the flowers were exploding in riotous colours. They passed through some of the garden, and the big dog took his place protectively beside the boy, who reached up and put his hand on the mastiff's neck. "If we don't catch any in our stream, Danny, we can go over to catch some in Squire Watkins's pond."

"Why, that'd be poachin'. It's agin' the law. We'd both go to jail."

"Not me."

"Yes, you. If you get caught poaching."

"Nobody can put a viscount in jail."

Danny laughed, reached out with his free hand, and tousled the boy's hair. "That's right, but I ain't no bloody viscount—and neither are you. Not yet anyways."

By the time they reached the stream, David had thought the matter over. He pulled his hand free and stared up at Danny, saying, "My mum wouldn't let them put me in jail. If they did, she'd get me out."

13

Danny was an astute young fellow. He had a great fondness for the boy and spent much of his time watching him. He had, in effect, become a playmate for the youngster. "You got that right. That's about wot she'd do, the viscountess. She'd blow the whole bloody jail up!"

The two laughed and then turned to pulling the lines out, checking the bait.

Septimus Isaac Newton had received his name in a logical fashion. He was the seventh son of his parents, thus the name Septimus. He was also a descendant of a close relative of the famous scientist Isaac Newton, thus the name Isaac. Septimus was a tall, gangling man of sixty-two. All of his movements seemed awkward, and it never ceased to amaze those who watched how delicate his touch was in a laboratory or when performing a surgery. He excelled in those two areas, having been a surgeon for a time, but he'd given it up for his experiments in science. He was a pathologist of world reputation and had written the definitive book on human anatomy. Right now he was sprawled on a couch, his white hair in no order whatsoever, except it fell, at times, over his broad forehead. He had forgotten to shave for several days, as the grey stubble on his face indicated. "What are you looking at, Alberta?"

Alberta Rose Stockard Newton, wife of Septimus, was ten years younger than her husband. For all her expensive clothes, she had a peasant's stocky figure. Her hands revealed the hard work she had done when she was a young girl, and even for a time after she had married Septimus. She tried to cover up this part of her past, since her husband had become rich and famous due to an experiment that produced something to do with coal mining that she never understood. She could buy any clothes she liked, although none of them ever concealed her background. Alberta always looked as if she were a washerwoman in a rather ridiculous disguise. Now as she stood at the window, she had several ropes of pearls around her neck that complemented the rest of her costume. The dress was the latest cut, but it was made for a more slender woman, full-sleeved at the shoulder, flaring at the knees and onto the ground. "I was just watching David. He's playing some game with Napoleon."

"Fine dog, that. I'd like to see the man that could harm David with him around."

Alberta watched silently and then said, "Danny's taking him down to the stream, I suppose."

"Danny's a good boy. Knows horses well as any young fellow alive."

Alberta turned and came over to sit beside her husband. She took a look around the room, and as she did, a memory surfaced from her subconscious. She thought of the room she and Septimus had shared when they were first married—small, crowded, and almost bare of furniture. But things had changed since then.

The parlor of the Trent house was large, the furniture of heavy dark wood. Embroidered antimacassars decorated the backs of the chairs. The pictures on the walls were of Italy, painted in hard blues—blue sky, blue sea with harsh sunlight. Over the fireplace hung an embroidered text: "The price of a good woman is above rubies."

Alberta always felt a keen pleasure in reading those words, for it was one of the few romantic things that Septimus had ever given her. She loved her husband and knew that he loved her, but he was of a scientific, clinical mind, not given to flowery or poetic expressions. She glanced over at the chiffonier bearing a vase of artificial silk flowers, delicate things with gay gossamer petals. It was a surprising touch of beauty that Alberta longed for in her life.

"Septimus, we've got to do something about friends for David."

"What do you mean?"

"I mean he needs other children his own age to play with."

"Why, Danny's a good playmate for him, and Serafina spends a great deal of time with him. I do the best I can, and I know you do. He's never lonely."

But Alberta, for all her husband's tremendous breadth of knowledge, was wiser than he in some ways. He might know chemical formulas and every bone in the human body, but she knew more about human nature than Septimus ever would. "A child needs other children around. Don't you remember having playmates when you were a boy?"

"Well, I suppose I do. Perhaps we could hire some children to come and play with him."

Alberta laughed and shook her head with slight disgust. "You do think of the oddest things! You can't rent a child as you rent a buggy."

"I don't see why not," Septimus said with a measure of surprise. "Lots of poor families would be glad to take a few pounds for one of their darlings to be David's playmate for part of the day."

Ellie Malder, a "tweeny" or teenage maid who could help with a variety of household tasks, appeared. She was an attractive young girl of fifteen with brown hair and warm brown eyes. "Shall I serve the tea, ma'am?"

"Yes, Ellie, please do."

Septimus lounged on the couch, listening as Alberta proposed solutions to finding friends for David. When Ellie brought the tea cart in, he sat up. The tea arrived in an exquisite bone china service, hand painted with blue harebells. She also served sandwiches about the size of one of Septimus's fingers and cakes no more than an inch and a half across.

"Septimus, you're eating like a starved wolf! Can't you be more dainty?"

"Yes, my dear, I'll certainly try." He picked up a tiny sandwich, bit off a fragment of it, and chewed. Suddenly Alberta turned to face Septimus. "Does David ever say anything to you about his father?"

"No, I don't know as he does. I don't believe he ever thinks of him."

"Yes, he does."

"He does? Has he talked to you?"

"Not directly, but I'm sure he thinks of him. Sometimes, when I read him a story, there'll be a family in it, and he'll ask a great many questions about the father in the story. It's as if he knows something important is missing from his life, but he doesn't know how to find it."

Septimus picked up one of the tiny teacups, holding it delicately between his thumb and forefinger, sipped the tea, and put it down. "You know, my dear, it's a terrible thing to say, but it's probably best that Charles died."

Alberta shot him a quick glance. "Why do you say that?"

"Well, I know you were happy when Serafina married into the peerage and became a viscountess, but there was always something missing, something wrong with the marriage, and I always thought it was Charles."

Alberta stared at her husband. She had thought the same thing herself. "He wasn't a good husband," she admitted reluctantly.

"No, nor a good father either."

The two sat there, silently thinking back over the years that had passed since their daughter Serafina had married Viscount Charles Trent. The marriage had been a disappointment to both of them, for the viscount had indeed not been a good husband. He had not been abusive, at least not in public, but something had been lacking in the marriage that neither Septimus nor Alberta could put their finger on. Alberta shook her shoulders as if freeing herself from some burden and said, "We must have a dinner soon. Lord Wentworth is back from France."

"That fellow? Why would we want to give him a dinner?"

"Because we have two daughters who need husbands, of course."

"No, we have only one, and she's too young. Aldora's only seventeen."

"I wasn't thinking of Aldora for Wentworth."

Septimus gave his wife a look of pure astonishment. "You're not thinking that Serafina might make a match with him!"

"Why, of course I was."

"She'll never marry again."

"Septimus, she's only twenty-seven years old. Of course she must marry."

"Alberta, she won't even speak of it. Have you forgotten how miserable she was while Charles was alive?"

Alberta could not answer for a moment, for the memory was painful. They sat there, and each of them was conscious of a failure that somehow seemed to be at least partially their fault.

"Serafina was such a happy child," Alberta whispered. "She went about singing all the time and laughing."

"Yes, she was a happy child. And before she was married, she talked a great deal about what it would be like to have a husband and children."

"Something—something happened in their marriage, Septimus. She won't even speak of it, but she lost the joy of life somehow."

"I've never had the courage to try to ask her what went wrong with the marriage. Perhaps you have?"

"I've tried, but she cuts me off. But she must marry again." She straightened up and said firmly, "Many women who've had difficulties with their first marriages take a second husband."

"Most of those women have romantic notions. They've read novels and love stories mostly written by Frenchmen and other perverts. Serafina is not guilty of that!" Septimus paused. "All she really cares about is David."

"Septimus, I sometimes think we didn't give Serafina the right education."

"Why, I educated her myself. I've taught her since she was a child."

"I know, dear. You filled her with your scientific notions. You're a good man, but you have no romance, and you've robbed your daughter of what a woman ought to have."

"Would you like for her to go around quoting poetry and falling in love at the drop of a hat?"

"No, of course not, but . . . well, she seems so *cold*. None of our children have any religion."

Septimus fell silent. Indeed, he had no religion himself. He was a pure scientist, and he passed this feeling along to all of his children. It had been a delight to teach Serafina, for she had the same type of mind as he, and now she was as much a scientist as he.

"I—I thought it was for the best, my dear." He closed his eyes and leaned his head back on the antimacassar. "But I sometimes think—"

Whatever it was that Septimus thought, Alberta was never to find out, for a muffled explosive sound interrupted his words, bringing them both to their feet. "What on earth was that?" Alberta cried.

"The laboratory! It sounded like an explosion." For all his awkwardness, Septimus was quick. He ran toward the stairs, followed by Alberta. He took the stairs two, three, and even four at a time while she was crying, "Wait for me, Septimus!"

He turned, and his face was pale. "D-d-d-" He tried to speak, but as always during times of crisis, a terrible stutter overtook him. "C-c-come on, Wife."

The two raced up to the third floor, and Septimus burst through the door to the room that housed the spacious laboratory where he did his work. He stopped dead still and put his arm around Alberta to support her. "Serafina, what happened?"

Elizabeth Serafina Trent, Viscountess of Radnor, was standing in the midst of a wrecked room. Her face was blackened with some sort of powder, and her eyes looked enormous. Her white apron also showed signs of the explosion.

"Are you all right, Serafina?" Alberta rushed to her.

Serafina raised her hand to push her hair away from her eyes. "Oh yes, Mother. I'm fine."

"What happened, Daughter?" Septimus asked.

Serafina turned to look at the laboratory. The shock of the explosion had not harmed her particularly, but her ears were still ringing with the blast. "I finished designing my gas oven."

"A gas oven! What in the world for?" Alberta demanded. She had little patience with the scientific work that went on in the laboratory, though her husband had grown wealthy by such inventions.

"Mother," Serafina said patiently, "you know all over England people are cooking with coal or wood. It's expensive, and England's running out of wood at least. The obvious thing is to design a stove that runs on gas. Well, that's what I've been making. Gas is the answer."

Alberta put her hand over her heart. "You look terrible," she moaned. "Are you sure you're not hurt?"

"Oh no," Serafina said. "I'm fine."

"Well, you won't be going to that dinner tonight," Alberta said.

"Why, of course I will. This is one dinner I won't miss."

Septimus shook his head in disbelief. "You hate formal dinners like this, Daughter."

"Not this one, Father. I'm going to meet the man I've admired for so long."

Alberta's eyes glowed, and she was smiling. "Is he . . . eligible?" she asked, hopeful that some man had created an interest in her older daughter's heart.

"He's a genius, Mother. It's Mr. Charles Darwin."

"Who is he?" Alberta frowned.

"He's the most brilliant scientist in the world—next to my own father, of course."

"Well, if I had known he was going to be there, I would have invited myself," Septimus said. "Perhaps you can invite him here."

The Viscountess of Radnor smiled. "I will certainly try, Father." She turned to her mother and shook her head. "But Mr. Darwin is married, I believe, so he's not eligible."

Septimus suddenly laughed, his face crinkled with fine lines. "Well, my dear, you go to your dinner and your Mr. Darwin, and I'll see what I can do with the mess you've made."

Alberta did not give up easily. "There'll probably be other gentlemen at the dinner. Maybe one of them would be a likely suitor for you."

Serafina came over and gave her mother an affectionate embrace. "If I find any man as brilliant as my father, I promise you, I'll marry him. Now—I must get cleaned up for Mr. Darwin!"

THREE

"Oh, it's a beautiful dress, Viscountess!"

Louisa Toft, Serafina's maid, stepped back, her green eyes glowing with admiration. She was a beautiful girl with red hair and skin like cream. "Don't you just love it, ma'am?"

"I suppose it's all right, Louisa."

Louisa shook her head. "You think less of clothes than any high society woman I ever saw."

"Clothes are to cover one up."

Louisa laughed with delight. "That's exactly the sort of thing you say that no other woman would say. All the other women I ever served saw clothes as much more than that, not just to cover up but to decorate, to entice, to allure." Her eyes ran up and down Serafina's figure. "And that dress will certainly do it."

Serafina indeed was dressed magnificently. The gown was a Nile green, elegant as water in the sun and stitched with silver beading and seed pearls. The waist was tiny and less than comfortable. The bodice crossed over at the front with the bosom low cut. The crinoline skirt formed the shape of a big dome, flowing from the waist to a wide hemline.

"You'll be the most beautiful woman at the dinner."

"I think I may be the only one."

21

Louisa stared with astonishment. "You'll be the only woman there! I don't believe it."

"It's a group of prominent men. When I heard that Charles Darwin would be there, I simply had to invite myself." Serafina smiled and turned to study herself carefully in the mirror. She was a tall woman, and at twenty-seven years still had the curves of a girl of eighteen. Her hair was an unusual strawberry blonde, and her eyes were her best feature. They were large, well spaced, and of an unusual violet tinge. Her face was too square for real beauty, but her wide, sensuous mouth made up for that. She touched her hair and said, "You've done a beautiful job on my hair, Louisa. You really deserve to have a more discerning mistress."

"Oh no, I only want to serve you, Viscountess," Louisa said quickly. "I am so glad that you are going out into society more."

Serafina shrugged. "This isn't really a social visit. As I said, I want to meet Charles Darwin."

"But you need a social life, my lady."

Serafina turned slightly and studied her maid. Her lips seemed to tighten, and she said, "A social life? Why would I need that? I have every-thing I want right here at Trentwood. My parents, my son, a fine home, and I have you to take care of me."

"But that's not all there is to life. There are other things."

Serafina knew that Louisa was carefully refraining from mention-ing a husband. When the girl had first come to serve Serafina, she had said something about Serafina's remarrying, and Serafina had cut her off so shortly that the subject had never come up again.

"Society is nothing but vanity. It is seeing who can spend the most money on the most ridiculous fashions. Look at this skirt." She turned and looked at the huge diameter spin around. "What a ridiculous thing to put on a woman's body!"

"I suppose some fashions are a little strange."

"Society itself is more than just a little strange. Just look at the way we auction off young girls for marriage."

"Auction girls? What do you mean, Viscountess?"

"In America they have slave markets where they take young black women and sell them to men ostensibly to be servants, but everyone knows what they're to be used for."

"But we don't have slavery in England."

"No, not of that variety, but every year young girls are put on the market. They are paraded around at teas and parties, they attend the races, they go to as many balls as possible, and for what reason? For enjoyment? Not at all! Most of the time they are miserable, afraid they will never catch a man, or not one who is suitable anyway. In the end the men look them over as if they were brood stock, able to produce a satisfactory heir. No, thank you, Louisa. I went through that once, and I would hope never to be again in such a position." Serafina suddenly saw that Louisa was disturbed. Her lips were trembling, and she said, "Why, what's wrong, Louisa? I haven't hurt your feelings?"

"No, my lady, but it's just that—well, ma'am, I've told you about Robert and how I love him. We're going to the park today. I think he's in love with me."

"And what about you?"

"Oh, Lady Serafina, I tremble all over when I think of him!"

Serafina opened her lips to make some cutting remark, for she had no use for such romantic notions. It was exactly this sort of thing that disgusted her, but when she saw the dewy-eyed young woman's trembling lips, she said merely, "Well, you go and have a good day, but be careful, Louisa. Don't expect too much out of married life." She turned to the door. "I'll go say good-bye to David."

Serafina descended the winding staircase and stepped out of the side entrance of the house. She went at once to David, who was playing some kind of a game with Danny. Her son's face was streaked with dirt. "David, what in the world?"

"It's my war paint. I'm a savage Indian."

"I'm sorry, Viscountess," Danny said. "'E got all dirty afore I could stop 'im."

"Danny's been reading me a book about wild Indians."

"One of Cooper's books, the American. You know, Viscountess?" Danny said.

"I know the books, and I wish you wouldn't read them to David."

Danny's eyes flew open. "Why, I fink they're a sight of fun. Nothin' immoral in 'em."

"I know, but make-believe games aren't good for young boys." Serafina turned and saw that David was staring at her with something like fear in his eyes. She went over and put her arm around him.

"Don't be 'ard on the boy. 'E's got a wunnerful imagination."

This, although Danny Spears did not know it, was exactly the thing that Serafina feared most. She believed in clinical logic and clear linear thinking, not make-believe stories. "Well, don't be upset, David. Why don't you take him fishing for trout, Danny? You'd like that, wouldn't you, Son?"

"Oh yes, Mum!"

She kissed him, and despite the dirt, she smiled and said, "You'll be asleep when I come home, but tomorrow you and I will go for a ride."

"Can I ride Patches all by myself, Mum?"

"Yes, indeed." She turned and said, "Danny, give this young man a lesson on Patches." Serafina had given the multicoloured pony to David for his sixth birthday.

As the two walked toward the stream, David talked a mile a minute. Serafina worried, *He has too much imagination—just as I once had.* As she turned to leave for the dinner, she thought of the girl she had once been. *There was once a girl full of joy and imagination and notions and romance. She loved fairy tales and high tales of romance.* The thought saddened her, and she whispered, "I wonder where that girl is now."

❧

Albert Givins, the coachman, pulled the landau up in front of the imposing mansion. It was indeed a spectacular home; it had once belonged to John Churchill, who later became the Duke of Wellington. The duke had moved to Blenhim, the most ornate and fabulous private home in all of England, and Sir Osric Wallace now resided in his mansion.

As Givins handed her down, Serafina thought about her host. Wallace had been a poor boy who made a fortune in coal mining. He had recently returned from America, where he had studied their coal mining methods. He had also carefully given large sums of money to the crown, for which Queen Victoria had knighted him as Sir Osric Wallace.

"It will be a rather long wait for you, Givins."

"That's all right, ma'am. Don't trouble yourself about that."

"If you go around to the kitchen, I'll have them fix you a nice supper."

"That's kind of you, ma'am. Indeed, it is."

The door was opened by a fine-looking footman, and Serafina was greeted at once by Lady Wallace, a dumpy, rather homely, but cheerful woman. She reminded Serafina of her own mother.

"Come into the reception room, my dear. You are the last to arrive."

"I didn't mean to be late."

"Oh, you're not late. It will be rather an odd affair. Just three of us women and the rest gentlemen."

Serafina wanted to say, *That's the way I like it,* but she merely said, "I'm sure it will be an enjoyable evening."

They passed down a hallway, the walls covered with paintings and sculptures of various kinds on shelves. They passed into a large open room with an interesting mixture of styles. On one side sat an old Chinese silk screen that had once been of great beauty but was now faded. Still, it held an elegance that gave the room charm and a comfortable grace. There was a Russian samovar on a side table, Venetian glass in a cabinet, a French ormolu clock on the mantel shelf above the fireplace, and a late Georgian mahogany table of total simplicity and cleanness of line that, to Serafina, was the loveliest thing in the room. Lady Wallace said, "Our last guest has arrived, the Viscountess Serafina Trent. Viscountess, let me introduce you to our guests. This, of course, is Mr. Charles Dickens."

Dickens stepped forward, a rather short man with a neatly trimmed beard, observant eyes, and a friendly demeanor. He smiled, took Serafina's hand, and bent over and kissed it. "I am delighted to make your acquaintance, Viscountess."

GILBERT MORRIS

"Thank you, Mr. Dickens. Might I say how much I enjoyed your book on the rulers of England."

"Very kind of you to say so. Which of my novels have you read?"

"Oh, I never read fiction."

A silence fell on the room, and Dickens seemed stunned. "And why not, may I ask?"

"I prefer reality to make-believe."

"That must cut you off from a great deal of pleasure. I find the world of art and literature invigorates me and amplifies reality."

"I'm sure it does for many people. Your success as a writer proves that. It's just that my father educated me to be a scientific thinker, and I find it difficult to move in other realms. But I congratulate you on the success of your latest book, *David Copperfield*. Everyone is talking about it."

"I wish you would try it, Lady Trent. I'll send you a copy."

"So kind of you, Mr. Dickens."

"And this is Mr. John Ruskin. I'm sure you've heard of him."

Ruskin was a man of medium height with mild blue eyes and an air of attentiveness. He kissed Serafina's hand and then said, "I'm very happy to meet you, Lady Trent."

"I must confess I haven't read your book, Mr. Ruskin. I have so many scientific books to read, I have little time for other areas."

"I assure you, you wouldn't like it." The speaker was a small man with quick black eyes and black hair to match.

"This is Mr. Clarence Morton, the reporter for the *London News*," Sir Osric Wallace explained.

"Why is it you think, sir, that I wouldn't like Mr. Ruskin's book?"

"Because he likes the old and hates the new, and I think you are just the opposite."

"I don't hate the new," Ruskin said quickly. "I just think it's ugly."

"You see, Viscountess? You like new inventions. Mr. Ruskin thinks that the older art was better because it was all done by hand. For example, he thinks the gargoyles on the Cathedral of Notre Dame are better

26

because they were done by individual artists. Nowadays a factory would turn them out, and they would be exactly alike."

"And they would not be art," Ruskin said, his eyes glowing with something like anger.

Serafina stared at the man. "I see no value in badly made artifacts."

Ruskin was displeased. "It's your privilege to think so, madam. I see art as a product of the human imagination, not the result of a machine."

"I'm afraid we will never agree, Mr. Ruskin. I believe in intellect and the machine."

Sir Osric was disturbed at the conflict and said quickly, "This is Lord Milburn, a leader in the House of Lords."

"I'm glad to meet you, Lord Milburn."

"And I you, Lady Trent."

"I've been reading about the Indian mutiny."

"Ah, yes, it's a sad thing."

The papers had been full of the news of the Indian mutiny. Many of the native troops had rebelled against their British masters, and all of England was buzzing with ideas about what should be done.

"It seems to me, if what I read is true," Serafina said, "that the solution should be fairly simple."

"Politics are never simple," Lord Milburn said rather stiffly.

"In this case I must disagree. If I understand it correctly, the trouble began over the cartridges for the new infield rifle."

Lord Milburn stared at her. "That is true."

"I understand the bullets were greased with the fat of hogs and cows."

"That is correct."

"But our leadership should have known that the Muslims and the Hindus are forbidden to eat such things, and that the cartridges had to be bitten before they could be inserted in the muzzle."

"This is far too difficult for a layman to understand."

Mr. Morton, the reporter, laughed. "It seems simple enough when Lady Serafina explains it."

Quickly, Sir Osric said, "This is the gentleman you've been anxious to meet. Mr. Charles Darwin."

At once Serafina turned her attention to the man who advanced to stand before her. He was not a handsome man, having a beetling brow and homely features, but she cried out with delight, "I am so happy to meet you, Mr. Darwin! I've read your books about your voyage in the *Beagle* over and over again ."

"I'm delighted to hear it, Lady Trent."

"I hope they have put us together at the table."

"Yes, indeed, we have," Sir Osric said immediately.

"But let me introduce you to a lady I'm sure you will recognise. May I introduce, Lady Trent, Miss Florence Nightingale."

"Of course. How do you do, Viscountess?"

"I've read so much about your work in the Crimea. I, along with all of England, admire you and encourage you in your attempts to improve the nursing situation. It is abominable."

Florence Nightingale was a slight woman with aristocratic features. Serafina's words brought a glow to her eyes. "I hope you can help me get that message across."

At that instant a butler entered and went to stand beside Sir Osric. "Sir, the dinner is ready at your pleasure."

"Why, thank you, Rogers. I believe we are ready. Come along. We can eat and argue at the same time, I trust."

Immediately Serafina took Mr. Darwin's arm and walked with him into the dining room. The room itself was sumptuously decorated in French blue and gold. The long windows were curtained in velvet, displayed in rich folds that skirted out over the floor in the approved fashion. The table glittered with silver and crystal. So many facets gleamed and glinted, the display dazzled the eyes. One could barely see the faces of the people at the farther end of the reflected light. Silver and porcelain clicked discreetly beneath the buzz of conversation as the meal began, footmen refilled glasses, and course after course came and went: two soups, two kinds of fish, partridge and duck, pudding, desserts, and fruits—pears, plums, nectarines, raspberries, grapes—all grouped in generous pyramids.

Darwin was monopolized by Lady Serafina, who said at once, "I read your paper on worms."

Everyone suddenly lifted their heads. Darwin saw the reaction and smiled. "I have written a paper on worms. I'm going to put it into a book. It will be entitled 'The Formation of Vegetable Mold through the Action of Worms, with Observations on Their Habits.'"

Morton laughed. "Mr. Darwin, I don't think people will rush out and buy extra copies of that."

"I believe you are right, Mr. Morton," Darwin said amiably, "but I found something congenial about worms. I became interested in them and wished to learn how far they acted consciously. Worms do not possess any sense of hearing. They took not the least notice of the shrill notes from a metal whistle which was repeatedly sounded near them. Nor did they know the deepest, loudest tones of the bassoon. They were indifferent to shouts if care was taken that the breath should not strike them."

"Somehow that is amusing, if you will forgive me," Charles Dickens said, chuckling. "The idea of the great scientist tooting a tin whistle for worms is somehow beyond my imagination."

Florence Nightingale had said little, but at one point she said, "I understand you are a scientist, Viscountess."

"I pass for one among women, Miss Nightingale."

"I wish you would do something in the medical field."

"Indeed, I've been studying that very thing. I read your report about the many men who died of infection."

"More died of infection in the Crimean War than were killed by bullets. The wounds were terrible."

"I've been conducting a simple experiment of my own. It's just beginning, you understand."

"Indeed?" Miss Nightingale said, her eyes intent on Serafina. "I'd like to hear about it."

"It involves maggots."

Every eye swiveled then to face Lady Serafina Trent, who spoke directly to Miss Nightingale and was unaware of the stares. "Maggots eat diseased flesh. I have introduced maggots into diseased flesh of animals, and have discovered that they have a therapeutic effect."

"We spend a great deal of time trying to keep maggots out of human flesh," Florence Nightingale said. She smiled slightly, amused at the pained expression on the faces around her.

"I think the answer lies in my initial experiments. I hope they may prove something different."

Charles Dickens suddenly cleared his throat, and his face was rather pale. "I think this might not be exactly the topic for a dinner conversation, Viscountess."

Serafina looked around the table with surprise. "Oh, I am sorry, Mr. Dickens. I have very bad manners in society."

Dickens began to talk of the literary world, his captivating presence entertaining everyone. Serafina was silent most of the time; she had not read most of the writers of whom Dickens and the others spoke.

Finally Sir Osric said, "Well, I confess I'm not as well read as most of you gentlemen here, but I did meet a rather famous writer in America. Mr. Edgar Allan Poe."

Dickens at once turned to face Sir Osric, a light in his eyes. "Indeed, you knew Mr. Poe?"

"Oh yes, we became friends of a sort."

"I have read his short stories," Dickens said, "and his poetry. I can't comment on the poetry, but he's a genius with words."

"He writes about such gloomy things," Lord Milburn said. "I tried one. It was about burying someone alive. I can't see the value in that."

"Well, he has a macabre imagination," Sir Osric said, "but he's very popular in America, or was. He died a few years ago."

Dickens was very thoughtful as he said, "The stories of the detective C. Auguste Dupin are excellent. They are almost a new genre."

"Indeed, they are," Sir Osric said warmly. "Mr. Poe told me he was tired of the bumbling of the police. He wanted to create a detective who would use pure mental powers, deduction, don't you see, to solve a crime."

Serafina listened as the talk about Auguste Dupin, the literary detective, went on, but she made no comment. Finally Sir Osric gave a self-conscious laugh. "Indeed, I wish there were such a detective as this Auguste Dupin." He looked at the faces around the table and said, "Of course there is no such man, but I have need of one like him."

"For what reason, sir?" Dickens demanded.

"Well, I managed to get from Mr. Poe, during our relationship, an original manuscript. His fame wasn't then what it is now, but the manuscript is worth at least ten thousand pounds. It'll be worth more later, but it's gone."

"Gone?" Morton, the reporter, said. "What do you mean, sir?"

"I mean a thief broke in and stole the manuscript just last night."

"Have you called the police?"

"Oh yes. They came and looked around, but they said it would be almost impossible to identify the thief or to recover the manuscript."

Serafina suddenly said, "I'm interested in this robbery. Could I see the room that was broken into?"

Sir Osric looked baffled. "Well, of course, Viscountess, if you'd like."

"I'd like to see it myself," Dickens said. He smiled and said in a teasing tone, "I think Lady Trent feels that she might have the kind of mind of Mr. Poe's fictional character, Auguste Dupin."

A smile went around the room, and Serafina said, "It's an interesting problem. All science is a problem, is it not, Mr. Darwin?"

"Indeed, it is, and many of them are never solved."

Sir Osric was embarrassed, but he said, "Perhaps all of you would like to come."

Indeed, the entire company did follow Sir Osric as he led Lady Serafina up the stairs. He opened a door, saying, "These are my private quarters." He crossed the room and motioned. "There's the broken window. The fellow obviously smashed the window, then reached in and unlocked it."

Serafina walked over and looked down at the window. She turned, and her face was stiff with concentration. "Where was the manuscript kept, Sir Osric?"

"Ah, that's the puzzling thing. See here." He walked across the room and opened the door of an armoire. Several garments were hanging there, but he swung back a door. The back of the armoire seemed to be hinged. It swung out, and Sir Osric smiled. "There's my secret safe."

Serafina moved closer. "How many people know the combination of that safe?"

"Only my attorney and I. I hardly think he broke into my house to steal."

"You must have written it down."

"Well, as a matter of fact, I did." He smiled ruefully. "My memory isn't what it used to be."

"I suppose you put it in your desk? Perhaps taped to the underside of one of the drawers?"

Wallace stared at her with amazement. "How in the world did you know that?"

"It was the first place I thought of to hide such a thing. Ergo, you would do the same."

Serafina walked around the room thoughtfully, and Dickens said jovially, "Well, have you determined who the thief is, Viscountess?"

Serafina turned and walked over to the window. "There's no glass on the floor. Was there any outside on the ground?"

Sir Osric nodded, and Serafina turned and stared at the butler, Rogers, who had followed them up the stairs. "The butler is the thief."

Everyone gave her an incredulous look and then turned to face Rogers. The butler's face turned absolutely pale.

"That's—that's not possible," Sir Osric stammered.

"Has he been with you long?"

"No, the man who had served me for several years died recently, but he came recommended by Sir George Philpot himself."

"Did Sir George recommend him in person?"

"No, but I had a letter from him that Rogers brought to me, and I know his handwriting."

"Why, this woman is entirely wrong, Sir Osric," Rogers said. "I'm not a thief."

"I'm afraid you've made a mistake, Lady Trent," Sir Osric said.

"The window was broken from the inside. A random thief would have had no idea about your secret safe."

"But he didn't know the combination!"

"I thought of the hiding place at once. He is a clever man and would have had plenty of time to find it. Only a person who lives here would know that, and one who had opportunity to find the combination."

"I didn't do it, sir. You must believe me, sir!"

"You must have more proof than this, Lady Trent," Sir Osric said, obviously disturbed.

"Rogers here is a literary man."

"How do you know that?"

"At dinner while you were talking about writing, he responded to your comments. When you mentioned one he didn't like, he shook his head. When you mentioned one he did, he nodded and smiled. Also, he's a Cambridge man, and he's come into a large amount of money recently."

"How can you tell that?" Dickens demanded.

"He's wearing a Cambridge tie, and that's an expensive new diamond ring."

"How can you say it's new?" the reporter, Morton, demanded.

"He's taken it off more than once. Look at his hands—they're tanned. If you have him take that ring off, you'll see that underneath, where it should be white, where the ring would protect the skin from the sun, it's not."

The man called Rogers suddenly let out a wild cry, whirled, and dashed out of the room. Everyone began to speak, and Sir Osric dashed out saying, "I must call the police!"

"He can't get far, Sir Osric. I'm sure the police will get out of him the name of the person who bought your manuscript."

Charles Dickens, in all probability the most famous writer in the world, came over to stand before Serafina. His eyes glowed, and he bent over, bowing deeply, and said, "I apologise with all my heart, Viscountess. You are, indeed, a wonder of intellect! A female Auguste Dupin!"

Charles Morton moved closer and offered his accolade. "I think, if you'll read the *London Times*, Viscountess Trent, you'll be interested."

Serafina took her leave soon after that. When she got to the carriage, Givins was waiting. "'Ow was the dinner, Lady Trent?"

As Serafina stepped inside and leaned back against the leather cushion, she shrugged. "Oh, it was all rather boring—except for the part about the worms and the burglar, of course."

✧ FOUR ✧

Light had begun drawing a faint line across the horizon in the east when Serafina rose. She had passed a restless night, which was not unusual for her. Moving over to the window, she stared outside, and her eyes fell on the tall trees over to the west of the park. They stood in disorganised ranks like a regiment at ease, and already they were laying their shadows on the ground in long lines. She stood there so long that the trees seemed to shoulder the sun out of the way, but then the light came through, and the sun put lambent fingers through the trees, touching the earth with gentleness. She turned from the window finally and began to dress. She knew that Louisa would be along shortly to help her, but she had an independence in her that would not submit to this. *A woman should be able to dress herself without help.* The thought sprang into her mind, and she smiled faintly at her own foolish ideas.

When she was dressed, she went back to the window again, as if reluctant to leave the sanctity of her room. She knew it would be a warm day, but an April shower was forming in the west. Torn shreds of clouds dragged across a clear azure sky, casting their frail shadows over the land. Serafina was always sensitive to the weather. A dreary day could darken her spirits and cause her to retreat into a shell. On the other hand, a cheerful, sunny day always lifted her spirits.

She turned and left her room, descended the stairs, then made her way to the kitchen. She stepped inside and was pleased with the warmth and good smells that already had begun to fill the room. It was a huge kitchen with a black cooking range big enough to roast half a beef and boil enough vegetables or bake enough pies and pastries to feed fifty people at a sitting. She ran her eyes over the rows of copper saucepans hung in order of size, every one shining clean. Open cabinets held services of crockery, and beyond the kitchen were sculleries, and larders—one specifically for game—and a bake house. There was also a room for knives, the entire laundry wing, a pantry, and a pastry room. Farther on was the butler's domain, which no human dared enter without fear of offending James Barden.

"Good morning, Nessa."

Nessa Douglas turned at once and greeted Serafina with a smile. "Good morning, mistress." Nessa was thirty-three, blonde with sky blue eyes, and somewhat overweight from sampling her own wares. She was a cheerful woman by nature and gave Serafina a bright smile. "You're up early this morning, ma'am."

"Can I help you with anything, Nessa?"

"And why would you be doing that, Viscountess? That's what you pay me for. You do your job, and I do mine."

"I'd like a cup of tea while I watch."

"It's already made." Nessa moved her bulk quickly around the kitchen and set a large mug of steaming tea before Serafina. "There, that's your favourite cup. You hate those tiny little china cups."

"I always say you can't have a cup of tea too hot or too large." Serafina sipped the tea and sat there and watched, her mind on something else. Nessa was aware that something was troubling the viscountess, but a servant did not inquire into the troubles of those who lived above the stairs.

By the time Serafina had finished her second cup of tea, she had watched Nessa throw together a breakfast with such skill and ease that it seemed a child could do it. Nessa had prepared fresh strawberries, steaks, scrambled eggs, fried potatoes, biscuits, buckwheat cakes, fried bread, and a fruit compote with strawberries, blueberries, and peaches with honey and milk.

"It looks like no one's going to starve to death." Serafina smiled. She had a good relationship with most of the servants. Only the butler, James Barden, was stiffly formal with her. He entered just as Serafina rose. He was a tall, dignified man with a wealth of brown hair neatly parted in the middle, and a pair of penetrating brown eyes. "Good morning, Viscountess."

Serafina said, "Good morning, James."

"Would you care to go to the dining room, ma'am? I'll have the breakfast brought in."

"I'll be there shortly. I have an errand to do first."

"Very well, ma'am."

The viscountess left the room, and as soon as she was out the door, James Barden sniffed. "Seems she'd have more to do than invade the kitchen."

"Bridle your tongue, Mr. Barden," Nessa said sharply. "She's a good mistress."

"She's too free with the help," Barden said. He liked to see the distinction between the family and the servants preserved. He looked over and said, "I think this will be sufficient. I'll have Rachel take it in."

❦

The knocking at the door disturbed Clive's restless sleep. The noise persisted, and finally he sat up and blinked his eyes like an owl brought into the sunlight. "Who could that be?" he grumbled. Slipping out of bed, he pulled on a blue silk robe and went to the door. Opening it, he found Serafina standing there. "What is it, Serafina?"

"I've got to talk to you, Clive." Serafina simply pushed by Clive. He shut the door, then said with irritation, "Couldn't it wait until after breakfast?"

"No, I'm leaving as soon as I finish breakfast. I'm going riding with David this morning."

Clive's fair hair was mussed, and a look of apprehension flickered in

37

his eyes. He cleared his throat before asking, "What is it? You never come here unless it's to tell me I'm doing something wrong."

"That's why I'm here."

"Well, what is it I've done this time?"

Serafina Trent had a direct way of approaching problems. She had heard it said once of her grandfather that he had a way of lowering his head and looking as if he were about to ram it through a solid oak door. There was something of this quality in Serafina as she turned squarely to face this younger brother of hers. Her eyes were fastened on him, and there was a severity in the set of her lips. "You're making a fool out of yourself with this actress, Clive."

"Serafina, that's none of your business. I'm twenty-one years old. I can do as I please."

"No, you can't. You're part of the family, and when one part of the family fails, all of us fail."

Clive tried to meet Serafina's gaze but could not. He dropped his eyes and mumbled sulkily, "There's nothing wrong with my seeing Kate."

"There's something wrong with stealing."

Clive reared back with shock. "Stealing?" he muttered. "What are you talking about?"

"I'm talking about the diamond ring that's missing from the safe. You took it, didn't you?"

Clive threw his arms out in a mildly eloquent gesture. "I have to do something to make Kate notice me. And anyway, no one ever wears that ring."

"So it's all right to steal from your own family? Is that what you're saying?" Serafina's voice was sharp, and she plunged the truth home relentlessly. "Don't you see what you've become? You've given up your honour for that woman—who is no more than a harlot if all I hear is true."

"Don't talk that way about her! You don't understand, Serafina." Clive put his hands before him as if to push Serafina away, and his voice turned to pathetic pleading. "You would never understand my feelings. You don't *have* any feelings, but I do."

"I have feelings the same as anyone else."

"You never show them for anyone except for David," he whined. "Well, I can't think of anyone except Kate."

For a long moment Serafina stood there wondering how to reach this brother of hers. His charge that she had no feelings hurt her, for she did have feelings—much deeper than anyone knew. But it was within her power to control them, and she saw that Clive lacked this ability. "You've got to stop seeing her."

"I won't do it, Serafina! Now if you'll leave, I'll get dressed."

Serafina put her eyes on him and saw the weakness in his face. "I'm sorry for you, Clive. Any man who would dishonour himself for a woman like that is in poor condition." She turned and left the room. Clive went over to the wicker chair beside the window and threw himself into it. He dropped his face into his hands. For a long time he sat there, Serafina's words burning into him as with a branding iron, and he knew that he would hear them over and over again. Finally he arose, thinking, *She doesn't understand. She's never loved anybody except her son.* He slowly began to dress, but dreaded facing the family. "I wonder if she'll tell them about the ring." He spoke the words aloud and then shook his head. "No, she's hard, but she wouldn't do that."

❧

The day had passed miserably enough for Clive Newton. As he had known would happen, he could not blot Serafina's words out of his mind. She had accused him of being a man without honour, and Clive had always prided himself on his honour. He had gotten away from the house as soon as possible after breakfast and had spent most of the day at the club, but late in the afternoon he had begun to drink. Now that the afternoon was closing down, and night would soon be here, he was on his way to the Old Vic. Deep in thought, he walked along the Thames embankment. From time to time he glanced at the steamboats on the river that were crowded with people enjoying themselves, wearing hats with streamers and waving to the shore. A band was playing, and he passed street peddlers selling lemonade, ham sandwiches, and various kinds of sweets.

All of this had little effect on Clive, for it was a struggle to put Serafina's charges out of his mind and to place his thoughts on Kate. As he approached the theatre, he heard the sound of laughter, music, and horses' hooves on the cobblestones. Open carriages passed with ladies displaying their fashionable hats and pretty faces. He passed a coster-monger pushing a barrow of fruits and vegetables. The man's shoulders strained against a coat a size too small, and his pinched face was thin with hunger and despair. Clive stopped at a public house and drank for half an hour, waiting for the time to pass. By the time he left, he was half-drunk. He knew that he did not hold his liquor well, but he chose to ignore it.

When he entered the Old Vic Theatre, he went at once to the side entrance that led backstage. As usual, though his mind was dulled by drink, he felt a sense of excitement as he moved through the crowd. He was in the midst of the business of the actors and actresses, along with those who handled the physical elements of the drama.

"Well, Clive, how are you tonight?"

Clive turned to face Dylan Tremayne, who now stood beside him. He nodded and muttered, "Hello, Dylan."

"A little early you are tonight. But I think you'd better go take your seat."

"Got to see Kate."

"Wouldn't be a good idea tonight. She's not in a particularly good mood." Dylan's eyes were fixed on the young man's face, and he said gently, "Put it off for a while, friend."

But Clive's mind was blunted by alcohol. He shook his head and mumbled, "Gotta see Kate . . ." He lifted his eyes and saw Kate just exiting from her dressing room. He felt numb, as he always did when he drank too much, and at some deep level knew he was in no condition to talk to the woman. But the alcohol had also dulled his sensitivity to tact. He moved forward, aware that Dylan was speaking to him, but he shook his head angrily. Walking toward Kate, he said, "Hello, Kate."

She turned and looked at him, then said with disgust, "You're drunk, Clive. Go somewhere and sleep it off."

"No, I've gotta talk to you." Clive was vaguely aware that others were listening, but he reached out and grasped Kate by the arm. "I want to marry you, Kate." His voice sounded much louder than he intended, and he heard several voices laughing.

"Another one with a proposal," someone said.

"Go away, Clive. I don't have time for you."

"I'm telling you I want to marry you. I want you to be my wife."

Kate laughed suddenly. "You're a young fool, Clive. We've had a good time, but it's all over. Now go away and be a good fellow."

"You don't mean that, Kate. I love you."

"That's not enough. I told you from the first that you were a silly boy, but you insisted on chasing me around. It's gotten tiresome."

Clive swayed slightly from side to side and focused his eyes on Kate. "You can't make an idiot out of me!"

"Nature's already done that," Kate said cruelly. She had beautiful features, but as she faced Clive, there was something feral in her eyes. "Now get out of here and leave me alone!"

"But I—I gave you a family ring."

"You want it back?"

"Yes."

"Well, you can't have it. It's the price you pay for education, Clive. Now I've got to go." She turned and made for the wings, but Clive reached out and grasped her. His fiery temper suddenly erupted. "You can't treat me like this! I won't let you!"

"Turn loose of me!"

"No, I won't! Give me that ring back or I'll break your neck!"

Clive began shaking Kate, who screamed, and at once strong hands were on Clive, pulling him away. He turned to see that Dylan and Ives Montgomery were holding him. "Take your hands off me!" he shouted furiously.

"Time for you to leave, Clive." The two actors turned him around, and Ives said, "You got off light, Newton. She took me for everything I had and then laughed at me."

Clive was struggling in the hands of the two strong men. "I'll get that ring back if I have to kill her!"

"Now you don't mean that," Dylan said. "Let me get someone to take you home." But Clive lurched away, muttering threats, and as soon as he was gone, Ives shook his head. "He's got to learn to handle his problems better than that."

Dylan was staring after the young man and said with compassion in his voice, "Probably the first thing Clive ever wanted that he couldn't get."

❧

Dylan knocked on the door of Kate's dressing room, and when he heard her voice, he opened the door and stepped inside. She was sitting at her dressing table and had changed her costume for street clothes. She rose from the chair and faced him squarely. "Well, what is it, Dylan? I suppose it's about that young fool who attacked me."

"Yes. I've come to ask you to give him a break. He is a fool, but we all are from time to time."

"What do you want me to do? The best favour I can do him is to not see him anymore, and I've told him that's the way it would be."

"You ought to give him the ring back, yes? I suspect it's a family treasure."

"Well, it's my family treasure now." She held up her hand and said, "Beautiful, isn't it?" Indeed, the ring was large and caught the reflection of the gaslight. Kate held it up, admired it, and said, "It's the pay I get for putting up with him. He was a real bore, Dylan."

Dylan tried to reason with Kate, but she stubbornly refused. "I'm keeping the ring," she said. She suddenly came over and took him by the arm, pressing herself against him. "I'm not going out to eat tonight. I'm going home. Why don't you come with me? I'll fix us something."

"No thanks, Kate."

Kate bit her lip and stared at the handsome man in front of her. Often, she had left the door open for him to make advances, but he never had. She believed that he was some sort of religious fanatic, but in Kate's mind all men were alike even if they were parsons. It irritated her that she could not ensnare Dylan, and she said, "Dylan, you're the first man who ever turned me down. I just can't believe you're that holy."

"Why, I'm not calling myself that, ay? You don't know the struggle I have to keep myself from going to rack and ruin as I was before."

"You weren't always a holy man, then."

"I don't call myself that even now. I was a sinner just as bad as any other man, you see."

His words caught Kate's attention, and as she watched him, she was acutely aware that something in him made him different from other men. She had heard men protest that they had no lust for her, but she had always been able to read that very thing in their eyes. Dylan seemed to walk in another dimension, and she asked impulsively, "What happened, if you were such a sinner, to make you so good?"

Dylan studied her closely. She was a beautiful woman, but he was well on his guard with her. "Well, it's this way, Kate. Sometimes a man bends over for a moment, and when he straightens up, the whole world has changed. A man can change that quick—and a woman too."

"What kind of change?"

"God can change a heart in a blink of an eye. The Bible calls it the new birth. Like being born again, it is. God takes away your old sin-stained heart and gives you a fresh new one. Now that's a glorious thing to happen to a fellow, yes?"

Kate stared at him. "I don't believe it."

"Oh, but it's true. The Gospel is the good news, Kate. Jesus died for our sins, and when you come to Jesus and ask Him to forgive you, there's no argument. It's done in a moment, and from that time on you're a new person, see? I'd like to see that happen to you, Kate."

Kate stepped away and eyed Dylan coldly. "I've got everything I want. I've got my looks, money, men chasing me. I could marry a dozen times tomorrow. Even a lord or two has been after me. You know that."

"But what about when all that's gone, Kate?"

"Gone? Gone where?"

"Why, you'll lose all of that. There'll come a time when you and I won't have our teeth, when we're all wrinkled and weak. Old age doesn't show any favourites. This black hair of mine will either be gone or silvered. Your good looks will fade as all things on this earth do. Then where will your admirers be? We'll lose everything in this world. Time takes it away from us."

Fear touched Kate Fairfield's eyes. She'd had thoughts like this but had always managed to put them away. "I don't want to hear about all that."

But Dylan was persistent. He spoke softly but with a fierce intensity that held Kate still. "Jesus is your friend, Kate. One day you and I will both stand before God. What will I be telling Him when He asks what I did? You know what I'll say? I'll say, 'Lord, I was a sinner. I committed every sin that I ever thought of, but Jesus bore all my sins on the cross—so I throw myself on your mercy because of what Jesus did.'" Dylan paused, and his eyes held hers. "What will you say to Him, Kate?"

Kate closed her eyes, and a tremor went through her body. She whirled suddenly, grabbed her coat, and gave him an angry look. "I'm not going to give up what I've got, Dylan! Maybe when I get older I'll have time for God—but not now." She hurried through the door, leaving Dylan standing in the middle of the dressing room. He went to the door and watched her sadly as she hurried away. "Poor lost woman. You have it all—and yet you really have nothing."

∗

As she usually did, Helen Morton arose early and fixed her own breakfast. She knew it would be useless to prepare a breakfast for her mistress, for

Kate did not rise early. Helen was a young woman of twenty who had become the personal maid of the actress almost a year ago. She had learnt that Kate demanded tact and discretion from her maid, as well as skill in hairdressing and wardrobe. She was expected to go blind when Kate brought a man home with her. The actress had warned her thoroughly that she would be dismissed if she ever spoke of anything that happened in the rooms where Kate lived in the south of London.

Helen fixed a good breakfast, then for a time she sat there reading yesterday's paper. She had always loved the cobwebby hours just before dawn. As soon as the morning began to break, she began to think of what clothing her mistress would wear. Rising from the table, she went to the door of her mistress's bedroom, slipped off her shoes, and silently opened the door. There had been times when there had been a man in the bedroom with Kate, but in the dimness of the room, she suddenly realised that the bed was empty. The covers were turned down and the bed had not been slept in.

She must not have come home last night. Helen shrugged, for this was not an unusual occurrence. She started across the room. A dim light from the gaslight in the street gave the room a pale opalescence. Something was different in the room, and Helen stopped. She looked past the bed and saw what appeared to be a bundle of dark clothes, blankets, or sheets piled together. She walked by the foot of the bed, and when she reached the pile, she realised that they were not clothes at all.

Helen's body seemed to freeze, for by the dim light she saw that Katherine Fairfield was staring up at her with sightless eyes. A terrible dark stain marred her graceful throat, and her bosom was saturated with blood.

Helen could not move for a moment, but then a bubbling scream rose to her throat. She backed away, holding her hands out as if someone were attacking her, then turned and fled from the silent room where the dead woman lay staring at the ceiling.

FIVE

"Mum, can I ride Patches this morning?"

Serafina was buttoning the jumper that she had just put on David. Shaking her head, she said, "Not today, Son. Don't you remember we're going to Buckingham Palace to watch the changing of the guard?"

"Will that be fun?"

"Oh yes, it will be very impressive."

"Will the queen be there?"

"I doubt it, David. She has many things to do."

"I'd like to meet the queen."

"Well, so would a great many other people, but she just can't get around to greet all of her subjects. I'm sure she'd like to, though."

"Does she have any little boys?"

"As a matter of fact, she does. She and the prince consort have a nice family."

"I'd like to go play with the queen's children."

"Well, I would like for you to, but it's very difficult to get in to see them. The prince and the queen are very concerned parents. They're very strict with their children."

"Don't they love them like you love me?"

"Oh, I'm sure they do." Serafina smiled. She suddenly felt a wave of warmth rising up in her. She reached out and pulled David in, giving him a hug and a resounding kiss on the cheek. "There, that's how much I love you. Now let's go down and have breakfast."

"Can we have the fish I caught yesterday for breakfast?"

Serafina laughed. "No, I'm afraid not, but I'm sure that Nessa has prepared a fine breakfast for us."

The two went downstairs into the smaller of the two dining rooms. The rest of the family were all there except for Clive, Serafina noticed. She felt a qualm, for she knew he had been going to the theatre frequently. She had gone early in the morning and found Clive fully dressed and sprawled across his bed. She had smelled the raw alcohol on his breath but had left him alone.

"Well, you two are late." Aldora Lynn Newton, at the age of seventeen, was a most attractive young lady. She was no more than medium height, slender but with a blossoming figure and a fine carriage. She had a wealth of auburn hair, warm brown eyes, and beautifully shaped lips. "And how are you this morning, David?" she said.

"I'm going to watch the changing of the guard with Mum."

"Oh, you'll like that. I'm sure." Dora smiled. She was a bright young woman, not scientifically minded like her father and her older sister, but as the servants often said, she was sweeter than the Viscountess. She turned and smiled at Serafina, saying, "I've got a present for you, Serafina."

Serafina turned to Dora. "It's not my birthday, Dora."

"I know that, but it's something I think you need to read. I think you'll enjoy it." She bent over and picked up a small package and handed it to Serafina.

"Did you get *me* a present too?" David piped up.

"Not this time, but I'll get you something nice if you're a good boy today."

Serafina carefully untied the blue ribbon that held the cream-coloured paper and stared at the small book with the rather garish cover. "Why . . . this is a novel, Dora. You know I never read novels."

"I know you don't, but you should read this one." Dora's face glowed as she said, "It's a detective story by Regis Stoneman. The heroine is a woman, and she's very smart, just like you are."

Serafina read the title aloud: "*The Mermaid in the Basement.* What a strange title—very fanciful."

"Everybody is reading Mr. Stoneman's novels," Dora said, her eyes glowing with excitement. "I've read all six of the novels in this series. The heroine is named Sabrina Diamond."

"Nobody would name a child that," Serafina murmured as she opened the book and read a few lines. "Why, this is a romance novel, Dora!"

"Yes, it is." Dora nodded. "She's a romantic detective. I—I thought you'd like a little romance in your life, Serafina."

Serafina gave Dora a hug and laughed. "I promise to read it—even if it does have a nonsensical title. Thank you, Dora. It was very sweet of you to try to put some romance in an old woman's life."

"You're not old!" David said. "And I like the title. I want you to read it to me, Mum."

Alberta listened as Serafina explained why some books shouldn't be read to very young boys, and then said, "I wonder where Clive is." She was dressed rather formally for breakfast, wearing a teal green dress trimmed with turquoise. It was expensive, as were all her clothes. The huge skirt swept around her as she moved across the room to the sideboard.

"I think he's sleeping late this morning, Mother," Serafina said.

"I'll go wake him up," David said.

"No, Son, he'll get up when he gets ready."

"He must have gotten in late last night," Septimus said. He was sitting at the end of the table, reading a book as usual. "I wish he wouldn't stay out so late."

As Serafina went to the sideboard, she noted the family's dining room with approval. It was not large but extremely elegant, with warm yellow paper, a golden wood floor, and heavy mahogany furniture. There were tawny bronze chrysanthemums in a vase over the sideboard, and she surveyed the breakfast that Nessa had prepared with satisfaction. She wondered if Clive was taking it all for granted. He had never faced any real difficulties in life, so perhaps he did not understand the value of what he had.

"Well, we're not going to starve to death at least." The sideboard was crowded with chafing dishes of kedgeree, deviled kidneys, scrambled eggs, poached eggs, bacon, sausages, smoked finnan haddock, kippers, and grilled mushrooms. She chose several items for David and returned to the table. "I don't want anything but the deviled eggs," David protested. "I don't want the rest of this."

"You need to eat some of all of it," Serafina nodded. "Now be a good boy." She went back, selected her own food, then sat down. Dora began speaking of a ball that she was going to, and Serafina studied her younger sister. She suddenly remembered that she had been just Dora's age when she met Viscount Charles Alden Trent. A poignant sadness came to her as she thought of how happy she had been, as happy as Dora seemed to be now. It seemed like another time and another age, when in reality she had been a widow for only two years. She did not like to think about the time of her marriage with Charles, so she blotted it out and listened as Septimus began reading from the newspaper.

"I see where our Royal Navy has destroyed a Chinese fleet over in Canton. I wonder why in the world the queen bothers to conquer China. All they do is ship opium over to us, and we certainly don't need that." He skimmed down the paper and remarked with satisfaction, "Well, they've done something worthwhile at last."

"What's that, Father?" Serafina asked, taking a bite of the deviled eggs.

"They've nearly completed that cable that goes under the Atlantic. Now *there's* an achievement that science can be proud of!"

"What's it for, dear?" Alberta asked.

"Why, it's to send messages."

"They go through a cable under the ocean? How could that be?"

Serafina thought, *After so many years of marriage, one would think Father would have learnt that Mother has no head for science whatsoever.*

She listened as Septimus explained the workings of electricity and how messages could be sent through a cable on the ocean floor, but the expression on her mother's face was one of complete puzzlement.

Finally Serafina interrupted by saying, "Did you read the story there about the Frenchman Louis Pasteur?"

"No, I haven't seen that yet."

"Well, he's proved that fermentation is caused by living organisms."

Septimus put his paper down, and the two of them began speaking of Pasteur's work. They might have been speaking in Sanskrit for all that Dora or Alberta understood. Septimus was just beginning another complicated explanation when James appeared. He cleared his throat and said, "Pardon me for interrupting, sir, but there are two gentlemen here to see you."

Septimus stared at him. "Who are they?"

"I believe they are from the police, sir."

Septimus could not have been more surprised if Barden had announced they had come from the moon. "The police!" he exclaimed.

"Well, sir, actually they're from Scotland Yard. One of them is Superintendent Winters."

"Oh, Mr. Winters!" Alberta exclaimed. "Why, I had lunch with Mrs. Winters just last Thursday. I wonder if anything has happened."

"I expect I had better go see," Septimus said.

"I'll go with you, Father," Serafina added quickly. "You finish your breakfast, David."

"Yes, Mum, but can I have more eggs?"

"Yes. Dora, get David some more eggs, please."

Septimus and Serafina left the room, and Serafina forced herself to control her agitation. Somehow she did not feel this was a social visit.

They entered the foyer, where the two men were waiting to greet them.

"Yes, gentlemen, what can I do for you?" Septimus said.

"I am Superintendent William Winters. You are Mr. Newton, I believe?"

"Yes, indeed. This is my daughter, Viscountess Serafina Trent."

Winters bowed. He was a tall, strongly built man of forty-four. He had aquiline features and icy blue eyes. "This is Inspector Matthew Grant." Grant bowed slightly but said nothing. He stood only slightly shorter than Winters, and his thick hair, obviously prematurely grey, glowed with health. He emanated physical well-being; strength was evident in his hands and in the thickness of his neck.

"Would you gentlemen care to come into the study?"

"I think that might be best, Mr. Newton."

Newton led the way into the study. It was a gracious room lined with bookshelves on two sides, the third being taken up with floor-to-ceiling windows curtained in rust red velvet. On the fourth side was a huge marble fireplace flanked by semicircular tables inlaid with exotic wood. A massive oak desk also sat imposingly in the room, complemented by a finely carved chair in green leather, its back to the windows, and also two large, leather-covered armchairs.

Serafina did not speak, but kept her eyes fixed on Winters and Grant. Of the two men, Grant seemed the most formidable. His attitude seemed belligerent, and his hazel eyes had an almost angry glint in them that she could not account for. Winters, on the other hand, despite his imposing presence, had a certain charm about him. She had heard her mother say that he had married a wealthy woman who had political ambitions for her husband.

"I know our visit comes as a surprise, but we need to have a word with Clive Newton. He's your son, I believe?"

"Yes, he is."

"We need to speak with him, sir."

"I'm afraid he's not up yet, Superintendent," Serafina said.

"I'm afraid I'll have to ask you to get him up," Winters said quietly.

"What's the problem, Superintendent?" Serafina asked. Her father seemed too stunned even to speak.

"There's been a crime, and we need to question your brother."

"I can't imagine what Clive could know about such a thing!" Septimus said, his voice troubled.

"I'll go get Clive," Serafina said. "Would you gentlemen be seated? I'll have the maid bring some tea."

"That would be most gracious, Viscountess." Winters bowed slightly.

Serafina ascended the stairs quickly. She did not knock on Clive's door but simply opened it and stepped inside. He was still asleep, and he groaned as she shook him. "Get up, Clive!"

"What? What is it?" Clive pushed her away and gave her an angry look. "What do you want, Serafina?"

"You've got to get up."

"Leave me alone." Clive tried to move away, but Serafina grasped his arms. "The police are downstairs. They insist on speaking with you."

Clive sat up and stared wildly around the room in confusion. "The police?"

"There's been a crime committed, and they want to question you about it."

Clive stood to his feet shakily, and the movement seemed to give him extreme pain in his temples. He raised his hand and held his head for a moment. "A crime? I don't know anything about a crime."

"Where were you last night, Clive?"

"I went to the theatre."

Serafina started to question him but shook her head. "You'll have to come down."

"I'll need to shave first."

"I don't think these gentlemen will wait. You can take care of that later. Come now."

Serafina waited until Clive had walked uncertainly to the door. He stepped through it and held the banister on his way down the stairs. "My head is killing me," he whispered.

"Be very careful what you say. These men will be listening carefully."

"I don't know why they want to talk to me."

"They're in the study. Father's with them."

Serafina took Clive's arm and led him to the door to the study. She released him and walked in with Clive close behind her. "This is my brother. Clive, this is Superintendent Winters and Inspector Grant."

Winters did not offer a formal greeting. "Mr. Newton, we have a few questions to ask you if you don't mind."

Clive's eyes were bleary. As always when challenged, he grew some-what rebellious. "I can't think why you need to speak with me, sir."

"We need to know your movements after you left the Old Vic Theatre last night." Grant spoke for the first time. He had a guarded manner that was somehow intimidating. His voice was low but demanding. "Where'd you get those scratches on your face, Mr. Newton?"

Serafina's eyes went at once to Clive's face. She had already noted the scratches—rather ugly wounds mostly on the left side of his face.

"I—I got into a little scuffle at a public house."

"Which public house was that, sir?" Grant demanded instantly. He set himself in front of Clive, and Superintendent Winters seemed content to let Grant do the questioning.

"I really don't remember. I had been drinking some."

"You must remember where you went, sir. After you left the theatre, which direction did you take?"

Clive's hands began to tremble. Even Serafina saw it, and her father said nervously, "What is it, Clive?"

"I don't like to be questioned like this."

Grant said at once, "It's either here or we'll take you down to the station."

"The station! You mean you'd arrest me?"

"There's been a tragic event, Mr. Newton," Winters said. His voice was soft, but his icy blue eyes were fixed on Clive. "You are acquainted with Miss Katherine Fairfield?"

"Yes, slightly."

"I understand that you've been seeing her quite regularly."

"We've been out together. What about it?"

Grant spoke, his words harsh. "Her maid found her this morning. She'd been murdered. Slashed terribly."

Serafina's eyes went at once to Clive. She saw him turn pale, and he ran his hands through his hair in a gesture she'd seen often in her brother when he was disturbed.

"I—I can't believe it . . ." Clive stammered. They all saw that he was shaken by the news, but Winters and Grant would see his behaviour in a different light. Even to Serafina, Clive gave the appearance of a guilty man.

"It's true enough," Winters said. "A great tragedy. A most brutal murder."

"But—why are you talking to me?"

"We understand," Grant said, relentless in his questioning, "that you had an altercation with Miss Fairfield at the theatre last night."

Clive swallowed hard and looked at his father and then at Serafina. He dropped his head and muttered, "We had an argument."

"Did you threaten to kill her?"

"Certainly not!"

"I'm afraid," Superintendent Winters said, "we have witnesses that will testify that you did make such threats. Mr. Newton, I think you'd better tell us all of your movements from the time you left the theatre."

Serafina's throat seemed to close as she listened to Clive stumble with his words. He was obviously making up the story, but one thing seemed clear. He had been drunk, and when he drank he usually could not remember what he did.

"I—I do remember going to the Seven Dials section."

"Why did you go there?"

"I—I don't know."

"What did you do while you were there, Mr. Newton?" Grant persisted.

Clive dropped his head. "A woman approached me. We went to get a drink together, and afterward we—we went to her room."

"What was her name?"

"I didn't ask her. But she gave me these scratches on my face. She wanted too much money, and I argued with her."

"Can you describe her, Mr. Newton?" Superintendent Winters asked quietly. "It's very important that we find her—important for you, I mean."

"I don't remember," Clive said. "I was drunk. I do remember she had blonde hair, and she was very tall. That's all I can remember."

"What street were you on?" Grant demanded.

As Grant fired direct questions, Septimus exchanged despairing glances with Serafina. They both were sick at heart. Finally Grant said, "We have a search warrant, Mr. Newton." He spoke to Septimus. "We'll have to search your son's room."

"Of course," Septimus whispered. "I'll take you up there."

The two detectives turned, but Winters said, "I have a sergeant outside. He'll have to stay with you, Mr. Newton, while we're searching your room."

"I'll call him in." Grant left the room and was back in a few minutes. With him was a small man, no more than five feet eight inches, with sandy hair, sharp light brown eyes, and a neat mustache. "This is Sergeant Kenzie. Kenzie, you will remain with Mr. Newton here while we search his room."

"That I will, sir."

The two detectives moved toward the stairway, and the maid came in at that moment with the tea. "Will you have some tea, Sergeant Kenzie?" Newton asked.

"That would be vury good, sir," he said in a thick Scottish accent. "I'm sorry for your trouble."

"Thank you, Sergeant."

❧

The two detectives had been searching the room for over thirty minutes. They were experienced and overlooked nothing.

"Doesn't seem to be anything here that would tie young Newton to the killing," Grant said, and he shook his head. "He's guilty, though. I'd stake my life on that!" Grant gave Winters a direct stare, then continued, "You know what they say about the death of Lady Trent's husband?"

"Of course." Winters shrugged. "I am familiar with that case."

"Some say he was murdered by his wife."

Winters shook his head, and regret tinged his tone as he said, "I'm one of those who believe that—but there wasn't enough evidence."

"What convinced you that she killed her husband, sir?"

"It was more of a feeling, Grant, and you know as well as I that in a murder trial, the prosecutor needs more than that."

Grant's lips drew together into a tight line, and he said, "I think Clive is guilty."

"Good! Then let's find some hard evidence."

The two continued to search, and finally Grant, who had pulled the drawer out of an armoire, spoke sharply. "Superintendent, look at this."

Winters came over and asked, "What is it, Grant?"

"Behind this drawer there's a cavity. And look, there's a bag here."

Grant pulled the bag out. It was leather, with a drawstring, and when he opened it and poured the contents into his hand, jewels glittered.

"That's bad news for Newton," Superintendent Winters said, shaking his head. "This looks like some of the jewellery on the list of what was missing from the victim's room."

"I've got the list, sir."

"Come over here and lay them out on this desk."

Grant emptied the bag, and the two men checked the contents against the list.

"There's no doubt about it," Grant said grimly. "They're the jewels that were taken from Kate Fairfield's room." He put the jewellery back, and had started to leave when suddenly Superintendent Winters stopped and said, "What's that?"

"What's what, sir?"

"There—stuffed behind that chest."

Winters went over, and Grant followed him. Winters reached down and tried to squeeze his hand behind it. "Some cloth back here."

"What would it be doing back there? Here, let me move this chest out." Grant gave a tug, and the heavy chest shifted enough for Superintendent Winters to pull out a garment. "It's a handkerchief," he said.

Grant leaned forward and took a short breath. "It's got blood all over it, sir. He wasn't very careful, was he?"

"We don't know that it's his."

"Why, of course we do, Superintendent. It's in his room. I just don't know why a man would be so careless as to leave a bloodstained handkerchief to be found."

Winters stood there holding the handkerchief. "It seems we have little choice."

"Well, we have more than feelings here, don't we, Superintendent?"

Winters nodded slowly. "I believe we do, Grant. I'm sorry for the family."

Grant shrugged. "There's always a family who gets hurt. Every criminal has some family who has to suffer."

"I suppose you're right." He gave the room a regretful look, then sighed deeply. "Well, Grant, let's go give the family the bad news." He stood still for a moment, then gave Grant a strange look. "I hate this part of our job."

"It's never easy, sir." The two went downstairs, and as soon as they entered the room, Clive stood to his feet. "Is this yours, sir?" Grant asked, holding up the bloodstained handkerchief.

"I—I never saw that handkerchief!"

"It has blood all over it," Superintendent Winters said quietly. "How do you account for that?"

Clive shook his head. "I don't know. I—I think I had a nosebleed."

"Well, why did you hide it behind the chest in your room?"

"I don't know. I was drunk when I got in. I didn't know what I was doing."

"We also found this in your room, hidden behind a drawer in your armoire," Grant said. He held up the leather bag, opened it, and poured out some of the jewels. "You recognise these?"

"No," Clive gasped, "I don't!"

"They were in your armoire," Grant said relentlessly.

"I'm afraid they're the jewels that were stolen from Miss Fairfield's apartment," Winters said.

Suddenly Septimus said, "Wait, let me see that."

"See what, sir?"

"Those jewels. Let me see them."

Grant looked at Winters, who shrugged and nodded. Grant poured out the jewels on top of the library table, and at once Septimus reached out and said, "This is my wife's ring."

"Your wife's ring? Are you certain, Mr. Newton?" Winters said.

"Yes, it's a family heirloom."

"How do you account for that, Mr. Newton?" Winters asked Clive.

"I gave that ring to Miss Fairfield as a gift."

"It was your personal possession?" Grant demanded.

"Actually, it belonged to the family."

"Did you give permission for your son to give this ring to Kate Fairfield, sir?" Winters put the question to Septimus, but he knew the answer before the older man spoke.

Septimus hesitated but answered truthfully, "I'm afraid not."

"So you stole the ring and gave it to Miss Fairfield?" Grant spoke harshly.

Everyone in the room saw the guilt on Clive's face. He tried to speak, and his voice was unsteady when he replied, "All right, I took the ring— but I didn't kill her."

"We have many witnesses who will testify that you demanded the ring back. When she refused to give it to you, you made threats. You said you'd kill her if she refused to give the ring back."

Clive's face was pale, and his hands trembled as he said, "I was drinking—but I didn't kill her."

Serafina went to Clive and put her arms around him. He was the picture of a guilty man, and the evidence was overwhelming—but she was a loyal woman. Clive had accused her of having no feelings, but he'd been wrong about that. As she held him, a well of compassion opened up, and she whispered, "Clive, it will be all right."

Septimus came then and put his hands on his son's shoulders. His voice was thin and filled with uncertainty as he said, "Of course it will be all right, Son."

Silence fell across the room, and finally Superintendent Winters took a deep breath. Regret touched his voice and was in his face as he said, "Clive Newton, I place you under arrest. The charge is suspicion of murder." Winters turned and faced Serafina. "I'm sorry, Viscountess." His eyes went to Septimus, who seemed stricken dumb. "I'm sorry, indeed, Mr. Newton."

"I didn't do it!" Clive whispered. "I swear I didn't do it!"

"You'll have a chance to prove that," Grant said. "Take him away, Sergeant Kenzie."

Kenzie came to stand beside Clive. As he did, however, Serafina reached up and put her hands on Clive's cheeks. "I know you didn't do it, Clive."

"I didn't, Serafina. I swear! I've done a lot of things wrong, but I did not kill anyone."

"You'll have to go with them," Serafina whispered, "but I promise you I'll find the real murderer. I'll find the one who killed that woman."

Kenzie held pressure on to Clive's arm firmly as Clive stumbled out the door.

Grant followed, but Superintendent Winters stopped and turned to face them. "I regret very much that this has come to you, Mr. Newton. Viscountess, I have heard your reputation of being a woman of great determination. I've even heard the story about how you solved the robbery at Sir Osric Wallace's house, but I strongly advise you not to get involved with police business."

Serafina raised her head, and her eyes flashed. "And I promise you, Superintendent, I'm going to do everything I can to bring the real murderer to justice."

Winters shook his head but said no more. He turned and left the room, and Serafina turned at once to her father. "We've got to tell the family. Shall you do it?"

"Yes, it's my responsibility. I—I didn't raise the boy right, Serafina."

"You can't blame yourself, Father."

"Do you believe he's innocent?"

"He has to be," Serafina whispered. "He just has to be!"

SIX

Dread crawled along Clive's nerves as he sat in the darkness. The cell into which he had been thrust was no more than ten feet square. He had never been fettered in any way, and with each passing moment, the room seemed more and more like a square coffin. He had paced the rough stone floor for what seemed like hours, and time seemed to move slower than on the outside. Clive stopped, looked about the room wildly, and felt fear clawing at him like a live thing. The walls, made of uneven bricks, radiated a nigrescent gloom, illuminated only by a stub of a candle with less than an inch left. The pale flickering light did not even lighten the ceiling, which was some ten feet high.

Clive leaned against the rough wall and tried to stop the trembling in his limbs. The cell was bare except for a single cot with a fetid straw pallet and a single worn grey blanket. On one side was a wooden bench with a hole in it that obviously served the calls of nature. Beside the cot was a pitcher that held tepid water. The whole cell was rank, and Clive, who had always been hypersensitive to bad odors, had been almost overcome during his first hours there. The bucket that held waste had obviously not been emptied, and the cell was clammy with dampness and mold. Clive suddenly stepped up on the cot. It sagged under his feet, but he was able to reach the solid steel bars on the single window no more than eighteen inches square. A tiny breath of fresh air came to him, and he inhaled deeply.

Clive hung on to the bars, listening for some sound, but only muffled echoes came through the thick walls. He had put his ear to the single door in the room, but through the thick solid oak he had heard only the cadence of footsteps and nothing more.

Clive had eaten nothing since the previous day and was so weak that his legs trembled. As he tried to step off the cot, it tipped over and threw him on the floor. He fell backward and struck the back of his head on the hard stone. The world seemed to explode in a display of yellow, red, and green spots that flashed before his eyes. Groaning, he rolled over, straightened the cot, and sat down on it. He wanted to shout, to scream, to beat his hands against the door, but he had already done that, and it had served only to increase his fear. He had slept some in fitful snatches, and he had walked back and forth. The candle had burned down at least two inches, but that gave him no hint of how long he had been encapsuled in the rank cell.

He sat there with his head in his hands, his eyes shut, and a wild concatenation of thoughts raced through him. *This is only a dream—I'll wake up, and I'll be back in my bed at home.* But the rank odors, the feel of the worn blanket, and the dead silence of the cell were reminders of reality.

He sat very still and wondered when his parents would come. He had been thrust into the cell without a word, although he had tried to ask the jailer when he could see visitors. The jailer had simply grunted, thrust him inside, and slammed the door, bolting it with a resounding clang.

Time seemed to crawl, and Clive forced himself to be still. He lay down and pulled the blanket over him. It was rough to the touch and stank of sweat and things even worse. Finally he heard a faint sound, and then the clang of the bolt outside. Eagerly he threw the blanket aside and stood to his feet. The door opened, and he was blinded by even the feeble light. "Bang on the door when you want out, sir."

"Thank you."

Clive blinked and stared at the man who had entered, then he whispered hoarsely, "Dylan, it's you!"

"Yes, Clive." Dylan came forward and put his arm around Clive's shoulder. Clive had never been one for giving or receiving this kind of salute from his male friends, but the strong form of Dylan Tremayne was all that was real in his world. "Dylan, I'm—I'm glad you came. I'm losing my mind!"

"I don't doubt it. It's an awful place, this. I've been in a jail or two myself, and this is about as bad as any. Maybe your parents can use their influence to get you a better place."

"You've got to talk to them, Dylan. I've got to get out of this place. I'm losing my mind!"

Dylan said, "Of course I will. As soon as I leave here, I'll go to them. I'm sure they can do something."

"It's all a terrible mistake. I didn't kill Kate! I swear I didn't!"

"I want you to tell me everything that you can remember about what happened after you left the theatre. *Everything*, Clive. Don't leave anything out."

Clive felt so weak he couldn't stand. "I've got to sit down," he gasped. He sat on the cot, and Dylan sat down beside him, keeping his arm on the young man's shoulder. "It's all like a bad dream. I was so drunk. I was drunk when I got to the theatre, and when I left there I went into a public house. I think the White Elephant was the name of it, but I'm not even sure about that. The White something."

"How long did you stay there?"

"I don't know. I stayed there until I was pretty drunk, then I got up, left there. All I could think of was what Kate had done to me. How she had led me on and made a fool out of me."

"Where did you go next?"

"Oh, I don't know. I just walked and walked. I thought I'd sober up and go find her again. That was the crazy thought that was in my mind."

"Did you go to her house?"

"No, I didn't. I'm sure of that." Suddenly he looked at Dylan and said, "Do you think I killed her, Dylan?"

Dylan hesitated. "I'll tell you this, Clive. I don't think you have it in you to murder a woman, but even if you did, it's your friend I am." The words came as a welcome relief to Clive. He felt the tears run down his cheeks and whispered, "I haven't cried since I was six years old."

"It's not wrong to cry. I do it myself sometimes."

"I don't believe that."

"Then you don't know me. Welshmen are pretty emotional, see? We laugh and we cry quite a bit. Now what about this woman? Do you remember anything about the district?"

"I walked a long time. I think it was Seven Dials, but I'm not sure. I do remember passing a public house with some kind of a bird out on the sign. I don't know whether it was a hawk or an eagle. It was a badly painted sign, but it was right about there I was so drunk I couldn't see straight and this woman came out and—I know it sounds crazy, Dylan, but I thought if I went with her it would somehow get me even with Kate. Stupid, isn't it?"

"We all do stupid things. This is very important. I've got to find that woman. She's got to testify that you spent the night with her."

"I wasn't there all night."

"Where did you go with her?"

"She had rooms. They were upstairs somewhere. She had more whiskey, and I drank it. I was about to pass out, but I found her going through my clothes, taking the money I had."

"What did you do then?"

"I hit out at her, and she came at me with her claws out. That's where I got my face all clawed up. The police didn't believe me, but that's the way it was."

"All right, Clive. Now tell me everything you can remember about this woman."

Clive was silent. He shut his eyes, and his face twisted in a grimace. "It's like trying to go back into a nightmare. I remember she was tall, nearly as tall as me, and she was built strongly."

"What colour was her hair?"

"It was—it was light-coloured hair, but I don't know if it was dyed or not."

"Can you remember anything about her face?"

"No. She wasn't beautiful. I know that. I thought she was ugly at the time."

"Was she wearing any jewellery?"

"She had on some kind of necklace. I remember it glittered in the gaslight, but I don't know what it was. Probably some cheap jewellery."

For some time Dylan persisted in his questioning, and finally he said, "I found out, Clive, that if you think on something long enough, your memory is like a deep well. You try to scoop something up on the surface, and it isn't there because it's sunk to the bottom. But it's still there, my boy; it's still there. You think on this, and maybe you can think of more details of where the woman's room was, what was outside. Did you see anyone? Did you pass anybody? Or remember something that you saw in the room itself?"

"I don't think I can remember."

"You've probably not been trying to. You've probably been trying to forget, but that's exactly what you must not do. I'm going to help you, Clive. I know that part of London pretty well, and I'm going to hunt for that woman. But I don't have much to go on."

"You can't help me, Dylan. No one can help me."

"The good God can help you," Dylan said simply.

But Clive had been too strongly taught by his father and by his sister. "I don't believe in God," he said, bitterness in his voice.

"Well, He believes in you, and I believe in you, Brother. I'm going to leave now. I'll go tell your parents to get you into a better place. I'm sure your father has some kind of influence."

"I remember my mother's a good friend of the superintendent that arrested me. His name is Winters. Maybe Mother can talk to Mrs. Winters and get her husband to get me a better place."

"I have no doubt that will happen. Good-bye for now." Dylan walked over and banged on the door and called out loudly. In a few moments the bar rattled. Dylan turned and said, "God hasn't forgotten you, boy. Not one to forget, the Lord God. He'll not see you perish."

The door opened then, and Dylan passed through it. As it shut, Clive sank back onto the cot. He thought of what Dylan had said, and he gritted his teeth. He began going back over his murky memories, trying to remember some detail that would help. Dylan's visit had brought a moment's hope, but now in the gloom of the cell it seemed to be slowly fading.

※

Dylan left the prison and hailed a hansom cab.

"Where to, sir?"

"The east side. I'll have to direct you when we get there. Drive as fast as you can."

"That I will, sir."

Dylan settled back, but his jaw was tense. He began to pray for guidance. His favourite Scripture had long been "Do any of you lack wisdom? Let him ask of God who giveth to all men liberally and upbraideth not." He shook his head and thought, *Well, Lord, it's wisdom I need. Help me to help that poor fellow. He's not one of Yours, Lord, not yet. But he's badly in need of Your love and mercy. So use me as Your instrument to bring him out of that prison.*

※

The household had been humming with the news. The servants, of course, knew more about the Newtons and the viscountess than anyone else. They sat in the kitchen eating the evening meal, and Albert Givins, the coachman, was holding forth. "I tell yer it's a terrible thing when a man gets accused of murder." He was a small Cockney with sandy hair and blue eyes, and when he ate he tasted nothing, as if he were storing food in his mouth for further use.

Mrs. Rachel Fielding, the housekeeper, shook her head. "It's a sad thing, but he's always been a wild young man."

Danny Spears was eating the lamb that was set before him, hacking it into pieces with a knife and stuffing it into his mouth. "Aw, 'e ain't killed nobody. 'E ain't no murderer."

"The police think he is." James sat at the head of the table. He was in charge of the male servants while Mrs. Fielding was in charge of the maids. "You should have seen him when they took him away. He looked guilty if ever a man did."

Nessa, the cook, sat next to Ellie, the tweeny housemaid. They made quite a contrast, Nessa large and fat and Ellie thin as a splinter. "I'll never believe it of the young man. He's got a good heart, he has, just a bit wild."

Albert glared at James. No love was lost between the two, and Albert said, "You don't know nuffin' about it, Mr. Barden. The police make mistakes all the time."

"This was Scotland Yard, not just the police, and they had all the evidence."

"Wot kind of evidence?" Peter Grimes asked. He was a tall, handsome man, as footmen should be, with black hair and brown eyes, and sturdily built. "What did they say?"

"They found the jewels," Barden said with some satisfaction.

"What jewels was that?" Mrs. Fielding demanded.

"The jewellery of the actress that was murdered. They found them in Master Clive's bedroom. They were hidden."

"Well, that's a bad one!" Peter said. "I expect 'e'll go down with evidence like that."

"That wasn't all," Barden said. "They found a bloodstained handkerchief in his room. He said it was from a nosebleed."

"How do you know all of this?" Nessa demanded. "Were you there?"

Barden looked discomfited. "They were talking rather loudly. I was waiting outside the door."

Nessa suddenly sniffed. "You mean you were eavesdropping."

"Call it what you will. It's our business to help this family. I thought I might hear something that might be of use to the master."

"Poor Mrs. Newton! She ain't stopped crying since they took Mr. Clive away," Mrs. Fielding said. "It's only right she should cry. If they hang him, she'll have lost her son. Mothers ought to cry over something like that."

"Well, 'e ain't 'ung yet," Albert Givins sniffed.

The servants continued to talk, until finally Mrs. Fielding said, "That's enough talk about this, and I don't want to hear of any of you talking to anybody outside. That goes for all of you women. It goes for you men also. This is family business. We will not speak of it to anyone outside."

❧

Serafina had spent much of the day trying to restore some sort of order. Her father seemed to be numbed by what had happened. He could handle a scientific problem of any sort with his massive intellect. But she had always known that handling personal problems was not his strong point. He had gone off into the laboratory, where she knew he was dabbling with chemical experiments as a way of trying to blot out the truth that was before him. Sadly, she realised that her father knew more about hiding from problems than about solving them.

She had stayed with her mother much of the day and had sent Danny outside with David, with instructions to keep him occupied. "Let him do anything he wants to as long as he doesn't get hurt."

"Yes, Lady Trent, I'll see to it. Don't yer be worryin' about the boy now," Danny had responded.

That left Dora and her mother, and the two women were weeping most of the time. Dora had cried over and over, "It can't be! I'll never believe it!" as if saying it would make it so. As for her mother, Serafina stayed very close to her. Finally the doctor came, and Serafina had called him aside. "You're going to have to give my mother and my sister something to make them sleep. I'd give them opium if I had any."

Dr. Maddox had said quickly, "I've got something just about as good." He had given her a bottle containing some sort of clear liquid. "You be very careful with this, Lady Trent. It's very powerful. Just a couple of drops in a glass of water will do it."

"Thank you, Dr. Maddox."

"What about yourself?"

"I don't need anything, thank you. I need a clear head."

"Well, you've always had that, Serafina, ever since you were a child. I'll keep in close touch with you. Send for me if you need me."

"Thank you, Doctor."

The day passed slowly, creeping by, it seemed, on leaden boots, until finally, late in the afternoon, Ellie entered, her eyes big. "Lady Trent, there's a man to see you."

"Man? What man, Ellie?"

"'E said 'is name is Tremayne."

Serafina straightened. "Bring him in here." She had been in the library thinking, trying to find a way to help Clive, and her nerves were stretched thin. When Tremayne entered the room, she was struck by his handsome features. He was tall, at least six feet she guessed, with an athletic figure. He had removed his hat, and his glossy black hair seemed, to her, as black as anything in nature. His eyes were a startling shade of blue, and he had a wedge-shaped face with a slight cleft in his chin.

"My name is Dylan Tremayne, Viscountess. I've come about your brother, Clive."

Serafina noted the Welsh accent and asked, "How do you know Clive?"

"I'm part of the Shakespearean Company putting on *Hamlet* at the Old Vic."

Instantly Serafina grew angry. "You're a friend of that actress Clive had been seeing—the one he's accused of murdering?"

"I knew he had been seeing Katherine Fairfield, and as a matter of fact, Lady Trent, I tried to discourage him."

Serafina stared at the man. He was possibly the finest-looking man she had ever seen—but he was an actor. "You're part of the crowd that has led my brother astray. I don't know why you're here."

"I've just come from visiting him."

She was amazed. "They wouldn't let anyone in. Father tried to see him earlier."

"He doesn't know the ways of the world, I'm afraid."

"Why would they let you in?" Serafina demanded.

"It wasn't too hard really. I simply told the jailer I was giving legal advice, and they took me for his lawyer."

"Isn't that a crime?"

Dylan shook his head and smiled slightly. "I didn't say I was a lawyer. I just said I was going to give him legal advice, which I did. It was the same advice you would give, I think."

"How is he, Mr. Tremayne?"

"He's in poor condition. I came because I believe you could use your influence to get him transferred to a more . . . amiable place of incarceration. A better cell, I mean."

"I don't have any influence."

"I think your mother does. Clive tells me she's a friend of the wife of Superintendent Winters. He has great influence."

Instantly, Serafina said, "That's true. I hadn't thought of that." She forced herself to say, "Thank you, Mr. Tremayne. I'll see that it's done."

Tremayne hesitated, then said, "I came for another reason, Viscountess."

"And what could that be?" Serafina found herself disliking the man. She had a low opinion of the theatre. She did not attend herself, but of course the newspapers usually flaunted the escapades and character flaws of actors and actresses.

"I don't know exactly how to say this. I've been practicing a speech all the way, but no matter how I say it, you're going to find it difficult to accept."

"Why don't you just say it and let me decide if I find it difficult."

Dylan was aware of her displeasure, but he took a deep breath, then said, "I don't know how you feel about things like this, but after I left your brother, I began to feel strongly that God wanted me to do something to help him."

Serafina stiffened her back, and her eyes narrowed. "God told you that? He spoke personally to you, did He?"

"Well, of course, not in an audible voice as He spoke to Moses on the mountain, but a strong feeling I had—"

"Mr. Tremayne, I do not trust feelings. I trust evidence, and feelings are not going to get my brother out of prison, nor are they going to discover who the real murderer actually is. That would require intelligence and mental ability." She hesitated, then said, "Of which I am not sure you have a plentiful supply."

"Well"—Dylan allowed himself a very slight smile—"you're right about that. I've never been called a genius, but I do know that God is real, and I feel very strongly that He wants me to be a help in some way."

"I thank you for going to see my brother, and I appreciate your bringing us the news that he needs better accommodations, but that's all I will require of you. I will see to my brother myself."

A flash of anger showed in Dylan's eyes, but he swallowed hard and said, "The only way that I can see with my limited intellect to help your brother is to find the woman he stayed with."

"Well, you figured that out all by yourself," Serafina said caustically. "That's exactly what I intend to do."

"It's help you'll be needing for that."

"I'm perfectly capable of asking questions, intelligent questions."

"You intend to go down to the Seven Dials and ask questions?"

"It's exactly what I intend to do."

"That could be very dangerous, Lady Trent."

"I'm not afraid. Now if you'll excuse me, I wish you'd go."

Dylan hesitated, but saw that it was useless to speak. He bowed his head and said not another word. As soon as he turned and left the room, Serafina felt a moment's satisfaction.

"The very idea that God told him! Just the sort of romantic notion I can't abide!" She immediately went to change her clothes. "I don't know that much about that side of town or that lifestyle, but I know they are human beings, and I know that money will answer most things. So I'll take money with me, and I'll find someone who will help me. I'll find that woman!"

As Serafina stepped out of the carriage, she said, "You wait here for me, Albert."

Albert Givins had stepped down to assist her out. "Lady Trent, I don't think you should go into this part of town. It ain't exactly wot you are used to. It ain't decent for you."

"Don't worry about me, Albert. You just wait right here."

She turned away, ignoring Albert's scowl of displeasure, and moved down the street. She had tied her hair back severely, and her dress was the plainest one she had, made of grey-blue, undecorated material. She still wore an opal necklace—a gift from her father—and a sapphire ring on her right hand.

She had never visited the Seven Dials district of London, and now she felt somewhat intimidated. It was a little after five and growing dark,. Many other people were on the streets, but they were people such as she had seen only at a distance. Some were idling in doorways, others peddling matches, bootlaces, and odds and ends. More than once she saw rough-looking men whom she suspected of being criminals. They looked like pickpockets and cutpurses. She passed by a woman, obviously a prostitute, looking tired and drab. She was terribly unattractive, with hair full of knots and teeth stained and chipped. Several gaps showed, and Serafina wondered, *Why would any man go to a woman like that? They must be totally depraved.*

The street seemed to narrow, and she walked more slowly. Water dripped off rotting eaves, and the stones beneath her feet were slimy. Doors hung crooked, and most of them were closed fast. People moved ahead of her and behind her like shadows, and as she turned the corner, she was aware of a man lying in the gutter. Her heart seemed to skip a beat, for he seemed to be dead, but he could be only drunk. The smells of rot and decay were everywhere, and fright began to touch Serafina's nerves. She hesitated and forced herself to walk more slowly. She found herself amidst a warren of alleys and passageways that all looked grim. She saw a big, hulking man standing with his back against the wall watching her. He did not speak, but his eyes were fixed on her. She stopped and asked him, "Excuse me. I'm looking for someone."

"Is that right?" His voice was coarse, and he moved away from the building and came to stand before her. "Who might that be, missy?"

"I don't know her name."

"You don't know 'er name? Why do you want 'er? Yer not a copper, I take it."

"No, of course not. I have a very personal reason."

The man wore dirty, shapeless trousers and a jacket so old and covered with dirt that it was hard to tell its original colour. He had a broad face; a scar trailed down from his eyebrow and disappeared into his dirty collar. There was a brutality about him and a force that Serafina could sense. "This woman I'm looking for has blonde hair, and she's very tall."

"Wot kind of woman is that? Yer don't know 'er name?"

"No."

"That's all yer know—she's tall and got fair hair? That ain't much for a man to go on."

"I'll be willing to pay liberally if you could help me find her."

"Is she a lissy?"

"Lissy? What do you mean by lissy?"

"Is she a whore?" he asked bluntly.

Serafina flushed. "Yes, she is."

"And do yer know how many of 'er kind there is in London? More than yer can count."

"I don't think there can be that many."

"Maybe all of 'em ain't full-time. Some of 'em works in the sweat-shops," he said. "They don't make enough to get by so they goes out at night and takes a man to get more money, don't yer see. Maybe I can help you though. Come along with me. We'll talk about it." He moved forward and took her arm. Suddenly the fear that had been lurking in her heart seemed to swell. "Please, turn me loose."

"Come on now, sweet'art. Me an' you will 'ave a nice little talk."

Serafina tried to pull away, but the man's strength was frightening. He was dragging her toward a door, and she began to call out. "Turn me loose! Help, someone!"

"They ain't no one to 'elp you. Come on in. I ain't going to 'urt you. I've taken a fancy to that ring on yer finger. We'll work out something."

Serafina struggled with all her might, but she might have been a child. The man's fingers dug into her arms, and she struck out at him, but he merely laughed at the feebleness of the blow. "That ain't no way for a lady to act. I'll teach you better manners than that."

"Turn her loose, George."

The voice seemed to come from nowhere, and the big man suddenly whirled, not releasing his grip. "Wot's that you say?"

Serafina twisted her head around and saw Dylan Tremayne standing there. She didn't like the man, but suddenly he was like a harbor for her. "Help me, Mr. Tremayne!" she begged.

"I said turn her loose, George."

"An' 'ow do yer know my name?"

"Oh, I know a lot about you, George. I know you did a stretch for robbing the Bentley house. That was a few years ago. Didn't improve your manners any."

The man called George suddenly released her, and his hand went into his pocket. He withdrew his hand and opened a knife and said, "On your way. We don't need yer 'elp 'ere."

"Now, George, let's not have any difficulty." Dylan stepped forward. His eyes were fixed on the big man. "The lady's coming with me, so let's not have any trouble."

"Trouble? I'll give you trouble!" George suddenly pushed Serafina aside, and she stumbled and almost fell. She saw him lunge forward, a bulking, menacing figure with the knife out in front. She did not see the blow, but she heard it, a muffled thud, and suddenly the man called George stopped as if he had run into a wall. She saw Tremayne reach out, grab his wrist, and twist it in a strange fashion so that the knife fell. He picked it up quickly and in one swift movement held it at George's throat. "You want to continue this, George, or do you want to go along like a good fellow?"

George's face was clear in the fading light. Sweat was on his forehead, and his eyes were bugging out. "I don't know 'oo yer are," he said. "Yer must be a copper."

"Nothing so dignified as that, I am. Just be on your way, or do you want to continue this . . . discussion?"

The big man took a step backward, glared hard at Dylan, and said, "This ain't over."

"I trust it is. Good night, George."

Serafina watched the big man twirl and step inside the door. She turned to Dylan and said, "Sir, I must thank you."

"Are you all right, Viscountess?"

"Yes, I am, but it's a good thing you came along."

"I think I'd better take you back to your carriage. There are others like George in this part of town."

"Thank you." He turned, and she walked silently beside him. Serafina tried to think of something to say, but the scene had drained her of logical thought. She was a woman who was in command of herself always, but she had stepped into a part of the world in which she was totally out of step with reality. She did not say a word until finally they reached the carriage, and Albert jumped down.

"What is it, miss? Are you all right?"

"Yes, Albert." She turned and saw that Dylan was holding his hand up to help her in. She stepped inside, and when he released her, she settled back. She turned to him and said, "I must thank you, Mr. Tremayne." Then she made her final summation of the problem. "I don't usually have to ask a man for help."

"We all have to have help, Viscountess. Good night, then."

Serafina leaned back and found that she had been drained of all energy by the experience. She said, "Quick, Albert, take me home."

"Yus, miss." As the horses leapt forward, throwing her against the back of the leather seat, she realised what might have happened if the actor had not suddenly appeared. She suddenly wondered how he had found her, but analytically put it to herself: *He knew I was coming to Seven Dials and knew I might be harmed. He waited outside and followed me. He's only an actor, but that was rather fine of him . . .*

Sir Leo Roth was, according to rumour, the finest barrister in England. He looked across his desk at Lady Serafina Trent and considered what she had just said. She had appeared in his office without an appointment, but Roth was in the habit of receiving countesses under any circumstances. He was a tall, lean man with fair hair and dark blue eyes. His dress was impeccable, and he was accustomed to women showing an interest in him. Now as he considered the woman across from him, he was taken both by her appearance and by her story. *She is a handsome one,* he thought, *but this story— well, I don't know.* Aloud he said, "So if I understand you correctly, your brother is in prison. He is accused of murdering an actress."

"That is correct, Sir Leo."

"And he was heard making threats against her life."

"I'm afraid so."

"And in his room, Scotland Yard found the jewellery stolen from this actress and a bloodstained handkerchief. Is that the case against him?"

"Yes. Do you think it's enough to convict him?"

"I will not deceive you. It will be enough, I'm afraid. Unless you can discover something else, your brother will be convicted."

"I've been thinking about this, Sir Leo. It seems to me that there are several possibilities. The murderer could have come from the aristocracy. The woman was acquainted with several people from that world. She could have been murdered by one of the cast. I understand there's a great deal of jealousy among those people. From what little I've heard, more than one of them had a great dislike for her. And the third possibility is that someone from the underworld killed her—perhaps hired by someone else."

"You seem to have thought this out very carefully."

"I must find the woman my brother spent the night with. She's a prostitute, and I made one attempt."

"Indeed? Would you tell me about that?" Sir Leo listened as she spoke and noted that her cheeks were flushed.

"I made a great mistake, Sir Leo. That is not my world. If the actor I mentioned, Dylan Tremayne, had not come along, I fear I would have come to great harm."

"Then it seems to me you need that man at least as much as you need a barrister."

"You think I need Mr. Tremayne?"

"That, evidently, is his world. You say he knew who accosted you?"

"Yes, he called him by his name."

"He must be a man of some force."

"He's a religious fanatic."

Leo suddenly smiled. "So were Martin Luther and Oliver Cromwell and John the Baptist, Viscountess. Give me a good religious fanatic every time! They always mean business, and they'll do what they set out to do or die trying."

"Will you take my brother's case?"

"I will take it, but I must warn you ahead: the odds are against us."

"Very well. What are your terms?"

She listened as he spoke of his fee, and then when he had finished, he added, "As your barrister, I must say we need to employ this man Tremayne even if he is a religious fanatic." He smiled as he said it.

"You're amused, but it's not a matter of humour to me."

"I beg your pardon, Viscountess, but I think you're going to have to come down to the real world."

"What do you mean, Sir Leo? I'm always in the real world. I'm a scientist."

"Seven Dials is part of the world, and it's a part that you haven't touched yet. For that, we need Dylan Tremayne."

"Very well. I'll ask him if he will help."

"Do you think he will?"

"Oh, I'm sure he will," she said, and her lips turned too tight. "He told me that God spoke to him and told him that he was to help me. That's the sort of man I'm having to use for help."

"He's also a good man in a dark alley at Seven Dials. I think you'll have to modify your pride a bit, Lady Trent."

"Very well. I will talk to him. Thank you very much, Sir Leo."

"I'll go see your brother today. Time is very short."

Serafina left the room, and as she went, she was thinking, *I'll have to go to the theatre and speak with Tremayne . . . and ask him for his help.* The thought infuriated her, but Serafina Trent was a woman of great force and determination. If it meant losing part of her dignity and letting a mere actor into her life, then so be it!

SEVEN

For a moment Serafina paused, standing uncertainly at the door of her parents' bedroom. She had steeled herself but dreaded the necessity of talking to her mother concerning Clive, for her mother was not one who could take hard things easily. Ever since Clive had been arrested, Alberta had been in a state of total disarray. It had taken all of the efforts of her two daughters and the maids—as well as the support of Septimus—to keep her from collapsing completely. Dr. Maddox's strong sedative had helped somewhat.

Taking a deep breath, Serafina knocked on the door. Hearing a faint response, she entered the room and found her mother sitting in a chair beside the window. She was wearing a blue dressing gown and a pair of leather house slippers. "How are you, Mother?" Serafina drew closer and stooped so that she could examine her mother's face.

"Daughter, what are we going to do?" There was such desperate anxiety in her mother's voice, and a tremor that she could not control, that Serafina felt almost helpless. She knew that during the early days of her marriage, her mother had been a strong woman. She'd had to struggle and work diligently to support Septimus during those difficult times.

"Could I get you some tea, Mother?"

"No—no! I don't want anything. I just can't believe this is happening to us. Poor Clive! We must do *something*!"

Serafina leaned forward and put her hand on her mother's shoulder. "It's going to be all right, Mother. You'll see."

"How can it be all right? Those policemen, they believe that Clive is guilty." She turned her eyes upward, and Serafina was shocked to see the sheer terror mirrored there. "You don't think he did that awful thing, do you?"

"Of course not," Serafina said firmly. "We're going to get through this all right, but it's going to take some strong action."

Alberta Newton looked up, and tears suddenly filled her eyes and ran down her cheeks. She snatched a handkerchief from her pocket and wiped them away. She blew her nose and asked, "What do you mean strong action?"

"The first thing we have to do is get Clive reassigned to better quarters."

"Better quarters?"

Serafina was tempted to tell her mother what Dylan had told her about the terrible cell her brother was in, but decided not to mention the actor. She modified the situation by saying, "Clive is being held in very squalid quarters. For some reason they put him in a cell with no comforts at all. Our first job," she said firmly, "is to get him out of that place and into a better one."

"But—how can we do that?"

"We're going to have to get someone with influence to go to the jail and have him put in a more comfortable cell."

"But we don't know anybody with that kind of influence."

"Oh yes, we do, Mother. You know Mrs. Winters."

"Mrs. Winters?" The name seemed to mean nothing to Alberta, but then she nodded. "Why—yes, of course. Her husband was one of the policemen."

"He's more than a policeman, Mother. He's the superintendent at Scotland Yard. He has great influence. They would listen to him."

"Then why don't you go to him and talk to him? Ask him to help us."

"I don't know his wife, but you do. You've gone to several teas and meetings with her, haven't you?"

"Oh yes, certainly. I don't know her that well, but she seems to be a very fine lady. Do you think she would help us?"

"Not personally, but she could persuade her husband to do something." Serafina smiled. "And I think she would if you would ask her."

"Oh, Serafina, I couldn't do that!"

"Why not?"

"I just couldn't face her. I'm so ashamed!"

Serafina hesitated, but she saw that it was hopeless. Her mother was totally unfit to face a crisis like this. *I'll have to go see Mrs. Winters myself.* "Very well, Mother. You stay here and try to get some rest. I'll go see Mrs. Winters to see if she can get her husband to help us."

Alberta reached out and seized Serafina's hand. She clung to it desperately, and it took some time before Serafina was able to get her to relax. "You do need to eat something. I'll go ask Nessa to send you up something very good."

"I don't believe I could eat anything."

"Yes, you could," Serafina said firmly. "You've got to keep your strength up."

She knew that she had to leave, but her mother was clinging to her. Disengaging her hand, she left the room and went down to the kitchen.

"Nessa, I want you to fix Mother up something very good to eat—something special."

"Why, 'course I will! I'll fix some of that special lamb that she likes so much. We've got some fresh."

"And fix her a nice dessert. Send it up by Daisy, and I'll give Daisy instructions to make sure she eats it."

"Will there be a full table for meals today?"

"I'm not sure, Nessa. I suppose you can just prepare whatever is easiest."

"Indeed, I won't do that." Nessa hesitated, then said, "We have trouble here, Lady Trent, but life must go on. The good God won't forsake us!"

"Yes, it must," Serafina said. She knew that Nessa was a faithful Christian, and though she herself did not share her beliefs, she knew the woman had a deep affection for her family. She smiled and gave Nessa a quick pat on the shoulder. "I do appreciate your concern."

She left the kitchen and went at once into the nursery. David did not sleep there anymore, but he kept all of his games and collections there. He was sitting on the floor with blocks, building some sort of structure. "What are you making, Son?"

"I'm making a castle. You see? This is the wall."

"Oh, that's very good. Do you suppose I could help?"

Eagerly, David cried, "Yes, Mum, I'll be inside the castle, and you'll be the enemy trying to break through."

Serafina sat down rather awkwardly beside David on the floor, and for the next half hour, she was fascinated by the quick and imaginative mind of this son of hers. Always she was careful to watch for signs that she dreaded, signs that he had some of his father's ways—but so far she was grateful that she found none of that. *There's more of me in him than there is of Charles!* Finally she said, "Would you like to go riding on Patches?"

Instantly, David jumped up, his eyes flashing, "Yes, Mum! Will you ride with me?"

"Yes, I'll get my little mare, and we'll ride together."

⚜

The ride had been a delight for Serafina. The time she spent with her son was always a pleasure, and she resolved to devote more of her time to him. David sat on the pony like a veteran, and Serafina guided her small mare beside him. The grounds were extensive, with riding paths carefully laid out, and finally they drew up at the trout stream. David said, "Mum, can I let Patches drink?"

"Of course you can. We'll water both of them. Can you get down by yourself?"

"Oh, Mum, you know I can!" David slipped off the pony and held to his reins. He led the pony forward, and Serafina did the same with her mare. The two horses lowered their heads and made slurping noises as they drank. As they did, she kept a close watch on David, wondering how much he knew about the tragedy that had overtaken their family. She finally said, "You're a very good rider, David."

David suddenly turned to face her. His dark blue eyes were troubled, she saw with concern, and he chewed on his lower lip. He was pondering some question, and she knew he would come out with it soon.

"Mum, was my father a good rider?"

The question caught Serafina off guard, for David almost never asked about his father. He had asked rather often some time ago, but it seemed that he had put away all thoughts of his father. She said quickly, "Oh yes, he was a very good rider. He liked to ride to the hounds."

David asked several more questions about his father's horsemanship, then he reached up and stroked the pony's nose. Suddenly he looked down and whispered, "Did—did he like me, Mum?"

Serafina at once went to David, still holding the reins, and put her arm around the boy's shoulder. His body was tense as a wire, and she said quickly, "Why, of course he did, David."

David looked up, and there was a desperate expression of hope in his eyes. She could not read him, and it troubled her. She had put all of her hopes in this young son of hers, and always there was the danger that some of his father might appear—especially as he grew older. She saw in his face nothing but innocence and a desire for a father whom she knew he could not have. Quickly, she said, "I've got to go to town today, Son, but how about this—I'll tell Danny to take you out to collect butterflies. Would you like that?"

"Oh yes, Mum, I like Danny, and will you read me some of that book with the funny title that Dora gave you—*The Mermaid in the Basement*?"

"No, but I'll get you a new book and read it to you."

"But I like that one, Mum! I want to know how someone got a mermaid in the basement. Do you think they kept her in a big bathtub?"

"It's just a silly romance, David. Now let's go back to the house."

The two rode back to the stable, and David insisted on staying with Danny, who unsaddled the horses and listened as the boy chattered.

"You two have a good time." Serafina smiled, then she went to the house. As she entered and moved down the foyer, she suddenly stopped, turned, and fixed her eyes on a large picture centered on the wall. It was a portrait of Viscount Charles Trent, her late husband. Serafina studied the handsome features, but even as she watched, a chill seemed to take her, and she gave a spastic motion of despair. She shut her eyes, swayed slightly, and whispered in a voice torn by torment, "Leave me alone, Charles!"

"Wot's that you say, ma'am?"

Serafina turned abruptly to see Rachel, the housekeeper, watching her. She said quickly, "Oh, just talking to myself. I'll be going to town, Rachel. You watch out for David when he comes to the house."

"Yes, my lady."

As Serafina hurried down the hall and turned up the steps, Rachel turned to the tweeny, Ellie, who appeared with a pail and mop in her hands. "Ain't it a shame, Ellie? Lady Trent misses 'im so much! She can't even look at his picture without crying."

"That's true, ain't it? She must really been in love with 'im, wasn't she?"

As Givins helped Serafina out of the carriage, she murmured, "I probably won't be too long, Givins."

"Yes, Viscountess. I'll be right 'ere waiting."

Serafina turned and studied the imposing house. It was a huge structure, made of pale stone in the classic Georgian style. The enormous front doors were flanked by long narrow windows, and areas framed by wrought iron rails abounded. The balconies were bright with boxes of potted plants, and the grounds looked more like a public park than a private residence.

As she stepped up to the door, Serafina summoned what knowledge she had of the Winters family—which was, indeed, not much. She had heard that Winters had been only a lowly inspector in Scotland Yard until he married Jewel Fremont, the daughter of an immensely wealthy railroad magnate. Mrs. Winters had become, so Serafina had heard, a moving force in society, and it was her influence and tremendous drive—as well as perhaps some money spent—that had paved the way for her husband's rapid rise to superintendent. She had also heard rather unsubstantial rumours that the marriage of the two was not always serene. She rapped with the heavy brass knocker, and a tall, dignified butler opened the door at once. He smiled and said, "Good afternoon, ma'am."

"I am the Viscountess Serafina Trent calling on Mrs. Winters."

"Oh, come in, Viscountess." He opened the door wider and, stepping aside, motioned her in. "If you'd care to wait, Lady Trent, I'll see if Mrs. Winters is at home."

Serafina could not restrain a smile at the form of the butler's address. *He certainly knows that she is home; otherwise, he would have said so. What he really means is that he'll see if his mistress wants to see me.* But she had learnt long ago to ignore the pretensions of society. "Thank you very much."

As she waited for the butler to return, she studied the foyer, which glittered in the sunlight that filtered through the tall windows. She noted also the variety of fabrics: satins, laces, and velvets. She took in the sweeping stairs, the chandeliers, and the dark portraits framed in gilt with acanthus leaves and curlicues.

The butler returned very quickly and bowed. "Lady Trent, would you come this way, please? Mrs. Winters is in the parlor."

"Thank you." She followed the butler down the hall, and when he stepped aside, she entered one of the most magnificent rooms she had ever seen. The design featured cool green colours, which were brightened by sunlight at this time of day. A large fireplace of polished marble gleamed directly across from her, and the paintings on the walls were seascapes and Dutch pastoral scenes. Long green velvet curtains were splayed out on the floor and swagged with braided sashes. Her eyes went at once to the woman who had risen to greet her. "I apologise for calling without an appointment, Mrs. Winters."

"Why, that's quite all right, Viscountess."

Jewel Winters was a remarkably striking woman of average height, with hair so fair it seemed almost luminous as it caught the light. Her skin, too, was unusually pale. She was dressed in an extremely elegant muslin gown of lilac and blues on white. Serafina noted that her smooth, rounded features also included a Greek nose.

"Please be seated. I will have the maid bring tea."

"Thank you, Mrs. Winters."

As the two women sat down and the maid brought the tea, Serafina was aware that Mrs. Winters was watching her with a cautious air mingled with curiosity. Her sharp, piercing eyes met Serafina's. Aloud Serifina said, "I'm embarrassed at the nature of my errand, Mrs. Winters."

"I take it your visit has something to do with the unfortunate matter of your brother."

"Yes, you've, of course, heard about that."

"My husband talks over his cases with me. May I offer you my deepest sympathy, my dear viscountess, and I intend to call upon your mother."

"That would be so kind of you."

"How is she taking it?"

"Not very well, I'm afraid. None of us are."

"Naturally, you would be distressed. Families must draw closer together when tragedy strikes."

"It is a tragedy indeed, but I've called on a matter that's very important to us."

"And that is what, Viscountess?"

"My brother has been placed in a cell that is extremely uncomfortable. Indeed, that's not the word for it. It's miserable."

"I suppose most prison cells are," Mrs. Winters said. She was waiting and turned her head slightly to one side. "What exactly do you have in mind?"

"My family has no influence in these matters, but it occurred to me that your husband might be able to help."

"My husband? But—he's the one who arrested your brother."

"I know, but I could tell that he's a kind man. It seems such a difficult thing for me to put into words, but do you suppose you could ask your husband to have my brother transferred into more comfortable quarters?"

Mrs. Winters' eyes instantly narrowed, and her usually full lips drew into a thin line. "I make it a policy never to interfere with my husband's work. He tells me things, but, of course, he must make all the decisions."

"I'm sure that's very wise, Mrs. Winters, but would it be possible for you just to ask him if there's anything that can be done?"

"I would not care to do that, Viscountess." Mrs. Winters had stiffened, and somehow a wall had been erected between the two women. "I would suggest that if you have a request, you go to the prison and speak to whoever's in charge."

"You don't think I should see your husband?"

"It would be pointless, my dear viscountess. Believe me, my husband cannot be influenced in matters like this." Mrs. Winters hesitated slightly, then added, "I trust that you have retained good counsel for your brother. I understand he's guilty, but a clever defense will, perhaps, be able to make some kind of an arrangement with the crown. Perhaps a prison term where there might be hope of parole."

Serafina knew that her errand was fruitless. She got to her feet and said, "Thank you, Mrs. Winters, for your advice and for your time."

"I'm sorry I could be of no help. Please tell your mother that our prayers are with her and that I will call soon."

"I will certainly tell her, and thank you again." Serafina left, and as the door closed behind her, it was clear that Mrs. Jewel Winters would be of no help. She had sensed a coldness in the woman, a steely quality that would permit no circumstances to interfere with her life.

Givins helped her into the carriage, and she said, "We'll go to Scotland Yard, Givins."

"Yes, ma'am."

The carriage moved out, and Serafina was thinking rapidly. *She didn't want me to talk to her husband, that much is obvious. She's a cold woman*

*beneath all of that charming manner of hers, but her husband seemed to have
at least some civility to him. The least he can do is tell me no.*

∞❧∞

Inspector Grant lifted one eyebrow and said, "You wish to see the superintendent, Viscountess?"

"Yes, if that's possible."

"Perhaps it's something I could help you with."

"I would much rather talk to Superintendent Winters, if you don't
mind."

Grant obviously was displeased. There was a hardness about the man
that Serafina could not like, and she was glad when he shrugged and took
her into an inner office. "Superintendent, Viscountess Trent is here to see you."

"Thank you, Grant. Please come in, Viscountess."

Serafina entered, and Superintendent Winters came forward at once.
He bowed and said, "I'm surprised to see you. Please sit down."

"Thank you, Superintendent." She took the seat he offered and said,
"I'm quite inexperienced in matters like this."

"Of course you are."

"And the family is very distraught."

"I quite understand, but why have you come to see me?"

Serafina felt almost helpless before his intent gaze. He was an imposing man, a man of strength and strength of will, but he had shown more
concern for her brother's well-being than had Inspector Grant.

"I've come to ask you a favour. It may be wrong of me to ask you,
even unethical in some way. I'm not aware of how the system works, so
please forgive me if I make a mistake."

"You may ask me anything. I may have to say no, but perhaps not."
There was a gentleness in Winters's manner, and he came over and sat
down opposite her. "What is it, Viscountess?"

"I'm very concerned about the awful cell my brother's in. A friend of
mine visited him, and it's a terrible, terrible place! I understand it's a

prison, not designed for comfort—but from the description my friend gave me, it's absolutely inhuman."

"Prisons often are." Winters shrugged wryly. "One of the unfortunate aspects of crime. But what would you like for me to do?"

"Could you tell me if there is any way I could get him put in a more comfortable setting? I'm not asking for luxurious quarters—just bare comforts."

"Well, I have a little influence with the jailer there, and I'm on good terms with the warden. Perhaps I could be of some help."

Serafina looked up, and her face showed the gratitude that she felt. "That would be so kind of you, sir!"

"Why, it's little enough I can do."

"I—I went to see your wife to ask her to intercede, but she tells me that she never does that."

"You should have come to see me first, but there was nothing improper in your seeing her. Let me take care of it, Viscountess. I think I can guarantee that your brother will be cared for in a much better fashion."

"How very kind of you! My family will be grateful when I tell them of your kindness."

"Have you retained legal help, Viscountess?"

"Yes, Sir Leo Roth will be defending my brother. Do you think he's the right man?"

Winters suddenly smiled, and his eyes twinkled. "You're asking me to recommend a man that I will be, in effect, competing against?"

"Oh, that would be wrong, wouldn't it?"

"My dear Lady Trent, I'm in the business of putting men in jail—or worse. But you know, I have a rather strange feeling about this case. I don't go on sentiment as a rule, and I doubt if you do either, but I will tell you what I could not admit to anyone else. It would please me to discover that your brother is innocent."

"How kind of you to say that!"

"It's a matter of justice, of course, but I have bad dreams sometimes."

"What sort of bad dreams?"

"Sometimes I have dreams that I arrest a man and do all I can to get him convicted, and he's executed. And then"—Winters rubbed his forehead in a vulnerable gesture—"evidence surfaces that he was an innocent man."

"Has—has that ever happened to you, Superintendent?"

Winters gave her a look that Serafina would never forget, a haunted look, strangely incongruous on a face with such strength. "Once it did. I shall never forgive myself! The evidence given at the trial was circumstantial, but it got the man death on the gallows."

"I'm so sorry."

Wearily, Winters dropped his head, and they were both silent for a moment. Then he seemed to stir himself and said, "I would recommend Sir Leo Roth. He's the best in London, and if I were you, I would hire a private investigator."

"I've already done that, Superintendent," she said, thinking of Dylan.

"Why, that's good news. You're moving right along, then. I must warn you that you're going against the stream, and it's going to be difficult. If you have, however, a good private investigator and a barrister such as Leo Roth on your side, that's the very best you can do."

Serafina got to her feet to leave, and he came over and put his hand out. He held hers and said, "I may go this far, my dear viscountess: if you need any help that doesn't conflict with my position here, I will freely give it. For instance, if you get any kind of line on that woman that your brother says is a witness, who could testify that he was with her, we have many resources here in the Yard. I'd be glad to put them at your disposal. We could probably find her more easily than your private investigator could."

"So good of you, Superintendent Winters! Thank you so much. I'll leave you now."

She left the office and saw that Grant was watching her with a hard glint in his eyes, but her mood was lightened, for Winters's kindness had been far better than anything she had expected.

Sir Leo Roth had listened intently while Serafina, who had come to his office accompanied by Dylan Tremayne, explained what she had done. She told him in great detail of her visit to Mrs. Winters, and when she did, he laughed aloud. "You went to see Mrs. Winters?"

"Why, yes, she's a friend of my mother's—well, an acquaintance really."

"And you asked her to intercede with her husband on behalf of your brother?"

"Yes, I did."

"And I am certain that you got nowhere."

"How did you know that?"

"You don't know Superintendent Winters and his wife as well as you should. She's a very wealthy woman. She has the money, and she's determined that her husband is going to rise in politics. She's also one of the most jealous women I've ever seen in my entire life. When a beautiful viscountess comes in and asks to form a union with her husband, she's not likely to agree."

Dylan grinned and said, "If you are having my opinion, the woman must be worse than a rat with green teeth!"

Sir Leo smiled at Dylan's words. "I'd hate to have her angry at me. She has influence in high places. She's going to give her husband a title, and then he'll be in the House of Lords. I don't know how much higher her ambition goes, but at least that high."

"Why did they put Clive in such a horrible place?"

"It sounds like Inspector Grant's doing. He's a merciless man."

"I can see that! He hates me."

"No, he hates criminals. His father was hanged for murder. He seems to see every suspect as being somehow responsible for that. It makes no sense." Sir Leo shrugged. "He has no wife and really no life apart from putting men in jail and seeing them hanged where it's appropriate."

Serafina asked, "What can we do, Sir Leo?"

Leo Roth leaned forward and began to speak. He had a mind as sharp as a razor, and he laid out the work that had to be done. Finally he leaned back and said, "We'll fight this with all we have, but it's going to be an extremely difficult matter."

"Thank you, Sir Leo. I know my brother's in good hands with you."

The two left Sir Leo's office, and as soon as they were outside, Serafina turned and said, "I want to meet the members of the cast. How can that be done?"

"Easy enough, it is." Dylan shrugged. "Come to the play tonight. We almost always go out and eat after the play. You'll be my guest, and you'll get to meet most of them."

"But—won't they think it's strange that I'm there, my brother in jail accused of murdering one of the cast?"

"Actors aren't particularly deep thinkers. I'll simply tell the truth. That always confuses them. Most people can't handle the truth very well—actors especially." He smiled and winked at her. "We actors always say one thing and mean another—which is pleasing the devil, ay?"

"But—what exactly will you tell them?"

"I'll tell them that you're convinced that your brother is innocent and you're hoping to find the real murderer."

"Won't they refuse to speak to me after that?"

"No, indeed! They'll all want to convince you that it couldn't be them. The fact is, Viscountess, we're all guilty of something. So we have to be willing to confess to small things to cover up the big ones."

She smiled at him; there was an attractiveness about the man that Serafina could not deny. "And what is your big sin, Mr. Tremayne?"

He grinned again, more broadly. "Call me by my first name, and I'll tell you."

"All right. What is your big sin, Dylan?"

"The sin of optimism." He saw her look of surprise and said, "I always think that the good people win, and the bad people lose."

Serafina stared at him. "But—you *know* better than that!"

Dylan looked down on her and said gently, "I find tongues in trees, books in the running brooks, sermons in stones—and good in every-thing. At least so says Shakespeare. My head may know better, but in my heart I always think that good will triumph over evil."

"I don't believe that," Serafina said at once. She bit her lower lip and looked up into his eyes. "But I'm glad you do, Dylan. I—I hope you always feel like that!"

EIGHT

I've never in my whole life been so confused, Daughter!"

Septimus Newton had sought Serafina as she was preparing to leave her room. She had admitted him to her bedroom and saw instantly that his face was drawn and his eyes filled with fear. This disturbed Serafina greatly, for although her father was a man who was often absent-minded and didn't always show affection for his family, Clive's tragedy had shaken him greatly. "What are we going to do?" he asked in a plaintive voice.

"We've all got to be strong, Father. Every one of us, but especially you and I."

Septimus shook his head. "I've never felt less able in my life, Daughter. This isn't like an experiment in a laboratory, you know. If you fail with that, you can always start over again, but this is—" He passed a hand over his face unsteadily and said brokenly, "This is life-and-death for Clive."

At that instant Serafina was aware that her father was a broken reed. As able a man as he was in the fields of science, as broad as his intellect had always been, he was ill suited to handle the problem that loomed before them. Going over to him, she put her arm around him, saying, "I want you to conceal your fears."

"Conceal them? I'm—I'm not sure I can do that."

"You *must*, Father. Mother is distraught. She needs to lean on someone."

"She's always leaned on you."

"Well, that must change. I want you to spend much time with her today. She'll want to weep and cry and talk about Clive, but you must put her mind on other things."

"How can I do that? All I can think of is that Clive may be convicted and sentenced to death."

"That's not going to happen, and you mustn't let Mother see that you feel that way."

"But what would I talk with her about?"

"Talk with her about Dora, about her chances for marriage. Talk about David and your plans for him. There are many things you can talk about. It would be good if you could get her out of the house, take her shopping. You and I are going to have to put the best face on this we can."

"I believe you're right, Serafina." Septimus pulled himself up and straightened his shoulders. "I'll do the very best I can."

"And keep in mind that Dora is very fragile. I'm worried about her. Get her involved. Go to her and tell her she's got to help keep Mother from grieving. Give her some responsibility."

"She's just a child herself."

"She's seventeen already, and this is the first real tragedy that she's ever faced."

"What are you going to do?"

"Well, Sir Leo is the best defense attorney in England. We're going to lean on him."

"What about that actor fellow, Tremayne?"

"He's not like anyone I've ever met, but he knows the world of London that we don't—the underworld, the criminal element."

"I didn't know that."

"He was brought up in the middle of it. It's a world that I know nothing about. And there's another world that is totally foreign to me, and it may be connected with the murder."

"What world is that?"

"The world of the theatre. It's quite possible that a member of the cast murdered Kate Fairfield. I need to talk to those people and look into their eyes and hear what they have to say about the situation."

"How are you going to do that?"

"I'm going to the theatre tonight, and after the play is over, I'll go backstage. Tremayne has said he can get me invited to the meal they usually have after a performance."

"You trust this actor?"

"Yes, I do." Serafina was surprised at how quickly she answered and at how strongly she felt. She was not a woman who leaned on anyone, but in the storm that surrounded her, she was searching desperately for anyone who would lend strength to her efforts. "He's a different sort of man, but he's honest, and he has an affection for Clive."

"But if he's a member of the troupe, he himself might have killed the woman."

"That's not possible," Serafina said firmly. "He was the one who came to me and told me about Clive's accomodations at the prison. Besides, he's very religious."

Septimus reared his head back and stared at her. "Well, Serafina, that's never been a recommendation to you."

"I know, Father. I don't share his views, but he came to me and said that God had told him to help Clive. I don't believe that, of course, but he could be useful. He knows the shady side of London and could help find that woman Clive was with."

"Perhaps I should go with you tonight."

"No, your place is here, Father. You need to shore up Mother and Dora and spend some time with David. He's very sensitive. He knows something is going on. Be careful that you don't say anything that would cause him to worry."

Septimus nodded. "I'll do as you say, Daughter. I hope you have some success." An odd look touched his eyes, and he chewed his lower lip thoughtfully. "At times like this, I envy those people who do have faith."

Serafina stared at him, for she had exactly the same thought. "We'll have to do the best we can with our minds. It's all we have, Father."

Superintendent Winters and Inspector Grant had arrived at the office of the prosecutor, Allen Greer. Greer was a tall, burly man with grey eyes and a mouth like a steel trap. He had the look of a rough longshoreman rather than an advocate. He was the man who would prosecute Clive Newton, and the three talked briefly of the situation.

"Well then," Greer said, "we're agreed. We're certain of a conviction."

"I believe so." Superintendent Winters nodded. He hesitated, then asked tentatively, "Have you met the accused man's sister?"

"No, I haven't."

"She's a viscountess. Viscountess Serafina Trent. A very fine family. Her father is a noted physician and scientist—as you well know."

"I expect this has set them back." Greer shrugged.

It was Grant who answered. "Very respectable family, sir, but the young man is a bit rowdy."

"I'd say that slashing a woman to death is a little more than 'a bit rowdy.'"

Grant flushed. "He's guilty. I'm sure of it."

Winters stroked his chin thoughtfully and seemed lost in some sort of problem. "Viscountess Trent, the boy's sister, came to me and asked me for help."

"She must be pretty arrogant coming to the superintendent of Scotland Yard to ask for help for a man who's being tried for murder! What did you say to her?"

"Oh, I offered what help I could. Young Trent was in one of the worst cells in the city." He suddenly turned and said, "Did you have anything to do with that, Grant?"

Grant flushed. "I may have. I didn't specify, but the jailer asked me, and I said treat him like you would anybody else. I take it he took it to mean handle him roughly."

"Well, he handled him roughly enough. I spoke to the warden and had him transferred to better quarters."

Grant shook his head. "I'm surprised at you, Superintendent."

"Why? Do you think I'm incapable of a generous action?"

"You've never been particularly concerned about the comfort of people we've arrested. As a matter of fact"—Grant stared at his superior—"people think I'm the hard man, but deep down you have more flint in you than I do."

"Oh, I think I would argue that with you." Winters smiled. "Somebody at the Yard has to be hard, and you seem to have earned that reputation."

Grant disliked what he was hearing. He was unusual in that the other officers at Scotland Yard were in awe of Winters. They knew his power and were hesitant to cross him. Grant, however, seemed to have no compunction about this. He turned to Greer and said, "Viscountess Trent has hired a private investigator to look for the woman that supposedly has the alibi for young Trent."

Greer stared at him. "If he finds her, that could blow our case. We need to find out who she has hired."

"You look into that, Grant," Winters said. "Find out who's working for her. If he finds her, it would give Newton an alibi."

"You two had better work on this," Greer stated flatly. "It would be a stroke of ill fortune indeed if they were to find that woman—for us, I mean."

"I think I may have done something a little underhanded," Winters said.

"You, Superintendent?" Greer's eyebrows lifted, and he showed surprise. "I can't imagine such a thing."

"What was it?" Grant demanded.

"I told her that if she got any leads about the witness from her investigator that we could probably find the woman more easily than an individual. I spoke to the viscountess about the efficiency of the Yard for finding people like that."

"And she believed you?" Grant demanded.

"Why, yes, I believe she did. So I think we'll find out if there's any development."

Grant snorted. "The fool! Doesn't she know we're the enemy?"

"She's no fool, Grant. But I've done my best to cause her to have confidence in us."

Greer laughed, although his eyes were hard. "Superintendent Winters, you're going to make a great politician. You have the devious character necessary for such an office."

Winters laughed. "I suppose I do. Well, we're agreed, then. There shouldn't be any trouble about securing a conviction."

The three men nodded, and as the two Scotland Yard detectives left, Greer muttered, "Well, thank God this is *one* case that won't cause me any trouble!"

❧

Serafina had discovered that she had nothing suitable to wear for her visit to the theatre. She was not a woman who paid a great deal of attention to clothes, most of the time wearing a plain dress and a white apron for her work in the laboratory. She and her maid, Louisa, had searched through her available wardrobe, and at Louisa's insistence she had gone shopping for a new dress. Louisa had helped her don the new dress, and the maid was absolutely ecstatic about it.

"It's the most beautiful dress I've ever seen, ma'am!"

"Well, the salesperson had more to say about it than I do. Do you really think it's suitable?"

"It is beautiful—like a dream!"

The dress was of a deep blue-green shade, cut high in the front with a sheer sleeve and decorated with delicate beading at throat and shoulder. She had also purchased an elegant pair of slippers, and Louisa stood back to admire her. "I've never seen you look so well, Viscountess."

Serafina turned and studied her reflection in the mirror, then shrugged. "Well, I'm not sure exactly what ladies wear to the theatre, but this does look very good."

She glanced at the ormolu clock on the shelf over the fireplace. "I must hurry. I don't want to be late."

She moved downstairs quickly, having already said her good-byes to David. Givins was waiting with the carriage, and he helped her in, bobbing his head and saying, "You look real fine, Viscountess."

"Thank you, Givins."

As she settled back for the ride to the theatre, her mind was working rapidly. She paid little attention to the scenery as the carriage moved from the estate into the interior part of the city. She was so caught up with going over the possibilities of helping Clive that it was a surprise when she found the carriage stopped and Givins saying, "We're here, Lady Trent."

Getting out of the carriage, Serafina said, "I hope you don't mind the long wait."

"Not at all, ma'am."

"I'm hoping to go out for a meal after the performance, so take this and buy yourself a fine meal."

Givins's eyes opened wide at the sovereign that she put in his hand. "Oh, you don't 'ave to do that, Lady Trent!"

"I want to. You enjoy yourself. I don't want you to be bored."

She entered the theatre, paid for her ticket, and moved forward with the crowd. She had bought a private box, and finally was forced to find an attendant to help her locate it. It was on a balcony over to the right side, and she could look right down at the stage. She was fascinated by the audience. Some of them, obviously, were well-to-do people, but many were less prosperous in appearance.

Finally the play began as the soldiers came out on the stage. She had read the play, although she had never seen it acted—nor any other Shakespearean production performed. The three soldiers who discussed the appearance of the ghost of the king were adequate, but when Ashley Hamilton first appeared, she studied his face carefully. He was in his thirties, as far as she could tell, and had light brown hair and sorrowful brown eyes. The action unfolded before her, but she kept watch for Dylan Tremayne to finally appear.

As soon as Dylan stepped onto the stage and said his first lines, something happened to Serafina. She had no idea what it was or how it happened, but there was an air or a quality about the Welshman that held her attention. It was a magnetic sort of feeling. He spoke his lines in a normal tone of voice, but there was something in him so vital that the audience could not take their eyes off of him—Serafina included.

As the play unfolded, she studied the faces of the actors. She paid particular attention to Elise Cuvier, who was playing the role of Ophelia instead of the murdered Kate Fairfield. Miss Cuvier seemed too young to play a woman like Ophelia, but as Serafina studied her closely, she saw that the actress was older than she had thought at first. There was an appealing quality about her, and she had a touch of dynamic magnetism. She studied the woman carefully, and by the time the play had progressed to the scene in which Ophelia loses her mind as the result of her father's death, Serafina was caught up in the drama completely. She sat there watching the action unfold, and when Laertes, played by Dylan, came back from France seething with anger, she was astonished at how much she entered into his feeling. Somehow the actor had the ability to draw from her emotions that she had not known she could have over a mere play.

By the time the end of the play had come, she was well aware that something was wrong. Hamlet, the central figure of the action, was forgotten the moment Laertes, played by Dylan, stepped onstage. When the duel took place, there was a grace in every movement of his body that was missing from the rather awkward swordsmanship of Ashley Hamilton. Finally, Laertes lay dying and made his last speech. He lay looking up at Hamlet and whispered huskily, "Exchange forgiveness with me, noble Hamlet. Mine and my father's death come not upon thee, nor thine on me."

When he slumped back, the play was over for Serafina. She sat there and watched the death of Hamlet unmoved, and finally, when the last words were spoken and the actors came for their bows, she noticed that two people received a great deal more applause than the others. One was Elise Cuvier, who had done a wonderful job, she thought. The other was Dylan

Tremayne, and the applause was absolutely thunderous. She saw he had a slight smile on his face and bowed gently, and then the actors disappeared.

She sat quietly in her box for a time, feeling sure that there would be many people rushing to the dressing room area to congratulate the actors. Finally she thought, *I've been missing a great deal. I didn't know that there was such power in the theatre!*

With some difficulty Serafina found her way to the dressing area backstage. It was packed with people, the air filled with the babble of voices. She passed by the actor who had played the role of Claudius and saw that he was much older than he appeared onstage. He was standing by the woman who had played Gertrude, and Serafina had seen by the program that they were husband and wife, Malcom and Irene Gilcrist.

Her eyes went to an area where a group was gathered around Dylan Tremayne. All except two of them were women, and it was obvious that they idolized the actor. Moving closer, she saw the women putting themselves forward, then suddenly his eyes met hers. She heard him say, "Excuse me, sirs, ladies, I appreciate your compliments."

Approaching Serafina, he said, "It's good to see you, Viscountess." He offered his arm. She took it and was shocked at the hard muscle concealed by the puffy sleeves of his costume. He led her behind what appeared to be a mass of ropes and painted backdrops. When he reached a doorway, he stepped aside, and after she entered the room, he followed her. It was evidently a prop room, for it was filled with costumes, wigs, and different pieces of furniture.

Serafina had prepared her speech, and she said quickly, "I am not good at asking for favors, Dylan, but my legal counsel, Sir Leo Roth, has told me that I need you desperately. If your offer still stands, I would appreciate your help in finding the person who killed Kate Fairfield. I'd also like to meet the cast tonight."

"Why, certainly. If I could help Clive get out of that old prison, I would rest happy in my grave." Dylan smiled, and Serafina was struck with the strength of his words. He was wearing a tight-fitting costume, a vest of a light violet colour and pure white tights that outlined his legs like a second skin. She noted that his hands were very strong, the fingers long. "As I said, most of the cast goes for a meal after the performance. I think it's good that you go. A woman sometimes sees things that a man misses. Think differently from men, they do."

Serafina did not know whether this was a compliment or an insult, but she said quickly, "You don't think they'll be intimidated by me?"

"More likely you'll be intimidated by them. Not a mannered lot, they are!" Dylan said with a wry expression. "Come along. You haven't been around actors much. Prepare yourself for egos the size of Ireland."

He moved out of the doorway and led her back to where the crowd seemed to be thinning out. The woman who had played Ophelia turned away from some of her admirers and saw Dylan. Her eyes fell on Serafina, and she paused. Dylan moved forward, saying, "I would like for you to meet one of your admirers, Elise. This is the Viscountess Serafina Trent. Viscountess, may I introduce Elise Cuvier."

Elise stared at Serafina and said calmly, "It's an honour, Viscountess."

"I enjoyed your performance very much. You gave a poignancy to the role that I didn't think possible."

"Thank you very much. Have you seen *Hamlet* performed many times?"

"No, not at all."

Elise hesitated, then said, "I am so sorry about your brother's trouble."

Serafina did not know how to answer this, but the words almost leapt to her lips, "I'm convinced that he is innocent, Miss Cuvier."

"I pray that it may be so."

"The viscountess is going to join our group tonight, Elise," Dylan said. "Perhaps after you change, you would introduce her to some other members of our cast."

"Certainly. Excuse me, Viscountess."

"She doesn't seem like a woman who could commit murder," Serafina said, watching the actress leave.

"You'd be surprised who could commit murder. From the words of Hamlet, 'I myself am indifferent honest, but yet I could accuse me of such things that it were better my mother had not borne me.'" The words flowed from his lips with such vigor that Serafina could only stare at him with astonishment. He smiled and said, "Now excuse me, Viscountess, while I change."

"Where shall I wait?"

"There's a chair over there. If you would just take it, the cast will be ready soon to go out."

The cast had gathered at a large public house called The Blue Parrot. Inside, pipe smoke mingled with the smell of cooked meat and alcohol. The troupe moved to a large room off of the main area. A long table that would seat the entire cast was centered in the middle. The proprietor, obviously proud of having such distinguished company, hustled about taking their orders. Before their meals arrived, everyone drank rather heavily—mostly wine, but several drank strong ale and other beverages.

Dylan had seated Lady Trent next to himself. At her right sat the new leading lady, Elise. Serafina's eyes roamed around the table, studying the cast carefully. She had been introduced to them, and they stared at her strangely. She saw that there was a close-knit quality in the group, yet a tension hung in the air—as if they were on the verge of opening a dark, malodorous box of fatal troubles. She leaned toward Dylan to ask in an undertone, "Are all these people close friends?"

"Bless you, Lady, no! They are in this play together, but when the run is over, they'll separate and go to different productions. You've noted that there's, more or less, a rigid air under all the laughter."

"I did notice that."

Claude Douglas was seated across from Serafina. He had played the role of Polonius—or had overplayed it, in Serafina's judgment. His voice had blared out and he had sawed the air with his hands as if he were cutting though a tough oak tree. He was staring at Serafina with a pair of small, rather suspicious eyes. He had given her only a brief greeting when he met her, but now he leaned forward and asked, "Did you like the production, Viscountess?"

"Very much indeed, Mr. Douglas."

"Have you seen a great many Shakespearean plays?"

"As a matter of fact, this was the first one I've ever seen."

"Do you tell me that? I'm shocked that a lady of your quality has neglected the art of drama." He lifted a huge mug of ale and drained it off, and when he slammed it down on the table, he glared around, saying, "You've seen the good and the bad as far as dramatic art is concerned, Viscountess."

Elise said quickly, "You're drinking too much, Claude." She turned to Serafina and smiled. "I am a little surprised that you've not seen a single play of the Bard's."

"I follow scientific pursuits, Miss Cuvier. I haven't had time for lighter things."

Something like shock ran around the company, and Ashley Hamilton, who sat at the right hand of Douglas, said, "You must have led a sheltered life. I thought the aristocracy entertained themselves more royally."

Elise smiled. "I think, Ashley, there are people who don't go to the theatre, but have other things to do."

"Why, that's heresy!" Malcom Gilcrist said. "Everyone goes to the theatre."

"I suspect," Dylan said quickly, "that the viscountess leads a very busy life. Her father is a very famous scientist, and he's trained and educated her to do the same. I believe you spend most of your time in your work with your father, do you not, Viscountess?"

"Yes. Ever since I was a child, my father trained me in the ways of science."

"I'm interested in how someone who knows nothing of drama feels about actors and the theatre—someone from your world, Viscountess." Irene Gilcrist was an attractive blonde woman, apparently in her mid-thirties.

She had played the role of Gertrude, the mother of Hamlet, well, and her chair was drawn close to her husband's as if she wanted to be able to keep control of him.

"I was very moved by it, Mrs. Gilcrist," Serafina said at once. "I must admit I was greatly surprised. I had read the play, of course, but that's nothing like seeing it. I've now discovered that I've been missing a great deal." She turned and asked, "Was it very difficult for you, Miss Cuvier, to step into Miss Fairfield's role after the tragedy?"

No one had mentioned the death of Kate Fairfield, at least in Serafina's presence, but now Serafina was aware of a web of increased tension that ran around the table. Ashley, who had already emptied his glass several times and was obviously well on his way to being drunk, said loudly, "It wasn't at all difficult. Elise has been lusting for the chance to step into Kate's shoes ever since the production started."

Serafina saw that Elise's face had suddenly hardened. She turned to face Ashley. "If you're hinting that I had anything to do with her death, then you should know better. After all, Ashley, you hated her worse than anyone. No one can hate a woman like an ex-lover."

An alarm touched Serafina's nerves, and she felt Dylan's elbow touch her slightly—a warning for her to conceal her surprise. The thought came to her that Ashley was terribly immature, a thirty-year-old teenager. And his hatred for Kate was reflected in his eyes.

Now that the subject of Kate Fairfield's death had been opened, they all began to talk. Claude Douglas said, "The police were here. Some inspector called Grant, Viscountess. He questioned us all as if we were suspects."

"I thought that was ridiculous," Irene said stiffly. "I don't want to be at all disrespectful, but all the evidence points to your brother, Viscountess."

Ives Montgomery, who played Horatio, was lolling back in his chair, a thoughtful look on his lean face. "That fellow Grant is a tough one. He pinned me down like a bug, wanted to know where I was after the performance the night that Kate was killed. If he didn't suspect me, I'd be surprised."

"Did you have a good alibi, Ives?" Dylan inquired with a smile.

"Not a bit of it. No more did you, I take it."

"No, I didn't."

"Did Grant question you, Mr. Tremayne?"

"Very closely indeed."

"He questioned all of us," Claude snapped. "I think we're all suspects."

"Why is that, Mr. Douglas?" Serafina asked quietly.

Claude was almost as drunk as Ashley and glared at her as if she were not sound. "We all despised the woman, that's why."

"Speak for yourself."

"Why, Irene? You hated her as much as the rest of us. You'd watched your husband chasing around after her like a dog with his tongue hanging out."

"Shut your mouth, Douglas!" Malcom Gilcrist shouted. He half rose as if to attack Claude, but his wife pulled him back into his chair. Her face was fixed in a furious expression, and she whispered forcefully, "Don't be any more of a fool than you can help!"

Angry words began to fly across the table, and each one seemed to be insulted that Grant had pressured them about their movements on the night of the murder.

Ashley obviously despised Malcom and his wife, Irene. "You had a motive for killing her, Irene. Your husband was in love with her. Where were *you* on the night she was killed?"

"Shut your foul mouth, Hamilton!" Malcom said. "You hated Kate more than all of us."

"No." Ashley shook his head, and a sadness came to his eyes. "No," he whispered, "I loved her."

The dinner, from that point on, was a disaster. They all changed the subject quickly, and Serafina felt stares of dislike. Finally, when the party broke up, Malcom came and said, "I apologise, Viscountess. We're like a family, don't you see? We have our spats, but afterwards we make it up. I'm sure you understand."

A deep sadness was reflected in the eyes of the man, and Serafina found herself pitying him greatly. "Of course. Don't trouble yourself about me, sir."

"I'm—I'm sorry about your brother."

"Thank you, Mr. Gilcrist."

As Malcom turned away, Dylan said quietly, "If you're ready to go, I'll take you to your carriage, Viscountess."

As Dylan walked with Serafina toward where Givins was waiting in the carriage, he asked, "What did you think of the cast?"

"They're not what I expected."

"They're a pretty vindictive crowd. It's a profession that breeds jealousy. Everyone wants to get to the top. But that's the way of the world, yes?"

"Why, you're exactly right. I know women who would kill to get their daughters married to an earl."

"The one that I suspect more than any other wasn't there tonight."

"Who was that, Dylan?"

"Sir William Dowding. The producer, he is."

"Why do you suspect him?"

"Difficult to say. It's really more of a feeling. He is a powerful man, very possessive. He hates to be crossed, and he holds what's his very tightly."

"And he was . . . in love with Katherine Fairfield?"

Dylan turned to face her, and she was caught by the intensity of his light blue eyes. "If you are having my opinion, not love it was he had for her. It was all flesh—and love is more than that. Many who talk of love know nothing of the real thing. He was having an affair with Kate, and that's not love. And a selfish, grabbing man he is too! If he found out that Kate was seeing another man, he could be very violent. I've seen it in him—anger jumping out like a snake striking. I suppose most powerful men are like that."

They reached the carriage, and Dylan opened the door. He handed her in. She leaned out and said, "I need to think about this, Dylan, but we need to talk. Can you come and see me tomorrow?"

"Yes indeed—but it should be early. Am going to start looking for that missing witness, I."

"Come for breakfast, then. You can meet my family, and we'll have time to talk."

"Your family—they may not like an actor coming for a meal."

She shook her head and seemed to be lost deep in thought. "I must tell you something, Dylan."

"Yes, what is it?"

Her voice was very low, and he had to lean forward to catch her words. She didn't face him but looked fixedly at the other side of the carriage. "I—I still don't believe that God told you to help Clive . . . but I find I need your help. I don't know how to function, and I know that there are things that you can do that I can't. We can't sneak around and hide that, Dylan. Come tomorrow. I'll make my family understand."

"I'll be there early, ay? May the good God go with you, Lady Serafina."

The carriage moved off, and Dylan watched as it went. He had seen a glimpse of a woman he did not know. There were two Serafina Trents. One was proud and rigid in her thinking, but he had seen another side of that same woman in her broken words—and he smiled at the thought that brushed against his mind.

✤ NINE ✤

Serafina stood before her dressing mirror brushing her hair. She knew that Louisa felt this was her job, but Serafina was not thinking of that. She had spent a restless night, troubled with very bad dreams, and her face was puffy from lack of sleep. She was thinking of how best to bring Dylan into her family's sphere, and was not certain that it could be done smoothly. Actors were not suitable houseguests in the world of high society, and Serafina knew that bringing Dylan into the tightly knit union of her family would not be easy.

With a quick movement, she put the brush down, turned, and left her bedroom. She moved quickly down the hall and descended the stairway—but as she reached the first floor, a loud female voice caused her to stop dead still. With a grimace she murmured, "Oh no! Not Aunt Bertha! Not *now* of all times!"

But no one had such a strident voice as Lady Bertha Mulvane. Her voice was loud, demanding, and easily overwhelmed any other voice in the Western world. She was the older sister of Alberta Newton, and a widow. Her husband, Sir Hubert Mulvane, had been knighted for something rather unimpressive, but in Bertha's eyes, the *Sir* before his name was the mark of royalty. Such a knighthood died with the man, so Bertha had no right whatsoever to the title Lady Mulvane, but this never troubled her. She was a selfish, overbearing woman of some sixty years who often invited herself for too-long visits with the Newtons.

Serafina paused at the door of the dining room, dreading the task of being polite to her aunt. She entered as Lady Mulvane was stating in a voice like a trumpet, ". . . and so you must not give in to weakness, Sister! We must bear the shame of Clive's disgrace with fortitude!"

Bertha Mulvane was always ready to bear with fortitude any sort of pain—as long as it was someone else's pain. When Serafina stepped into the room she saw that her mother was weeping silently, her face twisted with grief. Before Bertha could continue her exhortations, Serafina said loudly enough to drown her aunt's sermon, "Why, Aunt Bertha, I didn't know you were here." She advanced and took the hug and peck on the cheek that her aunt offered, but spoke quickly to head off any more jeremiads from her. "Here, come and sit down by me. I'll fix you a nice plate."

Serafina steered Lady Bertha to a place as far away as possible from Alberta and practically shoved her into one of the heavy mahogany chairs. "I came as soon as I heard of the disgrace—" she began, but Serafina simply spoke even more loudly, "No disgrace, Aunt. We're going to have the victory over this thing." Serafina raised the level of her voice each time Bertha tried to speak, and after piling a plate high, she placed it before her aunt. "There, Aunt Bertha, porridge, bacon, eggs, toast, butter, and preserves. You always like Nessie's breakfasts. Just start on that and there's plenty more."

Bertha was a voracious eater and attacked the food at once. Even with her mouth full of eggs, she still tried to sound a note of gloom, but Serafina's bright, cheeerful remarks simply overwhelmed her. Finally Serafina sat down by David and said, "We're going to have company for breakfast." Everyone looked at her with surprise, and Bertha said with indignation, "It must be a very thoughtless person—to intrude at such a time."

"Not at all, Aunt Bertha," Serafina said, her voice strong and her face marked with a pleasant expression. "It's a gentleman who's going to be of great help to our situation."

Aunt Bertha's double chin trembled with anger. "You shouldn't have a stranger coming at a time like this. I'm surprised at you, Serafina!"

"Who is our guest, dear?" Septimus asked. He had withered under Bertha's demanding charges and was very glad that Serafina had come to blunt some of Bertha's misdirected enthusiasm.

Serafina took a quick breath and plunged in. "The gentleman's name is Dylan Tremayne. I invited him to come to breakfast this morning because he can help us. He's a friend of Clive's, and he's offered to assist us in any way he can."

"The actor fellow?" Septimus said. "How could he possibly help?"

Alberta turned and stared at her husband. "What do you mean—an actor?"

"Well, the fellow's an actor. Isn't that right, Serafina?"

"Yes, he is. As you know, Clive went to the theatre a lot to meet that woman who was killed. Mr. Tremayne and he became friends."

"I don't think it's quite the right thing to have an actor having a meal in our house," Alberta said primly. "You know what a depraved group of people they are."

Bertha had been caught with a mouthful of mushrooms and gravy, so her response was delayed, but now she screeched, "An actor! I can't believe it! They are the most immoral people on this earth!" She waved her fan in front of her face as if she were about to faint. Bertha never fainted. She was far too solid—and too determined to have her say about the man Serafina had invited.

"I think you'll find Mr. Tremayne quite acceptable." Serafina tried to think of some way to prove this and finally said, "He's a Christian man, as I understand it. He does some mission work down on the wharf among the unfortunates there."

"I don't believe it! He's probably a ranting Methodist—some sort of enthusiast!" Bertha pronounced. "You can't have such a fellow in our home!"

Aldora was watching Serafina curiously. "But how could an actor be any help to us?" she asked. "I thought we might hire a private investigator."

"In effect, that's what Mr. Tremayne is, except that he's not being paid. He really has an affection for Clive, and I think that's important."

"Well, I would really rather you wouldn't ask him any more, Serafina," Alberta said. "I don't feel like having strangers around." She was nervous and twisted a handkerchief in her hands, and Septimus went over to her and put his arm around her. It was an unusual gesture of affection, and Alberta looked up at him with surprise. Then she glanced back and asked, "Where did you meet him, Serafina?"

Serafina related how Dylan had visited Clive in his cell and alerted the family about its condition. She was interrupted several times by Aunt Bertha, but each time Serafina simply raised the level of her voice. Just as she was ending the story, Barden came into the breakfast room and said, "There's a gentleman here, a Mr. Tremayne. He says he's expected."

"Show him in, will you, James," Serafina said quickly.

"I hardly know how to think of an actor in the midst of our family," Alberta said fretfully.

"It's unseemly, Serafina!" Bertha said loudly. "You should know better." She had no time to say more, for which Serafina was glad. James returned with Dylan and nodded. "Mr. Tremayne."

Serafina turned to face Dylan and saw that he was perfectly dressed. He wore a checked jacket of fine wool and a fresh cotton shirt. His trousers were a fawn colour and his boots gleamed, the fine leather catching the reflection of the chandelier. Serafina went forward, saying, "I'm glad you've come, Dylan."

"I hope I'm not late," Dylan said. He smiled, took her hand and bent over it, and turned to face her family.

"I would like for you all to meet Mr. Dylan Tremayne, a good friend of Clive's. This is my father, Septimus, and my mother, Alberta. This is my sister, Aldora, better known as Dora, and this is my son, David—oh, and this is my aunt, Lady Bertha Mulvane."

Serafina glanced at her family, and she saw that Dora's eyes were wide. She knew that the outlandish good looks of the actor had caught her attention. Her mother, she saw, was impressed by Dylan's appearance also, and her father's eyes brightened as he said, "We're glad to have you, Mr. Tremayne."

David said, "Can we eat now? I'm hungry."

"Yes, of course. Mr. Tremayne, this will be your seat." She had seated him next to her father, across from her, with Dora at his right side. But before he could sit down, she said quickly, "Come along, Mr. Tremayne, let me serve you."

"Very kind of you, it is. I'm very hungry." She led Tremayne to the sideboard and handed him a plate, and he filled it with food.

When Dylan was seated, Septimus said, "I haven't had a chance to thank you properly for the service you did to my poor boy."

"It was little enough, sir. I hope to be of further service."

David said, "Why do you talk so funny?"

"David!" Serafina said at once. "That's an impolite thing to say."

"It's all right, Viscountess. I'm accustomed to it." He turned to David and said, "I talk funny because I come from another country, ay?"

"You ain't an English person?"

"Well, not exactly. I come from a country called Wales."

"Does everyone talk like you there?"

"Pretty much, Master David."

David took a huge mouthful of eggs, and as he chewed it, he said, "Do you have any little boys?"

Dora leaned over and said urgently, "David, don't ask such personal questions."

"Why?"

"Because it's not polite." Dora turned to Dylan and said, "I'm sorry, Mr. Tremayne."

"No problem it is. How is the boy going to learn if he doesn't ask questions? No, David, I don't have any little boys, but I hope to someday."

David thought that over and said, "When you do, will you bring them here to play with me?"

"You may rest assured I will do exactly that, Master David."

"How long have you lived in England?" Alberta asked.

"Oh, I left Wales when I was but a boy of ten. Came to London, I did. Had a rough time of it for my growing-up years. Then I enlisted."

"You were a soldier?" Dora asked.

"Yes, I was. The Cavalry."

"Did you kill anybody?" David demanded.

Serafina was at her wits' end. She looked at David and said, "David, will you please not ask such personal questions."

"Well, if he was a soldier, he must have killed somebody."

"I was in some battles, Master David," Dylan said. He looked at the boy and smiled. "They were shooting at me, and I was shooting at them. I suppose I killed as many of them as they did of me."

Dora smiled at this and said, "There, David. Now don't ask any more personal questions."

"Have you been out of the Army long?" Septimus asked.

"Yes, for a couple of years."

"I understand that you're an actor," Aunt Bertha said. She pronounced the word *actor* as if it were something very unpleasant. "How did you get into that . . . profession?"

"Why, by accident mostly, ma'am. I got out of the service with no money and no profession really. I took up with some folks who were in the theatrical line, and they taught me a little bit about acting."

"Have you been in many plays, Mr. Tremayne?" Dora asked.

"Quite a few. I'm not the star of the one I'm in now, of course."

"I hope you'll all go see him in the play that's at the Old Vic," Serafina said. "He plays a rather dashing young man, sword fights and all sorts of things."

"I'll come and see you. Will you teach me how to fight with a sword?" David asked.

Dylan laughed and said, "I expect when you're a little older, your family will see to it that you have fencing lessons."

Dora leaned forward. Her eyes were large as she studied Dylan. She was excited, Serafina could tell. "What's it like being an actor?"

"Not as romantic as most people think. Mostly it's a lot of hard work, a lot of uncomfortable traveling, sleeping in uncomfortable, strange beds, and sometimes being run out of town."

"Disgraceful!" Bertha muttered under her breath, glaring at him.

"Not really!" Dora protested. "Run out of town? Why is that?"

"Some of the citizens have strong feelings against theatrical people and the theatre itself. I can understand that. Many of the plays are unfit to be seen."

"Then why do you appear in them?" Dora asked, a puzzled look on her face.

"I don't. I appear only in plays that I think are moral, upright, and can have some redeeming social value. Plays that can help a person be better."

"I hardly see how a person could learn morality from theatre," Aunt Bertha said stiffly.

"Well, ma'am, the first theatre was related to the church, so the history books tell us. Drama began, at least in our part of the world, with little sketches, always biblical. The story of Job and his wife, for example, would be enacted, or perhaps the history of Noah."

"That's true enough," Septimus said. "I read an account of that once, but the theatre's come a long way from its religious beginnings."

"I'm sorry to say you're correct, sir," Dylan said. "But there are some fine plays. Mr. Shakespeare has some rather raw things to say, but basically he causes people to think about right and wrong, God and eternity."

Serafina had to speak very little during breakfast. David and Dora continually asked questions, and Septimus and her mother did the same. Aunt Bertha, of course, had nothing kind to say. She sat there glowering at Dylan, but he smiled at her as if she were the most pleasant person alive. Between answering questions, Dylan was able to take a few bites, but was unable to finish his breakfast. Finally David said, "Would you like to see my pony? His name is Patches, and you can see my dog too. His name is Napoleon."

"I would like to see them very much, if that's all right with you, Viscountess?"

"Yes, David, go show Napoleon and Patches to Mr. Tremayne."

David looked up, his eyes bright and his face excited. "This way, sir. You'll like them. I promise you."

As soon as the two had left the room, Dora said, "Serafina, he's the most beautiful man I've ever seen!"

"Don't talk rubbish, Dora!" Bertha snapped. "He's not a proper guest for our house."

"Dora, don't talk like that!" Alberta said, shocked.

"Well, he *is*. Are all the actors that handsome, Serafina?"

"I don't think so."

Aunt Bertha lifted her voice and filled the room with reasons why it was disgraceful to have an actor in "our" home. She ended by pontificating, "I don't think we ought to admit him into our family."

Septimus very rarely went against the wishes of a member of his family. He was more prone simply to ignore difficulties, but now he turned to face Bertha and said sternly, "Bertha, the man is an actor, and actors have a bad name, but I'll tell you this—if he will be of any help in setting our son free, I don't care if he's the Antichrist!"

Bertha, for once, was silenced. She sat back, her mouth making a large O like a goldfish gasping for air.

⁂

Serafina watched through the big bay windows in the front of the house as Dylan and David moved from one location to another. She was amused at how, at one point, Dylan simply sat on the ground with David while the two played some kind of a game. She watched as Danny brought Patches out, and saw that Dylan made a great show over the pony, as he did over the big mastiff, Napoleon.

Finally she glanced at the clock and saw that it was time for her to leave for her appointment with Sir Leo Roth. Leaving the house, she went down and saw that Dylan and David had gone to the trout stream. Dylan was telling a story. He was sitting cross-legged on the ground despite his fine clothes, telling a story, waving his hands eloquently at times. David, she saw, was sitting before him simply spellbound. They did not hear her approach; reluctant to interrupt, she heard David say, "Tell me another story, please."

"Well, that I will. I'm just full of stories, me. Perhaps if I tell a good enough story, you'll take me back to the house and get me a lovely cup of tea."

"I will, but tell the story."

Dylan smiled and leaned forward, saying, "Well, once upon a time there was a king whose name was Midas."

"Was he a good king?"

"He was a very powerful king, as all kings are. One time, David, he had a chance to do one of the gods on Mount Olympus a favour, and the god said, 'I'm going to give you one wish. What would you like?'"

"What did he wish for?"

"That's what I'm about to tell you, Boy. He wished that everything he touched would turn to gold. Wasn't that a powerful wish?"

"Did it really happen?"

"In the story it did. The king started back to his house, and he touched a twig, and it turned to yellow gold. He picked up a stone from the path, and it became pure gold. Every clod he handled, every piece of fruit or flower became nothing but heavy yellow gold. He went to mount his mule, but when he touched it, guess what happened?"

"The mule turned to gold?"

"It certainly did. And Midas, he was such a happy man! He went home, tired from his journey, and the first thing he did was to call for some food. The servants brought the plates in. One of them brought a bowl of water for him to wash his hands, and when he put his hands in the water, it froze into golden ice. And so when he sat down to eat, Midas laughed at how his plates and bowls changed to gold. And guess what happened then?"

"What, Dylan?"

"He picked up his food and put it in his mouth—but it wasn't food

118

anymore. It was a lump of cold, hard, yellow gold. He tried to drink, but the water had turned to gold. Everything he put in his mouth turned to gold."

"What did he do then?"

"Why, it was a sad, sad king he was. He went hungry for a long time, and he envied the poorest kitchen boy in his palace when he saw him eating a piece of bread. He knew that if he touched the bread, it would turn to gold. He knew he couldn't touch his children because they would turn to gold. He became a very sad king."

"What did he do?" David whispered, leaning forward, and Serafina saw that his eyes were fixed intently on Dylan.

"He went back to the god that had given him his wish and begged him, 'Please take away the gift you have given me.' And that's the way it happened. He reached out and touched a flower and saw that it stayed soft and fragrant. He gave a shout, and he ran home and embraced his wife and his children. He called for food, and the plainest fare was better to him than all the gold in the world."

"Is that all the story?"

"That's all, but we can learn something from King Midas. Sometimes the thing we wish for is something we don't even need. So, Master David, be careful what you wish for. You may get it."

Serafina had listened to the story, and in truth she had become entranced by it. It was a minor miracle to her the way Dylan Tremayne could hold a person captive with his voice, his expressions, and his choice of words. She had never known an actor before, but she was sure that few of them had Dylan's power.

Quickly she went forward and said, "David, you're filthy. You've been rolling in the dirt."

"Dylan's been telling me stories," David said, his eyes bright. "He tells wonderful stories."

"You mustn't call him Dylan. You must call him Mr. Tremayne."

"Yes, Mum."

"Now, you go up and tell Dora to clean you up. I've got to go to town today, and I'll say good-bye to you before I leave."

David turned away reluctantly, then he wheeled and said, "Mr. Tremayne, will you come back and tell me another story?"

"I'll do that, boy, if it all works out."

Serafina watched as her son ran back toward the house, then she turned to Dylan, who said, "That is a fine son you have there, Viscountess."

"I'm very proud of him, but—"

Seeing Serafina hesitate, Dylan asked, "What is it? Is something wrong?"

"It's just that . . . well, I don't tell David stories like the one you just told him. I didn't want to interrupt, so I listened. I don't believe in fanciful stories about the supernatural such as the one you just told."

"I think it's innocent enough. There's a good lesson in the story of King Midas."

"It's just a story. I believe in what I can see or hear or touch."

Dylan was examining Serafina closely. Her face was a mirror that changed often. He saw pride in her, and yet still something seemed to touch her like a dark cloud. Suddenly she was, somehow, alone in the world, as if there were no other thing alive on the planet. It came to him that perhaps her life was composed of a search that she kept concealed—a search for colour and warmth and even for the comfort of some man's closeness, but instead she had a great solitariness. "I think there must be some exceptions to that, for you I mean."

"I don't understand."

"You're like the apostle Thomas."

"Who was he?"

"One of the disciples of Jesus. The other apostles saw Jesus after He was resurrected, but Thomas wasn't there, and when they told him that the Lord Jesus was alive after being crucified to death, he said, 'I won't believe it unless I see the scars in His hands and the wound in His side.' That's why people, for years, have applied the name Doubting Thomas to those who have no faith."

"I don't remember that story. I haven't read a great deal of the Bible. Did he ever believe?"

"Yes indeed! The next time Jesus came to the disciples, Thomas was there, and Jesus turned to Thomas, and He held out His hands, and He said, 'Thomas, look at My hands. You see the wounds from the nails. Look at My side that was pierced.' And Thomas believed!" A warm flush touched Dylan's face, and his whole countenance seemed to glow. "And Thomas said, 'My Lord and my God.' As soon as he said that, Jesus said something I've never forgotten."

"And what was that?"

"He said something like, 'You're blessed because you see and believe, but blessed are those who don't see and believe anyway.'"

Serafina was quick; she understood at once that he was talking about her attitude toward God, her lack of faith. She said defensively, "I've seen so many go wrong by blindly trusting in religion. I suppose I am like Thomas. I won't believe until I see the truth."

Dylan shot back at once. "Viscountess, do you think your brother will hang?"

"No!" She shook her head. "I don't believe that."

"But all your intellect," Dylan said, pressing her hard, "must tell you that he will. If he were not your brother, you wouldn't have any hope that he would escape the noose. But you do have that hope, don't you, Viscountess?"

Serafina dropped her head and nodded. "Yes," she whispered, "I do."

"You know, Lady Serafina, I've often thought that we know very well that people die physically if they don't have any food or water, but I think a spirit without hope can die just as dead as a body ."

"How can I hope when I have no faith?"

"It's possible. Men and women often have to fight against unbelief. I have myself." He suddenly asked, "Have you ever heard of a poem called 'The Darkling Thrush'?"

"No, I don't read poetry."

"That's a pity. It was written by a man called Thomas Hardy. Hardy was a man who had great doubts about God, but he wanted to believe. He wrote a poem called 'The Darkling Thrush.' I've always loved it. Could I say it for you?"

Speechless, Serafina nodded. She did not know what was happening to her, but whenever she was around this man, everything seemed to be changed. She knew some of it could very well be his good looks. She watched him, his eyes, so intent they held her, it seemed, almost against her will. "All right," she whispered.

Dylan half closed his eyes and began to speak, his voice almost a whisper, yet rich with sound:

> I leant upon a coppice gate
> When Frost was spectre-grey,
> And Winter's dregs made desolate
> The weakening eye of day.
> The tangled bine-stems scored the sky
> Like strings of broken lyres,
> And all mankind that haunted nigh
> Had sought their household fires.
>
> The land's sharp features seemed to be
> The Century's corpse outleant,
> His crypt the cloudy canopy,
> The wind his death-lament.
> The ancient pulse of germ and birth
> Was shrunken hard and dry,
> And every spirit upon earth
> Seemed fervourless as I.
>
> At once a voice arose among
> The bleak twigs overhead
> In a full-hearted evensong
> Of joy illimited;
> An aged thrush, frail, gaunt, and small,
> In blast-beruffled plume,

Had chosen thus to fling his soul
Upon the growing gloom.

So little cause for carolings
Of such ecstatic sound
Was written on terrestrial things
Afar or nigh around,
That I could think there trembled through
His happy good-night air
Some blessed Hope, whereof he knew
And I was unaware.

"I—I don't understand poetry much."

"Why, it's very simple, this poem," Dylan said softly. "A man is walking through the woods, and he's in despair and sees nothing but death and decay. And then he hears a bird sing, and he looks up and sees this old thrush, shivering with cold and probably hungry—yet his song is filled with joy. And man wishes that he had that kind of hope, yes? The last lines are pure beauty, they are: 'Some blessed Hope, whereof he knew/ And I was unaware.'" He sighed, and his eyes brimmed with tears. "That is beautiful, ay? Hope when all is lost!"

"I wish I had hope like that," Serafina said, almost against her will. The poem had moved her greatly, and she knew that part of the emotion that rose in her breast was due to the power of Dylan's words.

The poem suddenly seemed to take form in Serafina's mind. She seemed to see the man in the gloomy, hopeless land, held in the iron hand of winter that reflected his own gloom, and then she saw the bird—not much better off than the man physically, but singing a happy song. "I think I understand the poem," she said slowly. "The man wants to have faith and hope as he sees it in the bird."

"Right, you! That's what you need, Lady Serafina—hope!"

She noted that for the first time he called her by her first name, not

Lady Trent or Viscountess, and it did not occur to her to protest. She was moved by the encounter, and it disturbed her. She had been taught all of her life to believe in the scientific method, but Dylan Tremayne insisted that there was another and better world, which confused her. "We'd better go," she whispered. "I have to see Mr. Roth about Clive's defense."

"And I have to go find the woman that could save his life." Dylan hesitated, then said, "I like your family—especially your son."

Serafina looked up at him and smiled wryly. "How about Aunt Bertha?"

"Well now, she's a hard morsel to swallow, but I'll turn on my charm. I can charm the birds out of the trees, ay!"

"You looked like a small boy yourself sitting on the ground with David. What were you playing?"

"One of my favourite games—marbles." His eyes gleamed, and he said, "But, of course, you have to give up your dignity and sit on the ground."

She knew he was saying something to her that she could not grasp. She turned quickly and said, "Come along, Dylan."

He joined her, and the two walked back toward the house. Neither of them spoke, but Serafina knew that something had passed between them that she would think about for a long time.

TEN

James Barden, the butler of Trentwood House, was a man of intense dignity. There was a rigid solemnity about him that exceeded even that of other butlers. No one ever saw him in anything except perfect dress, but now as he sat in the kitchen, he found himself more relaxed than was usual. He had come in to talk with Mrs. Rachel Fielding, the housekeeper, about the meals for the day, and she had invited him to sit down and have a cup of tea with her. The two knew each other well as far as outward appearances were concerned, for they had served the Newton household for years. Barden was a strict taskmaster, although not unkind, but he could not remember a time, as he sat there, when he had had to correct Rachel for any reason.

It was a warm, delicious-smelling kitchen, and the kettle began to steam, singing its little song. Mrs. Fielding took a black-and-white china teapot out of the cupboard, rinsed it with boiling water, then spooned tea out of the caddie and poured in the rest of the water from the kettle and let it steep. She brought out cups, then milk from the larder.

"I hardly slept at all last night, Mr. Barden," she said as she set the cups down. She took a seat beside him and pushed a dish filled with sweetmeats toward him. "This matter of Master Clive has me so upset I just don't know what to think!"

"Neither does anyone else, I expect," Barden said. "It's most difficult for all of us."

Mrs. Fielding sighed. She was a fine-looking woman of forty-nine with black hair and brown eyes, a little heavy but still attractive. She had lost her husband many years ago and had never remarried. Her whole life was centered around her position as housekeeper for the Newton family. "Has that detective talked to you?" she asked.

Barden frowned and nodded. "Yes, he has. I don't like the fellow much."

"He's rather harsh, isn't he?"

"Unnecessarily so, I think. At a time like this, with the whole household disturbed as it is, you'd think they'd send a man who would have a little more tact. But we'll have to put up with him, I suppose."

"Who is he talking to now?"

"He's questioning Grimes, and little enough good that will do him!"

"Why in the world does he think a footman could tell him about this terrible thing?"

"I don't know, I'm sure. What did he ask you?"

"Mostly he asked about Mr. Clive. What sort of man he is."

"He asked me the same thing. I think he's asking everyone that."

The two sat there talking quietly until the tea was ready. Mrs. Fielding poured for both of them, and Barden added lemon and cream and sipped it carefully. "You make the best tea I've ever had, Rachel."

Her face glowed suddenly, and she said, "Anyone can make tea."

"Not like yours."

"Do you suppose," she asked, "he'll talk to the family?"

"Oh yes, I'm sure he will, but I can't see how he's hoping to accomplish anything." He sipped his tea, put the cup down, then put his hands on the table. Mrs. Fielding noticed that he had beautiful hands, with long, well-shaped fingers, and they made her think of a doctor or a musician. "I wish he'd go away," she said.

"I wish the whole thing would go away, but it's not likely to." He heaved a sigh and said, "Well, we'll have to plan for the meals, and let's try to keep the staff as calm as possible."

❧

"I must tell you, Inspector Grant, I'm not entirely happy with the manner with which you've been questioning our people."

Matthew Grant had spent the morning talking to the servants, and now, although it was almost noon, he was determined to start his questioning of the family. He looked steadily now at Serafina and had to admit that despite his distrust of the aristocracy, the woman did have a quality that he admired. Suddenly the thought crossed his mind, *She's the kind of woman, I think, who could draw a revolver and shoot a man down and not go to pieces afterward.* He was not impressed by the expensive clothes or jewellery, but there was a strength in Viscountess Serafina Trent that did impress Grant. He was a man who respected strength, and the woman who stood before him had more than her share of that quality. "I'm sorry you feel that way, Viscountess."

Serafina said quickly, "I know you have to investigate, Inspector. That's your job, but we're not accustomed to having things like this happen in our family. It's very hard."

"I'm sure it is, and I will do my best to be a bit more tactful." Grant's lips suddenly twitched, for it was the first time he could remember ever promising anyone to be tactful. He was a straightforward, hard-driving man who set a goal and pushed himself toward it with all that was in him. His reputation for this sort of thing was well known among his fellow officers and also among the criminal element. It gave him pleasure to think that when he walked down the streets of one of the rougher sections of London, petty thieves and prostitutes and others of that sort would duck into an alleyway to avoid meeting him. It always gave him a sense of pride, of work well done, when that happened. He had not, however, often dealt with the nobility, so he had not known what to expect out of Viscountess Trent. He was well aware that there were those who claimed she had murdered her husband. He had questioned those who were more familiar with the case, and they all had exactly the same attitude: *We think she did it, but we can't prove it.*

"You're using Tremayne to help you clear your brother, Viscountess, which surprises me. He's an actor, not at all trained to do that sort of work."

"I must take what help I can, sir."

Grant saw that she was resisting him in every way and gave what amounted to an apology, something he had never done before. "I seem hard to you, I know, but I have to be."

"Superintendent Winters isn't."

Grant smiled and shook his head. "He's running for office. He'll be asking for your support one day, Viscountess. Naturally he's going to be as gentle as he can with you, but I'm not running for anything. I just want to see justice done."

Serafina studied Grant clinically. She knew she was better at studying inanimate objects and doing experiments on physical things than she was at reading people, but she saw him as the enemy. He was not a tall man, but there was an impression of raw strength about him. She again noted his silver-coloured hair. She estimated his age at somewhere around thirty, so the silver hair was not a sign of old age. It was thick and glossy and held a slight wave. Grant also had strange eyes, perhaps the strangest Serafina had ever seen. They were well shaped, deep-set, and hooded—and the most unusual shade of hazel. "Superintendent Winters told me he had a fear of sending an innocent man to the gallows. Do you ever think of that, Inspector Grant?"

"I have thought of it, of course," Grant said quietly. "Any man would in my place."

"I'm glad to hear that. I ask you to be fair, Inspector Grant. My brother's not a . . . steady man. He's gotten into his share of minor scrapes, but he's never harmed anyone."

Instantly Grant said, "He harmed Edward Maxwell."

Grant's fast reply caught Serafina off guard. She blinked with surprise and clenched her teeth together in a sudden gesture of annoyance. She was shocked that Grant would know so much about her brother, but then she knew he had been asking not only her family but Clive's friends and those who were not so friendly. "It was a fight," she said, "over a foolish matter. Something about a cricket match."

"He broke Maxwell's jaw and had to be pulled off of him. One witness said he thought he was going to kill him before they could stop him from beating him any further."

"It's the sort of thing young men do. I don't deny, Inspector, that my brother is sometimes hot tempered. He is, but that's different from slashing a woman to death."

Grant felt slightly out of his depth here. They were seated in a cavernous drawing room hung with crystal chandeliers. Only one of them was lit, but it cast its gleam over the two who were facing each other beneath it. The wooden parquet floors were strewn with an assortment of oriental rugs in several shades and designs, all a fraction brighter than those that become worn with constant tread. The gleaming white antimacassars on the chairs were stitched in brown upon linen. "I deal with hard men, Viscountess Trent." Grant shrugged. "It's made me a hard man in some ways, but I'd like to think I'm a fair man."

"Superintendent Winters offered to help me find the woman Clive was with."

Grant responded smoothly, "Well, of course we could be of help, especially if we had more facts. I don't think your man Tremayne's going to be able to find the woman, not on the scanty information your brother has given. We don't have a name. The only physical description is that she was a tall woman with blonde hair. I don't think you have any idea, Viscountess, how many prostitutes there are in the city of London. Perhaps as many as a hundred thousand."

"That sounds impossible."

"That is not my figure, but the superintendent is right. If we get any more details about the woman, we do have the resources to find her, and we will do so. You think that's fair enough?"

Serafina considered Grant carefully. "Yes, that sounds fair. Will there be any more questions?"

"No, that's all." Grant stood to his feet and turned to leave. When he got to the door, however, he turned and made a most uncharacteristic remark. It was not the sort of thing he would have said to many people concerning one of his cases, but despite Serafina Trent's obvious strength, he had discerned the fear that was in her. It was something he had learnt when he was young in police work, to detect fear, and he was good at it. He had no wish to give her false hope, but he said, "I hope your brother's memory improves, Viscountess. It's your only hope."

As Grant left the drawing room, he had the impression that somehow he had been bested, a most unusual feeling for him. *She's a woman of great determination and a good mind,* he thought. *She'll do anything she can to save her brother.*

Grant left the house and started down the walk, but as he did, he heard a very slight sound to his right. He turned quickly to see a young woman sitting on a bench in the garden. The flowers were blooming abundantly, so she was almost hidden by the foliage.

Grant hesitated, then moved closer; but as soon as he approached, a huge dog suddenly planted himself in Grant's path, a low warning growl deep in his throat. Grant stopped immediately, for a dog this size was nothing to be trifled with.

"Napoleon, don't be that way." The woman rose, and he recognised her as the younger daughter of the house, whom he had already questioned during an earlier visit. He watched as she came and put her hand on the dog's head, saying, "Be quiet, Napoleon."

She straightened and faced him, and he took her measure at a glance. Her deep teal green dress flattered her auburn hair and her colouring. "What is it, Inspector?"

"You are Miss Aldora Newton."

"Yes, I saw you when you were here before."

She swallowed and was very vulnerable as she stood there before him. The fear that he had seen only a glimpse of in Serafina Trent was obvious in this young woman.

"Inspector," she said, her voice soft, a thread of grief running through it. "I have to tell you that my brother would never kill anyone."

Despite himself Grant was impressed with the difference between Aldora and her sister, Serafina. "It's natural you should think so," he said.

"May I ask why you are questioning the servants?"

"It's just routine, Miss Newton."

"I know nothing of police matters." She stood taller and took her hand off of Napoleon's head. Despite her agitation, Grant saw that she had a pleasantly expressive mouth, but there was none of the enormous will that he had seen in the viscountess. Her features were quick to reveal her thoughts, and she had difficulty hiding her emotions. It suddenly occurred to Grant that the distance between himself and this young woman was greater than the distance to the nearest star. His background, his whole life, had been lived in one world and hers in another. He did not know exactly how to talk to her, for he had the feeling that she had been weeping, and it would not be difficult to send her off into another paroxysm of grief.

"What—what's going to happen next?" she asked anxiously.

"There will be a trial, of course."

"Will my brother go to prison?"

"That will depend on the judge and the jury." Grant did not want to tell her that if Clive Newton were found guilty, he probably would be hanged. He had the feeling that if he told her this, she would turn pale as a sheet and perhaps even collapse. Grant knew he was good with hardened criminals, but this young woman was so vulnerable, he felt unable to handle her as he should.

"I can't help being afraid. I suppose you would be, too, wouldn't you, Inspector, if your brother were in such trouble?"

"I don't have any family."

"You don't have any family at all? What about your parents?"

Grant thought suddenly of the barren years of his childhood and shrugged. "Others have had worse times, I think."

"What happened to your parents?"

"I lost them at a very early age. I hardly knew them."

"I'm so sorry. Did you go to live with relatives?"

Grant could not understand how the conversation had taken this turn. "No," he said almost shortly, "I went to a workhouse."

"A workhouse? I read a book by Mr. Dickens, *Oliver Twist*, but it really wasn't that terrible, was it, not as bad as Mr. Dickens makes out in his book?"

"It was . . . unpleasant."

"I'm so sorry!"

Grant had heard people make that statement—"I'm so sorry"— many times. Usually it was the coinage of polite conversation. They weren't really sorry at all, and Matthew Grant liked all things to be as they really were. But he could see this young woman really was sorry, and it stunned him slightly.

He opened his lips to respond, but at that moment Serafina came out and called, "Dora, would you come inside, please?"

"Yes, Serafina." Dora turned and said in her small voice, "Good day, Inspector Grant."

Grant nodded, put on his hat, and walked away. As soon as Dora reached the steps, Serafina asked, "What was he saying to you?"

"He didn't say much."

"He's a very hard man, Dora."

"He's had a terrible life, Serafina. He lost his parents, and he had to go live in a workhouse just like in that book *Oliver Twist*."

"That would be hard for any individual, I think."

Aldora watched as Grant got into his carriage. She touched her hair, then said tentatively, "He's rather nice, isn't he?"

Serafina could not restrain a smile. She put her arm around Dora and said, "You would think Judas Iscariot was nice. Now come into the house."

❧

"So you really didn't find out anything new, Matthew?"

Grant had given Superintendent Winters his report. It had been brief, for he really had no new information.

"No murder weapon?" Winters asked.

"Not likely to find that, sir." Grant paused, then said rather awkwardly, "I've had difficulty with this investigation."

"What difficulty?" Winters asked quickly. "It seems like an open and shut case to me."

"Oh yes, as far as the evidence against young Newton is concerned, but talking to the family and the servants, I formed an idea of the suspect. He has a hot temper, but he doesn't come across, in my mind, as a murderer. The last person I talked to was Miss Aldora Newton. She's the youngest daughter. Very fragile young woman. She was crying when I found her."

Winters stared at the younger man. "You're not getting soft, are you, Matthew?"

Grant laughed shortly. "I trust not. I can't afford to be soft."

Winters came around the desk and put his hand on the inspector's shoulder. Grant had been his protégé, and Winters had spent considerable effort making him the best policeman the Yard had. "Don't get too hard, Matthew."

Surprised, Grant stared into Winters's eyes. The older man was taller and more powerfully built, and there was an air of power in him. "Well, the girl was . . . vulnerable, I suppose you might say."

"I suppose every murderer has some good relatives, but I don't have to warn you, surely, that it's dangerous to listen to your heart. Too many have said that you don't have one."

Grant saw that Winters was mocking him in a good-natured way, and he nodded. "That's me, the heartless Inspector Matthew Grant. Well, I'll keep you posted if I turn up anything new, but it doesn't look good for young Newton."

❧

"Viscountess, there's a man here who wants to see you."

"What man is that, Ellie?"

"I—I don't know, ma'am. He's not a gentleman. A rather rough-looking old man."

"Did he say what he wanted?"

"He said he has to talk to you. You want me to have Barden send him away?"

"No, I'll see him. Where is he now?"

"I didn't want to let him in the house, miss, so he's outside the servants' entrance in the back."

"I'll go out there and see him."

"Yes, ma'am."

Serafina made her way through the house and down the hall past the kitchen, and turned off toward the door that led to the back of the house. As soon as she stepped out, she saw the man, his hair dirty and dead-looking and his face grey as old bread. He was wearing the roughest of clothing, his shoes were terribly worn, and he leaned on a rough stick. When he turned to her, she saw that his head was turned to one side, apparently in some kind of permanent fixation. A shapeless old hat that he didn't bother to remove covered part of his face. As soon as she stepped out, he said in a cracked voice, husky and rough, "Be you the viscountess?"

"I'm Viscountess Trent. What do you want?"

"What do I want?" The old man cackled and winked at her. There were wrinkles in his face, and she guessed his age at somewhere past sixty. He took the stick and jabbed it in the ground. "I comes to do yer a favour, that's wot," he said, then he began to cough. He dragged a dreadful-looking rag out of his pocket and held it over his face while he seemed to strangle. Finally he blew his nose, hawked, and spat on the ground. "I got a bit of a cold."

"What do you want?"

The old man leered at her, leaned forward, and whispered huskily, "Wot would yer like better than anything in the world, Viscountess Trent?"

Serafina did not know what to make of this man. He was obviously a transient of some kind, and she said, "I don't have time for this. If you're hungry, I'll have them bring you something to eat."

"Well now, that's good of you, 'cause I could use a bite to eat, but you ain't found out why I'm 'ere yet, 'ave you now?"

"What do you want with me? Speak up, man!"

"Why, Viscountess Serafina Trent, I'm surprised that you be so cruel to a poor old, broken-down man."

Serafina gasped with surprise, for as the man stood up, she saw that he was taller than she had thought—and the voice was one she knew. She gasped. "Is—is that you, Dylan?"

"It's myself, I am—and nobody else."

Anger that he had deceived her rose in Serafina's breast. "What in the world are you doing in that awful garb?"

Dylan moved closer. "I'm going down to question some people in the Seven Dials section about the woman Clive was with. Too many people know me in that area. I've gotten respectable now, and they're not going to trust a respectable man. But they'll talk to a broken old man sometimes."

Serafina was shocked at his appearance. "I would never have known you!"

"Why, good to hear, that is. One good thing about acting, I've learnt to disguise myself fairly well, but nobody down in the Seven Dials will trust a toff—a swell, that is." His eyes were clear as he watched her, and he smiled suddenly, saying, "We never know who anybody is. An American writer said that, fellow named Melville. Wrote about a whale. He's right, I think. People are one thing on the outside and another on the inside."

"That's not always true."

"Maybe not always, but it usually is."

"Dylan, I want to see the room where Kate Fairfield was murdered."

"The police probably have the house locked. I doubt they'd let you see it."

"But I need to get inside."

"How badly?"

She stared at him. "What do you mean?"

"Well, I can get us in, but it will be against the law. Can't you just see the papers? 'Aristocratic lady and actor break into house.'"

"I must see that room even if it's risky."

"Very well. We'll do it tonight."

"What about your play?" she asked, surprised at his quick agreement.

"After the play's over, we'll do it. We'll wait until after midnight. Shakespeare had a great line about that time. He said the night is the time when 'thieves and robbers range abroad unseen.'" Dylan's magnificent voice rolled with the words, and he laughed suddenly. "That's us, Lady Serafina—thieves and robbers. Come to the play tonight. Afterwards we'll burgle the house. Now I must go to work . . ."

"I'll see you tonight, Dylan." She watched him go, bent over and hobbling as soon as he turned to leave her. She was amazed at how complete and effective the disguise was, and as she turned, she thought about what he had said. And then she straightened her shoulders and muttered, "If I have to be a robber to clear my brother, I'll do it!"

ELEVEN

Come inside, Viscountess Trent. There's something I have to pick up in my rooms."

Serafina hesitated. She had attended the play and, even more than at the previous performance, she had been aware of Dylan's power to move people. His role, of course, was not the key role in the play. That was reserved for the character of Hamlet, but every moment that Dylan was on the stage, he held the attention of the audience, herself included, with an intensity she would not have believed.

The two had waited until the rest of the cast had left, then Dylan had brought her outside and they had found a hansom cab. The night was dark, nigrescent almost, for there was no moon. When the carriage stopped, by the pale glow of the gaslight she was barely able to see the outline of a building. Dylan paid the cabdriver and dismissed him, then he took her arm and led her up the steps. "Why did you send the cab away?" she asked. "Is Miss Fairfield's house close by?"

"Close enough," he said, "but we wouldn't want anybody to give a testimony to the police that they took us there."

His answer disturbed Serafina. She had never even considered breaking the law, yet now she was set on a course that led her to do exactly that!

She steeled herself against such implications, blotting out of her mind the possibilities—which were dreadful indeed!

Dylan opened the door to the house, stepped inside, and then allowed her to enter. He shut the door and nodded at a flight of stairs dimly outlined by the lamp on the table in the downstairs hallway. "My rooms are upstairs," he said. He stepped back and allowed her to go up the stairway first. At the top of the stairs, he turned and said, "Down on the end to the left."

Serafina followed him, and when he produced a key and entered the door, he turned and said, "Let me go inside and get on a light." She waited there, and then she saw the blue spurt of a lighted match before the gaslights came on.

"Come inside. This will take only a minute," Dylan said.

Serafina stepped inside and looked around. It was not the sort of room she had expected, although she could not have said why. Everything was as neat as in her own room. The furniture was well chosen though simple, and good prints were on the walls. A door to the left apparently led off to a kitchen and dining area, and one on the right to a bedroom area. She watched as Dylan moved over to a desk. He reached behind it. She heard a faint click, and then he slid a part of the desk away. He brought forth what appeared to be a small leather bag. He closed the desk, came back, and smiled. "Now you know where my treasures are."

"You have a secret hiding place in your desk?"

"Yes. I think we're ready now."

"What's in the bag?" Serafina asked, unable to control her curiosity any longer.

Dylan untied the leather strap and unrolled the bag. It was not a bag actually but an oblong piece of leather with pouches in it. She saw instruments of steel gleaming in the night. Some of them were tiny as a hair, it seemed, and others were sturdier. Some had hooks and some corkscrews on the end. "It's a burglar's kit, Viscountess. I could open any door in London with these."

Serafina, startled, looked up into his eyes. She knew they were a light blue, but they seemed darker this evening. She saw that he was considering her, and his lips twisted slightly as if he were restraining a smile. He suddenly said, "I don't suppose you've spent many evenings with burglars?"

"No, indeed, but this is different. This is to save my brother's life."

Dylan nodded his approval. As he rolled the kit up, he said, "You're right."

"Why would you have those tools, Dylan?"

"Part of my misspent youth."

"You were a burglar?"

"Among other things. When I came to London, I didn't have a penny. I was starving on the street. A family took me in, fed me. Saved my life, I think." He reached up and ran his hand over his hair; memories stirred in his eyes. "I didn't know what they did at first for a living, but I soon found out. They were thieves. Since I was small, they used me in several ways. One was to put me into a small window of a house they were going to rob, then I'd go to open the doors and let them in. After I got older, my stealing got to be more complicated. I was taught to open a safe, a simple one at least, and it was no trouble for me to get through any door in London."

After hearing the terrible story, Serafina was silent for a moment. "Did it bother you to do that?"

"It was all I knew, Viscountess." His voice was even and calm. "I would have starved, I think, if they hadn't taken me in. Of course, later on when I came to know the Lord, I put all that behind me. The past is like a road. It's behind you, and it's not going to change. But the Lord Jesus forgives us our sins, and He's forgiven me for that."

Serafina was uncomfortable, as she always was, when he spoke of God or Jesus. It disturbed her, but she knew that this was no time to argue. She tried to think of a remark, but finally said simply, "I suppose it was something you had to do."

Dylan saw her problem but did not attempt to resolve it for her. "Come along," he said, and laughter glowed in his eyes. "It'll be quite an experience to see the Viscountess Serafina Trent burgling a house."

The house to which Dylan led her was no more than a quarter of a mile away. Some of the streets were lit by gaslights, but they were faint flickering things. More than once, shadowy figures stirred and moved toward them, and more than once Dylan raised his voice and said, "Move on there or it'll be the worse for you."

Serafina knew a touch of fear then. This was a world that she did not know, the midnight world of London, when—as Dylan had already told her—thieves and robbers ranged abroad.

Dylan led her down a side street and pulled her to one side. She felt the warmth of his hand under her arm, and it gave her some reassurance. Ordinarily she would have been offended that a man would take her arm, but this was no ordinary night—and this was no ordinary man.

"There's the house. You see it?"

"The big one there at the end of the road?"

"That's it."

"It's dark. I don't think there's anybody up."

"Probably not. Come along. Quiet now."

The two moved as quietly as possible until they reached the house. "We'll go around to the side," Dylan whispered. The darkness was so dense after they left the main street that she could see nothing. Dylan must have had eyes like a cat, for he led her to a side door and guided her through a small garden. "Wait right here," he whispered. She stood still, and he disappeared into the murky gloom for a moment. Far away she heard the sound of someone singing, but she could not understand the words.

Dylan was back then, appearing suddenly without a sound. "This way, Viscountess." He led her to a short flight of stairs, and she groped her way along, feeling the rail. They stepped inside, and there was no light at all. "We'll have to risk a little light," he said, "but I think it's all right. The house has been sealed by the police."

"What does that mean?"

"Until the investigation is over, nobody can come in except the police."

He fumbled in his pocket, and then she heard the sharp scratch of a match and saw the blue glow of a light. The light grew brighter, and she saw that he had lit a stub of a candle. He said, "Come this way. Her bedroom is on the second floor."

Serafina had never felt so strange and so vulnerable in her life as when they crept through the dark hallway. The small light from the candle made flickering shapes of their shadows on the walls, and as they walked up the stairs, one of the treads creaked. It sounded like thunder to her, but Dylan paid no attention. He moved quickly, efficiently, and when they were at the top of the stairs, he turned and said, "This way." They went down the hall and opened the door. "Not locked," he said. "Come inside."

They moved inside, and she found herself in the midst of a very large room. "This is the sitting room," Dylan said. "Her bedroom is over there. We're going to have to have lights for you to see anything. This candle won't do it."

"But someone might see!"

"We'll have to take a chance, but I do know that there are heavy drapes over the outside windows. Let me make sure those are closed." He moved catlike across the room, checked the windows, then said, "This way to the room where she was killed."

Serafina moved into the room, which was almost as large as the parlor. It was one of the largest bedrooms she had ever seen. The headboard of a large mahogany bed loomed on her right. Across the room were two windows, and she watched as Dylan arranged the heavy dark curtains over them. He lit the gaslights, and as they flared on, she blinked and felt a moment's fear. Still, she was a woman of strong nerves. "We'll have to hurry, won't we?"

"I wouldn't want to stay too long. What are we looking for?"

"I won't know until I see it," Serafina replied. She began moving around the room. She went to the large armoire on one side and went through it thoroughly. She examined the dresser carefully, and bit by bit she went over all the furniture, aware that Dylan was watching her closely.

Serafina moved to a small bookcase beside one of the windows. "She was a reader," she murmured.

"Are they classics?" Dylan asked.

Serafina laughed and held up one of the books. "Definitely not the classics. Look at this one."

Dylan took the book and read the title. "*The Mermaid in the Basement*—what a strange title!"

"It's by a novelist named Regis Stoneman, a writer of romantic detective stories."

"How would you know that?"

"My sister gave me this one for a gift. She's read them all and thinks they're wonderful."

"And you don't?"

"Of course not! They're silly and childish—full of romantic nonsense." She slipped the book back on the shelf and continued her search.

Dylan joined her, then suddenly said, "Look at this."

Serafina moved over to the table. It contained the stub of a cigar burnt down to within an inch.

"She certainly didn't smoke cigars."

Serafina took the small glass tray that held the cigar.

"That could be anybody's," Dylan said. "Could even have been left by one of the policemen."

"No, this is one of the most expensive cigars made. It comes from Cuba. It's called Roi Blanco—which means 'white king.'"

"How in the world do you know that?"

"I did a study on tobacco recently. I can identify over twenty brands of cigars, some just by the ashes. The man who smoked this is ostentatious."

"What makes you think so?"

"This brand of cigar is made to show people that money is no object, just like some people buy houses that are ostentatious. They don't buy them to live in; they buy them to make a statement about their wealth.

The same is true with jewellery, of almost any sort of object. A sensible person buys something that does the job. Only a man determined to display his wealth smokes Roi Blanco cigars."

For over an hour Dylan watched as Serafina examined the room. She reminded him suddenly of a dog on a scent. There was nothing doglike about her movements, but there was about the intensity with which she touched and smelled and moved from point to point, looking at everything in the room. Finally she straightened and looked at him. "Something's wrong here."

"What's wrong?"

"There are no personal papers."

"Maybe she didn't keep any."

"Everybody has personal things."

"Maybe she kept them in a bank in a steel box."

Serafina did not answer. She looked all over the room again and then suddenly stopped and looked down at what appeared to be an elaborate doghouse. "Did she have any pets?"

"She had a small dog once, but it died."

"That must be where the animal slept."

Dylan turned and said, "Yes, she spent over fifty pounds for this. I remember how she made fun of a man once. She said he was little enough to sleep in the dog's house."

Serafina looked at the doghouse, remarking, "Why would she keep the doghouse after the animal died?" She went back to the doghouse and stooped down, then got on her knees. "It hasn't been used recently."

"No, I suppose not since the animal died."

"Why did she keep it, then?"

"Maybe she was going to get another dog."

The doghouse itself was approximately eighteen inches wide and perhaps twenty-four inches long. It was made of walnut and adorned with hand-carved, ivory dog heads. "Very fancy for a doghouse."

"Katherine didn't mind spending money. She apparently had plenty of it."

"There's nothing on the outside," Serafina said. She pulled the pad out.

"What are you doing?" Dylan asked.

"There's something odd about this doghouse." She did not amplify her statement but pushed one arm in, and she was feeling around when suddenly she straightened up. "There's a false bottom here."

Dylan quickly knelt beside her. "What do you mean, Viscountess?"

"This floor is three inches above the bottom." She felt around some more, then said, "Wait a minute." Dylan heard a small click, and she said excitedly, "The bottom moved. It swings upward. It's on a hinge." Dylan peered inside and watched as she reached in. She came out with an elaborately carved wooden box some eight inches wide and twelve inches long. It was three inches thick, just the right size to fit in the false bottom of the doghouse.

"Now that's something," Dylan said. He watched as she opened the box, and the first thing she pulled out was a small leather notebook.

She looked at it and said, "It's some kind of a journal."

Dylan looked at the book she held open and said, "It's all numbers." The two studied the first page, both noting that the numbers were in groups of three, each separated by a dash.

"I can't make anything of it."

"I've studied cyphers for some time. Hopefully I can figure it out."

"Well, if it's a diary, I hope I'm not in it."

Serafina picked up a sheaf of banknotes and looked at the denominations. "Look, there's a lot of cash here."

Dylan whistled softly. "Well, devil fly off! There's enough there to buy this house."

Serafina also found several letters bound up with a ribbon. She scanned one. "The letters are from her lovers. This one is signed by Charles Atworth. Do you know him?"

"I know of him. He was interested in Katherine for a while. He's a wealthy man."

She scanned the letter and said, "He's a fool to put down his feelings for an actress on paper."

Dylan said, "I think we'd better get out of here. We can read those letters later."

"I believe you're right."

She closed the secret floor and put the pad back in the doghouse, and the two got to their feet. Dylan picked up the ashtray with the cigar stub and went over to the door. He waited until she had stepped outside, then lit his candle. As soon as it was lit, he turned the lights off. They left the house quietly, and as soon as they were out on the street again, he said, "We'd better get a good distance away from here before we get a cab."

"It's not too far to my house in town."

"Be better if we walked there." He hesitated, then said, "How does it feel to be a burglar—or is it a 'burglaress' for a woman?"

Serafina could not see his face clearly in the darkness, and her voice was husky as she said, "I know it's a crime to do this, but I'm going to see my brother walk out of that prison no matter what it takes! Come along, Dylan, let's get away from here."

❧

They had reached the door of Serafina's town house and she turned to him, saying, "Thank you, Dylan. I don't know why you'd risk so much for a man you really don't know."

"I told you. God told me to do it."

"It makes me feel uncomfortable when you say things like that."

"Maybe you'll not always feel that way."

She hesitated, not knowing what to make of his words, then said, "I'll study the journal, and tomorrow I'll tell you what I make of it."

"All right. Good night, Viscountess."

An impulse took her, and she put out her hand. When he took it in his own, she was conscious of the warmth and the strength of his hand. She had not touched him up to this point and was surprised at the sudden comfort that the gesture gave her. She was also disturbed, for she prided herself on her iron self-sufficiency. She had never spoken of it, but she well knew her pride was in her ability to take care of herself—without having to trust any man. Now as her hand was enveloped by his, it was as if she had given up part of her independence, but somehow she felt strangely assured by his touch. She looked up and saw that he was smiling at her. She at once withdrew her hand and said brusquely, "Good night, Dylan."

"Good night, Lady Serafina." Amusement tinged his voice, and she saw that he was well aware of her reaction to his touch. "Go with God," he said, knowing this was not something she wanted to hear.

She turned and entered the house, and as soon as she shut the door she leaned her back against it. She felt drained, for the tension of robbing a house had been great. But a sense of something else came to her. Her hand seemed to tingle, and she realised that she had acted like a weak woman, putting her trust in a man. The thought troubled her, and she moved away from the door, her mind not orderly but swirling with a vague confusion that was totally unlike her usual carefully controlled thoughts. *It's just the strain—and it was just a handshake—it didn't mean anything.* But her thoughts went back persistently to that moment when Dylan Tremayne's hand had held her own—in an embrace that had shaken her so greatly that she could not put it out of her mind.

❧

Inspector Grant appeared at ten in the morning, just as rehearsals began. He was met by the producer, Sir William Dowding. "What can I do for you, Inspector?" he asked quickly.

"I'm going to have to question the cast, Sir William."

"Whatever for?" Sir William's grey hair and light blue eyes made him look younger than his age of sixty-five, and he was quite accustomed to having his own way.

"There are still some unanswered questions about the death of Katherine Fairfield."

Dowding stared at him. "You've got Clive Newton in custody, I understand."

"Yes, but there are still some loose ends. Do you mind if I start with you?"

Dowding said, "Why, I don't think—"

"It'd be much more comfortable here than having you come to the station."

Dowding swallowed hard. He stared at Matthew Grant and saw something in his eyes that gave him pause. "Very well, Inspector."

"Perhaps we can find a more private place. But first let's inform the cast. I'll need to speak with each of them."

For an instant Grant was convinced that Sir William would refuse. "Very well," Sir William said in a resigned tone, "but I hope you'll be brief. We have a rehearsal."

"And I have a murdered woman," Grant said.

"Well, yes, of course." Grant waited there while Sir William raised his voice and informed the cast that Inspector Grant wanted to speak with each of them. "Go ahead and do what rehearsal you can while I speak with the inspector." He came back and said, "Now we can meet over here in this room, Inspector."

The two men went into a small side room that was used, evidently, as a dressing room for some of the lesser actors. Sir William turned and said somewhat aggressively, "Now please get this over as quickly as possible."

"Were you one of Katherine Fairfield's lovers, Sir William?"

The blunt question achieved exactly what Matthew Grant intended. The shock set the producer back on his heels. He glared at Grant, his eyes flashing, for he had not been expecting anything like this. Grant, although he did not show it by any expression, was pleased to see him thrown off balance.

"That is insulting, Inspector. My acquaintance with her has nothing to do with her death!"

"How can you be sure of that? Or better said, how can *I* be sure of that? There's always a chance that a cast-off lover will grow jealous. There have been any number of murders committed under such circumstances as this."

"Why—you're unsound!" A flush suffused Dowding's features, and he said furiously, "You have the murderer under arrest. I am insulted and shall certainly report your boorish behaviour to Superintendent Winters!"

"I'm sorry if I offended you, Sir William—but I notice that you have not answered my question. It would be very easy to prove me wrong." Grant's eyes narrowed, and he shot the words at Dowding as if they were bullets: "Were you her lover or not?"

Dowding appeared to be on the verge of striking Grant, but instead he took a deep breath and appeared to gain control of himself. "All right, Grant, I will answer your question. Yes, we were lovers." His lips twisted in a cynical smile as he asked, "Now where does that get you? If you arrest all the men Kate had affairs with, your jail will be overcrowded."

Grant studied the producer for a long moment, then said, "Thank you, Sir William, for your honesty. Now one more question. Where were you on the night that Katherine Fairfield was murdered?"

Dowding was no fool, and he said, "You know I took Kate out to dinner, I'm sure. But she wasn't feeling well, so I took her home early."

"How early, sir?"

"Somewhere around midnight."

"Did you go into her house?"

"I did not! As I said, she wasn't feeling well, and I dropped her off at her home, then went at once to my own."

"Can anyone vouch for that?"

"Why, yes, of course. My servants were there when I got home."

"And what did you do when you got home?"

Sir William grew frosty. "I went to bed as any normal man would."

"Did you leave your home after that?"

"Certainly not!"

"Can anybody testify to that?"

Sir William hesitated, then blurted out, "No, of course not. It was after midnight, and the servants all went to bed."

Grant turned his head to one side, and his voice was persistent as he said, "So you cannot prove that you were not with Katherine Fairfield when she was killed."

"I won't put up with this!" Dowding said, his face pale. "I cannot prove I was *not* with Kate when she was murdered, and you cannot prove that I *was*! You're intimating that I had something to do with Katherine's death."

Grant suddenly changed direction, for he knew that Dowding was exactly right. "Have you had any altercations with her?"

"Of course I did! Everyone had altercations with Kate Fairfield. She was a difficult woman. Beautiful, yes, but very difficult."

"What were you arguing about, if you don't mind saying?"

"I do mind saying, and I refuse to answer any more questions."

"Then answer me this." Grant decided to take another tack. "Did any of the rest of the cast have any difficulties with Miss Fairfield?"

Sir William gave a bitter laugh. "All of them."

"Oh, come now, Sir William. That's no answer."

"Well, it's almost true. You know she was engaged at one time to Ashley Hamilton."

"The actor who plays Hamlet?"

"Yes. They were very young, and it didn't last long." His expression changed, and he added, "She cast him aside when someone richer came along."

"And how did Mr. Hamilton take it?"

"He attacked her."

"You mean verbally?"

"No, I mean physically. He beat her up. She had him arrested. It looked for a while as if he would go to prison, but he got off somehow."

"How in the world did the two of them get parts in the same play? It seems like any producer knowing this would have avoided that."

"I don't know why, but Kate insisted that Ashley be asked."

"You must have some idea why."

Sir William threw his hands wide in an exasperated gesture. "The only reason that I can give you is that she wanted to torment him—which she did. She made fun of his acting. In their scenes together, she made him look like a fool and an incompetent performer, but I let her talk me into it."

"That's worth looking into. Anybody else particularly at odds with Miss Fairfield?"

"Well, of course Elise Cuvier was very bitter. Perhaps an understudy is always jealous of the star. She has to stand in the shadow of someone else. Her only hope is that something will happen—" Sir William broke off and looked confused. "I didn't mean to intimate that Elise killed her."

"Murder has been done for less. Anybody else?"

"Well, Malcom Gilcrist was practically mesmerized by Katherine. She could do that to a man, you know."

"No, I don't know."

"Well, there are women like that. Malcom and Irene Gilcrist have been married for years, but it was obvious to the whole cast that Malcom was chasing around after Katherine."

"Do you think they were lovers?"

"I don't think so, but Irene was convinced that they were. There's a possibility for you to work on."

Grant studied the older man carefully. "Thank you very much, Sir William. I believe those are all my questions for now."

"I'd appreciate it if you would keep all these things to yourself. I have enough trouble in this company without your setting us off against each other."

"Privileged communication, I assure you. Would you please send Mr. Hamilton in?"

Grant stood there musing over the information he had gotten from Sir William. He did not know exactly what it meant, but it was something he would think over.

Ashley Hamilton entered the room, and it was obvious to Grant that he had already begun drinking, although it was only a little after ten in the morning. "I understand you have a few questions for me, Inspector."

"Yes, if you don't mind."

"Or if I do mind?"

Grant smiled. "Yes, even if you do mind. I'll try to be as quick as possible."

"Perhaps I can save you some time."

"That would be most helpful."

"If you're looking for a killer other than young Newton, I'd probably be your next suspect."

"And why do you say that?"

"I have the feeling," Hamilton said, his lips twitching, "that you already know."

"I know that you were once engaged to the victim and that it was not an amiable parting."

"If you try to find everybody who wasn't amiable with Katherine, you're going to have more suspects than you have room for in your jail."

"Those are almost the exact words of another person. Where were you on the night she was killed?"

"I was here at the theatre until after the performance. I went out to eat with the rest of the cast, and then I went home."

"You live alone?"

"Yes, I do."

"Can anyone testify that you were there?"

"Not that I know of. So what do you do with that information?"

"I'll think about it," Grant said. "Did you kill your ex-lover?"

"No." The word leapt to Hamilton's lips. "I didn't."

"Assuming you're telling the truth, who do you think did?"

Hamilton stared at the inspector. "I didn't know you people asked questions like this. What possible use is my opinion to you?"

"It seems to me that the world of the theatre is a very close little circle. There are all sorts of currents going around. So I'm asking you who would you suspect?"

"I may be a drunk and a poor actor, but I'm not an informer. You're the detective. You find the criminal, although I thought you had Clive Newton."

"He hasn't been tried and found guilty yet. Until he is, the case is open. That will be all for now. Would you send in Mrs. Gilcrist."

"You want her husband too?"

"No, one at a time. Mrs. Irene Gilcrist first."

Irene Gilcrist, when she appeared, had a guarded manner. She was an attractive woman in her midthirties, and she had the mobile face of an actress. "You have questions for me, Inspector?"

"Just a few. I'd like to know where you were on the night that Miss Fairfield was murdered."

"I was at home. My husband and I left immediately after the performance."

"You were together the entire night?"

Irene smiled bitterly. "Yes, we were. Where else would a husband be but with his wife."

"I didn't mean to imply—"

"I know what you meant to imply. I also see that you're a young man who looks into things very carefully."

"That's my business, Mrs. Gilcrist."

"Well, go ahead and ask me any questions."

"I have heard that you were jealous because your husband paid attention to the murdered woman."

"You're exactly right. He's a fool! There's no fool like an old fool. She didn't care a flip for him, but she liked to keep men dangling on a string."

"You don't think there was actually an affair, then, between the two."

For an instant something changed in her face, and Grant caught it instantly. *She's not sure about that,* he thought. He waited for her to answer and saw that for all her talent as an actress, she could not cover up the bitterness. "I don't know. He would have had an affair with her, but I think she was just playing with him. She liked to do that with men, you know."

"So I understand. That'll be all for now."

"Do you want to talk to my husband?"

"I'm sure he would say the same thing, wouldn't he, that the two of you were together?"

"Yes, he would. He's not that big a fool."

"Thank you, ma'am. That'll be all for now."

For the next twenty minutes, Grant spoke to other members of the cast. Claude Douglas, who played the role of Polonius, confirmed what the others had said about the nature of the relationship between Sir William Dowding and Katherine Fairfield, and also about the jealousy of Irene Gilcrist. He spoke slightingly of Ashley Hamilton, and he himself had no alibi.

"I didn't know I was going to need an alibi." Douglas smiled. "If I had known it, I would certainly have provided one."

Ives Montgomery, who played Horatio, had a surface charm, at least. He answered all of the questions that Grant put to him and said, "I was out with a young lady."

"You can't give me her name?"

"Certainly. Her name is Maggie Monoghan. She's a barmaid at the Black Horse Tavern."

"Were you with her all night?"

"No, that would have been too boring, but I was there at the time Katherine was murdered."

"How do you know when she was murdered?" Grant snapped quickly.

"I heard a rumour that it must have been about two o'clock. I can account for that very well. Really, I didn't have anything to do with it, Inspector. I'm much too cowardly, and I have no motive."

"You weren't tempted by Miss Fairfield?"

"Not in the least. It was obvious to any man what she was. There's an insect called a praying mantis." A slight smile played on his lips. "I've heard it said that after mating, the female eats the male. That pretty well describes Katherine—except, of course, she's more attractive than any bug."

Grant shook his head. "I'll be talking to you later perhaps. Send Mr. Dylan Tremayne in."

"Glad to."

Grant waited, thinking about the cast, until Tremayne came in. "Yes, Inspector, what can I do for you?"

"You can tell me if you ever had an affair with Katherine Fairfield."

"No, I never did."

"Can you prove that?"

"I don't see how. It's easy to prove an affair, but I don't know how you disprove it."

"She never led you on?"

"That she did." Dylan's smile was innocuous. "Why not? She did that to practically every man she fancied. It was her way of life."

"But you didn't surrender to her?"

"I'm not as dumb as I look, Inspector. I've got better sense than to have anything to do with a woman whose habit is tormenting men."

"There seems to be little doubt about that. Who do you think killed her?"

"Well, not me."

"Where were you while it was taking place?"

"I was at the Water Street Mission. That's a place where I help sometimes with derelicts and women in trouble. Mostly prostitutes. We feed them and try to give them some direction, some help, you know."

"You've got a witness to that?"

"Oh yes, plenty of witnesses."

Grant studied the young man, thinking of his connection with Viscountess Trent. "What's your relationship with Viscountess Trent?"

"We are acquainted," Dylan said cheerfully. "I was a friend of her brother's, and I've offered to help her in any way I can."

"How could you possibly help?"

"Well, I could offer moral support and prayers."

Grant smiled for the first time. "I'm sure that's a comfort to her."

"Doesn't seem to be working too well."

"All right. That's all for now. You can go."

"Thank you, Inspector. Call on me anytime."

As Tremayne left, Grant stood there for a moment and thought about what he had. He knew that he had nothing that he could report to Superintendent Winters, but something about the nature of the woman who was murdered had emerged, and he thought it might be useful.

He left the theatre and walked back toward Scotland Yard wondering what he could do next, and then he wondered why he was doing anything. *We've got a suspect all sewed up, but somehow it doesn't seem right.* The thought disturbed him, and he could not shake it out of his head as he moved along the street.

﴾ TWELVE ﴿

The sun, beaming with a sidereal brilliance, was almost directly overhead as Dylan turned and walked toward the Trent mansion. He had gone through rehearsal and had been somewhat shocked to find that he saw almost everyone in the cast as a possible murderer. He knew Grant had seen the same thing, and it was obvious that the inspector was like a snapping turtle, hanging on to whatever he put his mind to until it thundered.

He gave three raps with the heavy brass knocker, then stepped back. It seemed only a few seconds until the door opened, and an attractive maid gave him a quick look, then smiled. "Yes, sir, can I help you?"

"I'd like to see the Viscountess, please."

"She's occupied right now, sir. Would you care to wait?" The maid had dark red hair and unusual green eyes. Right now those eyes were fixed on Dylan in a way that he had seen before. He was used to women being attracted to him, for an actor who was not completely hideous seemed to draw them like flies. "Would it be possible for me to see Mr. Newton?"

"If you'll step in, sir, I'll see."

Dylan stepped inside, removed his hat, and watched the woman as she moved away. There was a seductive movement in her walk that he had seen before. Women could speak with their lips, but oftentimes they spoke with motion. He pulled his glance away to look at the pictures and the statues that lined the spacious foyer, and the scene gave him an odd feeling. Here were people who had money such as he had never dreamt of. *I wonder what it's like to have money enough to buy anything you want.* He smiled and shrugged his shoulders slightly, knowing that he would never find out—and didn't care in the least.

The redheaded maid came back to say, "If you'll come this way, sir, I'll take you up to see Mr. Newton. He's in his laboratory." She smiled enticingly as if she were inviting him to an intimate meeting somewhere.

"Thank you," Dylan said. He followed the maid, keeping his eyes away from her rounded figure. He had been struck long ago by a verse in the Bible that said, "I will set no wicked thing before my eyes." Not that women themselves were necessarily wicked, but something wicked could happen if he allowed his gaze to linger on the maid. He had often wondered how biblical history might have been different if King David had turned away after his *first* look at Bathsheba in her bath. No man, he well knew, could help that first look, but the test of will came when he had to decide whether to take a *second* look.

They climbed two flights of stairs, and the maid said, "This is Mr. Newton's study. If you need anything, just let me know."

The innocent words included an invitation that Dylan read as plainly as if it were printed in large black letters on a white background. He had often thought that women spoke two languages—one of mere words that conveyed information, and a subtler one that a man could not easily resist. He said quickly, "Thank you, miss." She caught his glance, and her soft lips curved into a smile that would have stirred a mummy.

"My name is Louisa, sir."

"Thank you very much, Louisa."

He turned quickly and entered the laboratory. When he was inside, he stopped dead still, for it was an enormous room filled with benches, tables, filing cabinets, and all sorts of scientific equipment, including glass flagons and burners that were heating chemicals on a table. All was a mass of confusion to him.

"How are you today, Mr. Tremayne?"

Dylan turned quickly and returned the greeting. "Good afternoon, Dr. Newton. I hope I'm not disturbing you."

"Not at all. I'm just doing an experiment that takes a great deal of time. Oh, by the way, I'm not really a physician any longer—so no title is necessary." There was an awkwardness about the man, and his white hair seemed to be standing almost on end. His large head and very broad forehead created an intelligent appearance, and he had neglected to shave for at least one, perhaps two days.

"I've been at the prison this morning to visit my son."

"How is he, Mr. Newton?"

"Very low indeed—and no wonder. He's never had anything like this happen, and it's getting the best of him. I did all I could to cheer him up, but that's very difficult." Newton attempted a smile, but failed and shook his head. "It's hard to comfort someone when you're miserable yourself."

"Yes, it is."

"Excuse me. I have to make a change, if you don't mind. Can we talk as I work?"

"Of course."

Newton turned and went to a line of small cages. Inside each one of them was a white mouse. The professor picked up a tablet, pulled a mouse out, studied it under a large magnifying glass, then put the small creature back in the cage. He made a notation in a small book, then said, "I'm studying the effect of the lack of certain vitamins on mice."

"I wonder what the mice think about that," Dylan said.

The professor smiled. "It doesn't take much to make a mouse happy, Mr. Tremayne."

Tremayne had to smile. "I suppose not. Just a bit to eat and a warm spot out of the cold, is it?"

"Yes, human beings are a little bit more difficult." Newton went down the cages, looked at each mouse, and made notations in his notebook.

Dylan knew little of science, but he had heard Newton spoken of as one of the most brilliant minds of the Royal Academy. "Do you give the mice names, sir?"

Newton was surprised. He said at once, "Oh no, just numbers. If I gave them names, it would become a personal matter, you see."

"And that would be a bad thing?"

"It would be awkward. A man doesn't get sentimental over Mouse Number Six, but if he were named Joey, it would be difficult to be impersonal."

"I'm afraid I could never be a scientist, Mr. Newton."

"No, you're not the type, Mr. Tremayne. David has told me about the stories you tell him—romance and wonders of all kinds."

"Your daughter doesn't like such stories," Dylan remarked. "She asked me not to tell them—but David loves them."

The remark seemed to trouble Newton. He gave Dylan a rueful look. "Yes, I know. She mentioned it to me."

"A little difficult, it is. David loves my kind of fooling, and I have to tell him no."

Septimus looked down at the floor for a long moment, then said in a tone that was somehow sad, "I sometimes regret the way that I educated Serafina. She was quite imaginative when she was young. I thought that was a rather bad thing, so I spent years drilling into her that the only proper way to go at things was the rational, scientific method."

"A good job you made of it," Dylan said wryly. "She's not got much patience with anything like fancy or imagination now."

"I know that. I've thought many times that I took something from her that she needed." He turned his head to one side and looked like a curious bird as he studied Dylan. "I've seen some change in her since she went to your play. It's like a light went on in her. I think she doesn't want to see David grow up to be a man without that side to his nature."

Dylan saw something like longing and regret intermingled in the older man's face. He felt unqualified to tell a man like Newton how to raise his grandson, but he did say, "A man can have both imagination and a critical mind, sir. Your namesake, Sir Isaac Newton, had both sides to his character."

"How do you know that?"

"I had a friend who was fascinated with Sir Isaac. He said that he was the greatest scientific mind in all history."

"I believe your friend was right."

"He also said that toward his more mature years, after making some of the greatest discoveries about the way our world works, he turned to the Bible. He said that Professor Newton devoted many years to the study of the last book in the Scriptures—the book of Revelation."

Septimus was staring at Dylan with consternation. "Your friend was exactly right. I've been trying for years to understand how a man with Newton's gifts could turn to a book filled with exotic and violent images."

"I expect he found that science, for all that it's done for mankind, isn't the final answer. We need more than a chemical formula to give us hope about ourselves."

The two men talked for some time, much to Dylan's amazement. He became convinced that deep down, Septimus Newton had the same kind of hunger to know the deep things of God that Sir Isaac Newton had manifested.

"Do you ever talk with Lady Trent about things like this, sir?"

"No, I do not." Septimus seemed confused. "How could I? I've led her to become what she is. Can I go to her now and change all that I've taught her?" He seemed to slump, and with a strange look in his eyes, he said, "I must admit that all the scientific knowledge in the world doesn't do any-thing to help when your world falls apart." He suddenly cried out, "I'm not equipped to handle this business, Tremayne. To have your son accused of murder, it's getting to all of us, I'm afraid!"

"I know it's hard."

Newton threw his hands open in a helpless gesture. "Life is strange."

"Yes, it is, and not very pleasant. The Bible says man is born to trouble as the sparks fly upward."

"The Bible says that?"

"Yes, sir, it does."

"Well, I've read the Bible very little, but *that* is certainly true. Come over and sit down. We can be more comfortable." He moved across the room toward a big bay window with a table in front of it. There was tea brewing, and he poured them both a cup without asking and pushed one toward Dylan. "It's an odd thing," he said. "One moment you're a child out laughing and chasing butterflies, and the next minute you're an old man unable to handle the things that come up in life."

"Life is that way, isn't it? Man's like the grass in the field. He flourishes, and then the wind passes over him and he dies. Sometimes," Dylan added gently, "a man bends over to pick up something, and when he straightens up the whole world has changed."

The eyes of Septimus widened, and he said, "You're a very perceptive young man. Unusually so." He whispered in a tone of agony, "I feel so— so frustrated! There's so little I can do to help my son, and I appreciate your friendship for him."

"We haven't known each other long, but he has great potential. He just hasn't found his way yet, but I believe that God is going to step into his life."

Septimus sipped his tea, then said in a voice tinged with longing, "I wish I had faith."

"It's a thing that we all need, Mr. Newton. Have you ever called upon God?"

The question seemed to embarrass Septimus. He looked out the window and seemed to avoid answering. "Look at that chipmunk," he said. "He comes every day about this time." He moved over, opened the window, and put one of the cakes that was on the table outside. He stepped back and said, "I give him his dinner."

Dylan watched as the chipmunk streaked across the ground and scampered up a tree just outside the window. He made a rather daring leap, and when he landed, he looked up and saw the two men watching him. He tucked his front legs tightly against his chest so that only his paws were visible.

"He looks like a supplicant modestly holding his hat, doesn't he, Mr. Tremayne?"

"Yes, he does. He doesn't have many worries either, rather like the mice you have. Oh, I suppose all of God's creatures have problems, though." Dylan paused for a moment, then said, "Mr. Newton, have you ever read any of Mr. Burns's poetry—Robert Burns, the Scotsman?"

"No, I'm afraid I don't read poetry. What's the poem about?"

"It's about a female mouse who's made a burrow for her young. She gathered food for the winter. She's all set. Everything is prepared and she has no worries. Then suddenly a man with a plow comes along. The plow tears into the nest, scatters the food that the mouse has gathered, and I suppose it scatters the young ones out into the cold."

"Why would a man write a poem like that?"

"He was interested in the human condition, as all poets are. One line I've always remembered says, 'The best laid plans of mice and men often go astray.'"

A light suddenly flickered in Septimus's eyes. "That's very true. He was a very wise man to see that. Our plans don't take into account the calamities that are going to strike us." He gave Dylan a sharp glance, much like he had given to one of the mice in his experiment. "Tell me more about yourself, Mr. Tremayne."

Dylan gave a brief sketch of his life, of how he had come up the hard way, and he told him in great detail how he had found God. He finally ended by saying, "So now I have a master, the Lord God Jehovah, and His Son, the Lord Jesus. I try to be a good soldier for them, better than I was for the queen even, and I was a good soldier."

Septimus was watching Dylan as he spoke. He seemed to be drinking the words in as a thirsty man drinks cool water. He cleared his throat and said, "I admire your strength, and I honour you for it, sir."

"Oh, it's frail enough, I am, sir. But God wants us all. He made us all, and He wants us all to be His good soldiers. Even you, Mr. Newton. I encourage you to seek the Lord, and I'll pray for you."

Septimus Newton could not seem to find an answer. He had spent his whole life in the scientific world and had, more or less, ruled God out as a possibility. He had instilled this in his daughter, but now there were signs of doubt on his forehead. "I appreciate your sentiment, and I wish—"

Septimus never finished his sentence, for the door opened, and Serafina stepped in. She was wearing a simple dress of some light green material, and her hair was carefully pinned high on her head."Good morning, Dylan."

"Good morning, Viscountess."

"What have you two been talking about?"

"Oh, just man talk," Septimus said quickly. "I found out quite a lot about Mr. Tremayne."

"You have to be careful of my father. He's very nosy." Serafina went over and put her arm around her father. It was the first show of affection that Dylan had ever seen in her—except with David—and he thought it made a beautiful scene.

"Now I'm going to take Mr. Tremayne away." She gave Dylan a bright smile.

"I hope you can stay. David talks about you all the time," Newton said.

"He's a fine lad."

Serafina turned to go, and Dylan said, "It was good talking with you, sir."

Serafina led him to the library, and Dylan immediately gave an update. "Grant came to question the cast yesterday. He's a tough young fellow. He put everybody on the spot. Everybody's walking around in shock."

"Does he suspect one of them?"

"Oh, he suspects everybody, I think. But tell me about what you found."

She turned and said, "I've been trying to read the journal, and I've decided that we need to put everything back as it was—after I copy the journal, or the parts that I think are significant."

"Why would we want to put it back?"

"Because if it's evidence against the real murderer, the police need to find it. They're not going to think much of it as evidence if we rush in and say, 'Look, here are all the things you missed.'"

"Right, you! We'll think of some way. What's the next step?"

"I think we need to talk to Katherine Fairfield's maid. She was the last one to see Kate alive, and she's the one who found the body."

"She doesn't have to talk to us. We're not the police."

"I know, but we'll find a way. There's something else we should do," Serafina said. "We need to go to all the tobacconists in London and see who smokes the Roi Blanco cigars."

"There must be a hundred of them."

"You can rule out most of them. Only the exclusive shops handle this brand. If we find one tobacconist who sells them, he'd know who his competition would be."

"Good idea. We could start early tomorrow. Perhaps this afternoon we could see Katherine's maid."

"Do you know her?"

"Oh yes. She won't be hard to find."

They were interrupted suddenly when David came rushing into the room. He saw Dylan and ran to him. "Are you come to go fishing with me?"

"Not today," Dylan said with a sparkle in his eye. He glanced at Serafina and hesitated before saying, "But I'll tell you what. Why don't we go to the circus?"

David looked at him, his eyes wide. "A circus? I've never been to a circus."

"Everybody ought to go to the circus. I'll bet if you'd ask your mum, she'd go with us."

"Can we go, Mum, to the circus?" David asked, his eyes bright with anticipation.

Serafina paused before answering, then decided an outing would be good for everyone. "I think we should." She knew that David was hungry for companionship and said, "Let me go find Dora and see if she'll go with us. We'll make an afternoon of it."

David said, "Hurray!" and began to dance around. "Let's go quick, Mum!"

◆✿✦

The circus was held at the Crystal Palace, and the star of the show was Blondin, the world-famous tightrope walker. Dora had been reluctant to come, but she joined in the fun slowly and seemed to put her fears for Clive behind her. She was watching now as Blondin walked along a tightrope high in the air as confidently as a man walked on a paved roadway. "How does he do it?" Dora breathed.

"He has wonderful balance," Dylan said. "I read about him. You know he walked a tightrope stretched across Niagara Falls?"

"Really?" Serafina asked. "That must have been something to see."

"He tried to get the Prince of Wales to go across with him in a wheelbarrow, but, of course, the prince had more sense than to go."

"Did anybody go, Mr. Dylan?" David asked. "I would like to have gone."

"It'd be a long way down at those falls. You think you'd have been afraid?"

"I might be, but Mum wouldn't be. She's *never* afraid."

"Don't say that, David." Serafina smiled, and her lips made a delightful picture. "I'm afraid of a lot of things."

When the show was over, they stopped for beef sandwiches, and Dora took David to see the animals in the menagerie.

"I worry about David."

"He seems healthy and a bright young boy."

"He gets very lonely."

"You think he misses his father?"

Serafina almost flinched, and Dylan did not miss it. She did not answer the question, and he said, "Well, he wasn't lonesome today anyway. You're looking very well, Viscountess. The trip has put some colour in your cheeks."

Serafina laughed shortly. "I suppose you're used to young women chasing you around. My maid, Louisa, has fallen in love with you already—

and Dora thinks you're the most handsome man in the world. I suppose you're accustomed to that sort of adulation?"

"All that's for some actor. That's not me."

"You have a lot of women pursuing you. I've seen them after the performances. Do you have much trouble rejecting them—or *do* you reject them?"

"I don't think it's a healthy situation for a man to be pursued by women."

"It must be hard to say no when an attractive woman comes to you."

"It takes grace."

"Grace?"

"Yes, you have to get grace from God. It takes grace," he said, "as a man fills his cup under the waterfall. And I look on women as rather dangerous anyway—like tigers, beautiful but with deadly potential. I read once a story about a girl who was so beautiful she could fade the purple out of cloth and tarnish mirrors with her looks."

"She must have been quite a woman."

"Yes. The Talmud says that if a woman walks between two men and no appropriate prayer is said, one of them will die."

"So you have to pray to God to protect you from women."

"And from almost everything else," he said. "Look, David's coming back. I expect we'd best get you back home again."

"It's been a beautiful day. Thank you, Dylan. Tomorrow we'll see the maid and search for the tobacconist."

"Right, you." They turned to face Dora and David, both of them talking excitedly about the animals that were on exhibit.

"Can we go fishing when we get home, Mr. Dylan?"

"No, I have to go to work. I have to make a living, you know."

"Maybe we can pay you so you don't have to go to work."

Dylan laughed suddenly. "That would be great." He turned to Serafina, humour dancing in his eyes. "How much do you feel a broken-down actor is worth?"

"You're not broken down!" David protested.

"No, you're not indeed," Dora said. "It's been such a wonderful afternoon! I've almost managed to put Clive out of my mind. He's always there."

Dylan said, "God is going to do a work for your brother."

"Do you really believe that?" Dora whispered, her eyes pleading.

"Yes."

David said, "I want to see the elephant again, Mr. Dylan." He took Dylan's hand, and the two started off. Dora and Serafina watched them until they fell behind enough, and Dora whispered, "He's such a kind man—and so good with David! He's just what David needs, a man to pay him some attention."

Serafina could not answer for a moment, but finally she said, "Yes, and I hope he's the man Clive needs too."

"It's amazing how he's come into our lives at just the right time. It's almost like a miracle, isn't it?"

Serafina said, "He would agree with you, I'm sure." She watched the tall form of Dylan Tremayne and the well-known and loved form of her son, David, and did not speak.

✤ THIRTEEN ✤

The family had gathered for breakfast, but Serafina was not hungry. Rising from her chair, she moved across the room toward the open window. She looked out on the lawn as the heavy scent of wildflowers wafted inside.

It was a fine April afternoon, and the windows faced a long lawn set with trees sloping down to the brook. The willows made a cavern of green and reflected like lace on the barely moving currents. Roses covered a nearby pagoda, its white lattice arches visible through the leaves. As she stood there, Serafina was unmoved by the beautiful day. Her eyes fell on the blossoms of the garden with their riotous colours, and the brilliant flair of tulips caught her eye. The lupines were beginning to bloom, tall columns of pinks and blues and purples, and a dozen oriental poppies had opened, fragile and gaudy as coloured silk in a bed right below the window. Something like mild shock ran along Serafina's nerves as she realised that the beautiful day and the magnificent flowers brought her no joy. She could remember times when this sight had brought her a keen pleasure, but now it was nothing but an attractive scene.

From somewhere deep in her imagination, a thought came to Serafina—one of those unsought fragments of memory that formed part of her thinking process. She had read a book once about Iceland, and had seen drawings of the natives. She remembered vividly one of the pictures—a woman dressed in furs, her square brown face seamed with age and weathered like an old block of wood. She was sitting cross-legged in the snow, obviously enjoying her crude meal greatly. *That savage woman living on the very edge of death probably was enjoying her life at that moment more than I am now, even with all the conveniences that money can buy.* Serafina was grieved at the thought, for it was the sort of imaginative process that she had tried for years, under her father's tutelage, to root out of her mind.

The memory disturbed her greatly, and she closed her eyes for a moment, aware that the others in the room were talking about Clive's plight. When she forced herself to open her eyes, she saw that David and Danny were beneath a large yew tree, digging a hole. Even from where she stood, she could see the dirt on David's face as well as the bright smile he flashed at the groom, and she wondered what future lay before this son who, in one sense, was all she had in the world. The future was always a darkling place for her, one she thought of as little as possible. Although she was not a Bible believer, she had heard a verse of Scripture once that said, simply, "Give not thought for the morrow. Sufficient unto the day is the evil thereof." It had somehow taken root in her mind, and she had accepted it as one of the rules of her life.

As she watched David throwing dirt in arcs over his head and Danny Spears laughing at him, a cold touch of apprehension came over her. *Parents can do only so much for their children. Sooner or later they'll go their own way and make their own choices—and parents must stand and watch helplessly.*

She heard Dora say, "Father, I'm so worried. What are we going to do about Clive?"

The note of panic in Dora's voice pulled Serafina around, and she studied the face of her younger sister. *I was so much like her at her age. She's not a brilliant girl, but she has a sweetness that I once had —and lost somewhere along the way.*

"We'll just have to do the best we can for him," Septimus said. His voice, usually strong and vigorous, was weak and held a slight tremor. Serafina looked at his face and noticed lines that were not there before. He seemed to have aged very suddenly, and the thought frightened her. Her father had always been there for her. He had been her tutor, her teacher, her friend. She had never thought of him as being an old man, but now she saw the early signs of old age in his face, and the unsteadiness in his hands. *He's always been so certain. He's always been able to solve problems in his work, but this is different. I wonder if life will ever be the same for any of us in this house.*

Serafina glanced around the room. None of them except Aunt Bertha had been able to eat. They had consumed much of the tea, but it was Bertha who fed a steady stream of bacon and fairy cakes into her mouth. She also dominated the conversation with her loud voice. Suddenly she turned to Serafina and said, "Well, you're certainly not doing the family's name any good."

Serafina was accustomed to Aunt Bertha's charges, and she asked simply, "What are you talking about, Aunt Bertha?"

"Talking about? What am I talking about?" Aunt Bertha popped another fairy cake into her mouth and chewed it vigorously. Eating did not appear to have any effect on Bertha's speaking process. She could eat steadily and talk rapidly at the same time. "I'm talking about that actor you've been running around with all over town . You're going to ruin the family name!"

Serafina did not bother to answer, but Dora's face suddenly flushed pink. "Our family name isn't in good standing now, Aunt Bertha. At least Mr. Tremayne is trying to do something for poor Clive."

"What can *he* do? He's an actor." Bertha spoke these words as if she had said, "He's a leper," for in her mind lepers and actors were on the same plane. "He's a fortune hunter as well. He's after your money, Serafina, and one more thing—" She picked up a thick slice of bacon and, instead of taking a small bite, shoved the whole thing into her mouth. Serafina often thought she looked not like a woman who was eating for enjoyment but like someone storing food away for a future need. "It's him and those actors he lives with who dragged Clive down."

"That's not so, Aunt Bertha," Dora said hotly. She was a quiet, sweet-tempered girl, but whenever anyone attacked one of her family, a small tigress seemed to emerge. Her eyes flashed with anger as she said, "At least he's trying to help us, and he's not a fortune hunter."

At that instant Louisa entered the sitting room and announced, "There's a Sir Aaron Digby come to call. Are you at home, sir?"

She put the question to Septimus, but it was Bertha who answered. Her black eyes snapped, and she said vigorously, "Of course we will see him! Show him in at once." As soon as Louisa left the room, Bertha turned to Dora. "He's come calling on you, Dora. He's been trying to court you for weeks now."

"I'm not in the mood for Sir Aaron," Dora said. She started to rise, but Bertha arrested her with a sharp command. Her voice seemed to freeze Dora where she was, overtaking the young girl. "He's come to call upon you, and I will expect you to show the proper grace. He's quite taken with you."

"I don't want to talk to him," Dora said. But before she could even rise, Louisa entered and said, "Sir Aaron Digby."

The man who entered was somewhat under average height and wore the latest fashions. His face was full, and his eyes were close together, which gave him a squinty appearance. He bowed and said, "Good monring. I hope I'm not calling at a bad moment."

"Why, of course not, Sir Aaron," Aunt Bertha gushed. "We're just finishing breakfast. Sit right here and try some of these fresh fairy cakes."

"Thank you," Sir Aaron said. He moved across the room in rather mincing steps, sat down, and said, "I trust I find you well, Dr. Newton."

"Very well, thank you."

"And you, Mrs. Newton? But then you are always well."

"Thank you, Sir Aaron," Alberta said. She was watching the man curiously, for he had appeared in their lives some time ago in a rather minor way. He had called twice and had asked permission to take Dora to a concert and then to a ball. Both times permission had been granted, but Dora showed no enthusiasm for his advances. "I'm very well, thank you."

Sir Aaron took one of the cakes, bit off a tiny fragment, and chewed it thoroughly. "Very fine," he said. "You have an excellent cook."

"She's been with us a long time," Septimus said. "What have you been doing with yourself, Sir Aaron?"

The visitor gave the usual reply to such questions, and then he turned and put his eyes on Dora. "I must tell you how very much I enjoyed dancing with you at the Union Ball."

Dora dropped her eyes, and her voice was barely audible. "Thank you, sir. It was gracious of you to ask me."

"Not at all! Not at all! I know you all have been under considerable distress. I can't say that I know how you feel, for no man would until he's gone through something similar. I'm sure that you're all carrying on as well as possible under the dire circumstances of your son's problems."

"We do the best we can," Serafina said firmly. She had disliked the man from the beginning, although there was no reason for it. She had discovered he was forty-two years old and had been married, but his wife had died recently. Digby's wife had had money, and it had been rumoured that he had run through it with rather amazing speed. He also had two daughters living with him whom none of the Newtons had met.

"I think, Miss Dora, it would be good for you to get out, make yourself take part in activities. As a matter of fact, that's the occasion for my visit." He smiled at Dora and leaned forward slightly. "There's going to be a Wagner concert this week. I know how much you like the music of Mr. Wagner, and with your parents' permission I would like to escort you. It's next Wednesday afternoon at the park."

Dora said immediately, "I thank you, sir, but—"

"Of course she will go," Bertha interrupted. "What a thoughtful thing for you to do, Sir Aaron."

"Not at all. It will be my pleasure."

Sir Aaron stayed and talked to Septimus for some time, but it was obvious that his attention was directed toward Dora. Finally he got up and came to stand before Dora. "I will be here to call for you at one o'clock. Until then I remain your servant, Miss Dora."

He turned and left the room, and Bertha at once began speaking vehemently to Dora. "You sat there like a block of stone, Dora! What is the *matter* with you?"

"I—I don't like him."

"You don't *like* him? What is there not to like? He has money. He has a title, and he's obviously interested in you."

Dora looked up, and her lips were trembling. She had no ammunition to use against Aunt Bertha, but whispered, "He's twenty years older than I am, and he has two daughters almost as old as I am, and besides," she said again, "I don't like him."

"Nonsense! You sound like a green girl. Don't like him, indeed!" She turned and said forcefully, "Septimus, I think it's time for you to take a firm hand. Dora must learn that she should be guided by her family."

Serafina stood helplessly by, and finally Dora got up and mumbled, "Excuse me," and half ran from the room.

Septimus was the mildest of men, but there was something like exasperation in his voice when he said, "Bertha, I think you should be more gentle with Dora."

"Well, I see you're not in the least grateful for what I try to do around here! You don't care enough about your daughter, and that's your problem. Why, if it weren't for me, Serafina would never have married Charles."

The woman could not have said anything that pained Serafina more. She knew, indeed, that Bertha had been the prime mover of her marriage to Charles. It was she who had introduced them and had constantly filled her mind with how wonderful it would be if she could just become his wife. She would become the Viscountess of Radnor! She gave her aunt a cryptic look, then turned and left the room. She heard Septimus say, "I've been a bad father . . ." A moment's anger struck through Serafina. She had an impulse to turn around and confront Aunt Bertha, to tell her that her marriage counseling had led one of Septimus's daughters into one of the most terrible experiences possible. She knew, however, that it would be hopeless, and going to the laboratory, she sat down at the desk. She had been working long, arduous hours on the cypher in Kate Fairfield's journal, but with no success whatsoever. She had been highly interested in cyphers at one time and had learnt the basic form for them, but this cypher was such that the usual methods would yield nothing.

She looked up as her father entered, his face tense and his jovial expression wiped completely away.

"I feel so helpless, Daughter!"

"We all do, Father."

Her father whispered, "What can I do, Daughter? What can I possibly do?" Serafina saw tears in her father's eyes, and the sight shocked her to the core of her being. She had never seen her father weep. They were not a demonstrative family, but impulsively Serafina rose and went to her father. She put her arms around him, and he clung to her as if he were the child and she the parent. Serafina held him and thought of several times when she was a child and had had nightmares. It had been Septimus who appeared at night, put his arms around her, and comforted her until she went back to sleep. She had awakened the next morning to find that he was still there, and she still remembered those times as some of the most notable moments in her life as far as her father was concerned. But even as she comforted her father as best she could, a thought seemed to whisper into her mind. *Yes, but who will comfort me?*

❧

Dylan had brewed a pot of tea and was allowing it to steep when a knock at his door made him look up with surprise. "Who can that be, I wonder?" he murmured. Moving across the room, he opened the door and saw Viscountess Serafina standing there. "Well, good morning," he said, smiling. "It's a good surprise you brought me this morning. Come in, Viscountess."

Serafina stood there for one moment, and the sight of Dylan's smile, his athletic form, his coal black hair with the slight curl brought an instant thought. *He's probably the best-looking man in England.* The thought irritated her for some reason, but she stepped inside and said, "I had no way to tell you I was coming."

"No problem, ay. Here, I've just made a fresh pot of tea. Why don't you sit down and share it with me."

Serafina sat down and, glancing around the room, was impressed with the neatness of it. On the night they went to Kate Fairfield's, she hadn't taken the time to look around, but now she was curious. It was not a large room, and the walls were crowded by at least a dozen paintings that stirred her. They were modern impressions of sunlit landscapes, blurs of water lilies all in blues and greens with flashes of pink, and trees beside cornfields. All of them were highly individual experiments in art and were obviously the selection of a man who had very definite opinions about what constituted beauty in art.

"I like your paintings," she said.

"Thank you. They're done by a friend of mine."

"Perhaps you could take me to see him sometime. I might be interested in purchasing his work."

"Well, actually it's a young woman who does the paintings."

Serafina was surprised for no reason that she could identify. "Well, that doesn't matter," she said. "It might even make it more interesting."

"We'll do that."

As she sipped her tea, Serafina was aware that Dylan was studying her countenance. He did not do it covertly as many men might have, but faced her squarely, his trim shoulders set, his eyes steady, and she wondered what he was seeing. "Sorry I am to see how the trouble is wearing you down, Viscountess," he said finally.

She was caught off guard by his observation. In the mirror, she had seen little outward sign of the pressure brought by Clive's problem. "It's been very hard on all of us." She hesitated, then said, "I saw something today I've never seen before."

"And what was that now?"

"Something I saw in my father. We were talking about Clive's imprisonment, and Father had tears in his eyes. He could barely speak, but he whispered, 'What can I do, Daughter? What can I do?'" Serafina dropped her eyes and added, "I've never seen my father cry before."

"There's no escaping trouble," Dylan said. His voice was soft and gentle as a woman's, and compassion was in his eyes. "The old Hebrew said it well: 'Man is born to trouble as the sparks fly upward,' and women, too, of course. Plenty of unkindness in this world, there is. That's why all of us should help bear one another's burdens. Every man and woman is born the same, and we all go the same. The captains and the kings and the tinkers and the beggars, we all go alike."

"I—I never thought deeply about those things."

"Haven't you now? Well then, I think the very mention of time to come is like a spectre to some. We don't know what tomorrow will bring—or today for that matter—but the one thing we know is that time will bring its sorrow and grief." He added thoughtfully, "And we build bridges." His brow furrowed in a single ridge. "We build bridges until the river wets our feet, but there's no bridge to carry us over troubles and griefs and woes. All of us have to go through the depths of grief. It's the lot of all of us, Viscountess, and it seems God has no favourites in this. Indeed, sometimes He puts His favourites into the valley of humiliation, and the valley of pain, more than anyone else. Right now you're in that valley, and it's grieved I am for you and for your family."

Serafina listened to Dylan as he spoke with more gentleness than she had ever heard in a man's voice. It shocked her somehow, and at the same time brought her a measure of consolation. "That—that's what I've always thought, but I've been afraid to speak it out."

"We need to speak our thoughts out, Lady Serafina. That's what the tongue is, a miraculous organ that allows us to say what is in our spirits and in our souls and in our minds. The thoughts gather there, but unless they are spoken they fall dead at our feet. It's the tongue that makes man different from the animals, among other things, of course." He seemed very thoughtful now. "We can tell when animals are pleased by their bodily actions, but good it is to have a counselor bring news of comfort to us. As water to a thirsty man, so is a counselor who brings ease in the time of sorrow." He seemed to think deeply, then said, "But the times of sorrow need not be overwhelming. Have you read the story of King David?"

"No."

"He had many sons, but he had one son that he loved above all else. Loved him to distraction, King David did. This favourite son of David's was Absalom. David poured his love, his affection, and gifts upon that boy as he grew up, so that his whole heart and soul was tied up in the young man. David announced that Absalom would be the king after David died. But Absalom had a weakness. He couldn't wait for the blessing his father wanted to give him, so he made a conspiracy to kill his father and take the throne. King David awoke one day to find that Absalom had raised an army, and the old man had to flee his own kingdom."

"How terrible! What was in Absalom's heart?"

"Who knows what evil there can be in a human heart? The heart is deceitful above all things, and desperately wicked, Viscountess. Remember the words of Prince Hamlet on the wickedness of men? 'I am myself indifferent honest, but yet I could accuse me of such things that it were better my mother had not borne me.'"

"What happened?" Serafina asked.

"David was brought out of the city by some of his loyal followers. They crossed the brook outside of Jerusalem making for safety, but what agony must have been in David's heart. God Himself had identified David as a man after His own heart, and here David's own son had betrayed him and was out to kill him."

Dylan looked down at his hands and was quiet for a long moment. Serafina waited, and she saw that Dylan's hands were not steady. When he looked up, she was startled to see tears in his eyes. Tears in a man's eyes were a sign of weakness—or so she had always believed. She could not fathom it. Then Dylan said, "There's a psalm in the Bible recording David's prayer as he fled from his son Absalom. It says, 'Lord, how are they increased that trouble me! Many are they that rise up against me. But thou, O Lord, are the shield for me; my glory, and the lifter up of my head. I cried unto the Lord with my voice, and He heard me out of His holy hill.'"

Dylan was so moved that Serafina felt she could not breathe for a moment. This man had depths she had never encountered. But suddenly he smiled and said, "But I love what the Scripture tells us that King David did."

"What does it say?"

"It says, 'I laid me down and slept; I awakened; for the LORD sustained me.' Oh, there's a wonderful thing! David lay down and he slept! Glory to God for such a man who loved God so completely and trusted Him when death was at his very door!"

Serafina felt uncomfortable. Dylan's words were enigmatic to her. This God he spoke of she did not know—did not even believe in, and she suddenly felt an impulse to avoid such talk. She got to her feet and cleared her throat, saying more loudly than necessary, "That's very interesting, but I don't believe God's interested in me. I've not been interested in Him."

"There's wrong you are, Viscountess, about God anyway."

Viscountess Serafina Trent could not remember any moment in her life when she had felt as uncomfortable and as unable to speak as she did at that moment. She said almost desperately, "I think we need to go talk to the murdered woman's maid. I don't think we know all she knows."

Dylan smiled slightly. "Of course. We'll go at once."

❧

Helen Morton opened the door and stood looking at the pair for a moment. "What is it?" she said shortly. She was obviously distressed to see them and did not invite them in.

"I know this is hard for you, Helen," Dylan said quickly, "but I know you had a fondness for your mistress."

"Yes, I did. She wasn't the easiest person to serve, but she could be kind, at least to women."

"Could we come in and talk with you?"

Helen hesitated, then shrugged. "Come in," she said. She led them into the small sitting room and waved at a couch. They sat down side by side, and Helen's eyes were wary with distrust as she asked, "What is it you want me to say? I've told the police everything."

Serafina had a sudden insight. "Have you found another position, Helen?"

"No. They're not easy to come by."

"Perhaps I could help." Serafina smiled slightly. "I have a great many acquaintances. Would you like for me to see if I can find someone who needs a faithful maid?"

Serafina's words caused Helen to bite her lip and look down. Her hands were unsteady as she held them on her lap, as was her voice when she said, "That—that would be kind of you, ma'am."

"I'm sure we can find something."

"That's good of you, Lady Trent."

"You can't serve your mistress now, but you can help us find her killer. He needs to pay for this crime, Helen," Dylan said.

"What is it you want to know?"

"Tell us about the men in her life. We know there was more than one."

Helen's head tilted back, and a bitter smile turned the corners of her lips upward. "More than one! Yes indeed, more than a dozen. I lost count."

"Just tell us, if you will, about these men. Whatever you know."

The two sat there and listened, and finally Helen fell silent. Serafina saw that something was troubling her. "What's bothering you?" she asked.

Helen looked up. "You're very quick, ma'am. There was one man that I never saw."

"You never saw him?" Dylan asked. "How can that be?"

"Because she would never bring him to her house. She would get ready wearing her finest, and she would wait. A carriage would come to the door, and she would leave. I know it was wrong of me, but I was curious. I would go to the window and look at the carriage. She would get in, and they would drive off."

"Did you see the man?"

"Just barely an outline, but he wasn't any of the men that she allowed in the house."

"Can you tell us anything at all about his appearance?"

Helen closed her eyes and seemed to be thinking deeply. Finally she said, "One night they came back late. He got out of the carriage that one time, and I could see a little bit. He had his hat pulled down low and had on a dark cape. All I could see was that he was a tall man and seemed strong, but I couldn't see his face plainly."

Serafina asked, "Did you ever see Miss Fairfield write in a diary?"

"Oh, I know she kept one, but I never saw it. She kept it hidden, I think." Her fingers fumbled with her dress, and she shook her head. "She wasn't a good woman. She liked to make men suffer."

"And women too?" Serafina asked.

"No, just men."

❧

After they left the house, Dylan said doubtfully, "That's interesting, ay? A man that she would never bring inside."

"Obviously she didn't want the maid to see him."

"I wonder why?"

Serafina was thinking quickly as they got into her carriage. "It may be the other way around."

"How do you mean, Viscountess?"

"I mean perhaps the man didn't want to be seen."

Dylan turned and studied her. "Very quick, you are."

"I think we ought to go to some tobacconists and see if we can find a clue among those men who smoke Roi Blanco cigars."

"Right, you." He leaned out and said, "Take us down to the shopping areas, Albert."

"Yes, sir."

The two spoke little, and in the next two hours they went to four different tobacconists. They all sold Roi Blancos, but were reluctant to give the names of their customers. They were suspicious, and at one point Serafina said, "I wish you were a policeman instead of an actor. We could force them."

"Well, from that last one we have one clue. Sir William Dowding buys Roi Blanco cigars regularly."

"I think we should go and see him."

"Beard the lion? Are you feeling fierce this morning?"

Serafina turned. "Are you?" she asked.

"All he can do is turn us away with, perhaps, a rather sound cursing. I've heard him do it before."

"What's he like?"

"He's rich. That makes a man different. He's used to having his own way, and he will have it. He's a domineering man, and he can be cruel. Sometimes, though, he can be generous when he wants something from someone."

"And he was in love with Kate?"

"I don't like to use the word *love* that loosely. Certainly he lusted after her. He was one of many."

They did not speak again until they drew up in front of Sir William Dowding's home. They both were well dressed enough that when the butler opened the door, he at least invited them in, then went to ask if his master would see them.

"He doesn't think we're tradespeople or he would have made us go to the back or side entrance." Dylan grinned. "We must look very fine, indeed."

Serafina smiled. "Appearances can be deceiving."

"Sir William will see you now," the butler said as soon as he returned. He led them to the study, where Sir William was standing beside a window. He turned, and as if to confirm what they already knew, he was smoking a cigar that had the peculiar odor associated with Roi Blancos.

"Viscountess, it's good to see you." He looked with some surprise and said, "What are you doing here, Tremayne?"

"I know you heard, sir, that the viscountess's brother has been arrested."

"Yes, I read it in the papers." He was a tall, powerfully built man, and both Dylan and Serafina thought at once of the maid's description of a tall, well-built man. Sir Dowding at least fit into that category.

"I'm sorry to hear of it, Viscountess. How's the case going?"

"Not very well, I'm afraid, Sir William."

"Too bad. He's a reckless young man. Very likable, but he has a hot temper."

"We're calling on people who knew Kate," Dylan said carefully.

Sir William was not a fool. He looked at Serafina and said, "You're trying to get your brother off."

His words sounded like an accusation, and Serafina struck back at once. "You were seeing Miss Fairfield, I understand."

"That's no secret, but I knew she would turn me off." Dowding tapped the ash from the end of his cigar, studied it for a moment, and said, "She turned all men off sooner or later. That was her pleasure."

"When was the last time you were in her room?"

"It's been some time ago. I don't know how long. Why?"

"That's a Roi Blanco cigar you're smoking, isn't it, Sir William?" Serafina asked quietly.

Suddenly Dowding's eyes were wary. He looked like a wolf that had been brought to bay. "Yes, it is. What about it?"

"Someone smoked a Roi Blanco cigar in Kate's room the night she was murdered."

Sir William's face reddened, and the anger that lay buried not too deep came out. "Many men smoke these."

"Not many, Sir William—only rich men."

"I think we're through talking. I wish you would leave now."

"Thank you for seeing us," Dylan said. He offered Serafina his arm, and the two left the house. As soon as they were outside, Serafina said, "He's lying, I think."

"He may well be." Dylan shrugged. "I wish I could see into men's hearts, but only God can do that."

"What shall we do now?"

"We will go for a walk in the park. I don't believe in too much work in one day."

She saw that a lighter mood had come upon him, and felt herself in need of some lightness. "All right," she said.

The park was fairly crowded, the walkways filled with couples and families. Dylan said, "Come this way. I'm going to let you see my secret place."

"Is this where you come when you're angry?"

"No, I come here sometimes just because it's a beautiful spot, and I need to see some beauty."

He led her away from the main path down a smaller one that terminated by a small pond. The water reflected the blue of the sky, and he motioned to a tree that had fallen. "There's where I sit. Join me, Viscountess."

Serafina walked to the tree and sat down, and he sat beside her. "Tell me about yourself, Dylan."

"Why would you want to know that? It's not a very thrilling story."

"Women are all curious."

"Yes, they are. It's part of being a woman, I suppose. Well, I'll tell you about my life."

Serafina sat quietly, watching Dylan's face. He was facing out over the pond, his eyes moving from point to point as he gave her a brief history of his life. She was shocked at the hardness of his youth—orphaned at such an early age, working in the coal mines. He made light of it, but she knew the hardship that coal miners endured. He spoke of how he had fled to England and had become a criminal, forced into crime by the family that took him in.

"I got away as quick as I could. When I was seventeen I joined the Queen's Army."

"Did you see action?"

"Yes, I did, and bad it was. I didn't like the Army, and when my enlistment was up, I came back to England. I didn't know what to do with myself."

"So how did you become an actor?"

"Oh, I fell in with some friends who seemed to see something in me. One of them recommended me to a troupe, and I learnt the trade."

"And you've been successful."

"It's not a thing I care a great deal about. Some people, like Ashley and most other actors, make the theatre their lives, but I could be happy if I never saw another stage again."

"You've had a hard life."

"And so have you."

Startled, Serafina glanced at him. "How—how did you know that?"

"I've seen it in your eyes. I've heard it in your voice. Life is hard, my dear viscountess, but there's good in it. You have to search for it like a man searching for a treasure. He finally finds it in a field, and he goes and sells all he has to buy that field. That's what we all ought to be doing."

Serafina was shocked when Dylan reached over and took her hand. She let it lie in his, and he exerted a firm pressure. It was a liberty that would normally offend her, but the sound of his voice and the tale of his early life had softened her.

His voice drew her eyes to him. "You have so much to give, Serafina. All that a man could want. A lone man's urges move like the needle of a compass toward some women. Perhaps a woman just walks into a room, one he's never seen before, and he looks at her, and she catches his glance, and the old impulses rise. Perhaps in both of them. You're a proud woman, Serafina Trent, and your emotions run far beneath the surface. You have a power to stir men, but I don't think you recognise it."

"I—I don't know what you're talking about, Dylan."

"A woman is beauty, Serafina, and somehow all men look for beauty in their lives. Some men must stay a safe distance, afraid to go too close, and when they come upon it, the beauty fades and dies out. It's hard for a man to come into the shrine where a woman is and see that which he can never have."

Serafina was watching him and listening to him almost breathlessly. Her eyes were filled with shadows, and her bosom rose and fell with her quickened breathing. "There's a fragrance of you. You're a full woman, and a man feels strange things when he looks upon beauty and knows it will never be for him."

Serafina was intently aware of the warmth and strength of his hand as he held hers. She felt a strong impulse to leave it there and surrender, but at the same time deeply buried old memories troubled her, and she wanted to flee. "I—I must go back to the house." She pulled her hand away and stood to her feet. Dylan rose and said, "You've got all a man wants, Lady Serafina Trent, but you've built a wall around yourself. A wall so high that no man could ever climb over it."

FOURTEEN

I just can't do it!"

Serafina, with a violent motion, slammed the cover of the notebook shut, and for a moment sat there staring at it as if it were some sort of dangerous item. The sunlight streamed in from the window on one side of her bedroom. Ordinarily she took pleasure in the room, for she had spent many hours here at the small desk. Now, however, her lips were drawn into a tight line. She closed her eyes wearily and leaned back in the leather-covered chair. "It's just too hard for me!" she whispered.

A streak of frustration ran along her nerves, for she had always liked a challenge, and the journal, the secret cypher, that Kate Fairfield had used was indeed a challenge. She realised that this frustration was because her brother's life might well depend upon it. It was not like a problem in mathematics or an experiment in chemistry. She took pleasure in those things, but now the fear that had been lurking in her ever since Clive's arrest seemed to swell and rise to her throat.

She rose quickly and began to pace the floor. As she did, a strange thought came to her, one she had never had before. *It must be nice and convenient to believe in prayer as Dylan does.*

The thought brought with it an image of Dylan Tremayne, and she was confused at her thoughts, for she realised that Tremayne had impacted her in a way that troubled her. She did not analyse it, but actually she had built up a wall against admitting anyone into her intimate fellowship. But since the tragedy had struck their house, Dylan had come into her life, and she realised that he had come to play a much larger part in her thoughts than she liked. She stared out at the green grass and the flowers in the yard, but thoughts of Dylan would not leave her. "I can't be a fool," she whispered. "He's everything that I'm not."

A tap at the door broke into her thoughts, and Louisa came in. "The two policemen who were here before, ma'am, they're here again."

"What do they want?"

"Please, ma'am, they want to see you."

"What did you do with them?"

"I didn't know exactly where you'd want them, so I put them in the study."

"Thank you, Louisa. I'll come down." Serafina was aware that Louisa was intimidated by the policemen, and straightening her shoulders, she was determined to show no sign of weakness before the two men. Leaving her room, she walked down the hall and then descended to the ground floor. She made her way toward the study and found Winters and Grant standing in the centre of the room.

"Good afternoon, Superintendent, and you, Inspector Grant."

She saw that the two men exchanged an odd glance that troubled her, then Winters said, "I'm sorry to have to trouble you, Viscountess, but it was necessary that we have a word."

"Of course. Won't you sit down?"

"No, we'll not be here that long," Winters said. He looked handsome as he stood there—tall, well built, his eaglelike features highlighted by his icy blue eyes. No, *icy* was not the word. They were not cold, but bright and alert. He wore expensive clothes, far more expensive than a policeman would usually wear, and Serafina noted again the large diamond ring on his right hand. Grant, the smaller man, was also watching her cautiously.

"I'm afraid we have come on rather unpleasant business," Winters said. He shifted his weight for one moment and seemed to search for the right words.

"What is it, Superintendent?"

Winters nodded as if coming to some final decision and spoke in clipped tones. "I'm afraid we're here on official business."

"Does it have something to do with Clive?"

"Only indirectly. We've had a complaint from Sir William Dowding concerning the visit you and Tremayne made to his house."

A small alarm went off in Serafina's mind. She was not frightened but totally alert. "What did he say, sir?"

"He said that you as much as accused him of murdering Katherine Fairfield."

"That's not true, Superintendent. We asked him questions about some items that were troubling us."

"I felt this was important enough to come and warn you about. When a policeman comes into someone's house," he said with a slight grimace, "they automatically go on the defensive. That's natural enough, I suppose. We very rarely bring good news." Winters hesitated, then said, "I don't think he's going to bring any legal action against you, but Inspector Grant and I felt we needed to come by and warn you that this investigation that you and Tremayne seem to be determined to pursue can have unpleasant consequences."

"Exactly what are you telling me, Superintendent?" Serafina asked. Her voice was steady, and her eyes even more so as she faced the two men. She saw that Grant was watching her steadily, and she felt that she could not like the man much. He had a manner that seemed to be close to arrogance, but he kept silent as Winters continued.

"When people are in difficulties such as you and your family have been thrust into, they often make rash mistakes. I realise, of course, that your entire family is disturbed, but you can't run around accusing respectable citizens. We've already discovered that Sir William was at home at the time the murder was committed."

"And who told you that, Superintendent?"

"His valet." Winters immediately saw the disbelief on Serafina's face. "He's a respectable enough servant. He's not likely to lie about such a thing. Let us handle this matter, Viscountess. You're too emotionally involved."

"The man had an affair with the murdered woman."

"So did several other men, as you probably have discovered by now," Grant said. "But it's not against the law for a man to have an affair with a woman, and that's all the evidence you have."

A hot reply leapt to Serafina's lips, but she choked it off, saying merely, "I will take what you say under advisement, gentlemen, and I thank you for coming."

Winters smiled briefly. "I can see you're set on this thing, Viscountess, and I can only warn you again that it could be dangerous. If you did discover the murderer, he would be likely to turn on you."

"I'm not afraid of that."

"I'm sure you aren't. You're a strong woman, but there's another matter to consider, and that is that you may disturb evidence that we at the Yard need. You may give away something to the killer that would cause him to hide his trail even more cleverly."

"I'm sorry, but I can't promise you that I will stop looking for the man who killed Kate Fairfield. My brother's life is in the balance, and I will not stop until I have found the true murderer."

A silence seemed to fill the room, and the two men watched Serafina for a moment. Then Winters sighed and shook his head. "I feared this would be your attitude. We have no charges, of course. This is just in the nature of a warning. I hope you will listen to reason, Viscountess. Come along, Grant."

Serafina stepped aside, and the two men left, neither giving her a backward glance. She heard the front door close, then almost at once Dora came running in. She must have been waiting outside in the hallway. Her eyes were wide, and she said in an agitated tone, "What did they want, Serafina?"

"There's nothing to fear, Dora. Don't be troubled."

"How can I not be?" Dora said. She bit her lower lip in a nervous gesture that Serafina knew well from her childhood. "Did they come to give bad news about Clive?"

"Not at all. It was about another matter entirely. A minor thing."

Dora watched her older sister anxiously, and seeing no sign of trouble in Serafina's expression, she said, "I'm so glad."

"What have you got planned today, Dora?" Serafina asked. She went over and stood next to her sister and thought about how vulnerable she was, how she had always been that way. She was growing into a fine young woman, but still there was a dependency in her that Serafina saw and rather admired. Serafina had always been strong willed, and no one would ever call her vulnerable, but there was a quality of sweetness, of gentleness in Dora that made Serafina love her deeply, perhaps because she felt that somewhere along the way she had lost these qualities.

"I'm going to visit Clive," Dora said. "I've had Nessa make him some of his favourite dishes, and I'm going to take him some books."

"That's very good, Dora. You tell Clive that I'll be in to see him later on." She hesitated, then added, "That jail is a very depressing place. Are you sure you feel up to this?"

"Oh yes," Dora said quickly. "I don't mind it."

Serafina watched as Dora left the study, then returned to her room. She sat down before Kate's journal, opened it, and stared at the peculiar combination of numbers. "There's *got* to be an answer here somewhere that will save Clive," she muttered between clenched teeth. "There just has to be!"

❧

For one moment Dora hesitated, looking up at the cold, grey stone that composed the city's jail. She looked at the heavily barred windows in the front and had to push herself to continue. She mounted the steps, and upon entering the building noticed an odor that nearly sickened her. She had never smelled anything like it before, and she knew that Clive must be sickened by it as well. He had always been fastidious about such things.

A guard sat at a table reading the newspaper, and Dora walked over and said, "Please, I'd like to see my brother."

The guard, a burly man with beetling brows and muddy brown eyes, slapped the paper down and put his hand over it as if to keep it from walking away. "Wot's 'is name?"

"Clive Newton."

The guard's eyes half closed, and he said, "This ain't the regular visiting hours."

"Oh, I'm so sorry," Dora cried. "I didn't know there was a regular time."

The burly guard stared at her for a long moment, then shrugged his beefy shoulders. "I'll make an exception, but next time you'll 'ave to come when it's regular."

"Oh, I will," Dora said quickly.

"And I 'ave to look into those sacks."

"That will be all right." She watched as the guard examined the contents of the two sacks and was relieved when he said, "This way, then. I'll take you to 'im."

Dora followed the guard through a door and saw that the corridor led between two rows of cells. The stench here was almost unbearable, but she steeled herself against it.

"'E's up on the second floor. This way, miss."

The guard's boots clanged on the steel steps as he ascended, and when they got to the top floor, they met another guard there. "Woman 'ere wants to see Newton, Billy."

"It ain't regular visiting hours."

"Do you tell me that? Don't you think I know the rules? We'll make an exception this once. Take 'er to 'er brother."

The guard named Billy was as thin as the first guard was thick. He shrugged his shoulders and said, "Come on, then," to Dora. She followed him down the hallways, frightened by the feral expressions on the faces of the prisoners. Many of them were in cells with no windows whatsoever, and they stared at her as she walked by.

"You got a visitor, Newton."

The guard pulled the ring of keys from his belt, fitted one of them into the lock, and slung it open. "You sing out when you're ready to go."

"Thank you," Dora whispered. She stepped inside, and Clive came toward her.

"Dora!" It broke Dora's heart to see how he had changed. He had always been a happy-go-lucky, cheerful young man, but now his face was strained and his eyes seemed sunken into his head. She was carrying the bundles, and when he came to her, he put his arms around her and held her with the bundles between them. "I'm so glad to see you, Dora!"

Dora felt tears sting her eyes, but she blinked them back. She determined to be cheerful on her visit, and she said, "Here, you'll muss up the goodies I've brought to you."

Clive stepped back, and she saw that he was wearing clean clothes and was glad of that. The cell itself was spotlessly clean, and she saw a table for the parcels. "Come and see what I brought you."

Clive came to stand beside her as she unpacked the items from the sacks. "A kidney pie just like you always liked and a whole sackful of fairy cakes." She named off the items as she lifted them out and then said, "I also brought you a new book by Mr. Dickens. Everyone says it's very amusing."

"Thank you, Dora." Clive was standing there, and she noted that he had lost weight. She could see it in the hollow places in his cheeks and in how his clothes seemed to hang on him in a way that he never would have allowed when he had been free.

"I wish I could make you some tea, but you can eat something."

"All right." Clive sat down on the cot and watched as Dora busied herself fixing a plate for him. She talked cheerfully, but he saw the sorrow that was in her eyes, and when she came over and handed him the plate, he pulled her down on the cot. "Sit down beside me while I eat and tell me what you've been doing and how the family all are."

Dora felt a lump in her throat, but she put on a good face and forged ahead. She told him of the little things that made up her life, including stories of what David was doing and how the horses were. Clive merely nibbled at the food.

"Aren't you hungry, dear?" she asked.

"They brought our dinner not long ago. If I had known this was coming, I wouldn't have eaten it. But this will keep."

"Is the food very bad?"

"Not as good as Nessa's," Clive said, and a travesty of a smile touched his lips. "I don't think I ever realised how much we owe to Nessa. She's the best cook in the world, and I took it all for granted." He sighed suddenly and shook his head with a slight motion that was filled with sadness. "I took so many things for granted. When I get out of here, it will be different."

"Yes, it will," she said. She quickly kept the conversation going, aware that Clive was watching her intently. She was not good at covering up her feelings, and finally he interrupted her by saying, "What's wrong, Dora?"

"I—I've just been worried about you."

"But there's something else, isn't there?"

Dora had not intended to add to Clive's burden, but he questioned her gently and reached over and took her hand, and finally she said, "It's that man that I can't stand."

"You mean Aaron Digby?"

"Yes. He—he's courting me, Clive, and Aunt Bertha's insisting that I need to be nice to him."

"Don't pay any attention to her. She's the world's greatest busybody."

"I don't like him, Clive."

"Dora," he said and put his other hand over hers so that he held her small hands between his larger ones. "I've ruined my life. I don't want you to ruin yours."

"I'm afraid, Clive."

He squeezed her hands, then removed one of his and put it around her shoulders. "I am, too, Dora. I've done nothing but think about how mean and useless my life has been."

"That's not so!"

"I can't think of any kindness I ever did anybody. I've been so blasted selfish—so caught up with myself." His words were bitter, and he seemed to shrink inside himself, looking down at the cold stones of the floor.

"That's not true. You are a good brother to me, Clive. Think how many things you did for me when I was a child."

"I can't think of any."

"Yes, you can." She put her hands over his now and squeezed them. "You remember you always let me ride your pony? You wouldn't let anybody else touch it."

The memory stirred in Clive, and he said, "That's the sum total of my righteousness and my good deeds, I suppose."

"No, it's not. You remember how you used to take me out to find birds' eggs?"

Clive smiled then, and his eyes lit up. "I'd almost forgotten that. We climbed some tall trees, didn't we, to find those birds' eggs! Do you still have that collection?"

"Yes. Of course, it's still not complete."

A sadness swept across Clive's face, and he murmured, "You know, Dora, it's hard to believe that there was a time when the most important thing in life was to find a nightingale's egg."

The two sat there, and Dora yearned to simply throw her arms around him and cling to him. She wanted to weep, but she knew he had burdens enough without that. She stayed until finally the guard came down and said, "Time to go, miss."

Quickly Dora rose, and Clive put his arms around her and kissed her on the cheek. "Thank you for coming, Sister."

"I'll come back," she said. She left the cell, and she was aware now that the rain, which had started some time ago, was falling harder. When she descended to the main floor and went into the entry room, she saw that the rain was falling in slanting sheets, a regular downpour.

"You can't go out in that, miss," the burly guard said. "You'd better wait for it to slack off."

"All right. Thank you."

"You can sit over there on that bench."

Dora sat down, and the rain that fell was grey and grim and struck the earth with force. The downpour so burdened her spirit that she lowered her head and would not look up.

❧

Grant had come to the jail to get information from one of the prisoners. He had found the man unwilling to talk and had stayed for some time, trying persuasion and then threats. Finally he saw that he was getting nowhere, and he said sourly, "You're going down for this one, Johnson. All you have to do is tell me who masterminded it, and I'll see you're taken care of."

"I ain't no squealer."

"No, you're very noble and all that." Grant got up and called for the jailer. When the door opened, he left in a bitter frame of mind. His job required him to be with the worst of London's population. He had spent his life with the grimy side of the city, where virtue and charm were almost nonexistent.

He passed down the hall, thanked the guard, and was about to leave when he caught sight of a woman sitting on the bench. He was slightly shocked when he realised it was Dora Newton. He paused to study her and was struck by the sadness of her face. She was looking down. She had on a hat with a wide brim, but he could see enough of her face to know that she was devastated. For a moment Grant hesitated, then an impulse took him that he could not explain. He moved quickly across to her and said, "Well, the rain's pretty bad, isn't it, Miss Newton?" He saw her look up. There was a half-frightened look on her face. She reminded him, in that instant, of a frightened deer that he had once seen, a doe with a fawn. He had come upon them, taken them by surprise, and he had never forgotten that look in the beautiful eyes of the doe.

"Inspector Grant, isn't it?"

"That's right. Can I get you a carriage?"

"No, thank you, Inspector. I'm just waiting until the rain slackens a little bit. My carriage is just down the street."

"Well, you don't need to sit here. That rain might be coming down for quite a while." The impulse grew stronger in Grant, and he said, "Come along."

"Where?" Dora asked, giving him a startled look.

"To a room where you can have a little more privacy."

Dora rose and followed him as he walked through a door and down a hallway. He opened another door and said, "Come in, Miss Newton."

Dora entered and saw that it was a rather well-furnished room with tables, chairs, and best of all, a kettle on a gas fire.

"We sometimes take a little refreshment in here when we need to talk to one of the inmates. Look, let me make you some tea."

Dora whispered, "Thank you."

Grant made the tea with quick, efficient movements. He poured it into the kettle to steep, got two cups from the shelf on the wall, and said, "There. I'm not much of a cook, but I suppose anybody can make tea."

Dora said nothing. She was intimidated by Grant, and he knew it. It was something he was used to. Part of his job was to intimidate people, and he did it very well. He wondered now at himself as he looked at the young woman. He was not known for his softness, but he saw something in the young woman that stirred an old memory of some kind. He could not put his finger on it, but he had seen a young woman like this somewhere who had touched his heart. He tried to think of it, and finally it came to him. She had been a young girl, no older than Dora Newton, whose mother had committed suicide. Grant had been there to investigate, and the helplessness of the girl had touched even his hard spirit, and he had done his best to comfort her.

The tea was ready, and he poured it, saying, "How is your brother, Miss Newton?"

She took the cup and held it, and when she looked at him, he saw the sorrow and the grief that had marred her smooth features. Her dress was simple, well chosen, and he could not help but note the clean-running physical lines of the young woman. She seemed as thoroughly alone as if there were no other being alive on the planet. He had often seen this on the faces of those who came to visit family members sealed up in this prison. He studied her face as she drank her tea. He had noted before that she had a quality he could not name. It had something to do with the gravity that comes when someone has seen too much or has been given too much to bear—a shadow of a hidden sadness. There was a fragility about Dora Newton that pulled at Grant. Hardened as he was to most things, from time to time, he felt a love for fragile, beautiful things that he never spoke of to anyone. He had a few ceramics that he took out and examined from time to time, and this young woman had some of the same grace and beauty.

Dora lifted her eyes and whispered, "He's very well, thank you, Inspector."

"I know you and your family are worried about him, Miss Newton." He hesitated and tried to think of something to comfort her, but the man they had in the cell would soon be on trial for his life. A man, Grant knew, who had little chance of hearing a good verdict.

"Do you think there's any chance my brother will be found innocent?"

Grant ordinarily would have blurted out a resounding "Of course not," but he found he could not do that with this young woman. His mind raced as he tried to think of an appropriate reply that might give some comfort, and finally he said, with as much as force as he could muster, "I've seen men who came out well in situations like this." This was not altogether true, but Grant had seen a few instances. Grant found himself wishing that this would be one of them.

The two sat there quietly, and he inquired after her family. She was surprised at his interest, surprised indeed that he had stopped to talk to her and that he had shown a kindness. It did not show in his rugged features or in the determined quality of his eyes or the tightness of his mouth. The kindness caught her off guard, and she found herself warming to him. Finally she looked out the window and said, "I think it's slackened now."

"Yes, it has. I'll take you to your carriage." The two went out, and as they did, he picked up an umbrella from a stand. He opened the door, and when she stepped out, he opened the umbrella and put it over her. "Which way is your carriage?"

"That's it down there."

The two moved out into the rain. It had almost stopped, but it was still enough to ruin Dora's hat, so Grant kept the umbrella over her in a protective gesture. As they moved, he was aware that she was touching him, leaning against him slightly as if for protection. In another kind of woman he would have taken this as an invitation, but one glance at her face, and he knew that she was totally unconscious of the touch. She was the kind of woman Grant did not see often, and he knew that to her he was like an exotic specimen found in a museum. When they reached the carriage, he opened the door, and the coachman looked down. "Are you all right, Miss Dora?"

"Yes, thank you, Albert."

Grant helped her into the coach and then closed the door. Suddenly she turned and held her hand out, whispering, "Thank you so much, Inspector Grant." He had one hand free, and as he reached out awkwardly, he felt the fineness of her bones and the grace of her hand. For one moment he had the absurd impulse to bend over and kiss it. He had never done such a thing in his life, and he was stunned at his own thoughts. "Good day, Miss Newton."

He felt her squeeze his hand slightly, and when he looked at her, he saw that there was a tiny smile on her face. He nodded to the coachman, and the coach moved away. Inspector Matthew Grant watched it go. He had a low opinion of the aristocracy, but Dora Newton had shaken some of his preconceived and firmly rooted ideas of how selfish they all were. He shook his head, then turned and walked quickly away in the gentle rain.

❧

Dylan's performance had been poor that evening. He'd missed two cues, and his speeches lacked fire. Laertes, the role he played, was all fire, and when that was left out, he knew the performance was wooden and artificial.

As the cast took their bows, his mind was elsewhere. He ran his eyes down the members of the cast and could not get away from the fact that any one of them could have killed Kate Fairfield. It was a sobering and depressing thought. He had never been intimately close to any of them, but had considered them as benevolently as he could.

Finally he turned and walked away, and he was joined by Ashley Hamilton. "Well, Tremayne, thank you very much."

"What for, Ashley?"

"For not showing me up in the play. What's wrong with you?"

Dylan shook his head. "An 'off' night, I suppose."

"Must be that viscountess that's got you on the ropes. Well, good for her." Ashley was feeling good because he had performed well, and the bulk of the applause and the accolades had been for him. "Good for you. Marry her, and you'll be set for life."

"I just want to help her, Ash."

"Fine." Ashley grinned broadly. "She'll be so grateful she'll marry you. Then you can spend your life helping her—and spending her money, of course." He shook his head in mock sadness. "I wish I had a rich viscountess to set me up!" He laughed and turned away. Dylan watched him go and thought, *He's too lightweight to be a murderer, I think.*

❧

Dylan stepped out the door still thinking about Clive, as he usually was these days. He found Elise exiting her dressing room. She came over and took his arm. She had done well, as she did every night, and now she said, "Come along. We'll get something to eat."

Dylan did not want to go, but he was hungry and wanted to be gracious. "Right, you," he said. "Where shall we go?"

She named a restaurant, and thirty minutes later the two were sitting before a sumptuous repast at one of the better restaurants that kept its doors open late, mostly for the theatre crowd.

Elise had several drinks before the meal and continued to drink in a way that caught Dylan's attention. He knew she drank, of course, but there seemed to be something driving her toward oblivion.

Her speech grew slurred, and she could not handle her fork very well. "I'm lucky to have this role, Dylan."

"You're doing very well in it, Elise."

She looked at him with an expression he could not interpret. "I hate to tell you this, but I didn't grieve over Kate's death. I couldn't! I didn't like her, but then no woman ever did." She picked up her glass, drained the contents, and waved for another. She waited until the waiter had filled it, then said, "Her death was good for me, Dylan, but I didn't kill her."

"I'm sure you didn't, Elise."

"The police aren't so sure. They keep questioning me."

For some time Elise drank steadily, and finally she said, "Take me home."

Dylan had to support her on the way out. He found a cab, and she was so drunk that he had to almost pick her up to get her inside. He gave the address to the cabby and saw that she was slumped over, half drunk at least.

When they got to her house, an old brownstone used by many of the theatrical people, he had to support her again. He paid the cabby and helped her to the door. She was talking under her breath, and finally she simply collapsed, unable to walk. Dylan searched in her purse, found the key, opened the door, and then gave up on supporting her. He simply swept her into his arms and walked in. He had never been in her house before, but he found the bedroom with no trouble. Her eyes opened as he put her down on the bed. "I need 'nother drink . . ."

"No, you don't, Elise. You've had too much. Here, lie down and go to sleep. You'll be all right tomorrow."

But Elise was staring at him, trying to pull herself together. "I know . . . who killed Kate."

A thrill ran along Dylan's nerves. Perhaps this was the key they had been looking for. Keeping his voice normal, he said, "Who was it, Elise?"

"Sir William, that's who did it!"

"How do you know that?"

"He told the police he went home after the performance." Her speech was so slurred that Dylan had trouble making out the words. "But he lied, Dylan. He lied! He came here. He wanted to make love to me, and I told him no. He swore he was through with Kate. He told me she was doing something he wouldn't put up with."

"What was that?"

"He wouldn't say. We were both drinking, and when he left here . . . you know what he said?"

"What was it, Elise?"

"He said, 'She won't get away with it. I'll kill her first!'"

The words seemed to ring in the silence of the room, and Elise suddenly grew limp. Dylan threw a cover over her and left the house, but he could not get away from the words. *A threat to kill,* he thought. *It may be what we're looking for!*

⁕ FIFTEEN ⁕

Y ou missed, Mum!" David's eyes danced as he looked across the table at Serafina. "I beat you again!"

"Yes, you did, David. You're very good." Serafina leaned back in her chair and watched as David picked up the ball and a cue. He loved to play bagatelle, and he hit the green ball, sending it skipping along the table. There were nine holes, each one having a different value, and the object of the game was to knock the balls in with a small cue. As David chattered away, banging at the balls, missing some and sinking one now and then, she looked around the nursery and felt a sense of the passage of time.

This room had been the refuge of the Trent children for many years. It was like a world apart from reality. Wide curtains framed the windows, and sunlight caught the walls, highlighting faded patches and a rim of dust on the tops of pictures. Generations of young members of the Trent family were captured in paintings and drawings—little girls in crisp pinafores, two boys in sailor suits. Her eyes fell on one young boy. The artist had caught the gaze of a boy whose mouth showed a hint of an inner smile. She recognised the touch of auburn in his hair, and as she stared at the picture, time seemed to roll backward. In her imagination she saw that boy grow up into the man she had married.

Serafina quickly turned her eyes away, shutting them for a moment, then opened them. She glanced across the room at the dappled rocking horse by the window, its bridle broken and its saddle worn. There was a frilled ottoman in patched pink, and dolls that generations of girls bearing the Trent name had no doubt played with. Over on another table was a massive collection of tin soldiers that Serafina had spent many hours lining up while playing with David. They were now in orderly ranks, as David preferred. Next to the tin soldiers, on a shelf, were coloured bricks, and over to her left a dollhouse that opened up. On another shelf were two music boxes and a kaleidoscope.

From the open window the sound of men working on the lawn floated in to her. One of them had a rich cockney accent so thick she could barely understand him. The other was Peter Grimes, their footman, whose voice she recognised instantly. "It's your turn, Mum. I missed."

"You missed several times." Serafina smiled. She bent over the table and deliberately missed, at which David crowed, "You missed, Mum! I win again!"

"Yes, you do, Son. You're very good at this."

David gave her a smile, and she recognised in his features her own. He had the same facial structure, similar strawberry blonde hair, and his eyes were shaped like hers, though they were a deep dark blue instead of the violet tint of her own.

"What toys did you play with when you were a girl, Mum?"

"Oh, I loved dolls like all other girls when I was very small."

"Are any of them in here?"

"No, I didn't keep them."

"I wish I could have seen them. Don't you have any toys that you played with?"

"I'm afraid not. I wish I'd kept them, but I didn't."

David accepted this, then turned and went over to a chest and opened the top drawer. This was his "treasure chest." Serafina knew he kept all sorts of objects in there, and once she had found a live tortoise and had to admonish him that he couldn't keep living things in there. She watched as he picked something out and came back. "Look, I found this when Danny and I were digging for fish worms."

Serafina reached out and took the object. It was an ancient horseshoe that had evidently been in the earth for a long time. It had rusted down until it had lost its heft, and as she handled it, David said, "Danny said it would bring good luck. Do you think it will?"

"Mostly, Son, people make their own luck."

"I thought—" David hesitated, then broke off his speech.

"You thought what, Son?"

"I thought it might get Uncle Clive out of jail."

He bit his lower lip, a familiar gesture when he was troubled, and Serafina said, "You mustn't worry about your Uncle Clive."

"But, Mum, I heard Albert say that he could be hanged. He won't be, will he, Mum?"

Serafina's mind raced quickly. She tried to reassure him that there was every reason to hope that Clive would be found innocent. She watched his youthful face and saw that something was being formed in his mind. He had a mind different from hers, imaginative, quick to grasp at anything strange or unusual. Serafina remembered vaguely that she had had this kind of mind, though her father had managed to remove most of that sort of thinking.

"Dylan told me when he was a boy that there was an accident in the mine. He said it caved in, and some of the miners were trapped. His father was there."

"Is that right? What happened?"

"He said he prayed, and the men got out." David hesitated, then said, "Can't we do that, Mum?"

Serafina was seldom at a loss for words. She had seen this side of David years ago, when he was barely a toddler; he liked stories of the wonderful, and she had avoided giving him such things. She was not able to answer him, and now put him off and said, "Let's play another game of bagatelle."

"All right, Mum."

She allowed him to beat her again and then said, "I've got to go now. I have an errand to run. Give me a hug."

David was very responsive to such things. He threw his arms around her neck and buried his face against her. "You're the bestest mum in the whole world!"

His words touched Serafina deeply, and she said huskily, "I'm the bestest mum, and you're the bestest boy. Now I've got to go . . ."

As soon as Albert handed her out of the carriage, Serafina saw Sir Leo Roth waiting for her. He was standing in front of the prison to the left of the entrance, and he came toward her. "Good morning, Viscountess." He was wearing a velvet frock coat, a white linen shirt, a complicated black cravat with a small diamond stud, a pair of black britches pressed with a knife-edge crease, and black boots that reflected almost like a mirror. His fair hair was groomed carefully, and his classical face was sharply delineated by the bright morning sunshine.

"Good morning, Sir Leo. I'm a little late."

"That's the prerogative of a woman, isn't it?" He smiled at her, took the basket of food she had brought, then offered his free arm.

As they mounted the steps, she asked, "Have you been able to make any progress on a defense?"

Sir Leo opened the door, but before she went in, he said quietly, "Not a great deal." Something was on his mind, and he hesitated, then said gently, "Try not to hope too much, Viscountess. The odds are against us."

"I can't believe that, Sir Leo."

"That's as well. You have faith, then."

"I have faith in what you and I and Dylan can do to set my brother free."

He nodded slightly, and they entered the main building. The guard remembered them and bowed deferentially. "Good morning, Sir Leo. Good morning, ma'am."

"We'd like to see my client, please."

"Yes, sir. Right this way."

The two followed the guard out of the main room, up the stairs, and then down the line of cells. As always, the odor was rank, and Serafina steeled herself against it. "It looks like they could do something about the terrible smell in here."

Sir Leo shrugged his elegant shoulders. "I suppose they're not terribly interested in making the place nicer for the prisoners."

When they reached Clive's cell, the jailer opened it and said, "Just sing out when you're ready to go, Sir Leo."

"Yes, thank you very much."

Serafina entered first, with Sir Leo right behind, and the door clanged shut behind. Clive was standing, waiting for them. She went toward him and ordinarily would have given him her hand, but something came over her at the look of his thin, drawn face. She put her arms around him and gave him a hard hug. "Good morning, Clive."

Clive's arms tightened around her, then he released her and stood back. He had lost weight over the last three weeks in prison, and though his clothes were clean enough, they seemed to hang on him. He turned to Sir Leo, greeted him, and shook the advocate's hand. Then Serafina saw there was a measure of excitement in his eyes, and he was standing straighter than usual.

"Something has happened, Serafina."

"What is it, Clive?"

"I've been racking my brain trying to remember some of the details of the night that Kate was killed. I was a fool that night and very drunk. Last night I couldn't sleep. There was something that I was trying to touch in my memory, some sort of detail." Clive shook his head and turned it to one side, a familiar gesture to Serafina. He always turned his head to one side when he was excited.

"Did you remember something, then, Clive?" Sir Leo asked quickly, his voice animated. He wanted to win this case, but he knew there was no chance unless new evidence was unearthed. "What was it?"

"It came just before dawn. I was literally worn out trying to remember, and then it came to me like—well, it was like a picture. I remembered that while I was in that woman's room, a man came in."

"A man? What sort of a man?" Roth demanded.

"He must have been the woman's pimp, I suppose."

"Well, what did he look like?" Serafina demanded.

"I only saw him once and then only briefly. He came into the room, and I can only remember two things about him. He was a big man with blunt features—and instead of a right hand, he had a steel hook, like those you see in illustrations of pirate novels."

"That's wonderful, Clive!" Serafina exclaimed. She squeezed his arm and said, "Can you remember any more details?"

"No," Clive replied with chagrin. "But that ought to help some, don't you think? There can't be all that many men in London with steel hooks on their right hands."

"We'll have to pursue this at once. If we can find the man, we will have found the woman," Sir Leo said.

Hope shone out of Clive's eyes, and he seemed more alive.

Serafina took the basket of food from Sir Leo and set it on the single table in the room. "I brought some of the things you like best, Clive."

"Thank you, Sister. You know, if I could remember that one detail, I'm going to try to remember others."

"Good!" Sir Leo nodded vigorously. "We'll work on that. I know some men that are pretty well acquainted with the underworld of London. I'll talk to them immediately. You don't really forget a man with a steel hook for a hand."

"I remember," Clive said slowly, "he called the woman's name." He reached up and put his hands on his temples as if he could squeeze the name out of his brain. "I've tried and tried. He called her name. I just can't remember it."

"Try, Clive," Serafina urged. "It's very important. The trial will be starting soon."

"And we don't have much to go on, do we, Sir Leo?"

Sir Leo said honestly, "Not yet, but this will help, I'm sure. All we have to do is prove that you were at that woman's house during the time that Kate Fairfield was murdered, and no jury would find you guilty. The case, I imagine, would be dismissed."

"Oh, how wonderful that would be!" Serafina exclaimed. "I'll ask Dylan to help."

Serafina sat down on the cot with Clive, and Sir Leo leaned against the wall. He studied the two and saw that there was a strong family resemblance between them. Of the two, he knew for a certainty that Serafina was the stronger. He had found out a great deal about Clive from the members of the family and through asking about, and he knew that the young man was a wastrel, that he had never taken anything seriously in his life, and the thought suddenly came to him, *Well, he'll take this seriously all right. There's something about a noose being put around your neck that does tend to sober a man!*

∼✦∽

Dora had squeezed herself into the corner of Sir Aaron Digby's carriage. She knew that according to the etiquette of the day, when a man and a woman not related rode together, it was considered polite for the man to sit across from the woman, and she had expected that Digby would do exactly that. He had not, though, and had sat beside her. Now he was so close that his arm was brushing against hers, and she had to keep her lower body pulled away to keep his leg from touching hers.

"It was a fine concert, wasn't it, Dora?" Digby smiled. He was dressed at the height of fashion, as he always was, and looked elegant in a long black frock coat with a spotless white shirt. The coat was beautifully cut, without a wrinkle, and his boots were polished to a satin gleam.

"Yes, it was very nice."

Digby abruptly seized her hand and said, "You must know how much I admire you, Dora!"

Dora was startled and attempted to free her hand, but he was too strong for her. "Please, Sir Digby, let me go!"

"I will never do that! Why, I want you to marry me, Dora!" Before she could move, he seized her and pressed his lips against hers. He ran his hand down her back and laughed when she struggled. "You're a pure young woman, aren't you? Don't know a thing about men! Well, it will be my duty—and my pleasure—to teach you after we're married."

Dora freed herself, then said, "I don't intend to marry anyone for a long time."

Digby only laughed and shook his head. "I'll speak to your father. We'll settle the marriage between us." His smile was thin and suggestive, and he laughed as she tried to shrink away from him. "I'm anxious to have you, Dora. It will be an adventure for you."

Dora did not speak all the way to her home, and when she stepped out of the carriage, he came toward her. She whirled and fled, and his mocking cry came to her. "Run, little dove! Soon we'll be married and you'll be running to me."

❧

Serafina was startled when Dora burst into her room, her cheeks tearstained. "What in the world is wrong, Dora?" she cried.

"It's Sir Digby. He asked me to marry him—and I can't do it. Tell, me, Serafina, how does a woman know? You've been married. How do you know? How do you think about marriage?"

Serafina was quiet and did not speak. Finally she said in a strangely muted voice, "I'm not the right one to ask, Dora."

Dora stared at her older sister. "But you were married. You must know what it was like."

"I had ideas about what marriage was like," Serafina said, speaking slowly, and her face seemed to be fixed. "Of course I had some romantic notions—but I found out quickly enough that I had the wrong ideas. I—I knew how to perform scientific experiments, but I didn't know how to judge a man."

Dora stared at her sister. She realised that Serafina never spoke about Charles, and now she asked tentatively, "Weren't you happy with Charles?"

A long silence seemed to fill the room, almost palpable, and Dora saw the words were forced from Serafina. "No, Dora, I was miserable." Serafina shook her shoulders as if throwing off some burden and said, "You don't love this man, and none of us know him. I think you should put him out of your mind."

"Aunt Bertha won't let me do that. She thinks he's a wonderful catch."

"Then Bertha is wrong. All she sees is that he has money and a title, but there's more to a man than that." For a moment she hesitated, then said bitterly, "There has to be more to a man than that."

Dora turned slowly and left the room, and Serafina watched her go helplessly. "I wish I could help," she whispered. "I wish I could, but I couldn't even help myself!"

⚜

Dora slept little that night, for she feared what must happen the next day. She would have fled, but there was no place for her to run.

Early that evening, Sir Aaron Digby came and sought an audience with her father. Dora sat in the parlor with her mother, her aunt, and Serafina. Serafina had seen Digby come, and had come to the parlor and sat down on the couch next to Dora. She took her hand and smiled at her. "Don't be afraid."

Bertha was overflowing with excitement. "Just think—an earl! What a wonderful marriage that would be!"

Dora flinched, and Serafina said coolly, "I'm afraid you have an exalted idea of the peerage, Aunt Bertha."

"What are you talking about, Serafina? He's an earl! It would be a wonderful match."

Bertha went on and on about Sir Digby, and finally they heard the front door close. Septimus came to the door, his face grave. The women all looked at him, and Bertha said impulsively, "Well, did he ask for Dora's hand?"

"Yes, he did." Septimus turned to Dora. "He wants to marry you, Dora."

"Oh no, Papa, I couldn't marry him! I couldn't!"

"Couldn't marry him! What in the world are you talking about?

You're a foolish young girl!" Bertha cried out. The scene that followed was very painful. Bertha stridently demanded that Dora act like an adult and not a foolish child. It did not take much of her ranting to send Dora into tears, and soon she fled the room.

Serafina had endured all she could. She said, "Would you step outside, Aunt Bertha?"

"Outside? What for?"

"Because I have something to say to you."

"Very well." Bertha followed Serafina outside. Serafina led her to the study, and when the older woman came in, she shut the door, turned to her, and said, "Aunt Bertha, you will not urge Dora any more to take this man in marriage."

"I certainly will!" Bertha bridled, her face reddening. "It's up to the family to take care of matters like this."

"If you do urge Dora to accept Digby even one more time, you will leave this house for good, and the door will be shut against you forever. Do you understand me?"

It took a great deal to silence Bertha Mulvane, but when she saw the determination on Serafina's face, she turned pale. She could not afford to lose this relationship, and she dearly longed to bully Serafina into backing down. Aunt Bertha was accustomed to pushing her way through situations by raising her voice and demanding that others recognise that she always knew best. But Serafina's declaration seemed to hang in the air.

Serafina repeated in a voice as cold as polar ice, "Do you understand me, Aunt Bertha?"

Bertha swallowed and nodded. "Yes," she whispered.

"That's good, because I would hate to have a division in the family. But I warn you, one more word to Dora, and you will not be welcome in this house."

Serafina left the room, and Bertha stood there speechless for once. Anger rose in her, but she well knew she could not give up the advantages of being in the family of the Viscountess of Radnor, and she left and went to her own room at once.

❧

Dylan had come to visit with Serafina after she sent word to him. She had taken him to the library and shut the door, and there she had told him what Clive had said.

"He's a big man with a steel hook, Dylan. There can't be too many men like that."

"No, and people wouldn't forget it. I'll start looking at once." He paused and said, "What's wrong? You look troubled."

Serafina was not a woman to share her inner self, but Dora's plight had shaken her. She had put Aunt Bertha out of the picture, but she knew that Aaron Digby would not give up. She said, "Aaron Digby has proposed marriage to my sister."

"And you don't like that, I see."

"No, I don't. I don't like the man, and Dora despises him."

"Well, she doesn't have to marry him."

"No, she doesn't."

"She doesn't love him?"

"Of course not." Serafina suddenly laughed. "But I'm no authority on love, Dylan."

"Well, *I* am." Dylan smiled crookedly. "Let me tell you what love between a man and a woman is."

"I can't wait to hear it," Serafina said, smiling. She knew Dylan was speaking lightly to drive some of the grief out of her face.

"Well, you see, in the very beginning God made a creature, sort of like a paper doll. But then bad things happened. Original sin came to the world, and everything was torn apart. And this beautiful creature was torn apart. Half of it was called *man*, and the other half was called *woman*. Can you imagine, Viscountess, a paper doll torn in two, down the middle? You might have a million of them torn down the middle, but the only one that would really suit the male part would be the female part that was torn from it."

"I see. What does that have to do with love?"

"It's like this, you see. These two parts were scattered in the world far apart from each other, but the male part knew and the womanly part knew that somewhere in the world was the other half of itself. There were lots of other bits of creatures floating around, and they could each have made do, but the fit would not be perfect. But it finally happened that the original met the original. They came together, and they fit perfectly. So, you see, a man is looking for that woman that's a perfect fit, and the woman is searching for the man that will be a perfect fit for her."

"Are you saying that marriages are made in heaven, that God has in mind one particular person for each of us?"

"Oh yes. God's a romantic."

Serafina could not help laughing. "I've heard God called a lot of things, but not romantic."

"Oh yes," Dylan said. He looked handsome as he stood there with the sunlight on his features, one lock of his black hair hanging down over his forehead, and a teasing smile on his lips. "God's romantic, all right. He's got a woman in mind for me somewhere. No other woman will do but that one. So I don't have to worry about it. God will help me to find her."

Serafina, as usual, was fascinated by the way Dylan's mind worked. It was so different from her own processes. She said, "So you haven't found the woman God has made for you?"

Dylan's smile left his face. He looked down at the floor, but not before Serafina saw a look of sadness. It was the first time she had ever seen such a thing in Dylan. "What's wrong?"

"I thought I found the woman God had for me just one time."

"Who was she?"

"Her name was Eileen."

"Did you ask her to marry you?"

Dylan did not answer for a long time, but when he lifted his head, she saw that his face was totally still, and grief shadowed his eyes. "I was a soldier and had nothing." He blinked his eyes, and his lips went into a thin line as if something had pained him. "She loved me, though. She wanted us to marry, but I didn't have courage."

"What happened, Dylan?"

"She died, Viscountess."

"I'm so sorry." There was a sadness in the man that she had not seen even an indication of before. He once had happiness and joy, and it had been taken from him. "I am sorry."

"When she died, it was like the sun went out."

Serafina suddenly reached out and took Dylan's hand, something completely out of character for her since she had built a wall against men. "Do you think of her?"

"Think of her? I think of her every day." He looked at her and whispered, "You think I'm foolish, don't you?"

"No. No, I don't, Dylan. I—I didn't know a man could love a woman so much."

"He can, and a woman can love even more fiercely than a man, I think."

They stood there for a moment, she holding his hand, and then when she became conscious of his strength and his gentleness, she saw that sorrow made up part of Dylan's life too. "You'll have to tell me more if it's not too painful."

"Maybe someday, but it's possible for two people to find each other in this crazy world, just the two that will be right for each other."

Serafina dropped his hand and turned away, torn by emotions. Dylan's simple statement came to her. *When she died, it was like the sun went out.* She had known nothing like that in her marriage, but she saw in this man the truth that such love could exist.

SIXTEEN

Dylan studied his reflection in the full-length mirror and smiled. "Not a bad disguise if I do say so myself." He was wearing an ill-fitting jacket, a shirt with twice-turned collar and cuffs, and boots that were scuffed on the tops, their soles coming apart. His trousers were frayed at the bottom, and a soft battered hat hid his face. Turning swiftly, he left his room, his mind racing ahead. He had told Serafina he would throw his energies into finding the man with the steel hook for a hand. He headed for Seven Dials.

He threaded his way through a series of winding streets until he reached the Rookery, a rotting pile of tenements crammed one beside the other. The damp had warped and twisted the houses, and the floors and walls were unsteady, patched and repatched. The smell of human waste overwhelmed him, and the gutters down the alleys ran with filth. He was aware even before dark of the squeaking and slithering of rats.

Dylan did not move in an upright position, but walked all slumped over as he shuffled along the streets. Everywhere people were huddled in doorways, lying on the bare stones of the pavement, sometimes in groups, sometimes alone. He saw signs of starvation on the faces of even young children, and more than once he was approached by young girls, some looking no more than twelve, offering their bodies for sale.

A man finally approached him. He grinned, exposing missing teeth as he said, "You need some companionship? I've got a fine lady for you."

Dylan did not straighten up but twisted his face around. "Got no money for that," he said, making his voice hoarse, "but I'm looking for a man. I might pay a shilling or two if you could help me find him."

"Wot sort of man is that?"

"Don't know his name, but you can't miss him. He's got a hook instead of a right hand, you know."

"Don't know any men like that."

Dylan moved on down the streets. All afternoon he inquired, but the Rookery was immense, and he was not even certain that the man was from this district. There were other areas in London almost as bad.

The sun was going down, casting shadows on the narrow streets, when Dylan gave up. He turned to go back and walked down a street made more gloomy by the ending of the day.

A high-pitched voice came to him, and he turned quickly to see a young girl backing away from a man in an alleyway.

"You leave me alone now," she cried.

"Come 'ere, gal. I ain't gonna do you no 'arm."

The speaker was a hulking man dressed in clothing as rough as Dylan's own. He was advancing toward the girl, and Dylan's temper suddenly boiled over. He came up behind the man silently, then, planting his feet, he struck the man a terrific blow just over the belt where he knew the kidneys to be located. The man let out a muffled scream and fell to the ground, curling himself up. "You'll have trouble making water for a few days, but you'll live," Dylan said. "Come along, girl."

"Wot you want wif me?"

"I want to get you away from this man."

The girl came out of the shadows, and he saw that she was wearing a worn dress that she had practically outgrown. She was no more than twelve, he guessed, and was about to cross the line from adolescence to young womanhood. It was her face that caught his attention. She had striking eyes, large and almond-shaped with long lashes, and the colour of lapis lazuli. He was almost startled at their rich azure blue set off by her olive complexion. He stepped toward her, ignoring the man who was crying and keening. He was about to take the girl by the arm and lead her out of the alley, but as he reached out, she moved quickly. Reaching into a hidden pocket, she came out with a knife. It flickered in the fading light. "Get away from me or I'll cut you."

Dylan stopped. "I just want to help you, missy," he said.

"Yeah, I bet yer do! Men always want to *help* me," she snapped. She turned, and a young boy came out of the darkness.

"Are you all right, Callie?" He was no more than seven or eight. His eyes were dark brown, and his black hair was dirty and uncombed.

"Come on, Paco."

"Wot's wrong with 'im?" the boy asked, staring at the man writhing on the pavement.

"He was bothering your sister, so I discouraged him."

The young girl studied his face. It was as if she had spent many years learning to read expressions. Dylan did not move but pushed his hat back so she could see his face clearly. Her oddly coloured eyes were sharp, and she shrugged before the knife disappeared with a flick of her hand.

"We're all right now," she said and turned to her brother.

"Maybe I'd better walk home with you."

"Wot for?"

"To see that nobody bothers you." Dylan smiled.

Paco took the girl's hand and said, "Sister, I'm hungry."

"Come along, then, Paco."

The two started down the dark street, and Dylan joined them. He looked at the girl and said, "What's your name? My name's Dylan."

"Calandra Montevado."

"It's a big name for a little girl."

"Everybody calls 'er Callie," Paco said.

"So you're hungry, Paco?"

"Yus. I am."

"Well, come on. We'll find a street vendor."

"I knows where one is," Callie said defiantly and lifted up her head.

"Lead me to him."

The girl turned and, holding her brother's hand, moved down the street. Three blocks later she paused before a street vendor. "'E sells eel pies," Callie said. "They're good, they are."

The owner, a thin man with a battered stovepipe hat and an apron around his waist, said, "Wot'll it be, sir?"

A delicious smell issued from inside the containers in front of them. Dylan asked, "Callie, is there anybody else at home? Any more children?"

"Just my mum."

"Does she like eel pie?"

Callie nodded. "She's sick, and eel pie is her favourite."

"We'll have half a dozen eel pies."

"Right, sir!"

With alacrity the vendor removed six eel pies, wrapped them in old newspapers, and put them in a paper sack. He took the coin that Dylan offered him, bit it, and winked, "Right you are, sir. Best eel pies in London."

"Can I have some now?" Paco asked.

"Wouldn't you rather wait until we get home?"

"I guess so."

"Come on. Let's hurry," Callie said impatiently. She led them down a warren of streets until finally she came to a house with a set of stairs on the outside. "We lives upstairs."

Callie went in, followed by Paco, then Dylan. He had to stoop to enter; a solitary window threw the fading light of the sun over the room. It was a single room dominated by a table in the centre and a small bed on one side. A woman was in it, and she turned in the bed. Her face was thin, and fever showed in the brightness of her eyes.

"Mum, we got some eel pie!" Paco cried.

The woman struggled to sit up and drew the ragged covers about her. "Who are you, sir?"

"My name's Tremayne."

"'E bought us eel pies, six of 'em!" Paco cried with excitement. "Can I 'ave one now, Mr. Tremayne?"

"You surely can."

Callie drew a battered chair, one of three, up to the table. "You sit there," she said. Dylan grinned at her commanding tone but sat down. While Callie removed the pies, he said, "I'm sorry to find you ill, ma'am. Have you been sick long?"

"I'll be all right." The woman had traces of early beauty. He guessed that she was pure Spanish, and she spoke better than most people in the Rookery. "I haven't been able to work for a week now. Too sick."

"Who takes care of you?"

"I takes care of her," Callie said promptly. She had come over with one of the pies and helped her mother sit up. "Here, Mum, you eat this. It'll make you well."

Paco had already started on his pie with a vengeance. When Callie saw that her mother was eating, she came and said, "'Ere's one for you, mister."

"I'm not very hungry. Why don't you keep that for later." He watched Callie eat, and though she was very hungry, there was something almost delicate about the way she ate. She was going to be a beauty one day, though now the marks of poverty and want marked her strongly, as they did her brother and certainly her mother.

"Have you seen a doctor, ma'am?"

"No money for that."

"No doctor would come 'ere," Callie said.

"I know one who would. Why don't you eat up, and I'll go fetch him."

Callie did not answer, but her eyes followed Dylan as he left.

❦

"This is Dr. Carpenter, Mrs. Montevado."

Carpenter was a thin, lithe man of thirty with piercing grey eyes. He went over to the bed and said, "Let me see now how you are."

While the doctor examined the woman, Dylan sat down and began to ask Callie and Paco about their lives, about how they made it. He discovered that their mother worked in a sweatshop, and Callie and Paco went to the streets to pick up what they could.

The Rookery was filled with tragic stories like this, but Dylan found himself touched by their plight. As always, when faced with a difficult situation, he prayed that God would give him wisdom. Finally the doctor turned from the woman, came over, and said, "You taking care of her, missy?"

"Yus, I am."

Carpenter took out two bottles and said, "Give her a big spoonful of this once a day, and this one twice."

"Is she going to be all right?" Paco asked.

"I think so. She'll need some good food. Eel pie is good for anybody."

"Thanks for coming by, Carpenter." Dylan reached in his pocket and pulled out some money and offered it. Carpenter shook his head. "Buy some groceries for the family. Take care of yourself, Dylan."

The doctor left, and Dylan laid the money on the table. "There, Callie, use this to buy food for your mother and for yourselves."

Callie was staring at him. Her glance was a mixture of suspicion and awe. "Why you 'elping us, spending your money on us? We don't know you."

"Why, Callie, a man needs to help a woman when he can. Maybe you can help me."

Immediately she was suspicious. "Doing wot?" she demanded.

"I'm looking for a man. I don't know his name, but you might have seen him."

"Wot's 'e look like?"

"He's a big man, and you'll know him by the fact that he wouldn't have a right hand. He wears a steel hook."

"Don't know no man wif no hooks."

"Ask around. If you find him, there'll be a sovereign in it for you."

"A sovereign! Wot you want him for?"

"I need his help with something. Mind you, if you do see him, don't talk to him. Just get word to me."

"Where will you be?"

"I'll be at the Old Vic Theatre every night. I'm in a play there. Wait until the play's over and you'll see me coming out."

"You're a play actor?"

"A piece of one," Dylan said. He smiled and got up, then he reached out and tousled Paco's black hair. "You take care of your sister, Paco."

Paco swallowed hard. "Yes, sir. Thank you for the pies and for the doctor."

"Glad to do it."

Dylan left, and the young girl stared at the door. "Never saw no man like 'im," she whispered softly, then turned to go back to her mother.

⚜

Matthew Grant was not a man to waste time nor to think a great deal about matters beyond his control, but for some reason during the past few days he had been lost in some sort of haze. He was in the office of Superintendent Winters and was startled to hear Winters say abruptly, "You haven't heard a word I've said, have you, Grant?"

Grant shook himself as if he had come out of sleep. He was embarrassed, and mumbled, "Sorry, sir, I guess my mind's on a case."

"You haven't been yourself the last few days. What's wrong?"

"Nothing, sir."

"Well, maybe you don't have enough work to do."

"Probably right."

Winters was studying Grant. He liked the young man immensely. As far as he knew, Grant had no life outside of his work, and he wondered if the man had a woman or had lost one. "You haven't had a love affair that's gone sour, have you?"

Grant's lips tightened. "No, sir, nothing like that."

"Well, shake it off. We've got a lot to do."

Grant said, "What about the Kate Fairfield murder?"

"What about it?" Winters was surprised. "We've got our man."

"He still claims he's innocent."

Winters laughed. He lifted his hand to smooth his hair, and the large diamond on his finger caught the light and glistened. "Haven't you noticed we don't ever have any guilty men? They're all innocent—or so they say. We've got our killer. Leave that alone. I want you to look into this matter." He handed Grant a sheet of paper. "It's a burglary, but see what you can do with it."

"Yes, sir." Grant left the room, moved outside of the building that housed Scotland Yard, and heard a voice call his name. He turned around and saw Sergeant Sandy Kenzie scurrying toward him. "How aboot a bite to eat, Matthew?"

"I'm not too hungry."

"Well, you can listen to me and watch me eat, then." Kenzie grinned.

The two men went to a small eatery where the policemen often ate. The owner knew them and put them at a familiar table. Kenzie ordered pickled tongue and a bowl of suet pudding.

Grant discovered that he was hungry after all and ordered a piece of fried fish with anchovy sauce, spinach, and stewed rhubarb.

Kenzie gave Grant a report of what he had been doing, and finally he saw Grant's mind was elsewhere. "What's wrong with you? You act like you're half asleep."

"Nothing is wrong with me—"

"You getting along with Superintendent Winters?"

"Well enough. But today he thinks I'm not paying close attention to my work."

"Well, he's got his mind on other things. Sometimes he gets short. You've probably noticed. It's that wife of his."

Grant looked up. "His wife?" He had seen Winters's wife. She was an imposing woman with dark eyes. He had heard rumours and knew that she had inherited a fortune from her father. She also had no time for inspectors and Scotland Yard.

"She's a good-looking woman, and she has plenty of cash, but a man earns it when he marries a woman like that."

Matthew smiled slightly. "What do you mean by that, Sandy?"

"Well, in effect, Mrs. Winters went out and bought herself a husband. Slavery is illegal in any form except this."

"You're saying she dominates the superintendent? I find that hard to believe. He's a powerful man."

"Not where his wife is concerned. She makes his life pretty miserable. Sometimes she screams at him like a banshee, and he sits there and takes it."

Matthew chewed on a piece of fish, swallowed it, then asked curiously, "How do you know all this, Sandy?"

"Ah, Minnie told me."

"Minnie? Who's Minnie."

"She's the parlor maid for the Winterses. I've been taking her walking. I'm thinking of marrying her. Anyhow, she was pretty closemouthed about the family business, but she trusts me now."

"I didn't know all this."

Sandy shrugged and said, "Well, I wouldn't talk too much about it if I were you."

"No problem. My mind has been on the Newton case anyway."

Kenzie was surprised. His thin, intelligent face showed it. "We've got our man on that. I thought it was open and shut."

"I suppose it is." Matthew Grant pushed the vegetables around on his plate listlessly. "Something doesn't feel right about young Newton."

"Oh"—Kenzie grinned broadly—"so you're going on *feeling* now? That's not like you, Matthew. You're the man that always says 'evidence, evidence, evidence,' and now you're running your business by *feeling*. I can't believe it."

Grant had no intention of mentioning to anybody the impression that young Dora Newton had made on him. He said instead, "I've been trying to find a witness that saw something that night, but it was late. There weren't many people passing by that time of the night."

"I know one."

"One what?"

"One witness."

Grant stared at the smaller man. "What are you talking about, Sandy?"

"You know Jack Simmons?"

"Sure, I know Simmons. He's a burglar and a good one."

"Well, he slipped up this time. He was burgling a house on the night Kate Fairfield was murdered, and guess where the house was."

A bell went off in Grant's head. "Where?"

"Right across the street from the murdered woman's house. You know Jack. He's got sharp eyes. He'd keep an eye on that street while he's stealing."

"Where is he now?"

"He's in jail. He'll be tried and found guilty too."

Grant suddenly smiled. It made him look much younger, almost boyish. Sandy had seen that smile very rarely, and his eyes narrowed. "That means something to you, does it, Matthew?"

"It might, Sandy—it might!"

❧

Grant stared at Jack Simmons, who looked more like a teller in a bank than a burglar. He was a good-looking man of thirty, small and neat, and spoke better English than most. Grant had gone to the jail to see Simmons, and now Simmons was staring back at him. "I don't know what you're doing here, Inspector. I've already been caught."

"Maybe we can help each other, Jack."

Simmons seemed to sense there was some possibility for gain here. "I'm always glad to do anything I can to help you, Inspector Grant."

"You come from a good home, I think, Simmons."

"Yes, I did. I didn't live up to their aspirations for me. I had a good education too. Much good it did me. I was going to be a stockbroker. Instead of that, I became a burglar."

"Why did you do that?"

"You think I haven't asked myself that a thousand times? I lost my honour somewhere along the way." Simmons's eyes half closed, and he said dreamily, "You know, people don't lose their honour all at once, at least I didn't. There wasn't one day in my life when I suddenly said, 'Well, I've been a respectable man, and now I'm going to become a criminal.' No, it wasn't like that."

"What was it like, Jack?"

"I lost my honour a little morsel at a time. It's like a mouse comes in and steals just a little bit. Doesn't take the whole cheese, just a bite, and then he comes back and takes another, then another. So that's the way I lost my virtue, Inspector, a little bit at a time."

Matthew was wondering how to approach the man, and finally he said, "Can't you go back to your family?"

"No, I've got just enough pride to keep me from doing that."

"Pride's a cold thing to sleep with."

"What are you doing, Inspector, starting a society for reformed burglars? You want something. I can tell that. What is it?"

"The night you robbed the Sanderson house, you kept a good watch on the street?"

"Of course I did. I was a bad stockbroker, but I'm a good burglar."

"Did you see anything?"

"I saw everything." Simmons straightened up. "This is about that actress that was murdered, isn't it? She was killed the night I was burgling the Sanderson house. I remember it now. That's what this is all about."

"Yes, that's right, Jack."

"Rumour was you got your man. Clive Newton. A pretty high-flying young fellow, I hear. You looking for more evidence on him?"

"I want to know if you saw anybody entering the house of the murdered woman."

"What if I did?"

Grant suddenly leaned forward, and there was an intensity in his gaze. "I'd like to help you, Jack. I'd like for you to get out of this business."

Simmons studied the detective. "This is not your style, Inspector. Have you got religion or something?"

"No, but I've got an interest in the case. If you could help me, I think I could help you."

Simmons nodded and said, "All right. I saw a man who went into the house. He came in a carriage. I went to the window and watched. He got out and went up to the house, and somebody let him in."

"What did he look like?"

"He was a tall man. Had his hat on, of course, so I couldn't see much of his face, but I know he was big. Bigger than you, I think."

"Didn't you see his face at all?"

"Just a glimpse. It was dark, you know, and the gaslight doesn't throw off a lot of light."

"Have you ever seen young Newton?"

"The fellow that was supposed to have killed her? No."

"He's no more than five nine or so, a trim young fellow."

"Then he weren't the man I saw. The man I saw was big and tall, at least six feet. I did get a glimpse of his face. I didn't know him, though."

"Do you think you could identify him if you saw him?"

Simmons chewed on his lower lip. "It would be hard, Inspector. I've got a good memory for faces. I can tell you who it's not more than I can tell you who it is. I mean to say that I would know that a certain man wasn't the one I saw, but I'm not sure I could identify the man himself."

"Would you be willing to look at some people?"

"Can't do much looking from this cell."

"If I can talk to the judge and get you a suspended sentence on the grounds that you are working with Scotland Yard, would you help me?"

Simmons had an intelligent-looking face, sensitive in a way. Finally he whispered as if speaking to himself, "Is there such a thing as a second chance, Inspector?"

"I never thought so, but maybe there is, Jack. Will you help me?"

"Yes."

❧

Grant had left the jail and, not knowing what else to do, gone to talk to the judge. The judge liked him a great deal, and actually Simmons was small-time. He listened as Grant spoke, and then agreed to give him a suspended sentence. "If he gets in trouble again, I'll hold you responsible."

"I think there's a chance he won't," Grant had replied.

Now he walked the streets for a time, wondering what to do with this information. Finally it grew late in the evening, and on a whim he went to the theatre. He watched the play, and after it was over, he waited until Dylan Tremayne came out.

"Hello, Tremayne."

Dylan stopped and said, "Well, hello, Inspector Grant. Come to arrest me, have you now?"

"No, but I do need to talk to you."

"Well, I haven't had anything to eat. Why don't we get something?"

"All right."

The two went to a small restaurant and sat at a table off to one side. Dylan ordered his meal, but Grant was not hungry and took a beer. "What did you think of the play?"

"I don't go to many plays, and I didn't really understand that one, but I hated to see that fellow Hamlet wind up dead. He made some mistakes, didn't he?"

"We all do," Dylan said easily. "What is it you want from me, Inspector? I'm curious."

"I found a witness, Tremayne. He saw a man going into Kate Fairfield's apartment—it could have been the murderer."

Dylan instantly straightened up. "Who told you this?"

"He's a burglar. He was in a house across the street. He saw this man at Fairfield's."

"Can I talk to him?"

"Yes. As a matter of fact, I went to the judge and got him off with a suspended sentence."

Dylan stared at the policeman. "I don't understand, Inspector. Your job is to find proof. You seem to be trying to find something that will help young Newton."

Grant did not speak of his own feelings to anyone, and he was silent for a long time. Finally he said, "I—I met young Newton's sister at the jail, the one called Dora. I feel sorry for her."

"It's a good thing to feel like that about people. She's a fine girl, very sweet and tender. I think, Inspector, you ought to tell her how you feel."

Grant was startled. "How I feel! What are you talking about?"

"Obviously you feel something for Dora Newton."

"No, I don't!"

"You remember that line from the play where the man said, 'This above all: to thine own self be true'? I think you need to do that, Inspector."

"I can't do it," Grant said heavily. "I'm a policeman. She's quality, you know that. That kind looks on policemen as if they were grubby tradesmen."

"Dora won't feel that way. It will help her to know that you're on her brother's side."

Grant shook his head. "I don't know what's got into me. Everyone says I'm a hard man, and I am." Then he said abruptly, "I'll have to report all this about Simmons. I suppose Superintendent Winters will think I've gone around the bend."

"Do you have to tell him?"

"It's my duty." At that moment Grant looked to Dylan like a man with a heavy burden. "I don't have much, Tremayne, but I've got my honour and my job."

"Well, that's a lot. Many fellows don't have that."

Grant rose and left the room, his shoulders bowed. He didn't look back, and Dylan thought, *There's a man who's miserable!*

He left wondering what Jack Simmons could mean to Clive Newton's fight for life.

SEVENTEEN

Serafina wearily leaned back in her chair and closed her eyes. She had slept little after Dylan had come to tell her about Simmons, the thief who had seen a man going into Kate's apartment the night of the murder. The two of them had gone to Sir Leo's immediately. He had been cautious and had forced them to agree to let him handle this new development.

All the next morning, Serafina had tried to put Simmons out of her thoughts. She had been struggling to break the cypher but had made no progress whatsoever. As a scientist, she had been involved in experiments that involved more failure than success, but never before, in any of these, had the life of her brother been at stake. Restlessly she rose and began pacing the floor of the laboratory. Her mind went back to the interview with Sir Leo the previous day. She had sought him out and tried to win from him some kind of promise that would offer some hope, but though he tried to be encouraging, she read in his face the story that his words tried to deny. As she was preparing to leave, he had said heavily, "My dear viscountess, I wish I could be more hopeful, but I must say that if your brother is to be saved, it will take a miracle from God."

Serafina moved to the window, Sir Leo's final remark echoing through her mind. It was just the kind of thing that she had been trained not to believe in, and she stubbornly resisted accepting Sir Leo's dictum. By firm purpose, by sheer will and intelligence, she would find some way to help her brother!

May had come two days earlier. Ordinarily, when she looked out the window, she took pleasure in the fruit trees that decorated the garden and the ground with their lovely white and pink blossoms. But today they brought no pleasure to Serafina. She leaned forward on the window, and watched as Dylan and David played together. David was in the swing, and Dylan was swinging him mightily. She could hear his voice saying, "There you are, old man. Don't fall out now."

"I won't, Dylan. Higher! Higher!"

The sight of her son raised two opposing thoughts. One was pleasure that Dylan had brought out some things in David that had been lacking. Serafina knew that David admired Dylan, for the man had filled an empty place in him. On the other hand, as always, she was uneasy. She knew that David would grow into an adolescent and then a young man, and she thought of Charles and how attractive he had been—and how terribly their marriage had been marred by some traits that she had never shared with anyone else. She knew that David felt his lack of a father keenly, and at times when she had been courted by men, she had been tempted to remarry. But marriage loomed before her like a dark presence or a monster under a bridge, and she had given up on that idea. Now she watched David and Dylan leave the swings and pick up their fishing poles and head down for the pond. She was concerned about the future, about what would happen when Dylan left. How would David take that? She watched restlessly until the two reached the pond, then she turned back, went to her desk, and sat down. Wearily she opened the diary, pulled a sheet of paper from a drawer, and began struggling again to solve the mystery of Kate Fairfield's diary.

❧

"I caught him, Mr. Dylan! Look, he's a big one!"

Dylan had been standing beside David, not so much fishing as watching the young boy. David had become very significant in Dylan

Tremayne's life. He had little enough to do with babies or young people, and it had been a revelation to see how young David's mind worked. He knew the boy was bright and had an imagination that had been held back by Serafina and her father, who both seemed to be anxious about such things.

"Well now, that's a good fisherman, you are. Let me take him off."

"Let me do it, Mr. Dylan."

"All right, then. I'll hold him, and you take the hook out."

Dylan watched as David struggled to remove the hook, thinking, *He always likes to do things for himself. He's got a fierce independence, David has.*

Finally the fish was removed from the hook, and Dylan opened the top of a bucket and tossed the fish in with the others that had been caught. "That makes six," he said. "Don't you think that's about enough?"

David did not answer. The sunlight touched his fair hair, and as he turned toward Dylan, he asked, "Did you ever go fishing when you were little?"

"To tell the truth, I didn't do much of that."

"Why not, Mr. Dylan?"

"Because I didn't have anyone to take me. My father was a miner, and when I was very small, he worked very hard. In the free time he had, he had to do things around the house. A few times I went with other boys."

"Were your parents good to you?"

"Why, bless you, boy, yes, of course they were," he said, turning to look out over the pond, which was still as a mirror. There was no breeze for a moment, and he saw a fish break the water, making concentric circles, small ripples that continued until they reached the shore. "I lost my parents when I was just a little older than you."

"That was hard, wasn't it?"

"Very hard."

"Who took care of you?"

"I had an uncle. I went to live with him."

"Was he good to you?"

Dylan always tried to be honest with David, but in this case the truth would be too sordid. He remembered how abusive his uncle had been and how he had worked young Dylan until he could barely stand and had beaten him for the slightest transgression. "He was no worse than some, I suppose," he said carefully.

David stood for a moment, his eyes fixed on Dylan's face. He had that quality of watching and regarding, observing in ways that were far beyond his years. "I'm sorry you didn't have anyone to take you fishing, Mr. Dylan."

"Why, that's all right, old man. It's all right. I've got me a fine fishing partner now, haven't I?"

The remark pleased David. "Yes," he said. "Can we cook these fish and eat them?"

"I don't know if the cook would let us do that."

"She will if Mum tells her to."

The two turned and headed toward the house, Dylan carrying the bucket, and David carrying his pole. As they approached the house, Serafina came out. "Well, did you two fishermen catch anything?"

"Mum, we caught six! I caught four myself, and I caught the biggest one."

"Is that right? Let me see them."

David eagerly displayed the fish in the bucket and said, "Mum, I want to cook these fish myself. Will you tell cook to let us?"

"Why, she'd be glad to do it for you, David."

"No, I caught them, and I want to cook them and eat them."

"Well, can I have a bite if you do?"

"Yes! Come on. Let's go do it now."

David ran on ahead, and Dylan picked up the bucket. He started for the house beside Serafina, and she said, "I'm worried, Dylan."

"About Clive?"

"It's that blasted code, the cypher. I've tried almost everything I know, but I can't crack it. I can't interpret it. I've been thinking about going to an expert somewhere."

"I didn't know there were experts in that."

"Yes, I'm sure there are. There are experts in almost everything now."

"Well, I'll be leaving after lunch to go search for that man with a hook." He hesitated, then said, "I ran into a sad thing. A young girl named Callie and her brother, Paco . . ." He told the story of the children and of the mother who was so sick, and made little of his own part of it.

"She needs to see a doctor, Dylan. I'll be glad to pay for it."

"Oh, I took a doctor by, and he gave her some medicine. I'm hoping she'll be better, but I was looking at Paco. He's a fine-looking boy, and his sister, Callie, too. Her full name is Calandra Montevado. Her mother's full-blooded Spanish, I think. She's a beautiful child, well, not a child really. You know that age between twelve and thirteen, when a young girl turns into a young woman." He thought deeply for a moment and said, "That's no place for her."

Serafina had come to expect this from Dylan. She knew he had a compassion for weak, frail things, be they persons or animals, and she found it pleasing. "I'll give you some money, and you can use it to help them if you'd like, Dylan."

"They need so much. Clothes, food, medicine. Thank you, Viscountess, that's kind of you."

The two reached the kitchen and found David already explaining to Nessa, the cook, about the plan. ". . . So we're going to cook the fish, me and Mr. Dylan, ourselves."

Nessa looked up at Serafina, and Serafina winked and nodded. "Well, that is fine, Master David, just fine! I'll tell you what. I'll get all the pots and pans you'll need and all the spices, and if you need a bit of advice now and then, I'll be right here."

"Thank you, Nessa," David said, his face shining, and turning, he said, "Come on, Dylan."

"*Mr.* Dylan," Serafina said.

"Oh, that's all right when we're alone. He can put a Mr. on me if we're ever in company together. Come on now. Let's see how these fish are going to be turned into something good to eat."

Dylan, David, and Serafina sat down at the table in the kitchen. David had been so excited about cooking the fish that he had been almost unmanageable. Serafina had whispered once to Dylan, "He's so excited. It's good of you to do this."

"My pleasure, it is. He's a fine boy, Viscountess."

The fish had been fried in fat and was now on a platter. Nessa had gotten permission to make a salad, but David was interested only in the fish. "This is the big one. I know I caught him. Here, Mum, you can have half of it."

"Why, that's very generous of you, Son," Serafina said. She took the portion of fish and warned, "You be careful now. You pick the bones out."

"I will, Mum."

Nessa had fixed hot bread, and as they ate, David suddenly said, "Mum, Mr. Dylan didn't have anybody to take him fishing when he was little."

"Is that right, Dylan?"

"Well, you know I lost my parents when I was very young. I went into the coal mine. After a shift in one of those places, a boy's too tired to do much but sleep. Anyway," he said, "God's given me a good fishing partner now." He reached over and pinched David's ear.

David said, "Ouch," but grinned at the gesture.

They ate the fish, and afterward Nessa said, "I baked a plum pudding. Would you care for a little of that?"

"I would," David said at once.

"You're going to pop," Serafina warned, "but I guess a little bit won't hurt."

Dylan, as he was accustomed to do, gave a brief prayer of thanks just for the pudding. "Thank you, Lord, for this good, fine pudding. I doubt the angels have anything better."

David tasted the plum pudding, but it was too hot. He blew on the spoon and asked, "Did you ever see an angel, Mr. Dylan?"

"Not that I know of, but I may have." He leaned forward and whispered in a confidential tone, "You know angels come to this earth in disguise."

"They do?"

"Yes indeed. Sometimes you meet a poor fellow dressed in rags and looking like he's on his last leg, but under that disguise there may be a bright, shining, mighty angel. That's the reason," he added, "when I see a poor beggar I always try to give them something. You know what I'd hate?"

"What, Mr. Dylan?"

"I'd hate when I go to heaven to have an angel come to me and say, 'I was that beggar outside your door. You had money in your pocket, but you didn't help me. Why didn't you do that?'"

David's eyes were like saucers, and he began to ask questions about angels.

Serafina listened and marveled at Dylan's ability to weave his Christian beliefs into ordinary conversations. Most people she knew were nominal Christians at best. They had everything in neat compartments—so much time for work, so much for family, so much for playing games—and perhaps a little slice left over for God. She had always felt there was something wrong with this, but now she had met a man whose entire being was saturated with a love of God, and it disturbed her.

"I want you to pray for my Uncle Clive, Mr. Dylan. If you pray, you can get him home again."

Dylan was startled. He did not want to offend Serafina, whom he knew did not like religious talk, so he simply said, "Of course I'll pray for your uncle."

"And God will get him out of the prison?"

Again Dylan hesitated. He did not want the boy to see anything like doubt in him, so he smiled and nodded. "We know that God is good, don't we?"

They finished the meal, and David went upstairs to take his nap. Dylan prepared to leave. "I've got a lot of people to check with. I asked Callie and her brother to be on the lookout for a man with a steel hook for a hand."

"I thought about going to Superintendent Winters. He offered to help."

"I suppose he could."

Serafina shook her head. "I don't know, Dylan. I'm tired. I don't know what to do anymore."

"I can tell you what to do."

"What?"

"Go to church with me in the morning."

Serafina straightened and looked Dylan directly in the eye. It was the first time he had asked this. "You know I don't go to church."

"You're a scientist, aren't you?"

"Well, yes, that's what I am, I suppose."

"I thought scientists were supposed to examine all the evidence before they made a conclusion."

"They are, but what—"

"I don't think you examined the other side of the evidence. Your father has taught you about the material world, but there's another world." He was looking at her with a strange expression, a half smile but with a gleam in his eye that she could not interpret. "I wish you'd go with me, Serafina," he said quietly.

Serafina knew he would say no more, and impulsively she said, "All right, I'll go with you, Dylan."

"Fine! I'll be by to pick you up in the morning."

EIGHTEEN

Serafina had puzzled over how to dress for her visit to church with Dylan. She went through her wardrobe twice, and finally settled on a modest pearl grey skirt and jacket with dark green buttons. The only ornament was a touch of delicate white lace, edged with green, that showed at the opening of the tight-fitting, short jacket.

She paused before her mirror, studied her face, and passed her hand over her hair, which fell loosely down her back. "Well, I don't know if this is a proper churchgoing outfit or not, but it will have to do." Turning, she walked out of her room, and as she approached the stairs, she saw her father coming down the hall from the opposite direction. "Good morning, Father."

"Good morning, Serafina. Where are you off to this morning?" Septimus was carelessly dressed. He wore a pair of tired brown trousers with frayed cuffs, a white shirt with no necktie, and a green smoking jacket, although he never smoked.

For a moment Serafina was tempted to prevaricate, but she had always been able to talk with her father about anything, and anticipating his response, she smiled, saying, "Why, I'm going to church, Father."

As Serafina had expected, her father reacted strongly to her announcement. His eyes flew open, and she knew that he thought he had misunderstood her. "To church?" he said. "Why, you never go to church!"

"Well, I'm going this morning. Dylan wanted me to go with him, and I promised that I would. He spends so much time with David, Father, and that's meant a lot to him. And this is the only thing he ever asked of me. He wasn't pushy about it at all. He just simply asked me if I would go. I hated to say no, so here I am."

"Going to church." Septimus shook his head. "I don't remember the last time either of us went to church."

"Well, I'm going as an experiment."

"An experiment?"

"Yes. Dylan told me that a true scientist will look at both sides of a truth. I've looked at the rational side of man and his being for many years now, so I think it's time that I look at the other side."

Septimus stared at her and shook his head. "That may be a good thing, Serafina. I've often wished that I had given more attention to that side of man's being."

"Well, it's not too late, Father."

"No, I suppose not."

"Would you care to go with me?"

"No, I think one of us at a time will be sufficient."

Serafina kissed him on the cheek. "I'll tell you all about it when I get home."

She left her father with a puzzled look on his face and understood his problem. He had never been an anti-Christian man. He would never give a rebuke to those who chose to go the way of the church and of Jesus Christ.

Even as Serafina was on her way down the stairs, she heard the knock at the door and saw Daisy, her mother's maid, go to answer it. Serafina heard her greet Dylan by name. "Come in, Mr. Tremayne."

"Thank you, Daisy," Dylan said. He stepped inside and said, "You're looking very nice today." Daisy, a meek young girl of twenty-four years, smiled and looked down at her feet.

Even as Serafina approached, she could see the flush on the maid's cheek. *He has a way with women,* she thought, but she had noted that before. As she approached, she saw him look at her with approval in his eyes. "Good morning, Dylan."

"Good morning, Viscountess. You look very nice this morning."

"Well, I wasn't sure what kind of costume to wear to church."

"Almost any costume will do. You'll see some dressed in finery, others almost in rags. Are you ready?"

Dylan stepped back and opened the door, and as she stepped outside, she heard Dylan say, "Daisy, you'll have to come to Mr. Spurgeon's church one day. You would like it, I'm sure."

"Thank you, Mr. Tremayne. I would like it very much."

Dylan had hired a carriage, and he helped her into it, then told the driver, "New Park Street Chapel. Do you know it?"

"Why would I not know it? Everybody knows Mr. Spurgeon's church."

Dylan winked at him, got into the carriage, and sat across from Serafina. She noticed that he was versed in social amenities such as this. "Mr. Spurgeon seems very well known," she said. "Does he have a title?"

"You mean like Bishop, something like that?"

"Yes."

"No, as a matter of fact, he's never been ordained."

Serafina, who only knew the workings of the Church of England, was surprised by this. "Not ordained? I thought one had to be ordained to preach."

"Well, it is customary." Dylan shrugged. He was immaculately dressed in a black jacket and faintly striped trousers. His cravat was perfectly tied, and Serafina knew that he was one of those men who could put on any sort of clothing and make it look as if it were tailored especially for him. Other men, she knew, no matter how much they spent, always looked as if they were wearing somebody's cast-off clothing.

"I've been reading what the newspapers have to say about Mr. Spurgeon," she said. "He seems to have created quite a furor in the ecclesiastical world."

"Not of his making, Viscountess." Dylan shook his head firmly. "He's not a political man at all, but God has blessed him so greatly in building a great church that some in the Establishment are a little upset. They think that religion has to go through channels."

"I more or less thought that myself. What little I remember of church, everything is all done very methodically."

"I suppose that's true enough, but one of the things that I remember a preacher saying was, 'I'd like to see things in the service get out of control.'"

"Out of control! Why, that sounds like Methodist enthusiasm."

"What he meant was that we program our worship so strictly that there is no liberty to it. You'll find the services to be quite regular at the New Park Street Chapel, but Mr. Spurgeon somehow gives it an air of spontaneity. Still, he has his detractors."

As the carriage rolled along the street toward the centre of London, Serafina listened as Dylan spoke of Charles Haddon Spurgeon. It was not difficult to ascertain that he was an admirer of the man, and she was curious to see what sort of preacher Dylan would like. He himself seemed almost wildly unorthodox. In the first place, very few actors were active Christians, and then there was his tendency to just speak his faith wherever he was, in the kitchen with Nessa or talking about horses with the groom. It didn't seem to matter. For some reason she found this intriguing, and she questioned him gently about how he had come to know God.

"I wasn't converted when I was a lad, which would have been better," Dylan said. He frowned and shook his head. "When I came to England, as I told you, I fell in with a family that were basically burglars. They taught me their trade, and I thought that God was not interested in a man who was a thief, so I put Him off."

"What about when you were in the Army?"

"That's when I found the Lord, ay. I told you," he said, "about losing—" He hesitated as if he found it difficult to speak the words. "About losing Eileen."

"Yes, I remember." Serafina saw it pained him still to talk of the young woman he had loved. "Did she have something to do with your becoming a Christian?"

"Yes, in a rather indirect way," Dylan said soberly. He looked up, and she saw his eyes were filled with painful memories. "When Eileen died, I hated God for taking her. I'll not tell you all the things I shouted out at God in my grief. I thought I was going to lose my mind really."

"What changed you?"

"A very simple thing it was, Viscountess. I had left the barracks and gone out to walk. It was a day of rest for us, and most of the men were laughing and gambling. I couldn't stand it, and I left the camp and went for a walk. There was a copse there, and I entered into it and sat down on a log to think of nothing but Eileen and how I'd never see her again. I remember I put my head in my hands and wept like a baby. First time I'd done that in years," he mentioned. He fell silent then for a time.

"And then what?" Serafina asked quietly.

"I remember when I had just about worn myself out with grief, I had thrown myself down face forward on the ground and was crying out to God that He was unfair. Like a crazy man, I was, and then—" He paused, and a smile turned the corners of his lips upward. "And then something happened. Never have been able to explain it. There are instances in the Bible where God spoke audibly to men and women, but I've never had that experience. But somehow within my heart, which had been nothing but a raging storm, there was suddenly a quiet and a peace such as I didn't know existed. A verse of Scripture that I heard years before came to me. I didn't even know it was in my heart, but it seemed to mount up until it filled my mind."

"What was it?"

"A verse you probably know. 'God so loved the world that He gave His only begotten Son, that whosoever believeth in Him should not perish but have eternal life.' The words came to me as clearly as if they were printed on a page. I knew it was the Lord, so I began to pray, asking God why He had taken Eileen. I never did get an answer for that really, but I began to call upon God to ask Him to give me peace, and He did. I asked Him to save me, for I knew the Gospel, and when I called, He answered. I stayed out in those woods all day long praying, but the burden had lifted. I still missed Eileen as much as a man would miss his arm that he lost, but somehow the peace of God had come upon me, and from that day to this I have walked in it."

Serafina wanted to answer, but she did not know what to say. It was exactly the sort of religion that she had doubted. She was relieved, in a way, when the carriage pulled up, and Dylan said, "We're here." He stepped outside, helped her to the ground, and paid the cabby. "Come you, then," he said, and when she took his arm, they moved toward the entrance.

Serafina was rather startled as she watched the crowd. People from everywhere, from all walks of life, were headed toward the large building with the massive pillars in front—the New Park Street Chapel that housed Charles Spurgeon's flock had caught the attention of all of England. She held on to Dylan's arm and joined the people passing through the gates. It was still half an hour before the time of the service, and when they reached the doors, they were greeted by a man who said, "You can't get in without a ticket."

"Oh, I have tickets," Dylan said. He reached into his inner pocket and pulled out two tickets. The usher smiled and said, "Go right in, sir, and you, ma'am. Take your place."

"Is it always this crowded?" Serafina asked as Dylan led her to the seats.

"Always. Sunday mornings, Sunday night. Even on Thursday night for prayer meeting sometimes."

"I never heard of needing a ticket to get into a religious service. Why is that?"

"Too small the church is for all who want to come and hear Mr. Spurgeon. I've heard him urge people to go worship in their own churches. He wants the lost to hear the Gospel, see? And many times I've seen Christian people give their tickets to a sinner so they could hear the Gospel. I've done it myself, yes."

"He must be a great orator."

"That he is not," Dylan said. "You won't be impressed with his looks, for he is not a handsome man, he. And you'll be surprised at his sermon, how simple it is. He has a sense of humour, too, which I like."

Serafina took her seat with Dylan. The large clock on the platform pointed to ten minutes until eleven, and she was shocked to hear people talking in unabated voices, and even laughing. It was not at all like her memory of the Church of England services! Eleven o'clock came then. The doors at the back of the platform opened, and a stout, plain man stepped out.

"That's Mr. Spurgeon," Dylan whispered to her.

Serafina studied the famous preacher. He was somewhat under medium height, short from loin to knee, with a deep chest and a very massive forehead. He was not a handsome man, as Dylan had warned her, but his presence held her attention as he stepped forward and addressed the congregation. And what a voice he had! When he greeted the congregation and then gave the pastoral prayer, his voice was like an organ. Without effort it filled the massive building. It seemed to be not the voice of a man preaching to six thousand people; instead she felt as if the preacher were speaking to her alone, and she was relatively certain that everyone else felt the same way.

After the prayer, Mr. Spurgeon said, "We will now worship the Lord in songs of praise." The singing began then, and it was like nothing Serafina had ever heard. There was no choir. A middle-aged man simply stood beside Mr. Spurgeon, and his high tenor voice rose above the others. She took the hymnal that Dylan gave her, and she saw that the hymns were simple, not ornamented with flowery language as many she had seen.

She could not join in the singing, but she could hear Dylan and was impressed at what a clear, ringing, bell-like voice he had. As he was an actor, of course, she had expected this.

Finally it was time for the sermon, and the massive crowd grew still. Spurgeon read a Scripture verse: "Come unto Me all that labor, and I will give you rest." The sermon was simple, almost to the point of basic language, and personalized somehow. She listened as Spurgeon ticked off points, first saying, "I will give *you* rest. You all need rest. There may be in here a marquis, perhaps a countess . . ." When he said this, Serafina flinched and knew that Dylan felt it. "There may be a duke. There are certainly many of you this morning who barely know where your next meal will come from, but duke, marquis, countess, poor shoemaker, widow without any support—you all need this rest that the Lord Jesus has promised."

His next point was simple. "I will *give* you rest." And Serafina listened as Spurgeon spoke, his eyes gleaming and his plain features alive with passion. He paused often to tell simple stories to illustrate his message. She listened throughout the rest of the sermon, and all through it she noticed that the name of Jesus was often spoken. Everything was Jesus, according to Mr. Spurgeon's own words.

Finally, as the sermon went on, she felt herself seized by a peculiar sensation. *Have I missed something? Is there something to this religion after all?*

The feeling grew, and finally, when the service was over, she heard Mr. Spurgeon say, "Are you here this morning, and your heart is like a troubled sea? Jesus can calm that sea as He did the storm on Lake Galilee. He just simply said, 'Peace, be still,' and the sea abated. He will say the same to your troubled heart, my dear friends. Be you king or beggar, it's all the same. The ground at the foot of the cross is level."

The service ended then, and Dylan escorted her back to the carriage. He helped her in, then took his place across from her. He had a peaceful look on his face. "It always does me such good to hear Mr. Spurgeon. I'm glad I know one man that means every word he says."

Serafina wanted to answer, but she found that the *rest* that Mr. Spurgeon had spoken of was not something she possessed. She realised her emotions had been for many years like a troubled sea, exactly as the preacher had said. She found herself wishing that somehow she could find the rest that the passage of Scripture had offered. She looked up to see Dylan watching her cautiously, and knew that he would not question her. He did say, "Thank you for coming with me, Viscountess."

"It was . . . very nice," she said.

"Spurgeon is living proof that our way of selecting great preachers is wrong. We look for men of eloquence, and if they are tall and imposing with good looks, that's even better. If they are highly educated and can quote from all of the classics, that's who we think is the ideal preacher."

"Mr. Spurgeon doesn't fit that description. What *does* he have, Dylan?" She leaned forward and watched his face.

"He has within him the Spirit of the living God. I know that sounds like religious talk to you, but true it is. When a man comes to Jesus, Christ comes to reside in his heart. All believers have this presence, but some men and women are filled with the Holy Ghost so that the power spills out of them. I expect Charles Wesley had this and many others. Mr. Spurgeon has it. You could feel the fire of God, couldn't you?"

Serafina did not know how to answer. If she said yes, it would be perfectly logical for him to assume that she was on her way to finding God. She did not want to commit herself and stubbornly said, "Well, I'm glad I went. I see there is another side to Christianity than the one commonly believed by skeptics."

"There is," he said. "Jesus is the answer for all of us."

Serafina did not speak again. He let her out at the house and told her, "I'm still looking for our man with the steel hook. There's no performance today, so I've got all day and tonight. I hope that I'll find that man. The trial will be next week, and we have nothing really."

Serafina trembled at his words. "Yes, go look for him, Dylan. We must help my brother—and that man Simmons. He'll testify that Clive wasn't the man he saw go into Kate's house, won't he?"

"Yes, he will. I think he's our big hope, Lady Trent. He's out of jail now, and Sir Leo has been talking to him."

"How do you know that, Dylan?"

"I asked him." Dylan grinned crookedly. "He's a closemouthed man when he wants to be, Sir Leo is, but I could tell he's depending on Simmons to sway the jury."

"I—I hope so, Dylan." Serafina turned and walked away, and when she got inside, she closed the door and leaned against it. She felt exhausted, worn out, and could not understand why. Slowly she moved to the stairs and climbed them, and when she got to her room, she simply sat down in a chair and put her head in her hands. She wanted to pray but did not know how, and finally she lifted her head and said, "Dylan will find a way. I know he will!"

NINETEEN

A loud banging on his door brought Dylan Tremayne out of a deep sleep. He had spent all Sunday afternoon and late into the night searching for the man with the steel hook, with no success whatsoever. He had managed to go by and visit Callie and her family and had given them some money from the Viscountess Trent. When he had arrived home, it had been late, and he had fallen into bed exhausted. He was ordinarily a rather light sleeper, but the double strain of performing in the play every night except Sunday, and helping Lady Serafina Trent find something that would free her brother, had worn him thin.

"All right—all right, I'm coming!"

Rising from the bed, Dylan seized a robe and struggled into it as he moved toward the door. He threw the lock, opened it, and saw Albert Givins, Serafina's coachman, standing there. "Albert, what are you doing here?"

"I'm sorry to bother you, sir, but the viscountess, she wants to see you right now."

"What about?"

Givins smiled broadly, exposing a gap in his teeth. "I wouldn't be knowing that, sir, would I now? But she was very insistent."

"All right. Come on in, Albert. Let me get some clothes on, and I'll go."

"Yes, sir."

Dylan dressed hurriedly and, glancing at the pendulum clock on a table across the room, saw that it was just a little past five o'clock.

What in the world could she be wanting with me this time of the morning? It must be pretty serious. The thought touched his mind, and he pulled on his boots and then got up, saying, "All right, Albert, I'm ready."

"Yes, sir. I'll drive pretty fast on the way back. You hang on now."

As soon as Dylan was in the coach, he heard Albert call out to the horses, who lunged ahead, throwing him against the backseat with some force. "I hope he doesn't kill us getting there," he muttered. As they moved along, he saw that people were just beginning to fill the streets. The wheels rumbled over the cobblestones, and Albert drove the horses as if he were in a chariot race.

Finally the coach pulled up, Albert shouting, "Whoa there! Whoa!"

At once Dylan got out and gave Albert a cynical look. "Well, you didn't run over anybody."

"No, sir, I ain't never done nothing like that. You'd better go on. She's in a real tizzy."

Dylan walked quickly up the front steps and knocked on the door. Almost at once it opened, and Serafina herself answered. "What is it, Serafina?" he demanded.

Serafina laughed. "I take it Albert gave you quite an exciting ride."

"He did too." He waited and saw that there was a peculiar expression on her face. She was smiling, and her eyes were dancing. "It must be good news," he said.

"It is. Come along to the study."

He followed her down the hall into the study. She closed the door, and he saw that she was breathing quickly with an excitement he had never seen in her. "I've got good news, Dylan. I think I've solved the cypher."

"Why, that's wonderful, Serafina!"

"Well, I'm not 100 percent sure. Maybe 95. Come here and let me show you."

She moved over to a long hunt table with one chair before it, and she pulled up another. "Here, sit down, and I'll show you what I've come up with."

The two sat down, and he could smell the faint odor of lavender, a familiar scent with her. She did not use perfume as a rule, but her clothes always smelled like lavender, and he concluded that she put it, somehow, in the water when the dresses were washed. He looked down at the table and saw that it was littered with sheets of paper.

"All these are failures. I've been trying for days now to figure it out. Do you know how cyphers usually work?"

"I don't know much about them."

"Usually you just substitute one letter for another, or a number. In other words, in the simplest kind of code, you just assign the letter *A* to the number one, and *B* would be number two. So what anyone reading it would find is simply a series of numbers."

"That sounds simple enough."

"Too simple. What we have here is something far more complicated." She turned to him, and he could see a very faint line of freckles across her nose that he had never noticed before. He was aware of the beauty of her violet-coloured eyes, the only eyes he had seen of that shade, and she had a way of smiling, as she was now, that was desirable. Her chin tilted up, and her lips curved in an attractive fashion. A small dimple appeared at the left of her mouth, and humour danced in her eyes. "That kind of code isn't too hard to figure out."

"It seems to me it would be."

"Not really. You see, some letters appear very often in our words and others very rarely. For example, the most common letter, if you counted them all up in a book, would be the letter *E*. Probably the least common would be the letter *X*. So if you see whichever number, symbol, or sign occurs the most, in all probability, it's the letter *E*, and the one that occurs the least would be the *X*. Then you can figure out the second most common number, which might be *A*. You see?"

"It sounds easy the way you say it."

"Well, this wasn't that easy. Look at this, Dylan."

Dylan looked down at the diary of Kate Fairfield. He had seen it before and now shook his head. "It just looks like a meaningless bunch of numbers."

"Let's just look at the first line here," she said. She put the tip of her finger on the first line, which read: "123-16-4 210-10-2 323-5-6 98-7-1 269-21-5 322-18-3."

"I tried to find some pattern in these numbers, and, as usual, once you see it, it's easy. But seeing it the first time is what's hard."

"I just don't see any rhyme or reason to it," Dylan said. "Does each one stand for a word?"

"That's what I've always thought, but it's necessary to discover *how* the numbers make a word. I nearly lost my mind trying to find a pattern. When the answer came, it just came to me like a flash. It happens that way in science, Dylan. You wear yourself out and have nothing—and then out of nowhere, the answer comes. It can be frustrating."

"But you know how it works?"

"I think so. Just run your eyes down the page and you'll see that the first number is almost inevitably the largest number."

"Yes, I see that. What does that mean?"

"Let me go on," she said. "The second number is always relatively small compared to the first number. It hardly ever goes over twenty or twenty-five."

Dylan looked at the numbers and said, "That's right. What does it mean?"

"Look at the last number. It's the smallest of all. It never goes over ten or twelve at the most." She smiled at him then and said, "So we have one very large number and then two numbers much smaller, but the third much smaller than the second."

Dylan was aware that her arm was pressed against him as they sat at the table. "I'm not very good at games."

"I'm *very* good at them. I went to sleep last night thinking about this, and I woke up very early this morning, about four o'clock, and it was like a light went on in my mind. I suddenly was almost certain that I knew how to break the code."

"Tell me."

"The code is based on words in a book. The first number, which is always larger, is the page number of the book. That's why the first number may be as much as three or four hundred. The largest number I've found so far in the diary is four hundred and twenty. Nothing larger than that."

"What's the second number?"

"Why, you should be able to figure that out."

"I'm too tired. Tell me."

"The second number is the number of the line on the page. For instance, this one right here. The first number is one hundred and twenty-three. The second number is sixteen. So you go to page one hundred and twenty-three, and go down to the sixthteenth line."

"And the third number, four, is the word in that line."

"Very good! You can see how easy it is to find what the word is."

"But there would have to be one specific book."

"Ah, you're right about that."

"Which book is it?"

"I don't know."

Dylan stared at her with consternation. "There are millions of books in the world. The only way you could read this would be to find the particular book that Kate used to make the code."

"Yes, we must find that book."

Dylan's smooth brow furrowed. "There was a bookshelf in her room. We looked through the books."

"Yes, we looked behind them, we opened them up to find a note, but we found nothing. I believe that she had to keep the book in her room so that when she made an addition to her diary, she'd have the book there to make the code." Serafina then took out a single sheet of paper with a list of names written on it. Beside each name was what was obviously a nickname. The writing was brown, and the paper seemed to be brittle and tended to curl.

Dylan read the first entry. "James Fitzsimmons Hartwell. Why, he was a prominent member of the House of Lords, him! Where did you get this paper, Viscountess?"

"It was in the box where we found the diary. I paid no heed to it, then I wondered why she would have a blank sheet of paper in the box. Finally it came to me." She smiled, then added, "She had written the names in invisible ink. I tested my theory, and this is what I found."

"I didn't know there was such a thing as invisible ink."

"It's not too mysterious." Serafina smiled slightly. "Many things will work. In this case, I suspect, it was lemon juice."

"How do you make it visible?"

"You heat it up, usually over a hot stove, being careful not to let the paper catch on fire. You see how brown and crisp it is? I carefully warmed up part of it, and those few names are very legible."

Dylan glanced at the sheet of names before Serafina continued, "Now you know what we must do."

Dylan's mind was working quickly. "Yes, we've got to go look at those books again, but it will be dangerous to break in a second time. We'll raise our odds of being caught."

"Yes, you're right. We'll have to come up with something else." She sat there for a long moment, her mind racing, then said, "I'll go ask Superintendent Winters to let us look. He's been very sympathetic. I think he will give us his permission."

"Well, you have more confidence in policemen than I do, although I don't have any reason to distrust Winters any more than the rest. I would have thought that Grant would be the one to go to."

"I doubt if he has the authority. No, I'll go today and ask the superintendent for permission to look in Kate Fairfield's room."

⚜

"How are you, Superintendent?"

Winters had risen when Serafina entered his office. He was studying her face carefully and somewhat warily. "Good morning, Viscountess. You're up early."

"Yes, and like most people who come through your door, I have a favour to ask."

Winters smiled. He looked down at her from his greater height and said, "You're right about that. Does it have to do with your brother?"

"In a way it does."

"What's your request?"

"I'd like your permission to go to Miss Fairfield's room and look around."

Winters frowned. "Whatever for, Viscountess?"

"Oh, I think I might find a clue to what has happened in the bookcase. She had quite a few books, I understand."

"How did you know that?"

Serafina realised she had made a mistake but quickly recovered. "Oh, I overheard Inspector Grant talking to one of the sergeants. I think he mentioned it."

"And you think looking at her books would help find someone that killed Kate Fairfield?"

"I would like to think so. Time's passing very quickly. The trial is next week."

"I am sorry, but what you ask is a violation of our policy here at the Yard. We've also warned you about how dangerous your investigation could be for you." Then something changed in his face, and he stepped forward and put his hand on her arm. "I'm grieved over this, Viscountess. I will do what I can, but I can't break my own rules."

"Well, I can understand that, Superintendent Winters."

"Anything else I can do . . ."

"No, there's nothing."

Suddenly Winters said, "I understand your grief and your sense of fear. It's only natural. I wish I could do more to help."

"I'm sure you would."

Winters gave a strange gesture. He held out his hands to the side and said vehemently, "You must know your brother is guilty. All the evidence points to it. You are a woman of science, Viscountess. You must weigh the facts as you do in your laboratory."

Serafina knew that this was true, but she could not be so clinical when the life of her beloved brother was at stake. "I thought I was a pure scientist, but I find sometimes the heart overrules the head. Thank you for your time, Superintendent."

Winters watched as she left and shook his head. He gave her time to clear the building and then left his office. He moved down the hall and entered Grant's office without knocking. Grant was sitting at his desk writing, and he looked up in surprise. "What is it, Superintendent?"

"The viscountess has been here. She thinks she's got some sort of idea that will clear her brother's name."

An alarm went off in Grant's head. "What sort of idea, sir?"

"It had something to do with the murdered woman's books. There were a number of books in the room, as I recall."

"Yes, sir, but we looked in all of them. We examined every page, thinking maybe she had left a note, but we found nothing."

"Well, we can't have her destroying evidence."

"Do you want me to do something?"

"Yes, I want you to go to the woman's house and confiscate the books. Bring them in here. I don't have any idea what her thought was, but we'll have to look at those books again."

"I was supposed to go to Dillingham this afternoon. I wouldn't have time to get the books until tomorrow."

"That will do, I suppose, but make sure you have them here first thing in the morning."

❧

Grant was busy with his work all morning, but he could not stop thinking about Viscountess Trent's request. It troubled him, and he found himself unable to put his full attention on his real work.

Finally he said to Sergeant Kenzie, "I've got an errand to run, Sandy. I'll be back fairly soon."

"Don't forget you're going out of town."

"I know. I'll be there."

Grant left his office and the building that housed Scotland Yard. He rarely acted on impulse, but this thing in him was stronger than impulse. He finally came to a decision and took a hansom cab to the Trent estate. He said to the driver, "Wait here. I won't be long."

"Yes, Inspector."

He went up the steps and was admitted by a pretty parlor maid, to whom he said, "I'd like to see the viscountess."

"Yes, sir. If you'll just wait in the study." She led Grant down to the study and said, "I'll tell the viscountess you're here."

"Thank you."

Grant paced the floor, but almost at once a woman appeared. He thought at first it was the viscountess, but then he saw that it was Dora Newton.

"Why, Inspector Grant." Dora came toward him. She was dressed in dove grey, a simple dress that did not flaunt her youthful figure, but he was much aware of the young woman's lissome quality. "Are you here to see my father?"

"No, Miss Dora, I need to see the viscountess."

"I'm sure she'll come quickly." She hesitated, then gave a nervous laugh. She stepped closer to him and said in a confidential tone, "Do you know what, Inspector Grant? I was very afraid of you when you first came to our house. Very much so. You terrified me."

Grant was disappointed but shrugged, saying, "I guess a lot of people are afraid of me. I've got the name of being a hard man."

"No, that's not so," Dora said gently. "You're not hard, Inspector." She stepped forward impulsively and reached down and took his hand. She held it for a moment and said, "You've been so very kind to me!"

Matthew Grant, by his own admission, was a hard-driving man. He had come up hard and whetted his skills on the worst element in

London society. The woman who stood before him was the antithesis of all that he had learnt about women. Most of the women he contacted were of the criminal order—tough, loud, and without a thread of morality. This young woman seemed to exude an air of goodness and purity. Her lips were full and wide and were now turned up in a smile, and her eyes were fixed on him. He admired the smooth joining of her neck and shoulders, and her auburn hair glowed under the room lamps. There was a slight flush in her cheeks, and as it had before, her beauty hit Grant intensely. She had managed to stir his deepest and most reckless emotions, something that had happened against his will.

"I'm glad you feel that way, Miss Dora."

"I do." She held on to his hand, and at that moment something passed between them. She pulled back and gave a half laugh. "You must think I'm awful, being so forward."

"No, I would never think you were awful. I—I've never known a woman like you, Miss Dora."

"Really?" Dora took that as a compliment, which it was, and then she looked directly into his eyes and said, "And I've never met a man like you, Inspector Grant."

At that moment Grant's quick ears caught the sound of footsteps on the marble floor of the hallway. He turned from her, and as soon as Serafina entered, he nodded and said, "I apologise for coming at this unseemly hour, Viscountess."

"Not at all, Inspector Grant. Is there something I need to know?"

Grant hesitated, and both women were watching him. He seemed to see himself standing on the top of a thin wall high in the air. If he fell on one side, that meant one thing. If he fell on the other, it meant another. He knew well that for a policeman to give information to the relative of a suspect went against all the tenets of Scotland Yard—and against his own inclination. Still, his eyes went to Dora, and he knew he had no choice. He had never given up anything to a woman before, but now her gentleness had touched a part of him that he had not known he had.

"You went to Superintendent Winters about the books in Kate Fairfield's room."

"Yes, I wanted to look at them."

"Why?"

Now it was Serafina who was distressed. The man who stood before her represented the forces of law. She had thought he was a rigid adversary against whom she must throw her whole might, but as she watched him, she could not make up her mind. "I don't know how much I can trust you, Inspector."

At once Dora reached over and took Serafina's arm. "You can trust him, Sister. He's a good man."

Usually Serafina would pay no attention to such a recommendation. She would have said simply, "You think everyone is good, Dora." But there was something in the light of her sister's eyes, a light of hope and excitement she had not seen for some time.

She turned to face Grant and said, "I'm going to place myself in your power, Inspector. I trust you will not misuse it."

"I will not," Grant said firmly, and both women saw his jaw tighten as if he had made a vow.

"Some time ago a diary of Kate Fairfield's came into my possession." She very carefully did not tell how, although she saw that Grant wanted to know. "I can't explain how I got it. It might involve another person. In any case, it's written in a very complicated cypher. I can't read it, but I'm convinced the answer lies in one of her books. If we could find that book, Inspector, I think it might be the key to finding who really killed her."

Grant stared at Viscountess Serafina Trent. She was a strong woman, and he knew it had cost her greatly to put her trust in a policeman. His eyes shifted to Dora, who was watching him and smiling at him confidently. He cleared his throat and said, "I have orders to confiscate the books and take them down to the Yard. If they're there in the morning, my duty will require that. I'll say no more about it, and I'll bid you good day, Viscountess—and you, Miss Dora."

Dora put out her hand, and he took it. "Thank you so much, Inspector," she whispered.

Grant could only nod and make a quick farewell. As soon as he was outside, he stopped and looked up at the sky. It was all blue except for the large billowy clouds drifting with the breeze. A bird sang, and he looked up into a pear tree and saw a nightingale. He listened to the bird's song and then suddenly shook his shoulders in a gesture of annoyance. *Well, here I am listening to birds sing and giving away departmental information to a relative of an accused killer. I must be losing my mind!* But then he thought of Dora's soft eyes and her warm smile, and a smile touched his own lips. He walked down the path then, got into the carriage, and quickly drove away from the house.

~❈~

"I need your help, but I can't ask you to do it. Clive's not your brother."

Dylan stared at Serafina. "You do ask a lot of a man." He suddenly smiled, and when Serafina saw that smile, she understood how women would respond to it as she found herself doing.

"We'll have to wait until after midnight like we did last time. Besides, we can return the other items, as you said." He paused. "You know," he continued, "if we're going to burgle houses on a regular basis, I'd better buy myself a new set of burglar tools."

Serafina knew he was making light of the difficulty, and she said quietly, "Thank you, Dylan. It's like you."

"Is it now? A man will do anything for a beautiful woman, I suppose."

Serafina had heard compliments from men who pursued her, but there was a tone in his voice that caught at her.

"What is beauty, Dylan?"

"It's not in a pleasing form or smooth skin or beautifully shaped eyes. No indeed. It goes deeper than that. A man looks on a woman, and it's like she's the right woman for him. And when that happens to a man, he can't just walk away from it, or if he does, he carries it with him."

"As you carry the memory of Eileen," she said softly.

"You haven't forgotten that?"

"Indeed, no. It's beautiful to me that you can carry your love all this time, even when she's not there to receive it."

Dylan did not speak, and she saw that he was moved. He studied Serafina and saw the shape of her shoulders and the shining of her blonde hair, and moved by an impulse that was stronger than he, he stepped forward. He saw her eyes widen, but he reached out and pulled her to him. He put his arms around her and felt the firmness of her figure as she pressed against him. "A man finds beauty," he said, "and when he finds it, he has to respond to it or else he's no man at all." He bent his head, and she looked up. He let his mouth fall upon hers, and she did not resist. Her mouth, indeed, was soft and yet firm. Half of her came through, and half of her held off, and he did not put any more pressure on her. For the one instant while they were joined in that embrace, they were on the edge of a mystery that every man and woman faces, and neither of them knew at that moment what would come.

He stepped back and saw that her breath had quickened, and he said, "I'll be back for you after midnight." He waited for her to speak but saw that she had no intention of doing so. She was watching him, her eyes wide with something like shock, and he left without another word.

Serafina stood absolutely still. She had never been stirred by a man's kiss as she had by Dylan's. Something strong and unsettling had been stirred by his kiss, and she had felt something in herself crying out for surrender, softening her. Her stillness as she stood there was deceiving, for in her breast a turmoil was brewing. She had not known love in her marriage, for Charles had not been a loving man. He had taught her, if anything, to hate men, and for the first time in her memory, a man had stirred the deeper part of her that made her a woman. She looked down and saw that her hands were trembling. She held them together to still them, dropped her head, and closed her eyes. She knew she would be thinking of this moment for weeks.

Serafina stood close beside Dylan, her nerves stretched tight. They had entered the house of Kate Fairfield, Dylan having been extra careful that no one was on the street. It was a little after one, and the streets were deserted. Still, they had moved cautiously into the house, which was still sealed off. They had ascended the stairs, and now they stood in the centre of Kate's bedroom. Serafina looked over to the bed where the woman had died and felt a coldness.

"There's the bookcase," Dylan said. He moved toward it, and she joined him. It was a small bookcase, no more than four feet square. It sat on a mahogany table so that the books were at eye level.

"We went through these once before," Serafina said, "but we were looking for the wrong thing."

"What kind of books are they?"

Serafina scanned the books. "They're novels, most of them. Some romance. Some detective-type novels."

"They've got strange titles." He pulled one out and said, "*The Canary That Cried Wolf.*" He opened the front page and said, "Written by somebody named Regis Stoneman."

"I've never read one of his books, but my sister gave me this one as a present—*The Mermaid in the Basement*, remember?" she said with a slight chuckle.

"He must be popular, as many as there are. We don't even know if this is all. What do we do now?"

"It has to be one of these books." Serafina stood by the feeble light that he held and said, "How would the book she used be different?"

"I don't think she'd write on it 'This is the book that's the key to my code,'" he said wryly.

"No. Let's look at them individually."

Dylan set the lantern down, and the two of them began examining the books. They went through them page by page trying to find some connection, and finally Serafina said in despair, "We'll have to take them all."

"We can't do that. Grant would get into trouble."

"That's right. I forgot. Then we have to find which one is the key."

The two stood there before the books, and finally Serafina said, "Wait a minute. Something is odd about one of these."

"What is odd about it? They all look alike to me."

"Believe it or not, it's the book my sister gave me." She opened the book and looked up with excitement dancing in her eyes. "This must be the one."

"Why do you think so?"

"All the other books are very slightly used, as if they had been read once, but look at this one, Dylan. The spine is almost broken on it, and some of the print is smudged. Pages are turned down. It's been used a great deal."

"You're right. Here, how can we test it?"

"I made a copy of Kate's diary and brought the first page with me." She reached into the pocket of her dress and pulled out a paper. She pointed at the first line of numbers, "123-16-4 210-10-2 323-5-6 98-7-1 269-21-5 322-18-3."

"We can test it like this. I'll call out the numbers, and you find the page numbers and the lines and the word. All right?" She looked down and called out the first number. "One twenty-three, sixteen, four."

"No."

"You mean k-n-o-w?"

"Just n-o."

"Try the second one." She called out the second number. "Two ten, ten, two."

Dylan looked at the book. "One."

"No one." Her voice quickened. "Here's the next number. Three twenty-three, five, six."

Dylan quickly found the page. "Will."

"No one will." They both felt the glow of excitement. They worked out the next few lines, and when they did, she looked up and reached out and seized Dylan's arm as she read: 'No one will ever be able to read this journal.' This is it, Dylan! This is the key!"

"It is. You're a smart woman, Serafina Trent. Do we take it with us?"

"No. Dora gave me a copy of this book, so now we won't have to worry about the police discovering this one missing. And we can put the other items back too." Serafina moved over to the doghouse while Dylan put the books back in order.

"Let's hope we can get out of here without being caught," Dylan said.

She turned to him and said, "It's hard to believe that we found it."

"Why, it almost seems like we had help, doesn't it?"

She saw Dylan's smile that he tried to hide, and knew what he was thinking. "You think God had something to do with it?"

"He could. I don't think we ever would have found it without a little help. Look at it. The diary falls into our hands—that's a miracle. Secondly, you're a woman that knows how to do cyphers. That's a miracle. And then the greatest miracle of all, an inspector from Scotland Yard betrays his trust to give us a chance to find this book, which your sister already gave you. I'd say that God is helping us."

The Viscountess Serafina Trent bit her lip and saw that he was waiting for her reply. She discovered that all of her scientific training had no answer for this. She cleared her throat and said, "I—I can't explain this, Dylan."

He laughed softly in the darkness and took her arm. "Come along. You'll be able to someday." The two left the house, and as they did, Serafina felt a hope being born within her, a hope that this would lead to the freedom of her brother.

TWENTY

Dylan stepped into the Trent mansion and started to speak, but one look at Serafina's face gave him pause. She looked unhappy, which surprised him. She had sent him word to come, saying that she had made a discovery, and he had assumed that it was one that would be helpful in freeing her brother.

"Come into the library where we can be alone, Dylan."

The two went into the library, and as soon as she closed the door, she turned to him, saying, "I've translated all of Kate Fairfield's code."

"Well, God love the day, that's good news!" He saw that her full, composed lips were tight, and her eyes mirrored an unhappiness that ran deep. "What's wrong, Serafina?" he asked.

She hesitated, and in that moment the barrier she kept between herself and Dylan fell, and he became aware of the mystery that cloaks a woman. She finally said, "Come and sit down, and let me show you what I've done."

The two sat down at a table, and she spread sheets of paper out, saying, "At first the translation was slow, but then I got accustomed to it, and it went much easier. Certain combinations occurred over and over, so common words like *and* and *the* I didn't have to look up." She pulled over a sheaf of papers and removed the first sheet. "Here's the copy of her diary. Look at the first page."

Dylan took the sheet and read what she had written aloud: "No one will ever be able to read this journal, but it gives me pleasure to keep a record of the fools who chase after me. How pitiful they are! They come to me with lust in their eyes, promising me all sorts of wonderful things. At first I scorned them, but then it became a game to me. The first fool was a member of the House of Lords. I called him the Worm, which is what he was." Dylan looked up and said with some surprise, "She didn't give his proper name?"

"No, she didn't. She made up nicknames for them."

Dylan nodded and then began reading again: "He was disgusting, but I let him think I was in love with him. He was easy enough to handle. I got him to write me some letters, which would have been the ruin of him if they were made public. When I threatened to turn them over to the press, he curled up and begged. How I loved it! I bled him dry, then I taunted him with the threat that I was going to turn the letters over to his wife anyway. He got down on his knees and begged me with tears running down his silly face! I simply laughed at him and left him thinking I would have done that. Maybe I would, too, but the next day I read in the papers how he had died. The papers said he died of a heart attack, but I know better. The pitiful little grub worm probably put a bullet in his head or took poison. The Worm didn't deserve to live! Every time I look at the emerald necklace that I made him buy for me, I have to laugh. Men are dirt—all of them!"

Dylan read the words quietly, his watchful eyes half hidden behind their lids. His mouth was drawn into a tight line, and he looked up to meet Serafina's eyes. "A good woman I will leave my dinner to see, but a bad woman puts some kind of dread in me. I knew she was a bad woman, but I never thought she was this evil." He studied the page and said, "Mr. Worm. That doesn't help us much."

"She gave nicknames to all her victims," Serafina said. "I think it's probably because the names wouldn't be found in the novel. She was a clever woman to think of a code like this, but she made a mistake. Remember the list of names I found on the brown paper, Dylan? We put the paper back in Kate's room, but I made a copy first."

Serafina took out her copy. Beside each name was what was obviously a nickname. Dylan read the first entry again: "James Fitzsimmons Hartwell, a member of the House of Lords. Is he the Worm?"

"I remember reading about his death in the *Times*, but the paper never did say anything about suicide."

Dylan stared at the paper, then shook his head. "Is the rest of the diary as bad as this?"

A slight smile turned the corners of Serafina's lips up, and something like amusement touched her eyes. "You'll like one entry she made." She gave him a sheet and touched an entry. "Read that one to me."

Dylan read the passage: "I've always said I could get any man I want, but Apollo is different. He's the best-looking man I've ever seen, and the women fawn over him. But he resists them all. He's religious. I've tried all the things that lure men, but Apollo just smiles and ignores them. But I'll get him into my bed yet!"

"Apollo, that's you," Serafina said. She saw that for once Dylan was at a loss for words and laughed softly. "You're blushing, Apollo! I didn't think there was a man in all England who could still blush like a schoolboy!"

Dylan met her eyes, then laughed ruefully. "Don't be bringing this up to me, Viscountess, or I'll sling you into the river!" He cleared his throat and asked, "Are the rest of the entries as bad as Mr. Worm's?"

"Some of it's worse, but I've translated this entry almost at the end of the journal."

Dylan took the sheet she handed him and read aloud what she had written: "The Puppy comes sniffing around, his stupid face filled with love for me. I've gotten a few pieces of jewellery from him, but he won't be good for much. His sister has money, but I doubt if the viscountess will ever give him money to spend on an actress. He is amusing, and I will toy with him until he has nothing more to give, then I'll tell him I can't stand him and to leave me alone. It will be amusing to see the sick look on his face!"

Dylan glanced at the sheet with the names of Fairfield's victims, but he already knew what he would find. Next to Clive's name was the label

"Puppy." "Poor fellow," he whispered. "She tortured him, and then she laughed when she cast him off."

"I doubt this diary will help Sir Leo win Clive's freedom," Serafina said. "It doesn't prove he didn't kill her."

"But the name of the killer must be in there. She wrote everything else in there, didn't she?"

"Yes. You remember that Helen Morton told us that Kate had a secret lover?"

"Yes, I remember that."

"Read this, Dylan, the last entry in the diary, dated the same day she was murdered."

Once again Dylan read the passage aloud: "I've stripped many men of their money and of other things, but this one will be my masterpiece. He is my 'Secret Lover.' Even my maid, Helen, is curious about him, but she doesn't know who he is. He's more careful than the others, takes me to an apartment for our tryst. He's like a cow to be milked, and I've been draining him dry, the pious hypocrite! He will come for me tonight, and I'm going to laugh in his face. He will claim he can't get more money, but I know that he can. I have a letter from him, though it's not signed. There are handwriting experts, I understand, who can identify the writing of an individual. 'Secret Lover' I call him. He's secret, but he's no lover at all, the clumsy oaf! I'll tell him tonight that he's no man at all and that I've got to have more money. It will give me pleasure to see him squirm. He's grown tiresome, and I'll be glad to be rid of him."

Dylan finished and quickly looked down the list of names. "Why, there's no 'Secret Lover' on this list."

"No, there's not." Serafina's voice was flat, and when Dylan looked up, he saw the disappointment in her eyes. "The one name we need—and she never put it down," she said bitterly.

"Well, I think Sir Leo can use this diary at the trial."

"I don't think so. If she had put a name to Secret Lover, it would be enough to arrest him—but she didn't. We're not a lot better off, Dylan."

"Let's show this to Sir Leo," Dylan said. "He's a smart fellow, him, and

I think he'll find good use for this." He saw that Serafina was almost sick with disappointment, and he said gently, "There's a verse in the Bible that I like very much. It's very simple. It says, 'Wait on the Lord: be of good courage and He shall strengthen thine heart.' Isn't that a fine verse now?"

Serafina listened intently, but no cheer came into her expression. "I know you believe the Bible, Dylan, but I don't."

"You will someday, Lady Serafina Trent!"

Dylan spoke with such certainty, his voice ringing and his face fixed in an attitude of hope, that Serafina stared at him with something like envy in her expression. But she shook her head and said in a heavy tone, "We'll give this to Sir Leo, but I have no hope that it will save Clive."

❦

Sir Leo had listened as Serafina explained the diary and how it worked. He looked at it, then when she was finished, he said slowly, "This diary of the murdered woman tells quite a bit. It's a record of how she made men fall in love with her and give her expensive presents—and then she cast them aside and blackmailed them. She blackmailed many prominent men. She meticulously lists the dates and how much she made them pay."

"Will you be able to use it in Clive's favour?" Serafina asked at once.

"I think I'll use it, but it isn't conclusive. It doesn't name the killer, but it does show that your brother is a minor player in the murdered woman's scheme of things. It's all we've got now unless you find the woman that Clive was with. By the way, where did you get this?"

"This isn't the original. This is a copy."

"Where's the original?" Sir Leo demanded instantly.

"We think it's in the hands of the police."

Sir Leo stared at the two and asked, "And how did you get access to it?"

"I think it's better that you don't know everything, Sir Leo. The police have the diary; I've got a copy of it. That should be enough."

Serafina glanced at Dylan and saw that he was looking as innocent as possible. They had been in a quandary as to how to make sure the evidence got into the hands of Scotland Yard, and it had been Dylan who had suggested that Grant would be their safest bet. Serafina had spoken with him, hinting about what evidence might have been overlooked. She had not deceived Grant for one second—in fact, he had smiled at her, saying, "Wonderful how some evidence just turns up by chance." Serafina had no answer, and Grant had seen to it that the Roi Blanco cigar, the book, and the contents of the box hidden in the doghouse were "found" and taken as evidence.

"If I introduce it as evidence"—Sir Leo frowned—"they'll want to know what it means. Obviously they haven't been able to break the code."

"I'll be a witness. I have some small reputation as a woman of science," Serafina said.

"Yes, you do, Viscountess. Very well. It would have been better if Kate had named her so-called Secret Lover." He looked at them and shook his head slowly. "This trial is going to be a circus, you know. A famous actress, beautiful and rich, killed by a member of the peerage."

"Clive's not a member of the peerage."

"I know that, but the prosecutor will make it seem as though he is. He's the brother of a viscountess. That's all people will need to know."

"You'll have to overcome that some way," Serafina said.

Sir Leo looked at the copy of the journal, put his hand on it, and shook his head. "We need more than this. Find the man with the steel hook, get the name of the woman, and get her to testify. That's the only sure hope that we have. And remember, we don't have to prove who the murderer is—all we have to prove is that Clive is innocent." He stared at the two and saw that they were filled with doubt. "I wish I could give you better tidings, but that's the way it is."

"I know you'll be able to help Clive," Serafina said, her face intent. "You have the testimony of that man Simmons. That will count for a lot, won't it, Leo?"

Sir Leo's lips tightened, and he could not look Serafina in the eye. "I know this will come as a shock, Lady Trent, but we can't use Simmons as a witness."

Dylan and Serafina stared at Sir Leo. "But—why not?" Serafina whispered. The expression on Leo's face alarmed her, and she felt fear rising in her breast.

Sir Leo lifted his eyes and said in a voice touched with compassion, "We can't use him because he's dead."

TWENTY-ONE

Serafina felt that she had been struck a hard blow in the pit of her stomach. She stared at Sir Leo, and her voice was thin and strained as she whispered, "Simmons is dead? That—that *can't* be!"

"I'm afraid it is, Lady Trent," Sir Leo said quietly. "You know that I'd been to see him twice to go over his testimony. He was living in a boardinghouse on Oak Street, across from a pub called The White Owl. I must confess that I got to like the fellow. He came from a good home, but he'd made some bad choices and become a criminal. I think he might have been redeemed, really I do! I had him persuaded to go back and make things right with his parents, and I really believe he would have done it."

"But how did he die?" Dylan demanded. He saw that Serafina's face had paled, and he was conscious of a sinking sensation. "What happened to him, Sir Leo?"

"A heart attack," Sir Leo said, sadness in his tone. "I saw him three days ago, and he seemed fine. But when I went back to see him this morning, he was gone."

"Did he have a history of heart trouble?" Serafina asked abruptly.

"No, but the doctor told me that a bad heart can go undetected for some time." Leo leaned forward and said gently, "I'm sorry, Lady Trent.

It's a blow for our case—and a tragedy for a young man who might have had a better life."

For a time Leo and Dylan spoke of the death of Simmons and what it might mean to the case, but Serafina seemed totally overcome by the development. Finally she asked, "Will there be a funeral?"

"Why—yes, there will. I contacted the young man's parents, and they were quite stricken. The Simmonses will pick up the body tomorrow. The funeral will be on Thursday at St. Andrew's Church." He looked at Serafina and said, "There's no need for you to attend, Lady Trent. After all, you never met the man."

Serafina rose and said hurriedly, "We must go, Sir Leo." She moved toward the door, and Dylan hurried after her. Sir Leo watched them go, then shook his head sadly. "Too bad! Oh, too bad!"

Outside, Dylan said nothing but caught a glimpse of Serafina's profile. Her mouth was drawn tightly into a line, and colour was beginning to come back to her cheeks. She stopped abruptly and said, "He was murdered, Dylan."

"What? Simmons, you mean?"

"Yes. It's all too convenient. The one witness who might identify the murderer and he dies five days before the trial."

"You can't know that!"

Serafina stared up at Dylan. "I will know it—if you will help me."

Dylan was baffled but said, "Of course I will. You know that."

"It might land you in jail."

In her voice and in her expression was a determination that Dylan had never seen in her. "I've been there before, me. What about you?"

"I've never been in jail, but what I want to do could get us both there."

"Tell me, then. What's this plan that's going to get us in jail?"

Serafina began to speak rapidly, her eyes locked with Dylan's. Her breast swiftly rose and fell, and when she finished, she gasped and shook her head. "Well, will you do it, Dylan Tremayne?"

"Will I do it?" Dylan smiled. "Well, if the day ever comes when I won't help a beautiful viscountess in a crazy scheme, you can look for me on the floor!"

❦

Dylan drew the team to a halt and looked up at the sign over the pub. "The White Owl," he murmured. He turned his head and studied Serafina, half expecting to see some hesitation in her eyes. But she was looking at the house across from the pub.

"That must be where he lived," she said. She was calm, and Dylan thought about how she had directed their actions. She had insisted that they disguise themselves so that they would not be recognised. Dylan had decided to make them look like elderly people, and on the whole, he felt that he had done a good job. He wore a plain and worn snuff-brown shirt, with old shoes and a broad-brimmed hat to match. Serafina was dressed like a middle-class matron. Her dress was cotton, and its fullness diguised her youthful figure. Dylan had added some lines to her face and hidden her hair under a scarf. The shadows of the evening would also help conceal their true appearance.

"All right, Dylan, let's do it." Serafina started to leap down, but Dylan caught her arm. "Wait a minute, Mother," he grinned. "Remember your age and your rheumatism." He got down in a slow, lumbering movement as if he were in pain and then came to help her down. "Slow and easy, and let me do the talking."

Serafina nodded, and the two made their way up the steps of the brownstone. He knocked on the door, and within three minutes, it opened, and a large woman in a blue dress studied them. "Yes, you want rooms?"

Dylan cupped his hand over his ear and said in a voice cracked and thin, "What's that? Didn't hear you."

"Do you want a room?" the woman said, adding, "I'm Mrs. Williams."

"No, we come about our kin, Mr. Simmons."

The expression on the woman's face changed. "Oh, right. Sorry. Did you want to see him?"

Dylan hunched his back and said loudly, "Oh no, we've come fer 'im."

"Come for him?" Mrs. Williams was surprised. "Why, they're coming for him in the morning."

"We said we'd see to him, ma'am. Me and Mother want to do what we can fer him."

Mrs. Williams was confused, but somehow Dylan persuaded her that they had to remove the body at once. "Why, you can't move him. The two of you can't carry him to that wagon."

"Ain't you mebby got some menfolks who could help? I'd be glad to pay, ma'am."

"Oh, I don't want money." Mrs. Williams hesitated, then nodded. "I'll get my husband and my two boys—and my son-in-law is stout."

"We'd 'preciate it much, ma'am," Dylan said. "Jist have 'em bring the poor feller to the wagon."

No more than twenty minutes later, as the wagon turned down a side street, Serafina leaned back and gave a short laugh. "You are a convincing man, Dylan! They did just as you told them."

Dylan slapped the lines on the team, and as they leapt into a gallop, he said, "Well, being a disreputable actor has some benefits, ay?" He turned to face Serafina and saw that she was alive and excited. "Where now, Lady Trent?"

"Take us home, Dylan." She looked at the form of the dead man under the blanket and then looked forward, her mind working as she planned the rest of their plot.

❧

Night had closed in, and a sliver of a moon threw pale light on Dylan and Serafina as the team pulled to an abrupt halt beside an outbuilding some distance from the darkened main house. It was after midnight, and all were asleep. "Is this it?" Dylan whispered.

"Yes, wait here." Serafina stepped out of the wagon and moved toward the large door that broke the side of the brick structure. Fishing a key from her pocket, she inserted it and pushed the door open. Groping in the darkness, she found the gaslight, and light filled the room. Turning, she went to Dylan, who had gotten out of the wagon. "We'll move him inside."

Dylan rubbed his chin and gave a rather subdued glance at the dark form in the wagon bed. "I'll do it," he said. "Easier for one to handle a deadweight."

"All right."

Dylan moved to the rear of the wagon, grasped the feet of the corpse, and with one heave, lifted the body. Simmons had been a small man, and the weight was no trouble for Dylan. But the odor of the dead man caught in his throat. He moved quickly to the door and, stepping inside, gave a quick look around. It was not a large room, and was dominated by a metal table about three feet high in the centre of the room.

"Put him on the table."

Dylan quickly moved to the metal table and carefully laid the body on it. He gave a convulsive shudder as Serafina removed the blanket. He had seen enough men maimed in battle to endure the sight of torn flesh, and certainly Jack Simmons was not damaged. Indeed, he had been dressed in a rather formal suit. He wore a pair of new patent leather shoes, and his shirt was glistening white. His hair was neatly combed, and his expression was peaceful.

"We need to take his clothes off," Serafina said, her tone business-like. She moved forward and began to undress the corpse, removing his tie first. "Dylan, sit him up while I take off his coat and shirt." When Dylan was slow to follow her instructions, she gave him a surprised look. "Well, come on—help me," she said shortly.

Dylan obeyed, but as they stripped the clothing from the corpse, he felt repulsed. To him it seemed like some sort of violation of the dead man's privacy, though he knew the notion was ridiculous.

After the coat and shirt were off, Serafina said, "Lay him down."

Then she pulled Simmons's trousers off, and as she began removing his underclothing, Dylan protested, "You're not going to leave those on?"

"Certainly not!" Serafina stripped the clothing off expertly, and when the corpse lay without a stitch, she moved to get some instruments from a table. She pulled a white, full-length apron from a hanger, slipped into it, then came back and placed several instruments on a small table. Without a glance at Dylan, she picked up a scalpel and made a Y-shaped cut in the chest and stomach of the dead man. A muffled thud suddenly caught her attention, and she whirled and found Dylan on the floor. He lay on his back, his mouth open, and his skin a faint greenish colour. She checked to see if his head had been hurt, and when she discovered it had not, she turned back to the table. "Well, Mr. Dylan Tremayne, it seems you have a weakness after all." Serafina smiled at the thought, then she began to work swiftly on Mr. Simmons.

⁂

"You'll have to tie his cravat, Dylan. I don't know how."

Moving forward, Dylan did as he was told. His colour was still bad, but he finished the task and then stood back, refusing to look at Serafina. Minutes earlier, he had recovered consciousness, and after taking one look at what was happening to the body on the table, he had fled the room and vomited. Serafina came for him, and he had been forced to look at the neatly stitched Y-shaped pattern on Simmons but had said not a word as he helped Serafina dress him.

"Can you put him back on the wagon alone?" Serafina asked.

"Why couldn't I do that?"

"You don't look well."

"I'm fine—move out of the way!"

Serafina studied Dylan's face. He was different somehow, and she realised that he was humiliated.

"Don't let it trouble you, Dylan," she said. "Many people can't stand to watch an autopsy." She would have said more, but he lifted the corpse and left the room. She followed him and watched as he put the body in the wagon.

"What do we do with him now?" he asked shortly.

"We have to take him to his parents."

Dylan stared at her in outrage. "And tell them what?"

"The truth. That their son was murdered. And we'll convince them that what we did was the right thing."

"Why didn't we go to them earlier?"

"They would never have given their permission for an autopsy. People don't want their loved ones to go through that."

"This is crazy! We'll both go to jail!"

"No, we can do it. I'll go with you." Serafina's voice was hard-edged, and her lips were tight. "We'll convince them that we need to find the murderer."

"What will happen then?"

"I'll convince them to let my father do an autopsy. I don't have any credentials, but he's a recognised authority. He's done many autopsies. Of course, he won't have to do an autopsy because I've done it, and I've saved the evidence I found. That will be enough to prove that Simmons was murdered."

"But—we don't know who did it!"

"No, but this will help Sir Leo get an innocent verdict for Clive."

Dylan listened to her, then dropped his head. "Sorry I let you down. Didn't know I was such a baby!"

"You did fine, Dylan. I've never thanked you for all you've done—but I want you to know I'm more grateful than I can say." Then, as if she'd said more than she'd intended, she said briskly, "Now let's finish this job. The trial starts on Tuesday, and we've got to have all this evidence ready for Sir Leo."

TWENTY-TWO

The trial of Clive Newton began on the eighth day of May 1857. The day began with a warm breeze out of the south, but by ten o'clock rain clouds had gathered, and the spectators—those who did not have umbrellas— were drenched. The crowds swelled and contended over the few public seats in the Old Bailey that were available, and the air within the court-room was filled with expectancy, along with some laughter and loud jest-ing before the trial began. Outside in the street, newsboys were shouting the news of the trial, and the reporters had made it clear in all their sto-ries what was to come.

All of Clive's family were present, and Serafina glanced at them as they sat numbly watching the proceedings. Her father's face was still and fixed in an expressionless mood, but she knew that he was more troubled than she had ever seen him. Her mother was pale as a ghost, and her lips trembled when she tried to speak. Dora, as might be expected of one with such ten-der sensibilities, was so troubled that Serafina wondered if she could make it through the trial. Aunt Bertha, on the other hand, looked angrily at the officers of the court as though she would like to jump into the fray.

Finally the jury filed in and sat in two rows, their backs to some high windows, their faces pointed toward the lawyers' tables. To their right was the dock, which amounted to little more than a small closed-in balcony, its hidden steps leading down to the cells where prisoners were kept. The witness box was opposite the dock. In order to gain entrance, one had to cross the open space and climb some curving steps. The witness then stood isolated, facing the barristers and the public.

Highest of all and behind the witness box, surrounded by carved mahogany panels and seated on plush, was the judge. Serafina studied him carefully, for Sir Leo had told her a great deal about him. Judge Franklin Locke was in his fifties, a tall, lean man with an aquiline-looking face. His eyes were clear grey, bright as broken glass. A dark preoccupation shaded his face, which was marked by will and intelligence. "He's a challenging man," Sir Leo had said, "but he knows the law and plays no favourites."

Serafina shifted her eyes and saw Dylan, who had obtained a seat at the very back of the room. He smiled at her encouragingly, but she found herself unable to return his smile. She turned to the wall opposite the gallery. Everywhere there was a great amount of wooden paneling. It was very imposing, as little like an ordinary room as could be. She felt stifled by the presence of so many people. Every seat was filled. She straightened slightly when an officer stepped forward and said in a high-pitched nasal tone, "The court will come to order. Judge Franklin Locke presiding."

As the preliminaries went on, Serafina studied the jury, and some-how their faces frightened her. They were all men, and she noticed how they kept their eyes fixed on Clive, who stood in the dock. His face was pale, and he had lost weight so that his cheeks had sunken in as well as his eyes. Even as she looked, he turned and caught her eye, and she smiled with a confidence she did not feel.

The preliminaries were finally over, and the prosecution began. The prosecutor, Allen Greer, made his opening statement in a gravelly voice.

"My lord and gentlemen of the jury," he said, his voice seeming to fill the entire courtroom, "this case is a relatively simple one. You will have no difficulty at all arriving at a verdict of guilty. I would that all cases were this simple and easy for a jury."

"Objection, my lord." Sir Leo rose and said, "My worthy opponent is making assumptions. He may well make them, but the jury may not."

Judge Locke, who gave Sir Leo a steady look, said, "Objection sustained. Mr. Greer, you will let the jury arrive at their own conclusion."

Greer smiled at Sir Leo frostily but said, pleasantly enough, "Very well, my lord, I apologise." He then turned to the court and for the next ten minutes traced the crime from beginning to end. He laid out the murder and promised that he would present evidence against Clive Newton that the jury would find interesting. He smiled broadly, adding, "I trust my opponent, Sir Leo, does not object to that phrasing."

"Not at all, Mr. Greer." Sir Leo returned his smile.

"This is not a social event," Judge Locke said, his voice like a knife. "You will refrain from such pleasantries."

Greer was flustered by this and said, "I am finished, Your Honour."

Judge Locke waited until Greer seated himself, then said, "You may make your opening statement, Sir Leo."

Leo rose, and as Serafina studied his face, she marveled at his self-confidence and eagerness. *Why, he's more of an actor than Dylan!* she thought with astonishment. Indeed, Sir Leo laid out his plan to make it impossible for the jury to find Clive anything but innocent in their verdict. Both Serafina and Dylan knew that he was bluffing, but he was without doubt the best bluffer either one of them had ever seen.

After the opening statements, the judge said, "The prosecution may make its case."

Greer rose at once and began by calling a series of witnesses, most of them members of the cast of *Hamlet* playing at the Old Vic. In quick succession Sir William Dowding, Ashley Hamilton, Malcom Gilcrist, and Ives Montgomery gave testimony that amounted to the fact that Clive Newton had indeed been in hot pursuit of the murdered woman, that he had given her gifts, and that they had heard him make a death threat on the night the woman was murdered.

In each case, when it was his turn to cross-examine, Sir Leo flew at his task with a fierce energy. He was a relentless man when he was after a witness, although he had little chance to prove anything. He questioned the witnesses at such length that Greer protested once, "My lord, the defense is badgering these witnesses."

Locke turned to hear Sir Leo's reply, and when Sir Leo simply said, "It is my duty to see that all is brought out," the judge replied, "I think you have done that, Sir Leo."

"Yes, my lord," Sir Leo said and quickly sat back down.

The case for the prosecution went on all day, with only a break for lunch. After the judge had dismissed the court for the day, Serafina went at once and faced Sir Leo. "How was it, Leo?" she asked.

"All I could do was fight for time. In the meanwhile, I suggest you spend your time, perhaps, looking for that man with the steel hook."

Serafina stared at him. "You think that's our only hope, don't you?"

"I have never said anything else, have I, Lady Serafina?" He glanced over and saw the pale faces of the family. "Do what you can to comfort the family and find that man."

❧

The following morning a note came to Sir Leo before he even had his breakfast. It was brought by one of the jailers whom he knew slightly. He took the note, which said: *Give this man some money, Sir Leo, and come at once. I have news.* It was signed by Clive Newton. Sir Leo reached down to his pocket, pulled out a crown, and gave it to the man, who grinned and said, "Thankee, sir. Thankee!"

Sir Leo left the house at once, and upon arriving at the jail was admitted to Clive's cell. As soon as he stepped inside, he saw that there was an electric excitement in Clive's eyes. "What is it, Clive?" he demanded. "It had better be good to make me miss my breakfast."

"Sir Leo, I've thought of the woman's name."

The advocate instantly straightened up. "How did that happen?"

"I can't tell you how it was. I was awake all night, as you can imagine. I finally drifted off to sleep, and some time early this morning I had a dream, but it was more of a memory. I saw myself in the house with that woman, and the man with the steel hook entering the door when she called. When he came in, he said, 'Wot is it you want, Sadie?' That was her name—Sadie." Clive looked at Sir Leo. "Will that help, do you think?"

"It may help a great deal. I'll have to get word to your sister and Dylan. It will be a lot easier for them to find a woman called Sadie and a man with a steel hook than a woman with no name."

He left at once, and Clive watched him go with a bright look of expectation. But he realised that time was against them, and he sat down on the bench. After a long time he prayed, for the first time since he was a boy. "God, I have not been a good man, but you know I didn't harm Kate Fairfield. Give Dylan and Serafina a bit of good sense, Lord."

⁕

Sir Leo saw Serafina come into the courtroom, and out of the corner of his eye, he saw Dylan push and shove his way to one of the coveted seats. He got up and motioned to Serafina, then to Dylan. He led them out into the corridor, where he turned at once and said, "Clive got word to me this morning. He remembered the woman's name."

"That's wonderful!" Serafina exclaimed. "What was it?"

"He said her name was Sadie. That's all he knows. He dreamt it, so it may not be her name at all. I don't trust dreams all that much."

"Well, I do," Dylan said. "The best man in the Bible, in many ways, was Joseph, and they called him a dreamer. I'll go at once."

"I'll go with you," Serafina said. "I can do nothing here."

"I'll need you for a witness before the trial is over, so report in. I'll make sure you have notice before you go on the stand."

"Will the murder of Jack Simmons be of any help?" Dylan asked.

"The prosecution has convinced the judge that his death has nothing to do with the death of Kate Fairfield." Disgust thickened his voice, and he said bitterly, "It's one of those injustices that we find in the halls of justice. The judge said it was hearsay, not admissible in a trial."

"We'll just have to find the woman," Serafina said grimly. "It's our only hope."

The two left, and Sir Leo thought as he watched them go, *They're a strange pair. Different in every way, but God help them to find Sadie!*

❧

As soon as they were outside, Serafina said, "I'm going to send a note to Superintendent Winters."

"What about?"

"He promised to use his office to help find the woman."

"Did he now?"

"Yes. I know it's strange, but he seemed willing to help, and Inspector Grant also. They have many men in the Yard. If they were all looking for a woman named Sadie who lives with a man with a steel hook, they could cover more ground than we do."

"Send them a note. I'm going to put on some old clothes and go at once."

"I'm going with you."

"Go with me where?"

"I want to help you look."

"You can't go dressed like that."

"I'm going, Dylan, so let me hear no more about it!"

"Well, there's an old mule you are. Stubborn as I ever saw. Well, we'll have to get you some old clothes, and you're much too pretty. I'll have to unprettify you a bit." He smiled and said, "That might be fun."

Serafina stared at him, a hot reply on her lips. But this was his world, and she said, "All right. Whatever you say. I'll write the note and have it sent to Mr. Grant."

❧

Serafina had written the note, then gone to Dylan's rooms. Dylan had stopped on the way and bought her some old clothes from a shop specializing in such. She examined herself in a mirror on the wall. She had donned a shapeless grey dress that hid her figure well enough. The shoes had been patent leather once, but now were little more than scraps that she had to tie onto her feet. A ratty-looking shawl was draped around her neck, and Dylan had put a floppy mob cap on her, such as cleaning women wore. She stared at her reflection and then turned to face Dylan. "Will this do?"

"Almost, but you're far too clean." He kept some of his materials for disguises in his room, and he proceeded to dust her hands with something that gave them a grimy appearance. "Hold still now. Your face is far too clean."

Serafina stood still and felt his hands on her face. "Don't paw me!" she said angrily.

"Be quiet, woman, afore I bat you one!" Serafina stared at him, and he laughed. "That's the way you've got to talk. None of your fine English when we're out there."

Serafina saw that her face was grimy, and with the floppy bonnet on, she felt no one would recognise her.

"Rub some of that under your nails so they'll look like you haven't bathed. You really smell too good for a poor woman, but there's nothing we can do about that, is there?"

"Let's go, Dylan. Time is against us."

"Right, you. Come along."

The two left Dylan's apartment and went to the area of Saint Giles. It was another one of the slum areas of London, filled with filthy lanes and decaying tenements. "I was pretty close to some of these folks when I was a thief," he said. Serafina glanced at him and saw he was quite matter-of-fact about that time.

She followed him to a tenement house that seemed to be leaning precariously toward the street. "Still here," he said.

They went inside and were stopped at once by a hulking man with a brutal-looking face. "Wot's it yer want?"

"Come on, Baines. You remember me."

The big man called Baines squinted in a nearsighted fashion. "Why, it's you, ain't it? Where you been? In jail I reckon."

"Don't have time to talk now, Baines. Wot I wants to know is do you know a woman named Sadie who's kept by a man with a steel hook?"

"Wot yer wanna know for?"

"Wot do you care long as I pays?"

Baines stared at him and said, "You allus was a clever one. No, I don't know no such woman, nor no man wiv a steel hook."

"Here's a sovereign for you. There'll be another one just like it if yer find out anything. I'll check with you later on today. Be quick now."

"I keep this sovereign no matter," Baines said threateningly.

"Just find the woman. You'll get another. Maybe two."

Serafina followed after Dylan; she was completely out of her world. Most of the streets were narrow and required careful navigation. All of them were filled with costers, barrows, old clothes carts, peddlers, vegetable wagons, and clusters of people buying, selling, and begging. They all began to look alike to her, and the smell was terrible. Sometimes the pavements were only wide enough to allow for the passage of one person, and the open gutters that meandered through them were filled with the night's waste. The houses seemed to lean out over the streets, so close at the top as to blot out the sky.

Once Serafina stopped and looked at a child sitting in the gutter. The child was difficult to see in the half-light and was dressed in such rags it was impossible to tell whether it was a boy or a girl. A wave of compassion touched her, but Dylan pulled her away, saying, "Come on, woman."

They moved from point to point, each time Dylan finding someone he knew and promising them money if they found a woman named Sadie accompanied by a man with a steel hook. They passed by many prostitutes looking tired and drab. There was little beauty among them. Their hair was lusterless and full of knots, their teeth stained and chipped. They stayed at the job steadily, and finally Dylan turned and said, "You must be exhausted, Viscountess."

"I can go on," Serafina said, although her legs were trembling with fatigue, or perhaps it was emotion. She had never seen such misery or poverty at close hand.

"I have another call to make." He led her through the streets until he found the house where Callie and her brother, Paco, stayed with their mother. When he knocked, it was Paco who answered the door. "Hello, Paco, how are you this morning?"

Paco recognised him but looked past him at Serafina. "Who's she?"

"A friend of mine. Can we come in?"

Paco was suddenly joined by Callie. She had washed her face and donned a dress that was too small for her. "It's you," she said. "Wot is it yer wants?"

"I've come to visit with your mother."

Callie studied him carefully, then her eyes went to Serafina. "Is this 'ere your woman?" she demanded.

Serafina gave a gasp and was about to reply when Dylan dug his elbow into her side. "She's a friend of mine. Her name is Molly."

Serafina saw the girl staring at her in a clinical fashion, and she said weakly, "Hello, Callie."

"Are you 'is woman?"

Serafina was trapped. "Yes," she lied valiantly.

"Your face is dirty. Why don't yer take a bath?"

Suddenly Dylan laughed. "She hates bathing, Callie. Sometimes I just have to hold her down and wash her myself."

"We got some 'ot water if yer wants to wash 'er now."

Dylan was enjoying this, Serafina saw. He turned to her with his blue eyes bright. "You may have something there. What do you think, Molly? Could I wash your face?"

"Leave my face alone," Serafina said through clenched teeth.

"You see? She hates bathing." He looked over and saw Mrs. Montevado. "How are you today, Maria?"

"Much better." Maria Montevado was standing behind a table fixing some food. "The money you brought from the viscountess has been a godsend. We haven't ever eaten so well."

"Oh, she's a generous lady. Not like Molly here. Molly's stingy."

"Wot do you want 'er for if she's dirty and stingy?" Callie demanded.

"Well, I try to get rid of her, but she follows me around. Every time I try to hide from her, she finds me. She's so in love with me, you see, Callie, I just can't get rid of her."

Callie came to stand before Serafina. Only twelve years old, but she had the assurance of a much older person. Life in the streets had taught her that. "Why don't yer be clean and make yourself decent?" she said. "You like dirt?"

Serafina could feel Dylan holding back the laughter that showed in his features. She met his eyes, which were dancing with fun. "He's so pretty, 'e is, I can't bear to do without him, you see."

Callie considered this and said, "You ought to wash. It won't 'urt yer none."

"Will you let me fix you a bite to eat?" Maria asked.

"Oh no, we're in a hurry," Dylan said. He turned to Callie. "Callie, you remember I asked you to look for a man with a steel hook?"

"Yus, I remember that. I couldn't find him, though."

"Well, he lives with a woman called Sadie. She's a bad woman just like he's a bad man." He took a sovereign out of his pocket and held it toward her. "This is for you. If you find him, I'll give you five more just like it."

"Five sovereigns!" Callie exclaimed. She grasped the coin, stared at it, and then looked up at Dylan. "You must be rich."

"No, this is all from the viscountess. She's rich, and beautiful too. Not like ugly Molly here. She bathes a lot too."

"Well, why don't yer get rid of Molly and marry the viscountess?"

"Now there's an idea," Dylan said. "What do you think, Molly?"

Serafina glared at him, then looked over the poor surroundings, the two children, and the woman. The woman had traces of a beauty that had been worn down by life. Her heart smote her as she realised how little she knew about the poor. "I think you could afford more than five if she finds him."

"Ten it is! You see, Molly here is ugly and dirty, but she's got a generous spirit after all. Ten sovereigns if you find our man."

"We'll find 'im," she said, her eyes narrowing. "We'll find him. Don't you worry."

"Remember. You'll find me at the Old Vic Theatre at night. Come early, if you can, before the play starts."

"Wot if I find 'im some morning?"

"Here's my address. You come there and leave me a note. I'll check it every day, and if I get a note, I'll find you at once right here."

Callie nodded, then she turned and gave the sovereign to her mother. The woman said, "God must have sent you, Mr. Dylan."

"Like I say. It's the viscountess's money."

"Then God bless her," Maria Montevado said.

Dylan said, "I hope you find Sadie and the man. Come along, Molly."

They moved toward the door, and Callie came forward. She grabbed Serafina's dress and forced her to turn around. "You're dirty as a pig," she said, "but yer might look all right if you'd wash. You come back 'ere, and I'll 'elp yer look better. Mr. Dylan's too 'andsome to 'ave to have an ugly, dirty woman like you with 'im."

"There's a good offer for you, Molly." Dylan was laughing now, and he pulled her outside. As soon as they were clear, he turned to her and said, "Well, there's a fine young girl, that Callie."

"She's rude!"

"Just honest. Being in the streets makes you that way, I think. But you can see your money has done a good thing for that family."

Serafina stared at him and finally mustered a smile. "You enjoyed that, didn't you?"

"Me? I felt so sorry for you I could hardly keep from crying—and you making enough noise grinding your old teeth!"

"Liar!"

"I suppose I am. Let's move on. We'll get something to eat, and then we'll find some more people to ask."

Serafina trudged along, so weary she had to hold to his arm. Hope burned faintly within her, and she knew that without Dylan they would have no hope at all.

✦ TWENTY-THREE ✦

On Thursday afternoon the prosecution finally concluded its case. Allen Greer said in a voice edged with bad temper, "That is the case for the prosecution, my lord—and we might have ended much sooner if my worthy opponent had not kept interrupting with meaningless remarks."

Judge Franklin Locke gave Greer a look that could have cut to the heart. "If there is any rebuke to be made, Mr. Greer, I will be the one to make it."

"Yes, Your Honour," Greer muttered. He turned to the jury and grinned slightly, then took his seat.

"You may speak for the defendant, Sir Leo."

Leo rose slowly to his feet, his face filled with confidence, but then it always was no matter how poor a chance he had of getting his man off. He began by saying, "My lord, I will call as my first witness Mr. James Barden."

Barden, the butler, came in and took his place in the witness box. "You have been the butler for some time at the Newton household, Mr. Barden. Is that correct?"

"Yes, sir." Barden's face was pale, and he answered nervously.

"During this time you have had opportunities to observe the defendant, Mr. Clive Newton, very closely."

"Oh yes, sir. Since he was a small boy."

"Do you think Mr. Clive could be described as an evil man?"

"Objection!" Greer rose at once and said, "My worthy opponent is putting words in the witness's mouth."

"Sustained. Rephrase your question, Sir Leo."

Leo artfully changed the question so that it meant exactly the same thing. He kept the butler on the stand as long as possible until the jury began shifting nervously, then he said, "Do you have any questions, Mr. Greer?"

"No. There's no need. As we all know, any good servant will say nothing evil about his employer."

A murmur went through the room, but Sir Leo ignored it. He waited until Barden was gone and then started calling witnesses from the Newton household.

The trial proceeded at a snail's pace, and finally, after the judge dismissed the court with the notice that the trial would begin the next morning at ten o'clock, Greer moved over and said, "Well, Sir Leo, I don't believe I've ever seen a worse defense in my life."

Sir Leo simply smiled. "We will see, shall we not?"

"You don't have any secret weapons, Leo. Why don't you admit it and let the poor man confess everything, and we can all go home?"

"I don't think it will happen that way."

Greer shook his head and, going back to his desk, picked up his papers. As he stepped outside the courtroom, he saw Superintendent Winters. Winters moved toward him, asking, "How do you think it's going?"

"Very well for the prosecution."

Winters chewed his lower lip and sighed heavily as he said, "I feel sorry for the family. You know, Mr. Greer, one family member can destroy the rest. I can't think what Sir Leo is going to put up for a real defense."

"Oh, he has no defense to make. There's no way he can deny the evidence we have. He'll call in a whole parade of character witnesses. I've noticed he has put the Viscountess Trent on the list."

"I suppose just as a character witness for her brother."

"What else could she be there for?"

"Well, without giving away any secrets, Allen, she's playing detective."

"I beg your pardon?"

"She's been scraping around trying to find some sort of evidence that would free her brother. Made a regular nuisance of herself. If she weren't a viscountess, I would have stopped her long ago."

Greer grinned. "You can't afford to offend any of the nobility, can you, William? I mean, after all, the gossip is that you're right on the brink of receiving your knighthood."

"I can't speak about that."

"Oh, of course not. But after you become *Sir* William, things will be different."

Winters shook his head and looked rather downcast. "I've told you before, Allen. My wife is more ambitious than I am. I'd be content to stay at the Yard as superintendent, but she has political ideas. She wants me in the House of Lords. Not what I would like"—he grinned ruefully—"but we have to humour our wives, don't we now?"

"I don't."

"Oh, that's right. You don't have a wife."

"Well, there are times when I wish—" He broke off suddenly and said, "I'll be interested to see what the defense has. We've got this case nailed down, and I need a victory."

"Good publicity, eh? Especially with as spectacular a case as it is. Well, you needn't worry. We'll win this one."

❧

Serafina had hurried down for breakfast so that she could meet Dylan by eight o'clock and the two could continue their search. She was met by Louisa, her maid, who said, "There's a letter for you, ma'am."

"A letter? The post hasn't come yet."

"No, ma'am, it was slipped under the door."

Serafina took the envelope. Written on it in capital letters was her name: *Viscountess Serafina Trent.* The writing was blunt and blocky, impossible to recognise. Moving toward the smaller of the two dining rooms, she opened the envelope and pulled out a single sheet of paper. On it were written the words: *If you don't stop trying to get your brother off, something very bad is going to happen to your son. This is all the warning you will receive.*

A chill suddenly ran through Serafina. She stopped dead and read the message again, her hands unsteady.

"Is it bad news, Viscountess?"

"Oh, Louisa, never mind. I'm going to skip breakfast this morning." She moved to the hallway, picked up a cloak that she kept there, donned a hat, and left the house. Albert had the carriage all ready, and she said quickly, "Take me to Mr. Tremayne's house, please, Albert."

"Yes, Viscountess."

Serafina got into the carriage and leaned back. She put the letter back in the envelope and held tightly to it. The warning had shaken her in a way that she had never experienced before. She considered the idea of going to the Yard and telling Superintendent Winters or Mr. Grant what had happened, but she finally decided she would see Dylan first.

When she reached his house, she did not wait for Albert to help her. "Wait for me, Albert. I don't know how long I'll be."

"Yes, ma'am."

Serafina entered the house, walked to Dylan's room, and knocked on the door. He opened it almost immediately, and she said, "Dylan, something's happened."

Dylan stepped aside and scanned Serafina's face. She was more troubled than he had ever seen her. "What is it, Viscountess?"

"It's this." Serafina handed the note to Dylan, and he opened it and read it swiftly. "We must be getting close, Serafina. Whoever sent this knows what we've been doing."

"I don't know what to do. We need to find this woman Sadie, or Clive will die." She looked up, and fear was reflected in her violet eyes. "But I can't risk David's life."

"No, you can't do that," Dylan said. He stood there for a moment and then said, "We must protect David, but we're the only hope Clive has."

Serafina seemed incapable of clear thought. It was a new experience for her, but then she had never had her child threatened before. "I—I don't know what to do!"

A decision came to Dylan. "I think I have something that will answer. Don't be afraid!"

"I can't help it."

"Be of good courage. The Lord will strengthen your heart. I know you don't believe that now, but I do. So I'll just believe for both of us. Is your carriage outside?"

"Yes."

"Follow me, then. I think there's something we can do."

Serafina realised at that instant how dependent she had become upon Dylan. She, who had never wanted to depend on anybody and had prided herself on her ability to handle problems, suddenly felt as helpless as a child. She went outside, and as Dylan handed her into the carriage, she heard him give an address to Albert. Then he got in beside her and turned to face her as the carriage started out. "We've got to protect David, and we can't stay with him all the time and hunt for the witness, but there's one thing we can do. Some time ago I met a man called Lorenzo Pike. He was an expert thief and never once was caught. I knew what he was, though, and somehow we became friends. Lorenzo's wife grew very ill. I went to visit them many times, and while I was there sharing the Gospel with her, Lorenzo listened. To make a long story short, Lorenzo gave his heart to the Lord, and he's been a miracle to watch."

"Did he . . . stop being a burglar?"

"Indeed, he did! He bought into an establishment that sells and repairs locks and safes. He was good at that, him. He didn't need any education whatsoever. He has a friend called Yago the Gyp. He's a gypsy. He was Lorenzo's accomplice, but Lorenzo, after he found the Lord, bore witness to Gyp, and he also gave his heart to Christ, and now the two men are in business together."

"But how can they help us?"

"They were both thieves and they had to be experts to stay out of prison as long as they did. Their hearing is exceptional, they can see like eagles, and they're strong, tough men, able to handle any sort of trouble. I'm going to ask them, with your permission, that is, if they will be David's bodyguards while the trial lasts."

"You'll have to think for us, Dylan," Serafina whispered. "I can't think for myself, it seems."

He gave her a look filled with compassion, but his own eyes were bright with anger. "It's sad you are, and so am I—but I'm angry as well. I fight against being angry, but when I think of someone harming David, my heart is filled with murder. Deep down I've got fire like an inferno, and I can feel it rising to my brain. I want to take the man who wrote this note and drive a sword through his heart!"

Serafina was watching Dylan with something like shock. She whispered, "I feel something like that."

Taking a long breath, Dylan said, "It's going to be all right." He spoke of how able the two men were until they pulled up in front of a locksmith shop. "Lorenzo and his wife live above the shop with their three children. The shop won't be open because Lorenzo has a religious service at this time every week."

"We'll have to wait until it's over," Serafina said rather timidly.

"Not at all. We'll just join right in. Come you now." He stepped down, helped her out, and said, "There's a pub down the street, Albert. Go get yourself something to eat. We'll be a little while here." He flipped a coin up, and Albert caught it expertly. "Thank you, sir."

As they went up the stairs that led to the apartment over the shop, Serafina heard singing.

"They've already started."

"Can't we wait out here?"

"No, we'll go inside. It'll be fine."

The two knocked on the door, and it was answered by a large woman with a broad face and a generous mouth. Her eyes lit up at the sight of Dylan. "Why, it's you, Mr. Tremayne. Come in. We've just started."

"This is Viscountess Serafina Trent, Dorcas. Viscountess, this is Mrs. Dorcas Pike."

"I'm happy to meet you, ma'am. Come inside, and you can join in the service. I suppose it's Lorenzo you'll be wanting to see."

"Yes, but we can wait."

Serafina accompanied him into a very large room that was packed with people. At least thirty people were there, and several of them had instruments—a trumpet, a zither, a bass drum. She glanced at them, then put her eyes on a dark-featured man with black curly hair seated at a small organ.

Every eye turned to them, and Lorenzo Pike announced in stentorian tones, "Well, bless my soul, it's me dear friend Dylan Tremayne and his lady! Come in, beloved saints!" Pike was a very large man with merry blue eyes. Turning to the congregation, he boomed, "This 'ere is the dear servant of God that wot taught me of my wicked ways and led me to Jesus. Hallelujah! He's an actor now, but we must forgive 'im for his ungodly callin', for God can use even an actor."

"This is Serafina Trent, Lorenzo." Dylan grinned. "She's not an actress, I must say."

"Sister, we welcomes you to the meeting of the Church of the Living God." Lorenzo was wearing his best, a grey suit with a colourful red tie, and his hair was slicked down. He was obviously tremendously strong. His voice boomed, filling the room.

"Dearly beloved, let us rejoice that our dear brother and sister have found their way and that they, too, will have a home in the New Jerusalem. They will be there with all the saints when the rivers of water flow down from the throne. Hallelujah! Now then, we will sing the songs of Zion. Lift up your heads and your hearts and your voices, saints of God."

The singing was like nothing Serafina had ever heard. The instrumentalists were not the most accomplished, but they were earnest and made up in volume what they lacked in skill.

The first hymn was one that Serafina had never heard. The voice of Lorenzo Pike rose mightily:

Come, all ye soldiers of Jesus the Christ,
Come march to glory!
Our foes are defeated,
The Lord He is King!
Come march to glory!

And then came the chorus, at which the bass drum almost drowned
out the voices.

All praise to the King!
May He ever reign!
Praise His holy name forever!
Hallelujah! Hallelujah!
Oh, blessed be God
And the Lamb forever!

Serafina stood with the others, for they all remained standing, and
did not know what to think of such a service. She had been in her youth,
though not lately, to Anglican services, in which all was controlled and
peaceful and in order. This group of people, most of them in poor dress,
had faces shining with excitement. They lifted up their voices with enthusiasm, and this was obviously a thing of joy and a delight for them.

Serafina turned to watch Dylan and saw that he was enjoying himself immensely. She could not decide whether it was because he simply
enjoyed this kind of service or because he was the kind of man who could
fit into any situation. She suddenly decided it was the latter. He could
behave at an Anglican church with all propriety, but here propriety didn't
seem to matter much.

Again and again different songs and hymns of praise filled the room,
and despite herself Serafina was impressed by the earnestness these people
had. She had never seen people who enjoyed their religion so much!

The song service ended, and Lorenzo Pike stood up. He evidently
was the preacher of this group, and for thirty minutes he spoke, waving

8

his arms, pumping them up and down, lifting them over his head, and quoting innumerable Scriptures, most of which she did not know. She also did not understand his sermon, because his text was from the book of Revelation, but over and over again she heard the refrain, "Praise to the Lord Jesus. Praise to the Lord Jesus."

Finally the sermon was over, and she remained by Dylan's side as the crowd filed out. Many of them came over to shake hands with the visitors.

Lorenzo came forward along with the organist. "Miss Trent, this is my good friend Yago, sometimes called the Gyp. He also has been washed in the blood of the Lamb and is now a servant of the King."

"Happy to know you, ma'am," Gyp said. He was a smaller man than Lorenzo, but his lean body looked very strong and able, and his eyes were sharp as gimlets.

"Did you get a blessing from the service, my sister?" Lorenzo demanded, smiling at Serafina.

"Why, yes, I did. I've never been to a service like it."

"Well, blessings on thee, sister. You must come again, and we will continue our series of messages on the Revelation."

"We have a favour to ask of you, Lorenzo, and you, too, Gyp."

"Well, I was a black and awful sinner when you found me, Brother Dylan. You showed me the doorway to the kingdom of God's heaven. How I praise the day, and now am grateful indeed to return the favour. What can we do for you?"

Dylan carefully explained the situation. The two men listened without saying a word as Dylan spoke of Clive's plight and how he was certain to be convicted unless a witness were found to save him. "Her name is Sadie, and her man has a steel hook for a right hand."

"Don't know such a bloke," Gyp said, "but I can ask around."

"We can do that, but the viscountess here has received a threat against her son. We need someone to come to the house and protect the boy while we're searching for this witness. One of you could watch during the day, the other at night. You two could do more than a whole troop of policemen."

"It's a big favour to ask," Serafina said.

"Why, bless you, ma'am." Lorenzo nodded his head violently. "It's little enough for a brother in the Lord to ask of Gyp and me. We'll be glad to do it, won't we?"

"Nobody will get at the boy. I learnt some pretty mean, vicious tricks during my life as a sinner," Gyp said, "but now I'll have a chance to use them in the service of the Lord."

Serafina gave them her address, and they said, "We'll be there in an hour. You rest your spirit in the Lord, Sister Trent. The boy will be safe as if he was in the portals of heaven."

Dylan led Serafina out then, and as soon as they were outside, she said, "That was a strange experience."

"But it was a good one. No one will ever get near David. If they do," he said rather grimly, "it will be the worse for them."

The two left at once, and as they pulled away, Serafina was thinking of the enthusiasm with which the people had sung. *We're washed in the blood. We're soldiers of Jesus.* She had sung no hymns like that or, indeed, of any kind for years, but somehow a confidence came to her as she sat beside Dylan. "They'll take care of David, won't they?"

"They're better than an army for that kind of work. No one will see them until they try to harm David, and then," he said grimly, "the roof will fall down on them."

TWENTY-FOUR

As Matthew Grant drew the razor down across his face, he heard a tiny squeaking noise, and looking down he saw a mouse looking up at him. "Well, there you are," he said, a smile touching his lips. "You're getting to be quite a bold little beggar."

He cleaned the razor by drawing it across a towel, splashed water onto his face, and then dried it off. Turning, he moved to the desk, where he opened his box and pulled out a piece of cheese. Breaking off a tiny morsel, he came back and, leaning over, put the morsel before the mouse and watched. The mouse was a sleek grey with shiny black eyes, and for a moment she sat up with her paws folded, looking up at the man. To Grant she looked like a supplicant begging for a favour, and he smiled as she dropped onto all fours and moved over to the cheese and picked it up. She began turning the cheese rapidly, nibbling at it in tiny bites and pausing from time to time. Finally, when she had reduced the cheese to a small size, she took it in her mouth and whisked away to the hole in the baseboard that led to her nest.

"I must be losing my mind, becoming attached to vermin." Grant spoke the words aloud. As he straightened and moved toward the wardrobe that held his clothing, it occurred to him that there was probably no other man in London who had no companion but a mouse. The

298

tiny creature had appeared a month ago, and Grant, who had never had a pet in his entire life, on a whim put a bit of cheese down and then watched as she ate it. He had noticed then that she was a pregnant mother, and he found himself touched by her. As he opened the door of the wardrobe, he remembered vividly how he had been drawn into some sort of relationship with the tiny creature.

He had few friends and no family at all. His life was consumed by his work, and by some strange twist he had become attached to the mouse and had fed her. She would come out when he was seated in his chair, sitting up and folding her paws, her bright eyes expectant. Now he thought, *A fine thing when the closest friend a man has in his life is a mouse.* His thought did not trouble him, however, but then his lips turned upward in a smile, and he ran his hand through his hair. *The superintendent would be shocked to know that I have a gentle streak, and so would a lot of thieves and murderers in London. Old Matthew Grant's gone silly over a mouse.*

Putting those thoughts behind him, he paused before the wardrobe. All of his clothing was well worn, for he seldom bought new clothes. He had three suits that he wore on the job, and one suit that he wore for formal occasions, funerals, or the like.

Grant reached toward the best garment—an expensive grey suit—and then paused, his brow furrowed.

Who do you think you're going to impress? The thought touched his mind, and he moved his head as if to shake it off. He was a man of intense reality, and ignoring the expensive suit, he picked out a simple outfit and began to put it on. He knew himself well, and he realised why he had almost put on clothing he hardly ever wore. He was going to the Newton house, and his first impulse had been to wear his best and impress them.

Don't be a fool, Grant warned himself. *They're quality people and are not going to be impressed by a policeman no matter what he wears.* Quickly he put on the brown suit, added a dark blue tie, and then prepared to leave his room. He stopped by the mirror, however, and took one look, studying his squarish, stubborn-looking face, the silver hair, and the deep-set and wide-spaced hazel eyes. He suddenly laughed and spoke to his image. "So you're going to see Dora Newton again, and you're going to have something to say to the whole family. They'll probably have the butler show you out." Turning quickly, he left the room and walked rapidly along the sidewalk. It was midafternoon now, and the sun was bright. He passed by a group of sparrows on the curb. They were fighting over a bit of bread, it seemed, and Grant smiled. *Well, birds in their nest don't agree, so why should man be any different?*

Twenty minutes later he was standing at the front door of the Newton house. He took a deep breath and discovered that he felt anxiety running along his nerves. This was so unusual that he blinked, and for a moment did not knock. *You've gone after murderers and the worst in dark alleys, but now you're afraid to face a slip of a woman and her family?* A wry smile touched his lips. Firmly he reached out and knocked on the door. Almost at once Barden, the butler, answered it. "Inspector Grant," Barden said. "Won't you come in?"

"I'd like to see Mr. Newton if I could."

"The family are in the drawing room. If you'll wait here, Inspector, I'll see if they will receive you."

"Thank you, Barden."

Looking at the fine paintings in the foyer as he waited, Grant was impressed with the opulence of it all. He had known no other people in the very upper registers of society, and he felt out of place and awkward.

Barden came back and nodded. "The family will be glad to see you, Inspector. If you'll come this way."

"Thank you, Barden." Grant followed the butler down the hall and then entered a door that led to a rather large room. He had only been in the study of the Newton house and was impressed by the richness of the furniture, the paintings on the wall, and the thick drapes that were drawn back to allow the sunlight to shine upon the thick Persian carpet.

"I apologise for calling without notice," Grant said at once to

Septimus Newton, who had risen. He looked around and saw that the rest of the family was all there. *Just as well that I tell it to all of them,* he thought.

"We're glad to have you, Inspector. Is this an official visit?"

"No, sir, it's not. My visit has nothing to do with your son."

"Won't you sit down," Mrs. Newton said.

"Thank you," Grant said and took a seat on the very edge of a Queen Anne chair that seemed too delicate for furniture. He glanced over at Dora, and she smiled at him winningly.

"I have never felt so awkward in my life," Grant said, and his eyes swept the entire group. He saw that Lady Bertha Mulvane was staring at him with dislike. *She doesn't like policemen,* he thought, and then his eyes went to Alberta Newton, who was watching him with a nervous manner.

Septimus sat back down next to his daughter the viscountess, and Grant saw that she was watching him narrowly. She said, "There's no need to be nervous, Inspector."

His eyes went to Dora. "I try not to intefere with anyone's personal life, but something has come to my attention that I feel obligated to tell you." He hesitated and said, "It concerns something about Sir Aaron Digby that I think you should know."

"Why in the world would you be coming to us with this?" Bertha burst out. "Surely it's none of your business."

"You're right, ma'am, it is not, but if I see a tragedy about to happen, I like to think I wouldn't let my personal feelings keep me from stepping in."

"What's the tragedy you're speaking of, Inspector?" Serafina asked. She had not liked Grant at first, but the man had grown on her. There was certainly a stubbornness in him, and she had sensed that he distrusted and even disliked members of the aristocracy. But Dora had told her how kind he had been on two occasions, and now she studied the policeman carefully. "I've found out that if you have something to say to someone, it's best just to speak it out."

"Thank you, Viscountess. I believe you're right. Well, here it is, then.

I regret to tell you that your daughter will be ruined if she marries Sir Aaron Digby."

Everyone in the room stared at him, and Bertha gasped and cried out, "You're meddling in a family affair!"

"Yes, I know I am, but I would hate to see any woman marry Digby."

"What have you learnt about him?" Serafina asked. She was watching Dora, who was wide-eyed and seemingly could not speak.

"Sir Aaron Digby has a terrible record. The man is a sadist. He has two daughters who have been taken to the hospital since childhood many times, both of them, with bruises and even wounds. The same is true for his wife. The poor woman was battered, and Digby managed to cover it up by bribing people. This all came to my attention," he said, "through a man named Gerald James. He was a servant in Digby's household, and he was an eyewitness on at least three occasions when Digby beat the women severely. He tried to protest, and Digby fired him and hired men to beat him rather badly."

"I can't believe it!" Alberta Newton cried. "He seems like such a nice man."

"There's more," Grant said. "In addition to being a woman beater, he's a fortune hunter. All he had was his title before he married. He took all of his wife's money and squandered it. I traced some of it. I'm afraid I don't like to mention what he did with it, but there were women involved and gambling. Now he's in the hands of some very dangerous money-lenders. I spoke with one of them in my investigation, and he said that Digby was being threatened by other moneylenders. That's the man who wants to marry your daughter, Mr. Newton. I apologise for giving you this information."

"No, don't apologise," Dora cried. She stood up and came over and stood in front of Grant. "It was a noble thing, and I know it must have been very difficult for you."

Grant swallowed as he looked at the young woman and said, "It was difficult. No man likes to interfere in the affairs of others."

Septimus came then and put out his hand. "I thank you, Inspector, for coming. It would have been terrible for Dora to have married a man like this."

"I'd like to know why you have done this," Bertha demanded. She saw the futility of trying to go against the facts of Grant's findings, but still there was a bitter look on her face as she stared at the policeman.

A silence fell on the room, and then Dora turned and faced her aunt for a moment. "He did it for me, Aunt Bertha." Turning back, she looked up at Grant. "Isn't that true, Matthew?"

"Yes, it is."

Serafina smiled and came over and offered her hand. "I thank you very much. You've done the family a great service, Inspector Grant."

❧

"How are you, Callie?" Dylan was surprised to find Callie at his door, but he smiled and said, "Come in and have a seat."

Callie wore the same outfit she always wore, probably the only one she had, and she looked exhausted. There were dark circles under her eyes, and her speech was slower than usual.

Callie stepped inside, and as soon as Dylan closed the door, she said, "I found 'er and 'im too!"

For a moment Dylan could not imagine what she meant, and then his eyes narrowed. "You mean you found the woman named Sadie?"

"Yus, I found 'er, and she lives with a man wot's got a steel 'ook instead of a 'and."

"Where is she, Callie? How did you find her?"

Callie grinned then, in spite of the fatigue that was slowing her down. "I been looking, me and Paco, everywhere we could. I went all over to different districts, and I finally 'eard about a dolly mop named Sadie."

Dylan knew that *dolly mop* was a term used to describe the lowest class of prostitute. "Where did you find her?"

"I goes over to the east side, but I didn't find nuffin'. Finally I goes to Seven Dials and asked everybody wot I could think of, but it was over in the west end that I runs 'cross a woman wot used ter live next to us. I asked 'er about a woman named Sadie and a man wif a steel 'ook. She wanted money, and I had to give 'er the sovereign you guv me 'fore she'd tell me."

"You shall have it back," Dylan said. "What did you do then?"

"I gives 'er the sovereign, and then I goes to the place where she said Sadie lived with her man. I didn't want to ask too much, but I found out that the man with the steel 'ook has been real sick. Sadie's been going out taking men to keep 'em in food."

"And you found the house where they live?"

"Yus," she said. "I can take you to it."

"Right, you!"

"And what about them sovereigns?"

"Ten sovereigns, wasn't it? You'll have them today. I'll have to go by the bank and get them. Wait, we need to find the viscountess. You look so tired. Let's get you something to eat, then I'll give you the sovereigns."

"I'm a mite hungry," she confessed, "and tired too. But just think what I can buy for Mum wif ten sovereigns."

"You've done well, girl. Better than anybody. You found the woman when the rest of us all failed."

"You say I done good?"

"Very well indeed. I'm so proud of you! We'll have to buy you a new outfit, and Paco a new outfit, and we'll go out and celebrate. Take your mother, too, if she's able. If not, we'll bring her some good food back."

The girl smiled then, and he noted again her eyes, the colour of lapis lazuli, a rich azure blue, and saw that when she filled out, she had the potential of being a great beauty. Dylan decided in his heart that this girl would *not* go on the streets. He and the viscountess would see to that. "Come along, then. We'll get you something to eat. What would you fancy?"

"An eel pie."

Dylan laughed. He felt exultant and said, "We'll get it, and then I'll go to the bank, and you'll be ten sovereigns richer."

"This is the place that Callie said Sadie lived with the man with the steel hook." Dylan turned to see Serafina's reaction.

"It's a terrible place."

"Yes, it is." Dylan looked up at the leaning tenement. It looked as if it were about to fall down. "Let's find out if Callie's right."

"I pray that she is."

Dylan suddenly looked at her and smiled. "You pray that she's right? That's a good sign, isn't it?"

"I—I didn't mean that literally."

"Well, I do. Come along, Serafina."

The two entered the house and climbed a set of creaking stairs. Dylan knocked at the first door, and no one answered. Moving over, he tried another door, and after his knock, a voice inside said, "Wot do yer want?"

"I'm looking for Sadie."

The door opened then, and a woman stood there. She was large and gaunt, and her hair was unclean. She had lost most traces of her early beauty, but some of it was still there. "Who are you? Wot are you doing 'ere?" The woman looked over Dylan's shoulder at Serafina. "Why does you bring a woman 'ere for?"

"Is your name Sadie?"

"Wot's it to yer?"

"I think we might do you some good, Sadie."

"That ain't likely. You rich nobs come 'ere to satisfy your appetites, not to do me no good."

"Are you living with a man here with a hook on his right arm?"

Something like panic touched Sadie's eyes. "'E ain't done nothing! 'E's been here for two weeks, too sick to get out of bed. 'E couldn't hurt nobody or steal nothin'."

"I'm sorry to hear he's sick," Dylan said. "I don't know his name."

"'Is name is Oscar Bent. Wot do you care for? You ain't a copper."

"No, we're not the police. Sadie, could we step inside?"

"You might as well," she said, her voice filled with despair.

They went inside the room and saw a man lying on the bed. His eyes were closed, and he had not shaved in some time. Both arms were lying across his breast, and a steel hook glinted where his right hand should have been.

Sadie backed up as if to protect herself. "Wot do yer want? We ain't got nothing, and he's like to die."

"He needs to be in the hospital," Serafina said abruptly. She was touched by the awfulness of the situation. The woman was obviously worn out and had been misused, and the man, indeed, might even be dying. "We want you to help us," Serafina said, stepping closer to the woman. "And I hope we can help you."

"Me 'elp you? How could I 'elp you?"

"Several weeks ago a young man came here. You picked him up on the street, and he was drunk."

"I sees lots of drunks. Was 'e quality like you?"

"Yes, he was. He's not a tall man, and he has light brown hair and brown eyes and he's very handsome."

"Wot's it to you if I seen 'im?"

Serafina decided to be totally honest with the woman. "The man is my brother. He's being tried right now for the murder of a woman, but the murder took place while Clive says he was with someone. He didn't remember your name or where he was, he was so intoxicated. So you see, we've been looking for you for some time, and now we're going to ask you if you'll help us."

"And 'ow could such as me 'elp you?" Sadie demanded wearily. "I ain't got nothing to 'elp nobody."

"Would you be willing to testify that my brother was with you that night?"

"You means go afore a judge? I'd be afeared to do that!"

"You needn't be afraid, Sadie," Dylan said quickly. "You'll be doing the court a favour."

The man on the couch started to cough, and the woman turned and went over to him. She poured something into a glass and pulled him into an upright position. "Drink this, Oscar. It'll do you good." The man opened his eyes and reached out and took the glass. He managed to get most of it down, and then when she took the glass, he reached up and touched her cheek. "Thank you, Sadie. You're good to me."

"Lay down and try to sleep," Sadie said. She laid the man down carefully, and there was obvious affection in her, as well as worry. She turned again and came to stand before the two. "I remember 'im, all right. Wot will I get out of it?"

Quickly Serafina said, "We can't pay you money for your testimony, but I will tell you this. If you do testify, I will be very grateful to you."

"So will I, Sadie. We'll get a doctor here to look at Oscar, and if he says that he needs to be in a hospital, we'll see that he goes there. Things will be better for you both. And you'll save a good young man's life. Will you do it?"

Sadie looked at the two and then at the man. "If it'll get my man in a 'ospital, I'll do it."

"Good! We'll get some proper clothes for you to wear to the court," Dylan said.

"And we'll have a doctor here to look at your—" She started to say *husband* but faltered. "To look at Oscar, and we'll put him in the hospital if that's what the doctor says."

Sadie stared at the two, and suddenly tears came into her eyes. She dashed them away, saying, "Look at that. I ain't cried in many a year, but nobody ain't 'elped us. I still don't believe it."

"You can believe it," Serafina said. She came forward and put her hand on the woman's shoulder. "It will be all right. You'll see. We'll go find a doctor right now."

The two left then, and when they got into the carriage, Serafina was quiet. Dylan did not disturb her, but he could see that the viscountess had been moved by the pitiful condition of the two.

Serafina said, "She loves him, doesn't she?"

"She obviously has an affection."

Serafina seemed to be unable to speak for a moment. "It's hard for me to see how such people can have any love left in them. It seems it all would have been drained out by the hardness of their lives."

"I've seen love in strange places, but she does care for him, and he for her, it seems."

Serafina was quiet again, and finally she straightened up in the seat and turned to face him. "I know you think I'm cold, Dylan, but I wasn't always that way."

"What happened, Serafina?" Dylan's voice was gentle, for he saw she was struggling to get something out.

"I had a terrible marriage." The words came slowly, and Serafina had to clear her throat. "Everyone in the family thought Charles was such a wonderful match. He was rich, he had a title, and his family was high on the social scale. And he had a romantic way about him when he was courting me. I thought I was in love with him, but I was wrong."

Dylan saw that tears welled in Serafina's eyes. He pulled his handkerchief out of his breast pocket and said, "Here, take this."

"Thank you." Serafina wiped her eyes, then took a deep breath, but her voice was still unsteady as she said, "He married me to get an heir. He didn't love me." A touch of bitterness came to her then. "I was a brood mare to him. He liked—" Her voice broke, and she shook her head. "I hate to say this, but he liked . . . boys. After David was born, as he began to grow up, I was terrified that he would molest our son."

"How terrible for you!"

"I stayed with David constantly to give him no chance for that."

"How did he die, Serafina?"

"A man came to the house, a violent, angry man. I heard them shouting, and I listened at the door. The man accused Charles of molesting his son and ruining his life. I heard Charles laugh at him, and then the man cried out, and there was the sound of crashing. They had a terrible fight. When I went in, the man was standing over Charles, who was on his back and had a terrible wound. The man didn't bother me. He just ran away."

"It must have been awful for you."

"Everyone thought I had done it. They didn't believe my story about a man coming in, but I knew what that man suffered, so I refused to tell them what he looked like."

"I think you did the right thing."

"So if I'm cold, it's because of those terrible days. I—I feel like I'm frozen sometimes."

Dylan suddenly took her hand. He held it with both of his and said, "God will be with you, Serafina. We found the witness that can save Clive, and the Lord God is going to save you. He's going to take away those old memories and give you a rich, full life."

Serafina stared at him in disbelief, but with hope in her eyes. "Do you really think so, Dylan?"

"Of course I think so. God's not finished with either one of us yet. Now," he said, "we've got to get news to Sir Leo that we've found the witness."

"He'll be glad to have some ammunition for the battle, won't he?"

"I think he will, and it's going to be a glorious day when Clive walks out of that courtroom a free man! If you are having my opinion, the Lord God is giving you a miracle."

❧ TWENTY-FIVE ❧

As soon as Grant stepped into the superintendent's office, he saw that Winters was in a good mood. "Good morning, sir," he said at once.

"Well, good morning, Inspector Grant. How are you this fine morning?"

"I'm fine, sir." Grant smiled and said, "I suppose congratulations are in order. I understand that you're to be knighted very soon."

"Oh, well, that's true enough, but it means little. After all, it just means that you put a *Sir* in front of my name. I don't know if that's any great advantage to a man. But it's what my wife's been trying to bring about for quite a while. Sit down, Grant, and tell me what's going on."

Grant took a seat and went over three cases that he had been working on. He saw that the inspector was paying close attention to him, and finally he said, "Well, I have a bit of personal news."

"I can see that you look different. What's going on? Don't tell me you've found a lady that pleases you."

"Indeed, I have, Inspector."

"Well, it's about time. You've lived alone for so long I had about given up on you as a crusty old bachelor. I don't suppose I know the lady."

"Yes, you do, sir. It's Dora Newton."

Winters opened his eyes wide. "Well," he said, "that *is* a surprise. You're actually courting her?"

"I made my intentions known to her father and to the family yesterday."

"It's a wonder they didn't throw you out. A policeman doesn't rank very high on the social scale."

"That's true enough, sir, but I think highly of the young lady, and it seems she likes me too."

Winters turned his head to one side and studied Grant. He asked, "Doesn't she blame you for arresting her brother?"

"Oh no, sir. But her brother's not guilty."

"Why do you say that?" Winters's voice was sharp. "We have all the evidence. Allen Greer says it's a certain thing that he'll be found guilty."

"The woman's been found, sir—the witness that the viscountess and Dylan Tremayne have been looking for."

"What? She's actually been found?"

"Yes, sir, and she'll testify in court that young Newton was with her at the time the murder was committed. Sir Leo says the case will be dismissed for lack of evidence. But there's more than that."

"What else is there?"

"The secret journal of Katherine Fairfield. Viscountess Trent has solved it. She's translated the whole diary, and, sir, here's the good thing. The woman lists all the lovers she had. She had been blackmailing all of them, so there's going to be a stink over that when it becomes public."

"I wasn't aware that the viscountess was an expert in cyphers. We sure haven't had any success."

"She'll be a brilliant woman to Sir Leo tomorrow."

"Well, this is a surprising development. It looks like this case is out of our hands, doesn't it, Matthew?"

"I'm very happy, sir. I was convinced of Clive Newton's guilt, but it's not possible anymore to think like that."

"Well, we'll have to rearrange our plans, then."

"I don't think there's any rearranging to be done. With that diary and a witness that will possibly eliminate Clive Newton, we may have a new tack on this."

"Very well. Keep on top of it and let me know what you find out."

"Yes, sir, I'll do that."

Dylan had received a visit from Grant, who had a worried look on his face. "What's up, Matthew, or Inspector Grant, I should say."

"Matthew sounds good to me, Dylan. I've been worried about something. I thought I'd share it with you."

"What's that?"

"Well, things are looking good for Dora's brother, but you know this woman Sadie is the key to the whole thing. If something happens to her, Clive will probably be convicted."

"You're right about that." Dylan stroked his chin thoughtfully. "I think I'd better be sure that she has some protection. The viscountess has bought her some new clothes for her appearance in court. She looks pretty rough, but her word of testimony will save Clive."

"You'd better be sure she's kept alive. If the killer knew she was coming to testify, he'd kill her."

"Right, you. I'll take care of it."

Dylan went at once to the Newton house. He didn't see a sign of Yago, who was on the day shift, but when he called out, the man suddenly appeared from behind a hedge. "What is it, Mr. Dylan?"

"I've got a job for you, Yago. I want you to go to this address and be sure nothing happens to a woman called Sadie or to the man she lives with."

"What could happen to her?"

"Well, she's a key witness. I want to be absolutely sure that she's safe. Here's the address. Here's the money for the cab. Are you armed?"

"Yes, sir, I always am. I'm a servant of the Lord, but you never know when you'll need to protect yourself." He hesitated, then asked, "Who will look after the boy while I'm there? Lorenzo won't come on duty until midnight."

"I'll take over, Gyp."

"You got a gun, have you?"

"No, but I won't need one. Off with you, then."

"Yes, sir, I'll see to it."

~✖~

Dylan moved around the house, which was hooded with darkness. Pike would be due to come on the scene in an hour, but Dylan didn't want to leave his charge alone for even that short span of time. He moved as quietly as possible through the trees that grew thickly on the east side of the house, then stopped dead still. He wasn't certain, but he thought he'd seen the figure of a man moving toward the back of the house.

He moved forward quickly. Suddenly another shadowy figure appeared not more than ten feet away from him. He tried to see who it might be, but the moon was behind a cloud. He advanced toward the figure, wishing that he were armed. He could make out little about the intruder, but when the man passed within a few feet, Dylan launched himself forward with all his might. He struck the man with a blow that brought a muffled cry, and the two of them rolled on the ground. Dylan felt the strength of the man, and suddenly his adversary spoke in the darkness: "I'll put a hole in you unless you hold still!"

Dylan recognised the voice and cried out, "Matthew—it's you!"

"Dylan, you almost broke my neck!" Matthew Grant got to his feet, and by the pale light of the sliver of a moon, the two men stared at each other.

"What are you doing here, Matthew?" Dylan whispered.

Matthew put the gun back into his pocket and moved closer to say, "I came to be sure that the family was all right." He hesitated, then said, "I had a crazy idea. It made no sense, but I couldn't get it out of my head."

"What kind of crazy idea?"

"Well, I'm convinced that Clive is innocent, and so are you, right?"

"Yes, of course."

"But *somebody* killed Kate Fairfield, and it came to me that the only real evidence we had on Clive was the stolen jewellery and the bloody handkerchief Winters and I found in Clive's room. I was going over the possible suspects, and it came to me—something I should have thought of before."

Dylan suddenly understood where Grant was going with this line of thinking. "You think Winters planted that evidence, don't you?"

Grant's voice was tense as he said, "It *had* to be him! We were both in the room, and he planted the jewellery and the handkerchief while I was looking at something else. It would only take a minute." Grant said miserably, "I never once thought of such a thing, Dylan! Why would I? Winters— the superintendent of Scotland Yard! And he's a killer! And then I realised that I'd told him that you two had found the missing witness—and that the viscountess had broken the code of the murdered woman's journal."

A chill ran through Dylan's mind. "He'll have to kill Serafina now, and the witness as well."

"That's why I came. He doesn't know where the woman is who'll testify that Clive was with her—so he'll force Lady Trent to tell him, then he'll take the diary and—"

"And he'll kill Serafina and the witness!" Dylan whirled and made for the house at a dead run.

"Where are you going?" Matthew called out.

"To Serafina's room!" came the answer. Matthew broke into a run and followed Dylan toward the house.

⤟⬥⤠

Night had fallen, and Serafina had spent the evening with David. He had missed her since she had been away so much at the trial and looking for the missing witness. They had played games, and she had told stories, and now she was saying, "All right. Off to bed you go."

"Can't I stay up awhile longer, Mum?"

"No, you can't. To bed now." Serafina firmly took him to his room, helped him with his pajamas, and tucked him in. "Now then. Are you going to sleep tight?"

"Yes, I am. Mum, do you think Dylan will come tomorrow?"

"I think he will."

"Good. I like him."

"I'm glad you do. He's a good man. Now good night, David." She kissed him, and he gave her a hard hug. She turned and walked down the hall and went into her room. For some time she sat looking at the transcription of the journal and marveling at the evil that was in the actress. Sir Leo had given her the transcription and asked her to review it again before she gave her testimony tomorrow. It had been a grievous task for her. Finally the pendulum clock broke the silence; the house was quiet for the servants had all gone to bed.

Serafina put on her nightgown and then her robe. She moved across the suite to turn off the gaslight. The door opened suddenly, and Serafina stared at the man who entered.

"Superintendent Winters, what are you doing here?" Serafina's expression revealed her shock.

"I think we have some business, Viscountess." Winters moved quickly for a big man. He reached out and put his hands around her neck. "You're going to tell me where the woman is, the witness you and the actor found."

Like a flash of lightning, it all became clear to Serafina. "You're the one who killed Kate Fairfield! You're Secret Lover!"

"That's right, and I want your transcription while I'm here."

"I've already given it to Sir Leo."

"No, you haven't. It's here. Grant told me."

Serafina's mind was working rapidly. His big hands were around her throat, and he was strong enough, she knew, to break her neck. "If I give you the diary and tell you where the witness is, will you go away and leave us alone?"

"Yes, I will."

He released his grip, and Serafina moved over to the table. She picked up the transcript of the diary that she kept there, and turning to him, she asked, "Why did you do it, Winters?"

"I had to. She was going to tell my wife about our affair."

"I read that much in the journal. She bled you white, didn't she?"

"Yes," Winters said. His handsome face was set, and his eyes were unnaturally bright. "I embezzled funds from my wife's account to pay her off, and Kate knew it. She was going to tell my wife everything. So you see, I couldn't let her live. She was a wicked woman."

Serafina held out the diary, and he took it, glanced through it, and then stuck it into his pocket. "I'd like to let you live, Viscountess, but I can't. I've got the transcript, but you could retranslate it. I'm sorry it has to be like this. On one condition I'll let you live."

"What's that?"

"Tell me where the witness is."

Instantly Serafina made up a name. "Her name's Maude Simms. She lives in a room over The Blue Lion in the Seven Dials district."

A grim satisfaction swept across Winters's face. Perspiration had appeared on his forehead, and his face was almost grey with strain. "I'm sorry. I'm not a killer, but I'm fighting for my life." He suddenly reached forward to seize her by the neck, but Serafina twisted free. She picked up the lamp on the table and threw it at him. He ducked, but it caught him on the forehead and shattered. It cut a furrow in his face, and the blood ran down. Serafina screamed, and he lunged at her. He grabbed her by the throat, and she beat against him with her fists, but it was useless. She fought for air, and her eyes were filled with the terrible features of Winters as he slowly strangled her.

Just then the door burst open, and a voice said, "Turn her loose, Winters!"

Winters did not release her, but he turned. Serafina twisted in his grip and saw Dylan throw himself across the room. He threw a powerful blow that caught Winters on the side of the face. Winters's hands relaxed and he fell to his knees. He started to get to his feet, but as he did, he pulled a revolver. "I'll have to kill you both now," he cried in a deadly voice. He lifted the revolver, but Serafina threw herself against him. She caught his arm, and as she did, Dylan struck him a terrible blow just where his neck joined his head. The gun fired, but the bullet went harmlessly into the ceiling. The blow drove Winters to the floor, and Dylan quickly seized the revolver. At that instant, Grant rushed into the room. He took one look at Winters and said, "We were right, Dylan." He seized Winters by the arm and pulled him to his feet. He twisted the big man's arms and put a pair of cuffs on him.

"Shoot me!" Winters cried. "Shoot me, somebody!"

"No," Grant said coldly. "You'll hang, Winters."

Dylan moved over to Serafina and put his arm around her, for she was trembling. "Are you all right?" he asked.

"Yes. He was going to kill me."

They all three stared at Winters, and then Grant said, "You're under arrest for the murder of Kate Fairfield and the attempted murder of Viscountess Serafina Trent."

Winters stared at them and began to tremble. "Just shoot me," he whimpered. "I can't bear the disgrace."

"You didn't mind letting Clive Newton bear the disgrace," Grant said, his voice hard.

Grant led Winters out of the room, and Serafina suddenly felt herself swaying. Dylan gently said, "Sit down, Serafina."

As she sat down, Bertha came rushing in, along with Serafina's parents. "What's happened?" Septimus demanded.

"It's good news, Father," Serafina said. She was rubbing her neck, which she knew would later bear a bruise. "Clive's going to be set free. Superintendent Winters killed the actress."

"Superintendent Winters?" he asked in disbelief.

"Yes." She explained to them how it had all come about, and finally she turned and said, "If Dylan hadn't helped, it would never have happened."

Septimus came over and put his hand out. "God bless you, my boy," he said, wringing Dylan's hand with all his strength.

Dylan smiled. "I thought you didn't believe in God."

"Well, I've been wrong about other things. I may be wrong about that too. We'll have to talk about this, you and I."

"I'll be glad to, sir." He turned to Serafina. "Do you need a doctor, Viscountess?"

"No, but my nerves are so on edge I don't know if I can sleep." And then she gave Dylan a strange look. He could not read her expression, but he saw her smile. "Some stories do have happy endings, don't they?"

Dylan returned the smile. "Yes, they do, Viscountess Serafina Trent, and this is one of them, indeed!"

TWENTY-SIX

The formal dining room was extremely comfortable. The table and side-board were Elizabethan oak, solid and powerful. The carved chairs at each end of the table had high backs and ornate armrests. Mirrors on the wall reflected the gaslight from the magnificent chandelier. The curtains were dark green, and pictures adorned the walls.

Matthew Grant had been silent for most of the meal, although Dora, who sat next to him, chattered amiably. The food had been completely outside of Grant's experience. The first course, a bisque, was delicious. It was followed by salmon, and Matthew could not help but notice how much of the food was taken away. The family seemed to just sample a dish and then wait for the next. The fish was followed by an entrée of curried eggs, sweetbread, and mushrooms.

Dora smiled at Matthew and said, "Don't eat too much. There's a lot more to come."

"I'm not used to such rich meals, Miss Dora."

"Well, it's time you got used to them." She stared at him, and there was a winsome look on her face. "What's going to happen to Superintendent Winters?"

"He'll be tried and found guilty. He's already confessed."

"Well, who will be the new superintendent?"

Matthew smiled. "I will be," he said.

Dylan and Serafina, who were seated across from them, both exclaimed, "Wonderful!"

"They couldn't have made a better choice," Serafina added.

Septimus said, "Well, it is indeed an honour to have Superintendent Grant with us tonight."

Bertha had been prepared to cast disparaging remarks on a mere policeman, but the superintendent of Scotland Yard—that was something else again! "We're so happy to have you here, Superintendent Grant," she cooed.

Grant found her amusing. "Thank you, Lady Mulvane. It's kind of you to say so."

Clive was pale, but his eyes were alight with pleasure. "It will be good to have an official representation of Scotland Yard in the family. I propose a toast. Here's to Superintendent Matthew Grant."

They all echoed the toast to Superintendent Grant, and then Grant said, "If I may, I'd like to propose a toast to Viscountess Serafina Trent. She's the best detective of us all."

Serafina received the toast and then said, "We mustn't forget the man who came to our rescue like a knight in shining armor, Mr. Dylan Tremayne."

David, who had insisted on sitting next to Dylan, interrupted by saying, "Mr. Dylan, can we go fishing tomorrow?"

"Well, I don't see why not."

David's eyes brightened, and he looked up at Dylan with a pleading expression. "I wish you'd come and live here, Mr. Dylan. Then we could be together all the time."

"Well, I have a living to make, see?"

David thought this over and then blurted out, "Well, Mum, you've got lots of money. You could marry Mr. Dylan, and he could stay with us all the time, couldn't he?"

For once Lady Serafina Trent was speechless. Grant and Clive were trying not to laugh, but their attempts were not entirely successful. Everyone at the table seemed to be trying to hide their smiles. Dylan's face was flushed, and Serafina could not look up. Finally Dylan gave Serafina an inexplicable look, then turned to David. "Well, viscountesses don't marry actors, my boy."

"Why not?"

"Because actors aren't acceptable husbands."

"But you're nice, isn't he, Mum?"

"Yes, he is nice," Clive said, his eyes laughing, some colour in his cheeks now. "Since he's ridden to our rescue, I think it's something you might consider, Serafina."

Serafina knew she was blushing, and she hated it. She arose quickly and said, "I think we can move to the drawing room for dessert." They all got up and began to move, but Dora took Matthew by the arm and said, "I thought you were a brave man, Matthew."

"You think I'm not?"

"If you were really brave, you'd do more than just come courting me."

Matthew stared at the young woman with whom he had fallen so completely in love. It was an unexpected thing for him, and he was much more excited over the fact that Dora Newton liked him than he was over his promotion to superintendent of Scotland Yard. "If I asked you to marry me," he said, "people would say I was a fortune hunter."

"Oh, you could never be that."

Suddenly Matthew laughed and did a very uncharacteristic thing. "Yes, I am a fortune hunter, and you're the fortune I'm hunting for, Dora Newton." He leaned forward and kissed her, and then she laughed. "Aunt Bertha will go into spasms."

❧

David had insisted that Dylan put him to bed, and Dylan had picked him up and carried him up the stairs, followed by Serafina. He had watched as she undressed him, put on his pajamas, and then put him into the big bed.

"Now a story, is it?"

"Yes, a good story, Dylan!"

Serafina moved to the other side of the bed and sat down. She saw Dylan's face, mobile and expressive, and watched his hands as he waved them in the air telling a fanciful story. He was making it up, she knew, and she wondered again at the imagination of this man who had come into her life with such power and such force.

Finally Dylan finished the story, and David reached up and took him by the hand. "I still think you ought to marry Mum and be my father."

Dylan cast a look at Serafina and winked. "Well, maybe I'll be like the frog prince—you remember the story I told you about him? Maybe your mother will kiss me and turn an ugly frog into a fine, handsome young prince."

"You're not ugly!"

The three of them laughed together, then Dylan said, "Good night." He stepped back, and Serafina kissed the boy, then they left the room.

When they were outside, she asked, "Would you like to have tea?"

"Oh, that's good, it would be."

The two of them went to the kitchen, and she moved about heating water in the kettle, and they talked while it was steeping. She turned away from him and said, "I'm sorry that David embarrassed you with all his foolish talk, but David's wrong. I could never marry. I have terrible memories of my marriage. I've already told you why I'm cold. Sometimes I think my soul is frozen."

At once Dylan came to her. Her eyes widened as he turned her around, and his face was framed in her vision. His wide, mobile lips were smiling, and he pulled her closer and said, "But ice can melt, yes?"

"No—not in my case."

Dylan pulled her into his arms and kissed her. Something swirled rashly between the two of them, and once again, as she had before, Viscountess Serafina Trent felt a wonderful warmth that began somewhere in the vicinity of her heart and touched her face. At the same time there was a feeling of deep need that yearned to be satisfied. The loneliness of her past life seemed suddenly cold and barren. Dylan's arms were strong as he held her, his lips gentle. There was strength in this man, but a gentleness that drew her.

He lifted his head and said, "Many waters cannot quench love. Neither can the floods drown it. It's stronger than death, Serafina. Stronger than anything."

She stepped back, putting her hand on his chest, letting it rest there lightly. "I told you I'm nothing but ice."

"You're wrong about that, Viscountess Serafina Trent. I don't know what others see, but I see in you a woman of fire and imagination. You couldn't kiss me like that if you were cold."

"Dylan, we could never—" She broke off.

"We could never marry, you were going to say."

"We're too different."

"But one of us could change." He reached out and put his hand on the smoothness of her cheek, then smiled. "Good night, Serafina."

"You'll come back?" she asked quickly and then flushed. "To—to see David, I mean."

"Yes, to see David, and you and I will have more talk about a great many things." He did a strange thing then. He lifted his hand and ran it over her hair. His touch seemed to awaken something in her, and as he stood there smiling, it seemed to her that her heart beat faster. He turned and walked out of the room, and when he did, she walked to the window. She looked up at the stars spangling the heavens and whispered, "I'm not cold! Dylan said so—"

And then Lady Serafina Trent smiled and watched until he disappeared into the darkness.

She hugged herself and whispered, "He'll be back tomorrow. I know he will."

Excerpt from

A CONSPIRACY OF RAVENS,

Book Two in the Lady Trent Mysteries

O ctober, the harbinger of winter, had fallen upon England. A cold, blustery day swept across London and the many houses that bordered the city itself. Lady Serafina Trent had come to stare out the window, and the gloom of the day dampened her spirit. As she looked at the enormous oaks, they seemed to be specters raising skeletal limbs toward the sky.

A fleeting memory came to her as she thought of how she had come to Trentwood House as a young bride. She remembered the joy and the anticipation that had been hers when she married Charles Trent—but then a trembling, not caused by the temperature, shook her as a bitter memory touched her. She thought of her husband, now dead and buried in the family cemetery, then forced the thought away.

Serafina's eyes lingered on the grounds of Trentwood, the ancestral estate of the Trents. The grass was a leprous grey, the trees had dropped their leaves, and the death of summer took away the beauty of the world. Serafina suddenly turned, and with a quick movement moved away from the window and toward the large table where David sat scrunched up in a tall chair made especially for him. The blaze in the fireplace sent out its cheerful poppings and crackings, sending myriads of fiery sparks upward through the chimney in a magic dance, and the heat radiated throughout the room.

Serafina took a seat beside her son. She glanced around, and once again old memories came—but this time more pleasant ones. This was the room that she had persuaded Charles to give her as a study, and it was lined with artifacts of the trade of human anatomy. A grinning skeleton wired together stood at attention across the room. She and her father had put it together when she was only thirteen, and after her marriage it had come with her to Trentwood. Charles had laughed at her, saying, "You love death rather than life, Serafina."

Once again, the bitter memory of her marriage to Charles Trent brought gloom. She quickly scanned the room, noting the familiar bookshelves stuffed with leather-bound books, the drawings of various parts of the human anatomy on the walls, the stuffed animals that she and her father had dissected and put back together again. A table stretching the length of one wall was covered with vials, glasses, and containers. She remembered how she had labored in the world of chemistry during her early years at Trentwood.

"Mum, I can't do these old fractions!"

Serafina smiled and put her arm around David. At the age of seven, he had her looks—fair hair and dark blue eyes with just a touch of violet like Serafina's own. He was small, but there was a hint of a tall frame to come.

"Of course you can, David. It's easy."

"No, it ain't," David complained, and as he turned to her, she admired the smooth planes of his face, thinking what a handsome young man he was. She also noticed that instead of figures on the sheet of paper before him, he had drawn pictures of strange animals and birds. He had a gift for drawing, she knew, but now she shook her head saying, "You haven't been working on fractions. You've been drawing birds."

"I'd rather draw birds than do these old fractions, Mum."

Serafina had learnt from experience that David had inherited neither her passion for science, nor the mathematical genes of his grandfather, Septimus. He was intrigued more by fanciful things than by numbers and hard facts, which troubled Serafina.

"David, if you want to subtract a fraction from a whole number, you simply turn the whole number into a fraction. You change this number five to fourths. Now you want to subtract one-fourth from that. How many fourths are there in a whole number?"

"I dunno, Mum."

Serafina shook her head slowly and insisted, "You must learn fractions, David."

"I don't like them."

David suddenly gave her an odd, secretive look that she knew well. "What are you thinking, Son?"

"Will I show you something I like?"

Serafina sighed. "Yes, I suppose you will."

David jumped up and ran to the desk. He opened a drawer and took something out. It was, Serafina saw, a book, and his eyes were alight with excitement when he showed it to her. "Look, it's a book about King Arthur and his Knights of the Round Table."

Serafina took the book and opened it. On the first page, it read, "To my friend David," and it was signed Dylan Tremayne. "Dylan gave you this book?"

"Yes. Ain't it fine? It was a present, and he gave me his picture, too." David reached over and pulled a photograph from between the pages of the book. "Look at it, Mum. It looks just like him, don't it now?"

Serafina stared at the minature painting of Dylan Tremayne, and, as always, she was struck by the good looks of the man that had come to play such a vital part in her life. She studied the glossy black hair with the lock over the forehead as usual, the steady wide-spaced and deep-set eyes, and the wedge-shaped face, the wide mouth, the mobile features. *He's almost too handsome to be a man with those beautiful eyes.* The thought touched her, and she remembered how only recently it had been Tremayne who had helped her to free her brother, Clive, from a charge of murder. She remembered how, at first, she had resented Tremayne for everything that he was, all of which ran against the grain for the Viscountess of Radnor. Whereas she was logical, scientific, and reasonable, Dylan was fanciful, filled with imagination, and a fervent Christian, believing adamantly that miracles were not a thing of the past. She was also disturbed by the fact that although she had given up on romance long ago, she had felt the stirrings of a powerful attraction to this actor, who was so different from everything she knew.

She had tried to think of some way to curtail Dylan's influence on David, for she felt it was unhealthy, but it was very difficult. David was wild about Dylan, who spent a great deal of time with him, and Serafina was well aware that her son's affection for Tremayne was part of the latent desire that he had for a father.

Firmly, Serafina said, "David, this book isn't true. It's made up, a story book. It's not like a dictionary where words mean certain things. It's not like a book of mathematics where two plus two is always four. It isn't even like a history book when it gives the date of a famous person's birth. That's a fact."

David listened, but was restless. Finally he interrupted by saying, "But, Mum, Dylan says that these are stories about men who were brave and who fought for the truth. That's not bad, is it?"

"No, that's not bad, but they're not real men. If you must read stories about brave men, you need to read history."

"Dylan says there was a King Arthur once."

"Well, Dylan doesn't know any such thing. King Arthur and his knights are simply fairy tales, and you'd do well to put your mind on things that are real rather than things that are imaginary." Even as Serafina spoke, she saw the hurt in David's eyes, and her own heart smoldered. "We'll talk about it later," she said quickly. "Are you hungry?"

"Yes!"

"You're always hungry." Serafina laughed and hugged him.

"Dylan says he's going to come and see me today. Is that all right?"

"Yes, I suppose so. Come along now. Let's go see what cook has made for us."

❧

The dining room was always a pleasure to Serafina, and as she entered it she ran her eyes over it quickly. The table and sideboard were Elizabethan oak, solid and powerful, an immense weight of wood. The carved chairs at each end of the table had high backs and ornate armrests. The curtains that were pulled back now were dark green, and pictures adorned the walls. It was a gracious room, very large with the table already laden with rich food set out on exquisite linen. Silver gleamed discreetly under the chandeliers fully lit to counteract the gloom of the day. "You're late, Daughter. You missed out on the blessing."

The speaker, Septimus Isaac Newton, at the age of sixty-two managed to look out of place in almost any setting. He was a tall, gangling man over six feet with a large head and hair that never seemed to be brushed as a result of his running his hand through it. His sharp eyes were a warm brown and held a look of fondness as he said, "David, I'm about to eat all the food."

David laughed and shook his head. "No, you won't, Grandfather. There's too much of it."

Indeed, the table was covered with sandwiches, many of them thinly sliced cucumber sandwiches on brown bread. There were cream cheese sandwiches with a few chopped chives and smoked salmon mousse. White bread sandwiches flanked these. Smoked ham, eggs, mayonnaise with mustard and cress, and grand cheeses of all sorts complimented the sandwiches, as did scones, fresh and still warm with plenty of jams and cream, and finally cake and some exquisite French pastries. Serafina sat David in the chair, and James Barden, the butler, helped her into her own, then stepped back to watch the progress of the meal.

As Serafina helped pile the food onto David's tray, she listened to her father who chose at mealtime to announce the scientific progress taking place in the world.

"I see," Septimus said, "that London architects are going to enlarge Buckingham Palace to give it a south wing with a ballroom a hundred and ten feet long."

"That's as it should be. The old ballroom is much too small."

The speaker was Lady Bertha Mulvane, the widow of Sir Hubert Mulvane, and the sister of Septimus' wife Alberta. She was a heavy-set woman with blunt features and ate as if she had been starved.

"I'd love to go to a ball there," Aldora Lynn Newton said. She was a beautiful young girl with auburn hair flecked with gold and large well-shaped, brown eyes and a flawless complexion. An air of innocence glowed from her, though she would never be the beauty of her older sister. By some miracle of grace, she had no resentment towards Serafina.

Lady Bertha shook her head. "If you don't choose your friends with more discretion, Dora, I would be opposed to letting you go to any ball."

Aldora gave her aunt a look half frightened for the woman was intimidating. "I think my friends are very nice."

"You have no business letting that policeman call on you, that fellow Grant."

Indeed, Inspector Matthew Grant had made the acquaintance of the Newton family only recently. He had been the detective in charge of the case against Clive Newton. After the case was successfully solved, and the murderer turned out to be the superintendent of Scotland Yard, it had been assumed that Grant would take his place. Bertha Mulvane had been happy enough to receive him as Superintendent Grant.

Serafina could not help saying, "Inspector Grant was invaluable in helping get Clive out of prison."

"He did little enough. It was you and that actor fellow that did all the work solving that case."

"No, Inspector Grant's help was essential," Serafina insisted. She saw Lady Mulvane puff up and thought for an instant how much her aunt looked like an old, fat toad at times. She saw also that her aunt had taken one of the spoons and slipped it surreptitiously into her sleeve. "It's one thing to entertain the superintendent of Scotland Yard, but a mere policeman? Not at all suitable!"

Septimus said gently, "Well, Bertha, that was a political thing. Inspector Grant should have gotten the position, but politics gave it to a less worthy man."

Lady Bertha did not challenge this, but devoured another sandwich. She ate not with enjoyment but as if she were putting food in a cabinet somewhere to be eaten at a future time.

Serafina's mother, Alberta, was an attractive woman with blonde hair and mild blue eyes. She was getting a little heavier now in her early fifties but had no wrinkles on her smooth face. Her hands showed the rough, hard upbringing she'd had, for she came from a poor family. Septimus had not been rich when they had met, and she had pushed him into becoming a doctor and later into the research that had made him wealthy and famous. "Perhaps Bertha is right, Aldora."

"Of course, I'm right!" Bertha snapped. "And you, Serafina, I'd think you'd finally gotten some common sense."

"I'm glad to hear you think so, Aunt. What brings you to this alarming conclusion?" Serafina smiled, noting that her aunt had slipped one of the silver salt shakers into the large sleeve of her coat. She well knew that Bertha Mulvane's own house was furnished with items that had somehow mysteriously disappeared from Greenfield Hall and had taken residence at Lady Bertha's abode.

"Why, the fact that you have a suitor that's worthy of you."

"I'm not aware that I had such a suitor."

"Now don't be foolish, Serafina. Sir Alex Bolton is so handsome, and he has a title."

Serafina shook her head, picked up a cheese sandwich, and took a bite of it. "He's not calling on me. I danced with him once at a ball last week."

"But he's coming to dinner next week," Alberta said, a pleased expression on her face. "And, of course, I know that he's coming to see you."

"Oh, he'd be such a catch!" Bertha exclaimed.

Septimus looked up from his paper. "He's poor as a church mouse," he said firmly. "He lost most of his money in bad investments and gambling."

"Oh, you're wrong, Septimus," Bertha said. "He owns a great plantation in Ireland."

"I've heard he owns some forty acres of bog land good for nothing," Septimus said then turned to his grandson and smiled. "David, what are you going to do today?"

"Dylan's coming. We're going to trap some rabbits. He knows how to snare them."

Bertha's face was the picture of disgust. Her neck seemed to swell, and she barely spat out the words. "I have no doubt he's a poacher." She turned and said, "I would think you might choose your son's companions more carefully, Serafina."

Serafina said calmly, "You didn't object to Dylan when he was helping me to get Clive out of a murder charge."

Since Bertha had no defense for this, she left the room in a huff. David leaned over and whispered, "She stole a spoon, Mum."

"I know. Just don't pay any attention to her, David."